BRUNANBURGH

DAVID ANSON

AuthorHouse™ UK Ltd.
500 Avebury Boulevard
Central Milton Keynes, MK9 2BE
www.authorhouse.co.uk
Phone: 08001974150

© *2010 David Anson. All rights reserved.*

No part of this book may be reproduced, stored in a retrieval system, or transmitted by any means without the written permission of the author.

First published by AuthorHouse   9/7/2010

ISBN: 978-1-4520-5444-5 (e)
ISBN: 978-1-4520-5445-2 (sc)

This book is printed on acid-free paper.

SHEFFIELD LIBRARIES & ARCHIVES	
210100769	
Bertrams	
LOC	£13.49

Domine Deus omnipotent Rex regum et dominus dominantium in cujus manu omnis victoria consistit et omne bellum conteritur concede mihi ut tua manus cor meum corroboret ut in virtute yua in manibus viribusque mais bene pugnare viriliterque agere valeam ut inimici mei in conspectu meo cadent et corruant sicit corruit Golias ante faciem puere tui David et sicut populus Pharaonis coram Moysi in Mare Rubro. Et sicut Philistini coram populo Israhel ceciderunt et Amalech coram Moysi et Chananei coram Jesu corruerunt sic cadant inimici mei sub pedibus meis et per viam unam conveniant adversum me et per septem fugiant a me et conteret Deus arma eorum et confringret framea aorum et eliquesce in conspectu meo sicut cer a facie ignis ut sciant omnes populi tere quia invocatum est nomen Domini Nostri Jesu super me et magnificetur nomen tuum Domine in adversariis meis Domine Dues Israhel.

The original Latin version of Athelstan's prayer before the battle.
The English translation by Sylvia Becket is in
the text of Chapter 19 The Way South to War.

AUTHORS PREFACE AND ACKNOWLEDGEMENTS

On the 23rd September 937 AD the armies of King Athelstan the Saxon and his allies met in battle those of King Constantine of the Scots, Earl Anlaf of the Dublin Vikings and their allies. Whilst based around this historical fact, the following story remains a work of fiction and is intended to be so. Its inspiration lies in real history and information from the historians and archaeologists who have written about it. The location of the Battle of Brunanburgh, like many battles of the era, is said to be lost in the Dark Ages. I do not personally support the concept of "the Dark Ages." There is much research into the period by reputable modern historians and learned societies to show this is not the case and their work has inspired me. If I have made mistakes in the book as far as the history is concerned, this is of course my mistake and not theirs. Most of the detail I have made up in its entirety, of course.

I have set out to write a story, but at the same time advocate that Brunanburgh was the old Roman fort of Morbium at Templeborough near Rotherham in South Yorkshire. Michael Wood author of "In Search of England" and "In Search of the Dark Ages" believes this to be true, as did J H Cockburn in 1933 from place name research. Many other contemporary writers do the same. Local historians in Rotherham Leslie and Sylvia Beckett privately published research from Latin texts and other information they consulted in Dublin. This work points towards a site in South Yorkshire and particularly at Rotherham as opposed to Brinsworth, the site advocated by Michael Wood.

Leslie Beckett, particularly, drawing on his military experience concluded that an invasion intending to put Anlaf the Viking on a throne at York would first go there or at least near to it before moving on to a battle. Most of the medieval writers agreed the invasion ships moored in the Humber, and in many cases it was all they agreed on. If you, reader, consider the battle was part of a political campaign to re-establish the independent Kingdom of Northumbria with a capital in York, and not just an odd and isolated fight, a new perspective will open up for you, wherever you believe it was fought. After this battle in 937AD, Anlaf finally became king in York when Athelstan died in 939AD. Be like Anlaf and never lose sight of your real goal.

As an old soldier myself, the wider strategy of getting an army from what is now Scotland to middle England in 10th Century Britain, and vice-versa, would best choose the way, I describe in this story, in my opinion. It was good enough also for King Athelstan invading Scotland in 935 also. (I say this despite Prince Charles Stuart and his army coming the other way down the western side to Derby in 1745). The soldiers coming by sea would certainly have needed to have a place where they could meet up with the majority of their army marching down from the far north. Brunanburgh was most certainly the only surviving stone fort on the Don, located east of the Pennines. The agreed place to meet, however, did not mean it was the site of the battle. Critics of this approach should first imagine what Britain was like over a thousand years ago. Most of the north of England around the Pennines would be moor and forest. The Don Valley from Sheffield to The Humber would be nearly all marsh and filled with a wide, meandering, but in places, shallow, river. It would not be what we see today and perhaps more of a division between the prosperous south and the distant north than now.

I have also assumed the battle was not a chess piece conflict fought in a limited area as medieval writers suggest and many recent authors accept. Not "a field enhazelled," but groups of men spread out over a much wider area and just like modern battles, with problems of command and control. They would be fighting intermittently and trying to take advantage of movement. Large numbers of combatants are supposed to have been present and considering the number of enemies King Athelstan faced, this was most likely. They are all said to have turned up looking for a piece of his kingdom if not his wealth. He had considerably fewer men but had quality troops, equipment and a plan which he put into action. History has seemed to damn Athelstan for not acting fast enough when faced with the invasion, when really he was doing what Wellington did at Waterloo. He was waiting as long as he dare to get as many men together as possible, and then to meet the enemy on a field of his own choice. Harold Godwinsson should have done the same at Hastings. Athelstan is scarce remembered, as the English don't love a winner.

The personal names in this book are reasonably authentic for the time. Again the errors are mine, if they are not. The Celtic pronunciations may be strange to some readers. For example, Sine is Sheena, Brollachan is Brollack-awn, ending as in Dawn. Ceara is Key-ara and a variation of Kyra. Many Saxon, Danish and Norse names have been passed down as first or surnames and will not be too unknown.

Except for the kings the characters are not intended to represent anyone alive at the time who any person now living could claim as an ancestor.

My wife Angela helped with her tolerance and Leslie Beckett helped with inspiration and details but particularly with his book and unpublished research information. Sylvia Roddis Beckett I never knew, but her former pupils in South Yorkshire all remember her with the greatest affection and her knowledge of Latin was without equal. My shelves are full of history books which is a subject I have read constantly since a child. There are too many authors to mention but I thank them all. The various cats who inhabited our house over the time of writing, did their best to divert me. So to Athelstan, Balthazar, Morrigan, Zenobia and Tobias, I finished it despite your hours of interruption, you rascals. But most of all to my little son, Aylmer who was still-born at 39 weeks in June 2009 whilst I was writing, your character in this book is all I would ever have wanted you to be, noble and famous, as your name describes, and honourable and brave as a true warrior should be.

This book is dedicated to you, and to Sylvia Roddis Beckett and Leslie Beckett.

David Anson

Spring 2010

PROLOGUE

King Athelstan sat quietly for a while and began to think what he would say to the men who were starting to gather outside the little wood and stone church. He gazed through the darkness at the altar and felt a little tired. No different from how he had been feeling for the last five years. He had the place to himself and for a moment his mind wandered as he thought how far this journey had brought him. The words inside his head began to form and speak to him. They had done on so many occasions as he remembered his increasingly tired life.

"How I hate these people" he mused, "the Danes, the Saxons, the Britons, and the Angles most of all. People are starting to call the damned country after them. Why didn't God make me a Frank and king of a civilised country? A country with some real Roman heritage would have been nice, but the Romans just seemed to have passed through here just leaving a few walls behind, the odd building, a fort or two....."

"What about the roads?" The voice came out of his past.

"Oh yes, the roads, most of them go nowhere now!"

"There's lots of stone about for people to use. A few good forts. Some town walls. That bath place with a warm spring in the south west. Your Auntie liked it."

He remembered then his time fighting with the Franks, his visit to Rome as a young man and meeting the bishop, and all the friends he had made. He had always thought of it as an uncomplicated life until his father Edward decided he wanted him back home when his reputation as a warrior became apparent. Even in a backwater like Winchester, even though he was still then a young man, people then began to notice him.

"For almost the first time in his life he thought about me and considered I could be some use to him. It was Auntie Ethelfreda constantly reminding him that did it. What a woman! Give me a wapentake of Ethelfredas and I won't need an army! Grandad was right to marry her off to Uncle Ethelred. It was a surprise to everyone how much he loved her as well, even though she seemed to breathe fire at him most of the time. Dad was lucky the Witangemot didn't invite them to become King and Queen in his place. What a match, what a couple! If I never had much else going for me as a child, being fostered by them was the best thing ever happened to me. They taught me all I know... How I loved them both! Oh, how I miss them!"

Athelstan nearly allowed himself to laugh and cry in church at that thought. Edward had a new king created under his nose and had the decency to die early leaving the Witan nearly no choice but to chose him as king over Edmund his half brother who was still a child and the one or two other useless pretenders who were now safely despatched.

"This country always needs a warrior, Lord Athelstan," they said and those words constantly rang in his ears. He felt he had never been anything else and always claimed he could remember his grandfather Alfred giving him his first sword. In reality Auntie Ethelfreda had told about the occasion so many times, but he never lost the importance of it. It was the stewardship of the kingdom his Grandfather had rescued from the Danes. To Athelstan all the other kings in Britain were trying to rob the family of their birthright. It had been handed it to him for safekeeping.

The voice in his head said. "Well, they got their warrior and a bit more than some bargained for. You had better keep it that way!"

There was no doubt that someone was needed to complete the work of unifying the land of the Angles and Saxons, the Danes and the Britons. His grandfather Alfred had taken the title of their king after all. The work of his Father and Grandfather and most of all Auntie Ethelfreda was always in Athelstan's mind. He would constantly remind people how it was their duty to support him in this. It was to him a rebuilding of the Roman Empire in Britain. He had designs on the rest of the country where the Romans had never succeeded, the far north and across the western sea to conquer the Irish, even if he only dreamed. Athelstan was good at dreaming and occasionally managed to get some of his followers to share his dreams, especially the one about unity in the southern bit of the larger British Isle. They had a bit of difficulty with the bigger picture. In the happy part of his life, he sat with Auntie Ethelfreda discussing the detail. To Athelstan she never lost the picture or the plot. She always could comprehend the enormity of the task and played her part.

"Forts, trained men and armour," she would scream. "The lack of 'em nearly cost my Daddy the Kingdom. We won't make that mistake again.

We'll build more ships as well. We'll fight more battles. We'll hang more traitors and then people will know to stay loyal."

He knew she meant it. She had fortified everywhere she thought would hold off invaders into Wessex and Mercia, just to keep that base secure and she didn't trust the Danes, the Vikings and the Irish. It was also best never to mention the Scots and certain Angles in her presence. River crossings were her favourites to fortify, just like the Romans. Her knowledge of the land was encyclopaedic. Her grasp of strategy was a legend.

"Defence in depth, forts built for a refuge for our people," she said. "..... And big enough for a little army."

She had priests draw maps and write books about war. She had spies everywhere.

"What a woman" said the voice again.

"Yes and she knew how to deal with traitors too" though Athelstan. "She hanged enough her time and I have been glad to carry on that family tradition. Dear God, I wish she was here now, she'd know what to say much better than me."

Athelstan felt at peace in the little church. A devout believer like Ethelfreda, he always felt secure with the Church and they were now supporting him against his enemies. His friends in the old Roman Empire had not let him down during the past crises of his rule and now they were with him again. They were not slow to support him and promises of help were there, albeit secret at this stage as they had been before. This he considered gave him the confidence to act. Many of his followers, but especially his enemies, who were not aware of this support, did not understand the confidence it gave to him. Foreign diplomacy in politics was never important for them. Now it was more crucial than ever. Athelstan and the voice in his head understood this.

But what pleased Athelstan most of all, was even though she had been dead for nearly twenty years, Auntie Ethelfreda had second-guessed them all, the Welsh, the Vikings, the Danes, the Irish, the Northumbrians, the Scots, the complete nest of traitors, including the Angles. Anlaf Godfricsson and Constantine the Scot strut about pretending to be real kings, not the couple of bandits they really were. Holding courts and receiving ambassadors like real kings. Well, just like real kings they had courts full of traitors who would sell them out for a few pieces of silver. They didn't hang as many as he did it and so Athelstan knew all their plans. No one went around talking about Athelstan's plans. Kitchen boys did not listen at doors wherever he set up court, thinking to earn a few pieces of silver. Not if they valued their ears anyway.

"So, they can come to meet me at Brunanburgh if they want" he said out loud and then he whispered. "Auntie Ethelfreda had that Roman fort rebuilt and put up all those others on the Don and the land to the south. I can picture it in my mind. The valley has steep slopes on the northern bank and the old British fort at Wincobank which overlooked the rolling country to the south into Mercia and north into Northumbria. You can see everything from Wincobank. Brunanburgh is on a knoll pushing out into the river. The ford enters from gentle slopes on either bank and the river is wide and shallow. They will not cross at that point without a few arrows put in their direction and they'll find it difficult to get back across when I've done with them. Those that survive will anyway. It won't worry the dead……. It's such a pleasant place, in better times I'll put a palace there. I shall rebuild the fort again just like the Romans would have done. I'll use real craftsmen and masons not peasant labourers. It'll look nice and peaceful."

"Lord Athelstan, everyone is assembled now to hear you speak" a voice shouted outside the church and so Athelstan mumbled a prayer out loud and walked outside to stand on a small dais.

"My friends" he said, "I am so glad to see you and your followers here today."

CHAPTER I

THE DANES' DILEMMA

Athelstan looked briefly around him from the little church which was located on a hill just off the ancient north-south track to York and beyond. Generations had walked this way. Roman Legions still marched in his mind. He could see another track leading east down to the Trent River in the distance. It went on to Worksop to the west. Very well trod he thought. Danes move about a lot. He continued his speech:

"My friends, I have to come to speak on a serious issue which concerns us all, the security of our homes and families..... Some of you and your followers took part in my recent foray into the lands of King Constantine of the Scots. He is a man who I thought could be my friend but he has now treacherously allied himself again with the Vikings of Dublin. He previously threatened our peace with the *wealas* in the North and it was necessary for us to attack their country and his. He assumed the role of their overlord and made threats against us. We were forced to invade to keep our lands secure from his invasions, extract tribute and assurances of peace and security. Those of you who accompanied me had, I hope, what was a just share of that tribute. He threatens us once again, having broken the oaths he swore to be my friend. He is planning to raise a great army of all the people in the north and ally himself with *Jarl* Anlaf of Dublin and his Irish allies."

Athelstan allowed that point to sink home for a moment and continued.

"It is no secret *Jarl* Anlaf would be king in York as he pretends to be king in Dublin, and over many years has had plans to invade but has lacked men and resources. King Constantine is providing the resources for the invasion. Anlaf's own forces are small but he can call on many more………. who can only be paid only through plunder. They will not plunder lands which Anlaf seeks to rule around York. Your lands are the nearest to York and Anlaf does not want them……...or says he does not!"

Athelstan let those choice words register for a moment. It was a speech he had delivered before to his other Danish subjects on the borders of Mercia and always ensured he spoke correctly in their dialect of what was almost becoming a common language to some. He went on:

"You know for many years my father and my Aunt Ethelfreda organised the construction of fortifications from the hills to the western and eastern estuaries, the Mersey and Don Rivers. Those defences are now in place and we all sit secure behind them. They are, however, only as good as the men who are prepared to defend them and this is why today I have come to ask you to stand in their defence. King Constantine will try to bring his men raiding to the south of our forts while Anlaf resides in York. He knows he cannot pass too far or he runs out of support and supplies and will find his way blocked when he returns. He can only raid on the border after York is taken. We can defeat him wherever he decides to cross in either east or west. The place we may not know until the time. As your king I ask for your support."

A quiet murmur passed though the assembled Danish chiefs, most of who were from the area west of the Trent and north of Nottingham. Another good handful were from east of the river around Lincoln. They stood together, apart from the rest, with their men nearby.

Earl Thorold, a Danish *Jarl*, who was known for his support of the king spoke.

"Lord Athelstan, we need some time to consider your words amongst ourselves."

"*Jarl* Thorolf," replied Athelstan, knowing he preferred that term and the Danish version of his name, "thank you for that suggestion. I shall retire for a while and will be pleased to return to hear your advice."

When he had gone the short distance to his tent but well out of earshot, the Danes gathered. Thorolf spoke:

"No good us all talking at once we need someone to keep order."

"Grim the miller from Knaith never says a lot, he's the man," said someone.

"He does when he has something to say" shouted the same Grim.

"I've never understood why you all refer to him as Grim the Silent, he talks as much as anyone here."

"You only meet me when I have something to say *Jarl* Thorolf."

"Say your piece and then, my friend, preside over this meeting."

Thorolf realised that Grim would have his say and express a view many might agree with and set the tone of the meeting. The Danes in North Mercia felt vulnerable to invasion, even from people many saw as their kindred. The easterners were seemingly less at risk and might want not to get involved. Grim had his mill and lands by the River Trent in several places, easier to attack from the Humber, however. Everyone's grandfather had told them that was the way the ancestors had attacked, pillaged and finally settled around here.

Grim walked over and stood where Athelstan had been a few moments ago and everyone gathered around. So he began.

"A problem I have in all this, is trying to accept this Saxon King is correct in his assessment of the situation. If they invade from the eastern estuary as many have done in the past, they could go to York and circle around the marshes and pass west of Conisborough, or between there and Doncaster. Some of them could come around and up the River Trent over there. We could defend the banks or welcome them....... Kith and kin or not, but if their argument is with the Saxons they ought to go and attack the Saxons not us....... It would be just easier to take from us on the way, or as the King is suggesting, let their allies take from us. *Jarl* Anlaf would feign some innocence throughout that part of his campaign, protesting he and his men had remained in York. Having been to the Don valley and seen the forts, I can see the Scots and the *wealas* getting past them successfully, although not without some hindrance. The way back is another matter if they are defeated and running. The King will have a force waiting for them on the south side. We have to decide if we want to be part of it. This Saxon has won every other fight he's been in......and he's had a long time to prepare for this one. After the last invasion of the north I think he knew they would come looking for revenge and has been prepared better than we know. We also need to look to our own defence on the east of Trent."

At that point he looked out to his fellow Danes. A whole series of speakers came out of the crowd saying, how crafty Athelstan had been going round the Danes describing the threat from the north which might never affect them. It was only relevant if the east of the country was invaded. Someone pointed out the objective here is York and that is where the invaders will end up. It wouldn't matter where they land. York would be from where the looters and pillagers would set off. Athelstan had the west, the Mercian end of the country, well defended also, probably better than around here. He had his navy there for a start and the one or two still involved with seafaring said how good it was. Not a lot of it, but had it been around in Alfred's day, there would be fewer of us here. It was a good force and they reckoned Anlaf and Constantine knew it. They wouldn't risk meeting it on the open sea with a host of slow moving ships overloaded with men and supplies. Numbers wouldn't be any advantage. Anlaf was too smart to take on what is in the west, he might cause a diversion there.... but Athelstan wouldn't over-react to it. Besides it might not get past the forts because they were better in the west with larger garrisons. Athelstan had many spies; he would know the enemy movement. He would re-enforce where necessary. The Saxons had lots of horses to move their infantry and supplies around the country. They were mobile and could now outpace any invader. The Danes from east of the Trent didn't speak until Harald Edwinsson came out and took his turn.

"Friends, I am not too much a lover of the Saxons. They are deviously trying to win back the land we took from them in honest battle. They buy it up with the gold and silver Athelstan extracts from his enemies, but having said that, we can share the country with them. They took it from the *wealas* after all, and many of us who have settled by the Trent River have Welsh relatives from amongst the people who remained. All peoples can now live together if we try, and in fact in many places all three peoples seem to be getting on. It won't help if another load of invaders come passing through to steal what we are sharing. In the past I have fought for Athelstan, and was well rewarded with some of this gold he takes from his enemies. People envy me my wealth on occasions but everyone knows I share it with my followers.... It can be an advantage to be on a winning side. It does not mean that a man cannot have his own beliefs and aspirations. My father and grandfather fought against his, and like them, Athelstan will defend this land whether we help him or not......... I think it would be to our advantage to join this battle..... I do say this, however, we should prepare as he has done. We should not empty our villages of men to fill up his ranks. We should send men well-trained in war who know how to fight, and who will most likely come back. They should be well-equipped for the fight with good armour and weapons. The King I know has a stock and may even provide some where we are short. He will provide food and I do not think he will throw our lives away unnecessarily. *Jarl* Thorolf of us all knows him best and I think he will agree with me."

Thorolf came out to speak.

"You all know me as a supporter of the King. I am not afraid to say I have taken his money and like Harald, I think I and my men have earned it. Much of it has gone to support widows, orphans and aged parents. This king is mindful of that when he doles out his money. He is more of a Christian than many of us and he even reminds bishops of their duty. That is why you see so many wearing swords."

Laughter broke out at that comment. He went on.

"We cannot stand aside from this fight because I fear it might come to our doors. The defences on the Don are to deter raiders not invaders. Grim knows this well. The re-enforcement of the forts may prevent any invaders escaping but will not be sufficient to prevent them passing south in the first place…… The King means to deal with these invaders and not let them come back another time. You all should be there to profit by it. Take up Harald Edwinsson's advice on how you do it. We Danes can do well out of it and further our own cause now…..and on another day in the future. I have been present at the King's council and know what has been prepared. We just need enough men for the day. The northern allies come in great numbers but that is all. Only *Jarl* Anlaf has the real battle experience to lead them and the force may be so large as to be out of his control…….. They will fight like a rabble"

Grim spoke again. "Friends, have we reached any agreement on which I can speak to the King?"

After some more debate on how much support to give, Grim was asked to go to the King.

Grim walked over to the Athelstan's camp and walked up to him.

"Lord Athelstan, I am Grim the miller, a socman of Knaith, and I speak on behalf of my friends. They are all agreed to support you against your enemies and will do so with the best forces they can send."

"Grim, my friend," said Athelstan, "I am pleased to hear your words and I shall return to thank them. I should be grateful if you could assure them that food will be provided for all who serve me. Medicines and care for the wounded will also be given. But I would ask that only the best trained and equipped men are sent; those who are used to fighting as brothers. I would not wish for ill-trained and inexperienced boys to die for no reason, or old men who have given good service in the past to waste the happy years of their old age. Life has to go on and the villages should not be emptied."

"I will pass on those wise words, my lord" said Grim, thinking this is what we were going to do anyway. "My own, and only, son will be at the battle. I have no fear for his return from your service."

"Grim, my friend, he will return well rewarded. Let us now go to thank your countrymen."

Athelstan thought, yes, you rascal, you weren't going to be present in your tens of thousands, just enough to keep me on your side. I'll bet a son of yours is one of Edwinsson's berserks. They know how much I hate socmen as well. I'm sure they sent one to insult me.

"Watch yourself," said the voice in his head. "I know you don't like men without a lord. You can sort out his kind later. What did you think they were going to do? Refuse to defend their homes! They'll have a plan somewhere. Make sure you use it to your advantage. If it kills Vikings and apostates, why worry? What are a few Danes in the great scheme of rebuilding Rome? Do you really care how many die?"

"I do care," said Athelstan to himself. "I am the most Christian King in the world now the Great Karl is no more. God is looking out for all my enterprises against sinners and unbelievers. None of them will succeed against me. He sows dissension in all their plans. They will not succeed even if I do nothing."

"Don't be silly" said the voice. "You are a King of the Saxons. You are creating Angleland..... Saxons take action. They do not sit by in idleness."

"I hate that name" screamed Athelstan inside his head. "Why do these people insist on calling the place after the Angles? Whatever did they do to create it except live here and breed with the *wealas* and the Danes?"

"They plot against you with your enemies?"

"Do you think they do? Now who's being silly? Even the Scots can't tell us apart. They call us the same, *Sasseneach*."

The conversation would have gone on and on had Athelstan and Grim not returned to the assembly. Athelstan looked about. Thorolf gave him a knowing look and stared at Harald Edwinsson. Athelstan continued.

"My friends, Grim has conveyed to me your message and I was most pleased to hear it. Together we shall defend this land against the invaders from the north and maintain our peace and prosperity. Once again, I thank you."

He returned to his camp with Thorolf.

When he had gone, Grim spoke again. "He's got the better of us again, this Saxon. Whatever we do, he's one step ahead."

"We'll get our day in this country but not while they have kings like him," said Harald. "Let's all go home and get ready. Remember my advice!"

"He gave the same" said Grim. "Only the best fighters. Let us oblige him! But let's not forget the other issue for us, our own defence east of the river. I shall speak with Thorolf."

Athelstan and Thorolf walked on together. "Thorolf, I am always glad of your support. They followed your advice, I take it."

"I gave very little, my lord. Harald Edwinsson convinced them and I have no doubt for his own reasons. He wants no war east of the Trent, nor west of it, really. He would like to see greater Danish influence in the land."

"Well, he'd get that if I could get a tighter grip on York and the north. Men like him and yourself would do well out it. If Anlaf would cast his envious eyes elsewhere and stop stirring up trouble, the north would be more stable."

"I don't think we should set aside the threat of the Scots either, my lord, not just now but in the future. King Constantine is building up a unified country despite all his setbacks. I think he has difficulty with his influence in the far north and the western islands but the south is definitely coming under his direct control bit by bit. He looks longingly at Cumbria and parts of Northumbria. Moreover, he is not a man to take over now what he ultimately cannot hold. He is wise in many ways."

"I know he is very clever and experienced but frequently he is so poorly advised. He has underestimated our resolve and resources. I think he knows very little about us and we know a lot about him. We have the advantage of waiting for him to come to us now. We have been to see him and he knows what we can do as raiders. He does not know what we can do as defenders or on a battlefield. Neither he, nor Anlaf think we would want a pitched battle in a place we know, even though that place may not be of our choosing but theirs. They might think they are coming to split up and plunder but we shall not allow that. I hear nearly every cow-chief of the Irish has sworn to be Anlaf's man for the duration."

"True, my lord, but I for one do not intend to run about the Five Boroughs chasing cattle thieves if I can meet them all in one spot with a river at their back."

"Let's go and plan this battle, Thorolf, but not until after dinner. You are a wise man to want to meet them in one place. Let them all come to us. By the way what do you know about Grim the Miller?"

"Grim the Silent? He is certainly a man of few words unless he has something to say. His wife Emma is even quieter and it's rumoured all she has to do is look at you and she knows what you are going to say.........."

Good God, thought Athelstan, just like Auntie. I'll believe she can read minds as well. I'll bet her granny was one of the *wealas*.

"Athelstan," said the voice mildly. "You are getting pre-occupied with them. Most of them in Angleland are supporting you."

"……..He's been a warrior in his day but now definitely an advocate of the quiet life. He's much older than he looks. He's sixty if he's a day. Emma's a lot younger and some say she's a witch. They have an adopted son…… Grim is very clever. He's built a mill driven by water power. No one believes it works until they see it. It works by allowing the river to fill up a pool and then allowing it to slowly empty under his control."

"Do the priests call that witchcraft?"

"They would do, my lord, if he let them near it. He threatens to drown them in the pool if they come near. He tells them if they are true believers they will float."

Athelstan laughed heartily at that thought and saw church loads of floating priests in his mind. He laughed some more.

"Perhaps it is better for him, he keeps them away. They'll copy it and call it the wonder of God. Every abbey between here and Jerusalem would have one. The Romans had water power in corn mills but it went out of use here in Britain. I don't think the priests around here know that."

"King Athelstan, I really do wonder at what some priests know," said Thorolf, loud enough for one nearby to hear him. Tell that to the bishops, he thought. He went on.

"My lord, these men of God are creating a country within a country, they'll soon have more land than you. Make sure they return the service with soldiers to defend it and don't just sit on it getting fat."

"You're right, Thorolf, God is one thing and the Scotti kicking down the door is another. Anyhow Odo is here just in time for dinner again."

"My lord, some bishops can smell food cooking at a great distance."

"And when did you last say your prayers, you heathen," said Odo catching Thorolf's last comment on religion.

"Why, I said them only this morning, good bishop!"

"Yes, but to whom were they offered," he replied with some humour.

"I offered them humbly for the success of our King's enterprise and without a lot of fuss and dressing up in fine clothes."

"Come on to dinner, the pair of you. You are worse than children! No more of this until we've eaten. Then I must have had words with you and all the others here."

Athelstan's good humour never extended to anything to do with warfare. When questioned why, by those bold enough, he would say, war is too serious a business. It's not only the life and death of thousands but an issue of the immortal soul. He could never get to heaven if he sinned so greatly with war, that God thought he was not dispensing righteousness and justice at the same time. Athelstan believed the more penance you did on earth for war; the less you had to do before entering heaven. Some of his warriors often joked he would be sat waiting for them to arrive in heaven for a very long time, but not within his hearing. He was in reality gentle in some parts of his life. He took good care of his horses and his hunting dogs. His immediate servants he treasured and they were loyal to a man and woman. His personal chaplain never doubted his piety. His charity and concern for his friends and their families were legendary.

Bishop Odo took a similar view of war and no one seriously believed it was a teaching of the Church that war is good. The church just went along with it. He knew the enemies weren't really heathens and pagans anymore but he pretended. The church just picked one side and frequently chose both. Odo tried to have his priests and monks around to pick up the pieces, and even mediate the worst excesses when the battles were won.

Thorolf did not take that view. War was a violent extension of politics to him. Winning and being on the right side were important. The amount of the enemies' blood spilt in the process didn't matter. Thorolf's main aim in the coming months was to keep the invaders out of northern Mercia and the Trent Valley, and out of the Five Boroughs. Peace was very important to Thorolf. He thought short bloody campaigns were the best guarantee of it. Athelstan took a similar view. They talked often about it. Athelstan regretted sometimes one of his best supporters was a Danish warlord but realised he had to make do with what he had for followers. At least Thorolf was no traitor to him or anything he believed. Thorolf, he knew, understood the idea of recreating Rome and Britannia.

When the meal was over, Athelstan retired to the little church again. He thought to himself, the Danes don't deserve such a pleasant little place like this. Most of the rascals are still pagans at heart despite what they say. The place did have a well-used air about it and people were waiting outside to use it when he had left. After a few moments thought, he decided to go outside and talk to them.

"Good evening" he said. "I am pleased to see you come to prayer. This is a most pleasant place for a church."

"My Lord" said a woman at the front, "We believe there was a church here before we came to this land." She spoke in a Saxon dialect which pleased him.

"I did not realise this is a Saxon village," said the king.

"We all find we can live together around here. The land is good and there is enough to share at the moment without fighting over it," she added as an afterthought.

"Tell me more about the church?" He asked the audience.

Another man spoke and said. "This building was put here in your grandfather's time to replace one burnt down by the Danes. There was more stone in that one and it may have been built by the *wealas*. The Danes stole the stone for the foundations of their houses although many of the stones have now been returned. I can show you them."

He took Athelstan to what was obviously a more recently built part of the church to show him the neatly cut stones. There was a substantial wall with timber on top. Athelstan looked at the stone and thought, Roman, but where was it from, not originally from that first church surely?

"My friend," said Athelstan, "the Romans cut that stone but I think not for a church. Do you know of any ruins nearby?"

"I know of none too near, my Lord, but about a day's journey west is where this type of stone is found. I believe there were some great houses there but I have never seen any ruins myself."

"This is wonderful. I am so pleased to have visited this church and shall return to pray here again when I pass this way. I shall speak to your bishop to ensure this church receives money for its maintenance."

Grim the Miller had observed all this. He had not gone to the camp with the other Danes but had remained with Ivar his stepson to do some business in the village. They were staying with a villager and the three were maintaining some distance from the group outside the church.

His friend Edwin observed. "Our King knows how to talk to his people, Grim. Kings are bad news, however. They only bring war to your door…….. or demand taxes." Then he laughed.

"Edwin, sometimes I think your sense of humour betrays your pretended lack of loyalty to this man. You have fought for him and I thought a Saxon would not be so indifferent to a king's visit and interest in his people," said Ivar Grimsson.

"Edwin is worse than your father for looking at kings and lords with suspicion," said Grim. "He treats them all the same, Angle, Saxon or Dane, no wonder we get on so well. This Athelstan can't be bettered for getting people to like him unless you're a king of the Scots……… and then you just envy him."

"Watching kings tires me out," said Edwin, "especially the ones who have eaten and I haven't. Food should be ready at home now. Let's go and eat and besides, my people came from Angeln. What would I be doing, speaking too much good about any Saxon, unless it's my wife?"

"You like them really and the Danes as well. You are always friendly to us. It's well known how much you love your wife also."

"It's because we are all alike. We like doing business and eating and drinking," said Edwin with much more laughter. "And we all like being in love."

Athelstan returned to the few councillors he had with him. "Enough of us here to plan the next move in the war," he said gleefully. "We'll have our next major conference at Leicester in two or three weeks. We shall really need to look at strategy on land in detail. It looks already as if we have enough men to put inside the forts to defend the border on both sides of the hills. The forts won't fall if there are enough defenders. They don't have to stop the Scots and the Scots may not bother with them. While they are intact the invaders will be nervous and looking over their shoulders. We have enough for a good defence in depth, especially around here where the country is less hilly than in the west. I think this is the way they will come. Only the Romans have never invaded this island through the Humber and they used it for their navy once they discovered what a wonderful anchorage it is. It's too tempting not to put a large fleet into it, considering how windy the west coast can be at any time of year. I'd like you all to go away and consider the problems of putting together your parts of our forces, where to station them and how quickly we can bring them together east or west of the hills. I don't care if Anlaf goes directly to York. It doesn't follow he will invade south of our forts in the east or if he will invade at all. He could leave that bit to Constantine...... and we could scare off that old cow stealer in no time."

He invited ideas from everyone else but no one disagreed with his assessment and said they would meet with him in Leicester.

After they had gone Athelstan sat alone in his tent with his thoughts.

"Done it again," said the voice. "Your auntie would be proud. Grandad would be proud. You're the best of the line. Even God's on your side, my friend."

"I know," said Athelstan, "but why didn't he make me a Roman."

"You can make yourself into a Roman anytime you want. You and your friend Henricus can do this, and he's as crazy as you about it. It's the only way civilization can return to the world. You speak Latin better than most churchmen. You can do it."

"Yes, I can!" said Athelstan. "I'm king of Greater Britain, Britannia, not just of that awful Angleland"

"Athelstan, Athelstan, don't be so dismissive of the Angles. They are your allies and most of them are loyal. All the real traitors to you were from our own people....." said another much sweeter voice.

"What about the Cornish and the *wealas*, I have had to deal with them?"

"You over-react to a few malcontents."

"What about the Danes? How many did Grandad and my father have to kill before we had peace? Hundreds if not thousands?"

"Well, you haven't killed too many."

"Not yet, I haven't."

"Athelstan, listen to your Aunt, like people more. Why haven't you married? A woman in your life would make a difference."

"Auntie you know the reason, I love her still after all the years of loneliness."

"She was a slave you fished out of the sea after a battle. She was not royal or strong enough for childbearing. You just exalted her above all the other women around you."

"She was better than them all. Just like you, she could take care of me. She never scolded me or denied me anything. Everything I did was good and right for her and she would pray in church with me. She was a warrior's woman and by God, do I need her now!........And I've never met another like her! I wasn't just her king. I was her lover, the only man she ever loved. I'm so tired, Auntie, and there you and Uncle Ethelred are, ensconced in heaven with each other."

"I would not believe that if I were you, Athelstan."

Athelstan felt sad at that thought although no sadder than he had been for years. The years without a home or a real family had begun to tell on Athelstan. Campaigning, living in tents or just out in the rain, worry about the constant fights, too much poor quality food; it was all beginning to tell. The nights he spent alone missing Juliana without sleep began to tell also. It told on his spirit.

"Don't worry, all this won't go on forever" the voice called to him. "This is the price you pay for being king of Angleland and not just king of the Angles and Saxons."

Athelstan bellowed at the voice. "Don't keep mentioning those traitors to me!"

"Don't be a fool as well as a king, they are your people."

"If they are not on my side in this battle, they will all die."

"Athelstan, my Athelstan," said a still small voice, even quieter. "This isn't like you to hate people so much. Love your people for me who could never be their queen."

On hearing Juliana's voice Athelstan fell asleep peacefully until the dawn.

CHAPTER 2

ANLAF'S DILEMMA

Anlaf Godfricsson was not famous for having a happy frame of mind. For that reason he got on worse with the Irish than many others of a more cheerful disposition might have done under similar circumstances. He had profited from their divisions and seemed likely to do so for some time to come. Just like Athelstan he had his vision of an empire but his had nothing to do with the Romans. His world view ran from Ireland to northern Britain and back to Norway, and back to Orkney. He was content, but not happy, to share the land in between with Constantine and his mix of Scots and Picts and his Welsh and Anglian allies. He would abandon Dublin if all else failed but what he wanted most of all was Yorkshire and York as a capital, and just that. Some territory across the larger British island, sea to sea, would be enough, if all else failed. Athelstan could keep Mercia, Wessex, Anglia and what else was around it. It was impossible to capture all the lot. The place was so rich they could buy an army, just like they were doing now. If he wanted soldiers, he had to persuade, promise, threaten but he was good at that. So he thought he was!

After the last meeting of his Council he began to think that perhaps he and his fellow Vikings weren't really in charge around here. Events were just taking over. He had to call the meeting when a letter arrived from Athelstan and one from Constantine, King of the Scots, with an ambassador nearly on the same day. His plan originally was just to go to York with his forces from Dublin. He was going to land in the west but Athelstan suddenly put his fleet in the Dee and the Mersey. The Northern Welsh in Cumbria and Strathclyde were ready to help and the Northumbrian Angles in Bambrugh were prepared to stand aside. A simple plan, land a small army, march in, and take over with some local support. Then he would make a peace. The Danes in Mercia and Anglia wouldn't worry too much, as there would be no invasion of their land or the south. They loved the Saxons in the south as much as the Northumbrians loved them. Once the dust had settled, especially if it was done quickly, Athelstan might have thought twice and learned to live with it, especially if there was no invasion of Mercia. The Danes in the Five Boroughs could stay on Athelstan's side and persuade him to accept it.

But Anlaf had foolishly waited on the Scots to raise an army, promising destruction of the Saxons, righting the old wrongs done to the Northern Welsh, their southern cousins, their friends, and many other issues he never knew existed until his new allies had voiced them.

Athelstan's letter seemed to sum up for him the problems he now faced. It was surprisingly direct for a diplomatic letter, although perhaps it was the Latin language of its composition, he thought. It accused Anlaf of having designs on the lands of the Angles, Saxons, Danes and Britons which Athelstan's grandfather Alfred, had brought together in peace. Territory, which had accepted him as its overlord and paid him taxes and tribute, was under threat of invasion. Anlaf, he said, was conspiring with his subjects and with others who had sworn him friendship, causing them to break sacred oaths made before God. It went on to accuse him of harbouring his enemies and those of Christ and the Roman Church, a variety of heretics, apostates and sacrilegious heathens.

"Dear God, he's going on about the Romans again," said Anlaf when he first heard the translation. Anlaf was not really very religious in the Christian sense and he did think Athelstan took it too seriously. Previous correspondence in better times had mentioned Rome. In fact it always mentioned Rome and the Roman heritage.

It concluded by asking for his assurance this conspiracy would not continue and that he would open up Dublin for more trade and to priests from the true church. This last bit angered the monk who read and translated the letter for him. Anlaf thought the contents of this letter will be all round Ireland before the end of Sunday unless he murdered him here and now.

Not a good idea and so he decided instead he had better invite some of the bishops to the council.

It had not been a particularly friendly occasion but he consoled himself by thinking such a meeting to discuss war and the life and death of thousands, should not be joyous. It was the dissension amongst his fellow Vikings which distressed him most of all because he knew they could never hold on to their conquests if they were divided. His title as king was nominal, most of his supporters and sympathisers called him *Jarl*. Only a few sycophants had persuaded him to take the title of king to impress the foreigners. Athelstan's letter certainly never used it. It addressed him as always as "dear cousin" and not "dear brother. But then Athelstan knew how to send a letter to stir up trouble and cause dissension. Anlaf always wanted to be clever like Athelstan, to be able to read and write properly....... and own books he could read and understand.

Constantine's letter wasn't much better and in the view of some of his men, contained as much bad news. It asked him to delay his invasion until he, Constantine, could assemble his forces. Athelstan's last raid had cost him dearly in terms of men and money. People were beginning to lose confidence in his leadership and he need to cajole a bit more support out of the Picts who had been united into his country by his great-grandfather Kenneth McAlpin. They had always been a bit rebellious, thought Anlaf. The in-roads into their land by his fellow Vikings had always been strongly opposed if generally in vain. He didn't doubt Constantine could get the numbers together but he was concerned about the quality of the warriors and the equipment. He would have liked some horsemen. They would have been worth the wait but he suspected the crafty old devil was holding them back. Constantine knew today's friends soon turn into tomorrow's enemies and he'd often said to Anlaf that he made sure the Picts never got hold of horses in great numbers. Their expert use of them in the past had defeated the Scots many times. He'd even forbidden their leaders to ride them in battle when fighting for him. Anlaf thought that was strange. It didn't help that Constantine was also his father in law. Anlaf always felt Constantine had so many children, he had lost track of them. He couldn't remember who he'd married off to whom, and somehow he never treated Anlaf like a son. He was more like a vassal.

At the Council two of his most loyal men, Howerd and Toolig had argued for a quick invasion with the support of the northern Welsh. The Northern Angles might come in greater numbers as well, if only the capture of York and some of the land north of the Mercian defences running from the Mersey to the Humber were involved. No one should invade south of the forts as they had heard many were too strong to take and the country beyond them would be very hostile. They argued that by allying with Scotti and the Picti, it would lose us friends amongst Danes and Angles. They would expect their lands south of the forts to be pillaged because it was the richest. Anlaf suspected that was what Constantine wanted. Revenge on the Saxons, steal everything, and then turn on us. He's been getting too cosy with the Irish already. They want to go raiding in Mercia and they haven't yet boarded a ship. Haven't they heard the western sea is too wide to swim over the cattle they steal?

Toolig particularly worried about the Danes. They are quite united on both sides of the Mercian defences. If we attack the ones to the north, their southern relatives will take fright and be keener on Athelstan. We could send emissaries to re-assure them and deal honestly with them. We ought to try to get the Southern Welsh to rebel and not fight for Athelstan, if it's only to threaten Chester. We can spare them some men to help if Constantine and Owen are providing so many men.

Most members of the Council didn't agree. They didn't want the army spread so thinly. Anlaf also suspected that Constantine's ambassador, Callum the Red as he styled himself, had been spreading money about and making promises. Anlaf also suspected some of Athelstan's gold was also washing around the shores of Dublin. In the end he was talked into waiting for a large force to assemble and taking his ships around the north to collect some of it.

One of the few aspects of the plan to make real sense to him was a seaborne invasion via the Humber. Vikings had been doing that before the Romans came to Britain and since. The Saxons don't control it so tightly as the Dee and the Mersey, he thought. Callum's argument was that the Saxons only had such a small fleet; they couldn't dare to split it to become non-effective. This led him to think that was the reason why they stationed it as near to Dublin as they dare. The western harbours are the best place on the whole coast. It was a danger to Dublin. The fleet was small but it was good. They could, therefore, land unopposed in the Humber with the Saxon fleet on the other coast. However, they still had to leave a force behind to guard against these ships attacking Dublin or land one near them as a threat to their base at Chester.

So they agreed this would be the wider strategy with a diversion on the west coast to threaten the Saxons in Chester and Manchester, and the rest of their western defences. Most of that force would march down from

Cumbria. Anlaf thought these were the strongest of all the defences across northern Mercia and his plan had always been to march across to York avoiding them. Callum, who seemed to know his geography to well for his own good, said he could sail up the Ouse to York. Everyone but Anlaf got excited by that suggestion. No point in sitting in York, he thought while Athelstan's army gets larger. I know what he'll do. He'll dare us to invade and the longer we sit in York with him massing an army, the quicker we'll have to do it. He'll get stronger, the longer we wait.

Callum thought from such a base they could march south on the same route, Ryknield Street, which Athelstan had used for his invasion of the north. It would be the quickest way to get to the line of forts to establish control over the land north of them. Furthermore, if they could arrange supplies or take enough with them, there would be no need to live off the land and irritate the local Angles, Danes and Britons. Anlaf began to worry more and more. The details of the route and the timing of all this are being shared with more people. Too much can go wrong over the next year. We should have gone this summer past, not next year. Athelstan knows too much already.

Anlaf, as was his right, had spoken last. "So as far as our strategy is concerned, we need to agree now that a force from ourselves will land on the west coast and with some Cumbrian help will watch the western forts. The Strathclyde Welsh and Scots will march down the east coast. Our fleet with our main force will sail to the Humber; pick up ships with Scots and Picts on the way....... and food supplies from King Constantine. We'll all meet at York by the middle or end of August once the harvest is in."

Anlaf thought that was that and the meeting dispersed.

After the usual feasting, a few days had passed and Anlaf began to have more second thoughts. He had had a string of visitors from his own men and the Irish. Callum the Red had not gone home either which irritated Anlaf. He despised the man and had already wondered how he could get rid of him.

Firstly his men worried about the detail, despite nearly a year to collect the men and ships.

So he said, "My brother's son Hakon will lead the force to the west of the country. He's headstrong, I know, and it will keep him from doing anything rash in the real battle. We shall have this big battle with Athelstan unless we negotiate a peace. Perhaps, it is best if we can avoid a fight. We shall have the biggest army, and so he won't be able to rest while it is threatening his Mercian borders. He may not fight against such a large force."

There were worries about the weather and the northern harvest. No one trusted the Scots and particularly not the Picts. They had too much bad blood with the Scots to fight well for them and with the Vikings. They'll run at the first sign of a pitched battle was what most of his men thought. Anlaf's reply was the Irish are coming to fight for us and we don't trust them. But he acknowledged they were doing it for the loot as well as the glory. He secretly worried how they would perform against Athelstan's legionaries, as he had heard the man called them.

The bishops came about the religious dimension to it all. The Celtic Church was feeling vulnerable. The uneasy peace with Rome had begun to break down long ago and missions to their territory under the excuse of converting pagans were getting common. If people followed the old Gods and Goddesses, they were seldom found and very much hidden way in isolated parts of Greater and Lesser Britain. They were concerned Athelstan was getting support to challenge their power from the Franks and Germans. The Roman church gave more than moral support, they gave men and money. Saxon bishops were forgetting the teachings of Christ and becoming warriors, raising armies and carrying swords.

Anlaf's family had been nominally Christian for a couple of generations. He couldn't imagine churchmen behaving like that and said they made it up. Bishop Neal came clean and admitted to him they had many agents in Wessex and Mercia and knew what was happening. They had one or two in Francia and Brittany also he admitted.

This angered Anlaf to the point he screamed at them "not as many as in my city."

They left somewhat hurt after this observation and he thought, did they think I didn't know? Every servant listens to our conversations but we didn't come here conquering to plant our own barley and wash our own linen, so we'll live with the problem. At least they are telling the *Clans* to fight for us. I can sort out the problem from York. They won't come to pester me there.

Irish chiefs came in by the handful. The all asked the same question. How much they were likely to bring home? Anlaf gave them all the same answer, as much as they wanted as long as it came from his enemies and not his potential subjects. After the battle they could pursue the defeated army, attack the forts which he made out to be poorly constructed and defended....... take as much as they could in fact. And so every cow-chief within about twenty days march of Dublin turned up after this, swearing to be his man. This lot will have to walk down the west, he thought. They are not going by ship, they eat too much. They haven't a plan to get back either unless I provide the ships.

Sitric Oslacsson, however, came later with a problem which seemed trivial but as they talked it through, Anlaf began to wonder. Sitric he knew he could count on. They had seen a few bad times and neither were young. Sitric, he knew was a follower of the old ways, although he held no animosity to the Christians that he ever showed. He had a band of good followers who served well in Anlaf's cause. He had been away at the time of the council meeting and Anlaf had wished him there a number of times. He had a menace about him which Anlaf admired in a warrior, even though Sitric never saw himself more than a trader. He was rich and spread it around. His men were loyal but it wasn't just the money. When he spoke most sensible men listened.

"Jarl Anlaf, the man Callum the Red is treacherous in any lord's camp, including the king he pretends to serve. He knows too much of the Saxon's country for a man who claims never to have been there. Men are dancing to his tune on both sides of the western sea, and he seems set on bringing us to battle with Athelstan. Traders tell me that King Athelstan dreams of recreating the Empire of Rome in Britannia. It is said the Romans nearly conquered the whole of Greater Britain. Only the Picts held them off, and did finally beat them back to one of their walls. It's even said they completely destroyed one of the legions. I am sceptical of this myself."

"Sitric, nearly every kitchen boy in Dublin has heard of Athelstan's dreams. The traders once talked of nothing else."

"I've come really to talk of what Callum the Red speaks, when he has had too much of our ale……..

Now this I do want to hear, thought Anlaf.

"He talks of a red fort originally built by the Romans which guards the main eastern river crossing out of Mercia towards York. He says it's the only stone one in the whole string across the country except for Chester but I know that isn't true. I went first to trade in Chester with my father when I was fifteen and having been going back since, and we know that one is stone. There are others inland. His idea is that we should capture this eastern fort to hold the crossing for the rest of the army to move over. It's apparently the widest and shallowest ford and there are two more, maybe three, nearby to the north east, good but not as good as at this fort. It's so wide an army could cross on a broad front, especially if we are talking about large numbers. There are also some earthwork defences to the north, built by the Britons. These run from the hills to the marshes where some rivers meet to go into the Humber. There's an old Welsh fort as well which the Saxons hold."

Anlaf commented. "It is the way the Saxons moved against the Scots last time. Now either he was there, or he knew someone who travelled with them. There are few men of honour left on the earth, my good friend."

"Jarl Anlaf, I think this Callum wants us to hurry on the invasion of Mercia. Despite all being agreed that you are commander and the objective is York, he has his own plan or he has Constantine's in mind."

"Sitric! Watch this man, and report to me anything he says when his guard is down or even if it is not. I am certain he purposely plants foolish ideas in the minds of even more foolish men."

"He has come out with another one guaranteed to upset many of the army if not sow dissension. He laughs when he tells it, but I do not, nor do many of my men."

"Tell me the worst."

"Constantine has agreed the Picts can bring their Mhor Rioghain priestesses to the battlefield to fight with them."

"What? Do they exist anymore? Didn't that Saint Adomnan persuade them to stop worshipping the Great Queen and taking women into battles? Wasn't it some ten generations ago?...... That'll upset the Christians!" Anlaf laughed, forgetting he was supposed to be one. "Oh no, you think some of our lads will not like the Pictish Valkyries wandering about the battlefield."

Anlaf thought for a moment and said. "Christianity is on the surface with us in many respects. Everyone listens to the skald. The Irish and Welsh hear their bards. Women on battlefields are always bad luck. Before the battle they are a sign you are to die. They strip your body afterwards to give the crows and wolves an easier meal."

"I think this will just stir up problems. There are apparently about two score or more at last count who have been training in secret with weapons and magic. Constantine will know but I suspect he's gone along with the idea to get the Picts to come and fight," said Sitric. "The interesting bit which is going to cause the problem is that they fight naked and eat berries to go into a frenzy."

"That sounds fanciful," said Anlaf, "but the whole thing is getting out of our control and the Scots want us to run this campaign. Their troops will outnumber ours and be out of control once the battle starts. They are already picking the site of a battle and an invasion of Mercia we don't want. Athelstan is sure to find out, or it could even be his plan his spies put about. We can't hold on to the middle of the country even if we win the battle."

"They want Athelstan to sue for peace and give them back their tribute but he'll have spent that paying the Danes."

"By Odin, Sitric, you think of everything."

"Jarl Anlaf, how can we all have stayed alive so long if we didn't?"

"Sitric, in this battle I am beginning to think I can lead the army but will have no control over the fight. I will watch my own back and what I require of you is to watch the Scots. Whether we win or lose, deal with any of their treachery. You and your men stay close to Constantine and his family. If the Saxons don't kill them, we can if necessary, and come back another day. Keep the plan to yourself until nearer the time, hang back from the fight even if you have to.... and spare your forces. There'll be enough on our side to kill the Saxons. Well, if they all turn up, at least I hope there will."

"I'll work out something and let you know near to the time, *Jarl*."

"Organise a defence for this place for me. Put someone we can trust in charge who can't be bought off. You'll have someone."

When he'd gone Anlaf thought, I'll have his men watch over the whole army and deal with the dissension. He was right about the women. The Morrigan wash the armour of the dead. First woman who goes near a river or a pool to wash clothes, the men will kill her. I suspect the Picts will guard them well, so it may not be a problem till the battle. By then everyone should have staying alive on their mind. Afterwards there will be the usual chaos but that's what Valkyries do, bring chaos. Whichever way this battle goes, I need to profit by it.

But just in case it all goes wrong a way back to Dublin must be planned for our army and planned in secret. I need to talk to the Cumbrians and Strathclyders, I can trust them. I'll talk to Sitric about it soon. He'll know what to do. The rascal will have planned his way out in case of a defeat. He's clever but his father was too smart for his own good. He took too many risks with the Saxons. Look what happened to him. They killed him when he thought he could change from trading to pillaging overnight. Sitric always thought they had been watching him for a while and had the men ready. A traitor was suspected as well. The Saxons have too much money and buy the loyalties of weak-willed men.

Off he went lost in his thoughts, and wondering why I don't just settle on my own plans. My father in law is going to get me and mine into all kinds of difficulties, I can see it. Why don't I just do things my way? It works around here. Must talk to Sitric again about all this!

CHAPTER 3

SITRIC GIVES HIS ORDERS

Anlaf wondered who he could trust to consult with the Cumbrians. Despite the land being occupied by mainly Celtic peoples, many of the Vikings and some Angles had settled there. They were all living peacefully together at the moment. There had been a lot of friction in the past and the issue of a Saxon invasion might just be enough to bring unity. The Scots' King Constantine, his father in law, laid claim to the country and many there did not mind being his ally, provided he kept some distance from them. Ultimately Anlaf saw himself in York, allied with them and any Angles who had settled nearby. They had not much love for their southern cousins. The Danes there should naturally be his allies but they had their own agenda for power in Britain. He wondered if he could ever really divert them from it. For ambassadors, Anlaf settled on two of Sitric's sons. He chose two as he didn't want to appear favouring one over the other. He thought them both good men and wanted to help them, explaining to Sitric they should build up connections in the country. He wanted one to stay as a permanent ambassador and the other to return with the reply to his message. They could decide who did what at the time. He knew he could trust them as they were very direct in their approach to most of the problems of life, just like their father.

This pleased Sitric and when he was happy, the whole world was a better place. Sitric had no great hopes for the venture against Athelstan. He knew a fighter when he heard of one and a man who could inspire others. Sitric knew men's loyalties could be bought, but he set about the task Anlaf had given him to watch Constantine and his allies. He made a start by discussing the problem with his sons going to the Cumbrians, the other two staying with him and some of his leading men.

"*Jarl* Anlaf has many concerns about the coming invasion of Greater Britain. He wisely does not trust our allies. They cannot make a distinction between stealing and conquering. The Saxons and the Danes over there know the difference and we should learn this from them. It is the dilemma we face here in Dublin. Because we are strong, everyone wants to be our friend. We must therefore not weaken but I fear this campaign will do exactly that. When that happens, the Irish will come wanting the return of this place again and we will be too weak to prevent them from taking it back. However, this invasion is unstoppable. We should therefore do a number of things.......

.......Ragnold and Stigand will go to the Cumbrians and let us know what they think about the invasion. One could come back or send a messenger, to me first, not the *Jarl*. He has too many men looking over his shoulder and listening in corners. One of you might be better employed talking to the Welsh and the Angles on the border with the Scots and the ones from Bambrugh if possible. You do that Ragnold! Watch out for problems. There are men for and against Athelstan. Stigand, build us up a base with some support amongst the Cumbrians. They could be desperate to keep the Scots and the Strathclyders at arm's length. We could help......

.....Guthric and Siward I want you to stay here until we sail, train up our forces and make better allies of the Irish we can trust. Recruit some smaller forces to command direct. Soldiers, not cow stealers are what we need. There are plenty of them about at a time like this. Try not to pick too many Christians. Find out if there are any more pagans left in this country, if you can.........

....That's got the family sorted out. All know what we are doing? Good! Speak to me later about detail if necessary.........

.......Osbern and Sweyn! You've got the job of watching the Scots and their Pict allies on the way and at the battle. We shall pretend we are helping them but any sign of treachery on the way to the battle report it to me. Keep your ears open. On the battlefield, get your men and just deal with it........

......The rest of us, we just have a battle to fight and that is what worries me. Everyone is determined to meet the Saxons head on....and it will all end in misery. I know this Callum the Red talks about numbers being about sixty thousand on our side but how many will be any good. Its twelve legions and only the Romans ever had that many soldiers and never all together in the same place in Britain. Who is capable of managing so many men and camp followers? Most will be starving. We are not going hungry. Beorn you are going to be in charge of the supplies for us. Not because you can cook but because you can fight to get food and hold on to it. Better than anyone I know……..

……Hemming and Sweyn, you have the hard job of getting us better equipped. See me together about the money and don't tell anyone how much we are spending. Hemming you are going to have to stay here in Dublin with some good men and hold on to all this. We don't want the Irish taking it back the day after we sail and we are only taking warriors. Get the young lads in training. They'll look fierce from a distance and they'll be more than a match for a lot of the locals. *Jarl* Anlaf's got most of the ones we can't trust coming with us anyway but you could look for some who could be on our side…..Any questions?"

Sitric's men never interrupted as he spoke. It was his custom to have his say and once finished they could argue as much as they wanted. They all knew that he was careful with words.

Guthric spoke first."Father, that Scot, Callum talks about women warriors coming with them, almost making it sound like an advantage to us. We know the stories of old. I think they are trying to frighten us somehow, even though it's not working in my case."

"I am pleased to hear that, son. At nearly twenty you should be at the age of understanding these things. We don't quite know why this is just yet. We shall probably be involved with picking up these women. Anlaf plans for us to all sail around the north to the Humber. Have any of you ever been there?"

Beorn said. "That's sensible, it's shorter travelling time. We can be there in ten weeks at the right time of year and weather. You did say Athelstan's fleet is in the western sea?

Sitric nodded and then said, "next to the Thames, the Humber is the biggest anchorage in Britain and one of the safest, especially late in the year. It's wide with marshes on all sides and sand bars, any amount of rivers flow into it they say, seven or eight. Remember it needs careful navigation. Warn all our crews."

"We should get food on the way?"Asked Guthric.

He nodded again but spoke. "Constantine has promised supplies but I doubt there will be enough."

"We'd better talk about the details of watching the Scots when we land. We'll have a feel for what's happening by then."

"If I march down with the allies, am I right in thinking that is the route back if all fails. If it is, I can make some preparations and I can make sure we don't make too many enemies getting there," said Stigand.

Everyone mmmmmed at that idea and Sitric said proudly.

"A good suggestion, son. Whichever way either of you lads come, don't leave the doors shut. We just never know and we are with friends. Try to make sure the rest behave, but that will be difficult. I'll talk to Anlaf about all this. I wish I had more confidence in the outcome. Remind every soldier, that the Saxons are training. Some of them may be farmers but they are training to defend their homes. There are also the mercenaries. Athelstan saves his money for rainy days like the ones he sees coming. If we weren't committed to this side, I'd sail everyone to Chester and we'd sign up for some of this money."

"Dad," said Ragnold! "If this all goes wrong, you might see me carrying King Athelstan's standard."

"Son, no one would blame you if you managed to stay alive."

Everyone laughed and someone said, like father like son, which Sitric took as a compliment.

Ragnold spoke again and said.

"You've trained us all well father and it seems some simple mistakes are being made here. Red Callum seems to be talking too much in public about the plans and a brown fort in the Don River valley. Grandma seems to know about the river and says it's a sacred one to the *Welsh*. She says it demands blood every year like the Liffey, the Dee, the Shannon and the Severn but that's a side issue. Callum's ideas must have got to Athelstan's spies by now."

"Callum's convinced we will have enough men to win a pitched battle, so better to fight it on ground of our own choice. There is said to be some rolling open country to the south of The Don according to him" said Stigand. "He hasn't convinced me we can win, but he's probably convinced King Athelstan to turn up."

They talked a bit longer and Sitric closed the meeting before word got around Dublin and the spies came to listen.

Ragnold and Stigand went for a walk outside the camp where no one was listening. They sat on rocks overlooking the river. Ragnold spoke first.

"Stig, the more I think about this, the more I know Dad and Uncle

Anlaf are right. King Athelstan wants the *Scotti* and the *Welsh* to come for a pitched battle and King Constantine involving us is just to his advantage. He gets Uncle Anlaf's generalship. We ought just sneak over next month and grab York, rebuild the defences properly and offer some sort of peace to all the neighbours."

"King Constantine's price for supporting us is that he takes part in it; him and his allies. They won't rest till they have had vengeance on the Saxons. No good will come of such desires, Brother. Grandma's been having bad dreams about it all for weeks now."

"I'd be the last to suggest we live our lives around Granny's dreams but they do serve as a warning to take care, especially where we are going. Has she seen we are going to die?"

"She has warned young Guthric to be careful about women on the battlefield but he's her favourite anyway. She wouldn't worry too much about us, would she, Stig?

"Ragi, this does remind me we had better travel lightly, swiftly and secretly across to Cumbria. Remember we are real spies, and not princely ambassadors masquerading as them. I'll pick a handful of men we can trust and let's go before anyone knows we were even thinking about going, or I'll be expecting a ship full of Saxons waiting over there to greet us. We are going to be away for six weeks with the best of weather. The crew in the boat are not going to know till we're at sea. I'll tell them first we are going to Donegal to look for warriors. They'll understand the need for secrecy."

"Too many people around here wanting foreign gold they don't have to take with a sword, as Dad would say. It worries me that Athelstan has put his fleet in the west and nothing is happening with it. A man like King Athelstan does nothing without a reason. He's up to something and murdering us he would do in passing, like his father did with grandad."

"I agree, Brother, and I am going to sharpen my sword. You never know with Donegal men or Saxons. You need a sharp sword when dealing with both."

"If we are going even near Donegal, I am sharpening mine also. Let's go and invade the kitchen. Granny could be baking today."

Guthric, Siward and Hemming had left Sweyn talking with Osbern and some of the others outside the hall. Sitric had put Hemming in charge of training his two younger sons some time ago. He had been big brother and surrogate father and nursemaid to them for 10 years since their mother died. Hemming wasn't disappointed to be left behind. He knew the great value

Sitric put on having a home and a base, and to be trusted with it, was to be as good as being on his side in battle. He had only been seventeen when Sitric asked him to care for his sons. The other young men laughed a little until they saw how much Sitric valued what he did. From the beginning he was always at Sitric's council with the boys and on the high table at a feast. Hemming had always been quiet and slightly distant from the other boys when younger.

His father had been Sitric's steersman and had been killed in some almost-forgotten sea battle with the Scots and Picts when Hemming was a baby. Sitric never forgot his friends and supporters, or his enemies and he hated traitors. His choice of confidants seldom failed him and Hemming was no exception. People guessed Sitric had no great hopes for the invasion where a pitched battle was involved. Quick conquests were his and Anlaf's real strength. To choose Hemming to command his base would say everything to those who knew Sitric. People knew Sitric was coming home whatever happened in Mercia. Hemming knew now that he was going to left in charge of Dublin also. Sitric would be asking his *Jarl* in a way he could not refuse him.

Siward the younger of the brothers looked a bit miserable. "Hemming, you won't be with us at the battle."

"It's time now for you to stand up for yourselves. You must fight with your father! I have done this many times. You don't need me with you. Your father has given you some tasks. I shall help you in them and then when you sail, we shall part as men and as friends. When you return, we shall go into battle together. Remember I was about your age when your father asked me to watch over you. That task is over for me once you sail as warriors."

Guthric said. "Hemming, I am always inspired to hear you talk. Dad always said he told you your main job was to inspire us. We had better discuss what we are going to do. But let's go somewhere quiet and you little brother, stop looking like you've fallen over your feet and don't tell anyone what we say, not even Granny and certainly none of the servants. Every washerwoman between here and the big ocean will be talking about it."

"Yes," said Hemming. "There are enough secrets in this camp which are secret no longer. If your father suspects anyone of blabbing, they'll wish they were dead and if it's either of you two, I'll take him the pieces for your Granny to put back together. We need not concern ourselves with the invasion or what your brothers do. We want men and equipment. I am going to take you out west to meet some men who are anxious to make names for themselves in this country and need some money to do it. Cattle are still the main currency around here but that is going to change. The best source of money is the Saxons. These men don't have the means to get over there and enlist with King Athelstan, but they can be convinced that "King" Anlaf is the next best."

Like his chief, Sitric, Hemming never thought of Anlaf as King, only *Jarl*.

"So when do we meet these people," said Siward.

"All too soon, my young friend. Your father has had me working on this for a while. You can guess I can keep a secret around here. It is best for you to follow my example. People will find out soon enough what we are doing. Just make sure they don't hear it from you. We'll talk here just before evening meal. The servants will be too busy to spy on us......... Until then!"

Hemming went back to his hut where he knew Bronagh was waiting. Many of the older Vikings were a little uneasy about him living with a woman they saw as local and a chief's sister. She was actually from about two weeks march west from Dublin in the middle of the island. Hemming treated her as a wife, not a slave or some woman he found around camp. He had found her while out trading with Sitric. Only the three of them really knew the circumstances and it was a secret they shared. She went around dressed as befitting her status. Her long red hair and pale skin made her an attraction in Dublin but only the foolhardy would have dared to make advances. Hemming was well known for his skill as a warrior and Sitric was never known to avoid a fight where the honour of his men, or their women, was concerned. Sitric liked to build up fear around his men. Hemming and one or two more of his men, were good at assisting him. Only strangers or fools tended to challenge them.

Bronagh's history was simple and straightforward. A trading mission to the middle of the island had gone wrong and Sitric found himself in the middle of a fight between the local chiefs. Having an instinct to be on not just the winning side but the side he wanted to win, Sitric and his men fought also. Sitric chose the apparent losers who then became the winners, knowing the result would be two weak clans he could influence. The winners were grateful for help and the losers were grateful he had killed so few of them. Somewhere in all this Hemming found a frightened girl hiding in a burnt-out hut and fell in love. Bronagh often said to him she didn't know who to fear the most at the time; her own demoralised family or the other side... Or even him. She was glad of a way out and never said at the time which side she had been on or her real name. Bronagh, the sad one, was a name she chose because of her situation and certainly away from Hemming she was seldom seen to smile. She was overjoyed to find he would be staying, but less happy at the news that he planned to take Guthric and Siward back to where she was born. Her family had been assisted by Sitric and her brothers still lived as the clan leaders. She didn't want to go back. Hemming explained he was to take the boys to recruit the soldiers for Sitric to take to invade the Saxons. She seemed fine with that. She was never frightened of Hemming and Sitric treated her like a daughter. Even his mother had always been there for her. Her own mother had been killed in the same raid as her father. She had hidden under some skins in a part burned hut and had survived. All the time she planned her revenge. Peace may have broken out in the west but not in Bronagh's heart. She was just waiting her time.

Ragnold and Stigand wasted no time setting sail for Cumbria and getting on with the job. It came as no surprise to them that no one loved the Saxons, the further north you went. The *wealas* really wanted to be independent but knew they had no hope beyond being clients of the Scots. The thought of Anlaf as king in York brought them little joy as they expected to be fought over between him and the Scots. They did not expect the current alliance to last beyond the war. The Norse in Cumbria were suspicious of Anlaf's alliance with the Scots. They would have preferred him to invade Yorkshire and just wait and see what a peace could bring. They didn't feel too threatened by Athelstan. The Angles on the other coast and bordering Northumbria feared that at any moment they might find themselves prisoners of the Saxons. They knew the fate of spies in Athelstan's country. After a round trip of some weeks they were glad to be safe in Cumbria with some Scots despatched by King Constantine. They were all on the same business to ensure the Cumbrians of all shades were on the side of Anlaf and Constantine.

The Cumbrians were quite happy to keep open the link back to Dublin which Sitric wanted but many of them were looking for the rewards that the war might bring in terms of Saxon loot. They wanted some assurance the Saxons would be defeated and were not easily persuaded. The gold brought by the Scots helped a little but for the long term they wanted the protection of either the king of the Scots or from a king in York.

Stigand went back home to Dublin with the news. Ragnold stayed behind to try to build up some more support.

Neither Sitric nor Anlaf were totally surprised with what he reported. Threats and money were the only solution as far as Sitric was concerned. They would change their minds with a Scots army marching through and a Viking one marching back but for the moment, keeping on good terms was the best remedy. Not the outcome Sitric wanted but at least he had Ragnold on the ground, and sent a message for him to stay and not move from there. He wanted to develop the original plan to keep open an escape route. It was beginning to look more necessary than ever. Sitric was going to work on the basis no one really knew what was going to happen in that space between the Scots and the Saxons where his *Jarl* was trying to put himself.

At least things were looking better in the west of Ireland. Hemming was getting a good number of recruits. Men were starting to flock to him on the basis there was some good booty to be obtained in the land of the Saxons. Many who had tried their hand at piracy in the past attested to this, and the one or two who suggested they would have to fight very hard for it, were ignored. He got mainly fighters and not adventurers, but found he could not chose too well as Bronagh's brothers did not want to deplete their own forces to much. The men seemed to lack no courage but equipment was going to be a problem, especially armour of any sort. Hemming didn't worry. He knew enough of war to know that even many well-equipped men only went on a one way journey to a battlefield. They could find something to fit there.

He found more support amongst the neighbours who were a bit jealous of the prosperity the connections with Dublin, had brought to Bronagh's clan. They were clearly seeking wealth to improve their situation. He thought they would be disappointed whichever side won. As time went on Hemming could not think anything but, why don't we just walk into York whilst all this chaos is taking place in the Isles of Britain? We could abandon Dublin before it abandons us and set up there. Once there we'd get enough allies. The Danes for a start. Most of the Angles would be with us. The Cumbrians also. The Scots would be angry they had no part in it and had no chance to raid in Saxon territory.....That was the problem, but where would they would be without us. It was, he suspected, this threat from the Scots which was uniting the Saxons, the Danes and whatever Britons remained south of Cumbria. They were all doing too well under Athelstan's peace. They would be turning out to fight for him as well. Moreover, they would be well equipped and not hungry. War and starvation went all too well together in Ireland.

Sitric's name seemed enough to bring in some support and the presence of his sons was the correct signal to the Irish of his sincerity. Ten score of men were signed up fairly quickly and the promise of as many more at the time. A dozen or so formed a little band with Guthric and Siward and agreed to come to Dublin at once. They would return to fetch the rest after the winter. They would come by sea and return overland. Anlaf's money would buy them a safe passage and for the men returning with them. All ran smoother than Hemming thought it would which made him worry a little. He didn't trust Bronagh's brothers and had to say on some reflection that she had warned him. She did believe that the war which had caused their parents' death had been as much their causing as their enemies. He was quite glad to leave when a message came from Sitric for him to return without the boys.

CHAPTER 4

CONSTANTINE'S DILEMMA

Ever since the Saxon invasion or raid the year before, the definition depended on whose opinion was given, Constantine's country had been in chaos. Not that the Saxons did too much damage compared to what they might have done, it just took a lot of money and goods to persuade them to go away. Constantine was not surprised they didn't want hostages as he knew Athelstan wouldn't set much store by them. He knew Constantine wouldn't give him anyone important so no one would be too unhappy when he had to kill them. So he never bothered to ask. He had his men kill anyone who resisted and who he saw as a future threat. It came as a shock to the Scots just how ruthless Athelstan was in his instructions. Many of Constantine's supporters failed to understand the message behind the invasion and continually clamoured for revenge, the moment Athelstan's army left and the supporting fleet sailed back to the Thames.

Constantine made the initial mistake of giving in to all this clamour and clatter and allying himself with Anlaf Godfricsson who, if left to his own devices would have sailed for York and caused enough upheaval for the next seven generations. The Scots could have stayed at home and consolidated their place further south of their country, making alliances with the Welsh and the Angles around there. These Angles at least had more sympathy with him than their distant relatives to the south. It did irritate the Angles that the Scots continually referred to them as Sassenaech, Saxons.

King Constantine had none of this wisdom and pressured Anlaf into holding off his invasion while he got his forces, and those of his allies, together. He sent his man, Callum the Red to Dublin with enough gold to bribe Anlaf's men if necessary. Callum thought their vanity and the prospect of power in York would be enough, but he was of the revenge party amongst the Scots. They had extensive influence in Dunnottar, Constantine's capital. His advice to his king had been for Anlaf to lead the campaign and then the Irish and the rest of the north would come on board. The southern Welsh and Cornish might take a chance also. Seemingly all it would take was one defeat. They all had grievances against the Saxons and the Mercians, and some of the Danes. Callum was in reality unsure of the southern Danes and Anlaf was no help. Anlaf had written off their support. They had got too settled and cosy in the Five Boroughs. They were not seeing themselves as invaders any more. Anlaf in a period of oversight had agreed to wait and set aside his own plans............ He just hoped the Danes would support him once he was over there.

Anlaf had written to Constantine suggesting that they limit their forces to the better quality troops and not put out ideas of raiding into Danish Mercia. Athelstan might let them be and they should move immediately to invade. However, events were out of the control of both men. A campaign had been preached for some years already by men anxious for glory, and the bards and Celtic church had taken it up. Athelstan had, of course, heard about this and his attack on the Clyde valley and the east of the country had been an attempt to frighten off a potential invasion. However, the momentum was unstoppable as everyone built up their little armies, failing to understand Athelstan's large effective one never really stood down. They failed to see he enlarged it further with help from his continental allies and the Roman church.

When Constantine counted the spears he felt vindicated by his decision and despatched Callum to Anlaf with the news in case he might be tempted to change his mind. He needed Callum also to sort out the strategy with Anlaf. All that was going well in his view but he need to settle a few internal matters of politics while Callum was away. He was concerned the man was getting too big for his boots. He had answer for every question and was getting too popular by far.

Callum had worked out the strategy himself and the choice of meeting place to assemble the armies to invade Mercia. The area of Yorkshire around the old Northumbrian forts was ideal to him but he voiced it too many times for Constantine. Athelstan was bound to hear of it. Callum's answer was what does it matter with the size of the army we are taking? It's the greatest assembled in these islands since Roman times. He said that and people believed him. This army in Constantine's view was nearly all a rabble compared to several Roman legions. What was worse, the good troops were likely to be spread so thinly to make no difference, if the bad ones ran away at sight of the Saxons. What Constantine could not quite understand was the idea of meeting to fight near a fortress, probably the best one on that eastern part of the defensive system, Athelstan's Roman wall, just because everyone seemed to know where it was. No one seemed to know whether or not it could be taken, despite the size of the army they were marching up to it. In fact no one knew anything about it, except it existed. Someone was bound to suggest forcing the crossing it was guarding without knowing how well it was defended or what they were going to do once they were over and past it. It would all get out of control. He just hoped numbers counted because he had never got the Saxons to a pitched battle with a large army, and Athelstan had been careful to avoid one. When they were up north, they never waited around for a large force to assemble. They purposely kept on the move.

Constantine had never lost sight of the need to consolidate his hold on his own country by conquering the land to the south as his grandfather had done with the north. It had been a mixed blessing taking in the Picts but it was helping to keep out the Northmen. He needed to repeat that process and get a border with what Anlaf may capture and hold. The people were a mixed bunch but they were not always against him. They were more worried about what was happening in the south of Britain and so was he. He persuaded himself he could help Anlaf in a time of need. No one else at his court seemed to trust the Dublin Vikings, despite them being really few in number and the marriage alliance. The local Angles and Welsh he really wanted on his side. He spent hours musing on the issues and what to do, almost in fear of asking his supporters. Their advice was always conflicting.

The problem of raising armies had generated some resurgence of nationalism amongst the Picts and some indifference in the western islands. Constantine had some grudging respect for Picts as fighters in a small scale conflict. His grandfather Kenneth macAlpin had persuaded them into a form of unity by both negotiation and fear of the constant Viking incursions which hadn't really stopped. Allied with the Scots they were better able to resist in the interior of the country. The coasts had always been difficult to defend even with the ships they had, although Kenneth did make the mistake occasionally of allying with the Vikings. Constantine always felt that was inviting the wolves into the house and really preferred to keep a distance from them. The thought constantly on his mind was how he could use them.

He knew Athelstan was a clever diplomat and how he envied him his alliances and the way he had of dealing with his neighbours. The offer of friendship always backed up by a real threat of force if necessary. No bluff or bluster with Athelstan. He always did what he said he would do. Constantine put some of this down to the quality of his advisers and the endless amount of resources he seemed to have from a wealthy country. Accumulating wealth seemed no good to you in the north. It always cost you too much to guard it from the thieving neighbours. He really felt he ought to have made a friend of Athelstan once again and not repudiated the treaty, when all his supporters wanted to do was go south and rob as much as they could. Cattle stealing and slaving was about as much as many of them were good for. They had no view of a bigger picture; to create a country with some stability and peace. They thought a campaign in southern Britain was like a skirmish with the Welsh and Northumbrians. The one taste they had of Athelstan's power had no effect on their thinking. Many of them hadn't even been present when the Saxons arrived. They'd never counted the mercenaries and looked at the quality of the equipment. What was even worse they hadn't counted the dead on the little battlefields or met any of his ruthless supporters. They had lost no family or followers.

Callum the Red's idea was that after the victory, the country in the north would accept Constantine as its overlord, Anlaf would have York and be a buffer between the Scots and the Saxons and Athelstan, after defeat, would content himself with the south. The simplicity of this was not appealing to Constantine. He had been a king too long to be taken in by such a simple strategy. It didn't account for Athelstan winning or wanting revenge if he lost. One battle would never decide all the issues and no one knew how much support Athelstan had in his own country. Probably he had already sold his supporters the idea of unity, similar to the one being advocated by Callum for the north, and they were no doubt in agreement. His hadn't grasped it yet. They just wanted a fight and some loot.

Despite his name Constantine was no Roman but he would sit many hours wishing he was. He wondered how they could have held on to such diverse groups of people for so long when the Picts his nearest neighbours, were so much trouble to him. They had never forgotten they ruled the country and held off the Romans from the far north. The Welsh settlement of the southern lowlands had only been with Roman connivance. Some even thought the Romans had encouraged the Sassenaech to settle as a buffer between them and the Picts. What diplomacy he thought! If only I could get Anlaf to do that for me between us and Athelstan without having to march an army so far south. Constantine felt old and lonely with his thoughts and his dreams.

A deputation of Picts had been waiting for two days to discuss the invasion but he was refusing to meet them to talk in detail until another from the Welsh and Angles arrived. They had a woman with them whose presence was putting the whole court on edge. The priests said she was a witch and in the same breath, that the others in the deputation were Roman Christians and not to be trusted. Athelstan was a Roman Christian. Constantine just wondered how far the man's influence was stretching. One of his men Fergus macCaennath had said his daughter frightened her children to sleep with threats of Athelstan the bogeyman. Hardly anyone but Fergus and the warmongers thought that was remotely funny. Fergus had never met the real one. Constantine knew he was old but as the days went on he just felt older and older.

After another week the rest arrived and Constantine felt comforted by the numbers and the genuine declarations of support. Even the Pictish woman he considered to be welcome by this time. Her presence still unnerved many of the men and some wanted him to send her away, but he was fascinated by what she might think, and what was her purpose at the assembly? No one involved who knew her was letting on. Most others suspected she was a *clan* chief. The Picts had a more equal view of men and women in the past, although the influence of the Roman Church was ending all that. Sometimes the atmosphere at his court was falsely lightened by one of the factions playing a game of Spot the Traitor, every time a new deputation arrived. Constantine could not laugh at this. It was too close to the truth. Someone was running with information to Athelstan and he didn't really think it was the local Sassenaech. They could gain nothing by it except ruin. Someone was gaining money or power in the north from this particular bit of treachery, but for the life of him, he couldn't work out who it was.

When his Council and the deputations finally came together, tempers were fraying, in many cases just because of the waiting, but at least Callum the Red was not there to stir up more trouble. He had given him the name of Red, not only because of his red hair, but to distinguish him from Black Callum, another of his allies, a macNeill from the Isles. Black Callum, called so because of his lack of humour, was Constantine's conscience. He could always be called on to look at the darker side of a problem which the optimists would never consider. Constantine valued him greatly as a supporter. He had a bad habit of being right in the view of many people, especially those who thought he had more influence and control of events than was apparent. His prophecies seemed self-fulfilling. Constantine felt tired and put Black Callum in charge of the meeting.

Constantine set aside his right to speak first and this was his first mistake. The Pict woman requested to speak and no one challenged her. Even Black Callum felt he had no choice but to allow her. She began in the language of the Gaels and not her own Pictish.

"My name is Brigid and I am *Cailleach*."

A deathly hush fell on the meeting. She continued.

"Too long we have all suffered the oppression of the *Sassenaech* and the Northmen who come at us from the land and sea on all sides. It is time for us to take our destiny in our hands and return to the way of our ancestors and oppose this. We repelled the Romans and their legions. They were only made up of the same people and these are not such an army. They only defeat us because we do not expect them. We suffer them when they take us by surprise. If we now present them with no surprise in sufficient numbers in their own country, what choice do they have but fight us in a battle we can win? In their own house they have nowhere to run. When we defeat them we must take it over. We turned out the Romans once before and we can do the same to those who pretend to be them. Our ancestors broke through the last Roman walls and they lie now in ruins. A string of forts with enough space between should present us no problem if we hold our force together and move as one. Their country is rich and we can live off it. There we may even find friends who would provide for us and plundering would not be necessary, unless from our enemies."

Sweet Christ, thought Constantine, they'll eat out of her hand. She went on.

"We must invade before they get too strong and organised. We cannot wait for the self-styled king of Ireland when we have our own true noble King who has sufficient years and experience for the task. Constantine and his sons can lead us. Who else do we need?"

At this point the Scots, Welsh and Sassenaech nodded in agreement, the Picts just smiled. Brigid continued:

"We must return, however, to the ways of our ancestors in our preparation for battle. Everyone must train well and prepare for death and no one should fear it. All the soldiers must attack with the name of the Great Queen on their lips. My priestesses are prepared to attack and die in order that the victory may be ours. The soldiers should not fear to follow them. This is the way we defeated the Romans. We can defeat this pretender Athelstan the same way!"

She sat down. The members of the war and revenge party almost to a man stood up enthusiastically demanding to be the next to speak. Constantine felt trapped. Black Callum was made of stronger stuff than his king ignored them all and acknowledged Murdoch macEanruigh who had sat in silence like him. He thought he would talk some sense to the meeting and not just clamour for war.

"I have sat listening to this woman and thought she was advocating we all go out and get ourselves killed. I thought she should save her words for shouting at warriors on the battlefield and not for the councils of kings. This is what I originally thought. But I examined her words and took out of them some wisdom. She is right we should go to the land of the Angles, Saxons and Danes with a great and organised army. We should equip one and train it. We should also inspire it. We could stand a chance of beating the Saxons, but we must not go with a rabble which falls apart at the first signs of difficulty. We need unity of force and purpose. I agree with her, only our Lord Constantine can lead this army not that Viking bandit from Dublin. I think he is too treacherous. Once he is installed in York, he will forget his friends. I do not rate him as a commander just because he claims he puts fear into what he calls, a bunch of disorganised cow stealers across the western sea. Our kindred over there will have their day with him and this may come soon if he becomes pre-occupied with being king of York. His own men fight well but only for him. I think they will not fight so well for us. This army we plan is getting very large and most it will come from our lands. We are proposing to let him command it for his own ends."

He sat down and the war party clamoured again to speak. Constantine got up.

"Countrymen," he said, ignoring Brigid, "the strategy in this venture is ours. We have decided to put an army into the middle of Athelstan's kingdom by the best means we know, a march overland and a fleet into the Humber. This is the weaker half of his defences and the Danes to the north of them are likely to be on our side if we deal honestly with them. York is a fortress and a good base. People say it has walls just as the Romans left it. We may have double or almost three times their force, if we have time to assemble it. Red Callum is organising the sea transport of a good number and the rest will march down through land sympathetic to our cause. The Vikings intend to create a western diversion to keep some of the Saxons occupied near the forts on the western border. We can break through in the east. He has to fight us there. We must make sure we pick the time and place."

Constantine sat down and Black Callum spoke, almost forgetting previous reservations.

"Friends, we must make sure we fight as soon as possible in a summer before a winter sets in. We cannot over-winter with a large force next to such unfriendly territory."

He acknowledged Angus macCullen without thinking one of the leading lights of the war party is going to speak. The rest of the meeting fell silent for Angus.

"Lord Constantine, I worried when I saw this lady appear at your court. I worried that our northern brothers...or sisters, were not on our side in this campaign to revive your fortunes. I suspected their loyalty to you, but now I have heard their position put by the Lady Brigid, I regret my mistrust of their motives to want to hold this meeting before today. I am glad everyone present has been able to hear this declaration. Out of this campaign we should try to unify ourselves against the threat from the south. King Athelstan's power increases as his country becomes stronger and he has many allies amongst the Franks and Germans as well as in Rome. All we have is ourselves at this council and some of the Welsh. We have to trust each other for this venture as we can all gain from it. We should try to rekindle the flames of past glories. Remember if once we are defeated, the southern rulers will try to extend their power north. They want an empire and in our country, and that of the Welsh and Irish, is the only place they can create it. Athelstan dreams of success where the Romans failed. We know who and where our enemy is. We should go and attack before he comes again to us."

Black Callum gathered himself before the next speaker thinking, how has this Brigid charmed us all? We are gasping for war without a thought. "Duncan macFinlay." He said, hoping to hear some restraint. Duncan did not disappoint him.

"The best thing we can hope for in all this is for there to be chaos in the land of the Angles and Saxons. Why don't we just let Anlaf get on with it?"

Constantine thought what a relief, he's broken her magic. We don't have to go rushing off south when Anlaf and the Irish will do it for us. We won't upset the Danes that way by stealing what's theirs, just to be able to eat. They could all turn on the Saxons. They went there to conquer, remember? We can stay at home and recover from their last foray. My lands and followers suffered from them. They stole everything they could and burnt the rest and you lot were no help. You only crawled out of your holes when they had gone"

These comments caused some unrest which Callum had difficulty in containing until Brigid spoke softly.

"My friends, Duncan macFinlay is genuinely aggrieved here. You did not come to his aid as you should to an ally and a brother. This should be a lesson to you all not to show weakness to Athelstan. Even though it is a great distance to Winchester, the kings of Wessex can still cause dissension in this place. If he brings his army again, your lands will be as Duncan's, so show him more sympathy. Athelstan has spies everywhere. Someone will report this meeting to him and who has said what. We can only prevent this by going to him."

One of the bishops, Strachan, indicated he wanted to speak. Black Callum signalled his agreement.

"Athelstan seeks to further the power of the Church of Rome. Already its priests and monks are in the north amongst this Brigid's people. They are causing her and her ilk to cause discord in this meeting for we have not yet discovered her real purpose. That is to revive witchcraft and pagan beliefs in our land. God will not give us victory if we allow this to happen. Holy Saint Adomnan forbade women on battlefields. If we go against the words of saints, God will curse us all. The Roman Church is strong in the north and our true church is being pushed out. They are stirring up heresy to confuse us. Athelstan is making this battle about religion when it really is about his own base desires to rule the whole of this island and God has not granted it to him."

One of the Pict *Clan* leaders signalled. Moray, Muireachadh, the leader of their delegation, Callum stumbled over his name.

"We are letting this southern king set the tone of this meeting. It is no secret he sends his priests to come up north and spy for him whilst converting the people. King Constantine, you do little to prevent them and you, bishop, do not send your own church's priests amongst our people as if you are in fear of all this. Our people are turning back to their old beliefs and we believe it is the path to victory over our enemies."

Constantine suddenly felt uncomfortable. Moray went on.

"We shall use this coming battle to revive our former glory and will fight as our ancestors fought, on foot and horseback with our women at our side. This is how we defeated the Romans."

The war and revenge party were on their feet again showing support. Constantine thought what a rabble and was disturbed to see his sons amongst them. The war party had grown larger as the meeting progressed. Constantine wanted to retire for a nap. Black Callum spoke again.

"We all seem anxious to die and make a country full of widows and orphans. It's too far to drive home cattle, you fools. You'd have to eat them on the way. There can't be enough gold and silver for us all and Anlaf won't want us to take his people as slaves. Someone show me the profit in all this!"

The meeting went quiet and just as Constantine thought, perhaps they'll come around, and God appeared not on his side in spite of all his past piety. Ironically, a messenger from the border had brought a letter from Athelstan earlier that week. It was written in Latin and needed a translator to be read to the meeting. Strachan was no help complaining his Latin was confined to the mass and the meanings of the gospels.

"The language is not the same as we have learnt, its more Roman," he said. "I suppose ours has become debased over time."

He sent for a younger monk to enquire if he could understand it. Fortunately he could but he was nearly overlooked when Brigid offered, on the basis she was raised in a convent. Constantine thought it was pointless sending all the Pictish hostages to convents. They just learn things to confuse me.

Brother Andrew the monk read the letter with some care to get the correct meaning and imagery. It began:

"To my brother Constantine, I have heard that you plot against me despite you having sworn holy oaths to be my friend and ally. Do you deny that you are allying with your neighbours and countrymen against me and these are people who have also sworn to be my friends? You are consorting with my enemies in Dublin who seek to steal part of my kingdom from me, lands which my father and grandfather have held. You are causing dissent in my realm and threatening the peace and wealth of my subjects. Furthermore you continue to persist with heresies and support false beliefs amongst your own subjects. I insist that you do

not prevent the messengers of the true church from converting the unbelieving people in your country.

Write to assure me this is not the case and punish your subjects who advocate heresy and dissent. Your brother in Christ, Athelstan, Rex Totius Britanniae."

Dear God, thought Andrew, the letter is from a madman. King of All Britain, who does he think he is?

"You don't read Latin very well, Brother Andrew," said Brigid cautiously.

Angus macCullen without waiting for permission from either Constantine or Black Callum, spoke out.

"That's it! War! Doesn't matter who wants it or not. King of all Britain! That's a declaration! He's saying, come south and invade..... My lord Constantine, write and say we're on our way."

A dozen Scottish voices echoed as well as the Welsh and the Sassenaech. Only the Picts were totally silent and smiling. Brigid was looking radiant and every man in the hall looked at her from time to time.

"The magic worked, Moray," she said. "With a little help from Winchester, we can now have our war."

Constantine felt washed out and looked at Brigid. "Mhor Rioghain, the washer at the ford, she's washing my clothes," he whispered to Black Callum.

Black Callum said nothing, thinking perhaps it's time to go home.

Moray and Brigid walked out of the meeting with everyone else after the niceties had been observed. A thin figure slipped out from the side of the building and walked by their side without speaking. Black Callum was walking next to them and looked at all three, especially the girl.

"So your little fairy spy has returned to her mistress with the news from her latest mission. I have been watching the way she finds her way in and out of places. Why do I always feel she is listening at my door?"

"She probably heard you talking in your sleep," said Moray.

"She wouldn't have heard too much wisdom" said Brigid. "Brollachan has the sense to stay quiet unlike many in this place."

"Now there is something on which we can agree," said Black Callum. "Just keep her eyes and little ears away from what I do or there will be a little body to bury before we set off for a battle." With that he walked off.

"Child, have you discovered anything today," said Moray?

"Nothing you haven't guessed already, Lord Moray. While you were all together, the king's grandsons and their friends sat and talked about the same matters. They were all saying they wanted to issue a challenge to Saxons to meet them at this Brunanburgh fort. They are going to ask their grandfather to issue a challenge to the Saxons to meet in battle and give a date and time. They said something strange about marking out a field and in the same breath they spoke of what the other Callum who has gone to the Vikings had said about it."

"Only young hot-heads and Scots would think they could win a battle by telling the enemy the time and place and then ask them to be there on time" said Moray.

Brigid looked grim and said "I think Red Callum is informing Athelstan directly or indirectly. I think he is confident we can win a pitched battle. We ought to let the Vikings and the rest fight the battle while we invade the middle of the country. He'll have to leave troops behind everywhere if we threaten this. He'll have no men on the battlefield.......... Carry on, Brollachan!"

"They didn't say much more except that all the other young men are ready to go. *Cailleach,* they want to fight with us. I think they have watched us training our armies. They know they won't get a victory unless they break up the Saxon forces. They said also there is some rolling country on the hill tops south of the river next to Brunanburgh which would be ideal for a battle. They can't know that. They have never been there."

"That river is a sacred one, Brollachan. If we cross it, payment in blood will be demanded. Remember that if you go near it. I have not seen it myself but I know the Romans stopped at it when they invaded until they appeased the people nearby and their Goddess Brigit."

"Sounds like I am correct, Red Callum has some knowledge of the country, and he's been filling their heads with thoughts of an easy victory," said Moray.

"They said as well there are some ditches and banks on the north side of this river they could use to hold up the Saxons if they cross over. I can't see the point of that if they want a battle so much."

"Brigid, Brollachan, we have got to have more proof its Red Callum who's double dealing here. If the Saxons pick the field, they could beat us. I am going to speak to the King."

Off he went in the direction of the other Callum.

CHAPTER 5

THE DANES CALL TO ARMS

The day after the meeting with King Athelstan, *Jarl* Thorolf went and spoke to as many of the Danish leaders as he could find. He went with the king's offer of weapons and armour. It came as no surprise to him that very little in the way of weapons were needed. It was the issue of armour that concerned his countrymen most of all.

Grim the Miller or Grim Therkellson to give his proper name, had sought him out the previous night and put to him a proposition which he did not want to suggest to the king directly but which all the Danes present would like Thorolf to think about first. The matter related to the garrisons on the border and the defence of North Lindsey. They were prepared to prevent the navigation of the River Trent and put a force on the eastern bank to deter an invasion on that flank. They would put together a force more lightly armed, of older men and some of the older boys and would not expect them to be used in a pitched battle but to defend a fort or attack small groups. The invaders wouldn't know how they were made up. Grim knew that was how Athelstan was making up his forces in his other forts. They could put about 500 extra soldiers together and a few river boats which would act more like warships. When Athelstan heard this from Thorolf, he laughed.

"You Danes never fail to surprise even me who thinks he has seen much and learnt more. You teach things, I could never learn from books. It was that old fox Grim who came with this suggestion wasn't it?"

Thorolf nodded.

"I think I am glad he is on our side, and if he wasn't I would ask God that he was stood aside and not with Anlaf. He has a way of bringing people together which a king could envy. When this is all over, we must use his services more often. You said he has a son. We must ensure a good future for the boy. I have no doubt that with such a father, he lacks neither courage nor skill."

"He is one of Edwinsson's men, one of his personal guard" said Thorolf.

"Doesn't surprise me either, and I suppose what they want is armour for this cohort. Something a bit better than a leather jerkin? Tell the rascal he can have what he wants but the quality isn't too good. We got it off the Cornish and the Welsh. We've given the main army most of the best stuff already. The ones coming to the battle can have the best if they are short. We'll help with food as well but not to disadvantage the main army. Organise this for me, Thorold. I am going for prayers now."

"Yes, my lord," said Thorolf. He left him and thought, was he going to talk to God or that aunt of his? I am sure he thinks she isn't dead. He's still enough of a Saxon to know the boundary between life and death is a near one despite what the Christians say. Perhaps the king believes also you can cross back and forth. Is he still a believer in Odin at heart? Is this piety all to get the Roman Church to support him? Is it part of him wanting to be a Roman? It's a pity he never married. A good woman like the one he fished out of the sea off the coast of Marsallia, would have brought him to earth. What a pity this northern climate ruined her health, he thought. She was from the east where the Romans still had an empire and he was a different man with her around. She looked like the pictures of women, the monks had in their books of saints and women on the walls of the buildings the Romans had left in Britain. Everyone gave her a second look and the King would have married her except the Witangemot were not in favour. They believed she was not royal, although she never pretended she was. Athelstan made her out to be so because of her beauty. Even his aunt loved her and she was a comfort to Ethelfreda in the last months of her life. Thorolf thought how much he missed her as well. Her joy spilled over into everyone's life around her. It was only in this one thing he ever envied Athelstan, even after she was dead over twelve years.

The following day Thorolf walked around the Danes camp and with one of the king's clerks made out several lists when he had spoke with his countrymen. It was well past midday before he had finished and he went to see Grim and Ivar. They were still at Edwin's farm in the village. He looked tired and hungry and Edwin's wife produced some food for him and he didn't speak till he had finished.

"For an earl he is almost like one of us," said Edwin, loud enough for Thorolf to hear. "He likes his dinner."

"I like a good dinner of roast lamb and buttered beets the best of all and usually eat it in silence to show my appreciation," said Thorolf when he finished. "In fact I nearly love it as much as baked trout in honey and mustard sauce with a baked apple to follow."

"You have brought us the king's answer," said Grim, changing the subject.

"He agrees to your suggestion and will provide some armour and food. The armour may be none too good. It's from the *wealas*."

"As long as the food's good, lots of beef and cheese for me," said Edwin. "I've seen some good Welsh armour and some fierce Welsh on the inside of it, Earl Thorold. They wouldn't have given it up easily."

"Are you in on this part of the plan, Edwin Bruningsson," said Thorolf?

"We all are around here. Did you think we want the Scots sailing up the Trent or sneaking across from it? They might eat all the trout for a start...... There's still a bit of fight left in some of us despite our age. Life is good around here in times of peace. We want no war to make it harder and foreigners walking over the land."

"The king will be glad to know that and I know just how you feel about age, serving that Saxon begins to tire me sometimes. Who's going to command this force anyway?"

"In Lindsey, Wilfred Egbertsson, and he's acceptable to all parties, Angles, Saxons and Danes. On this side of the river, the king needs to appoint someone who is linked to his existing forces," said Grim.

"The king was right about you, Grim. It's much safer having you on our side. Where are you fighting?

"I am too old to fight in a pitched battle but you can be sure I'm watching from a distance in case I am needed for anything. I was never used to standing inside a fort waiting for the enemy to come over the fence."

"You're as fit as anyone for your age and I know you have a sword to match anyone's as well," said Thorolf. "And you know how to use it. I have seen you use it against pirates on the Trent. You could throw a spear as far as most men I know. I suspect you still can."

"We go back a while, do we not *Jarl* Thorolf? But there are younger and better men who will be all the happier in the fight to know that we older men are looking after what they have at home, having said all that. Has the king ever considered what might be happening to the south of the Humber? Has he no plans for the east coast?"

"He has a plan of waiting to see how events would unfold once he knows the enemies intentions. It seems everyone is guessing the invasion will come by sea to the Humber. There is no other safer place nearby on the east coast. We think not even the Scots are bold or desperate enough, to use the Thames."

"We thought that too," said Grim "and expect them to try to come by our gate. We might have welcomed Anlaf but he will come with some unwelcome friends. So he had best stay away, I think."

"Five hundred old men and boys won't put him off, Grim."

"They will with everyone else and besides we can watch what his main force are up to. It's too wet on our side of the Humber if you want to land a large army. They won't all come by sea and what does, will be the smaller part. They'll join the rest on drier ground to the west and besides, Anlaf will go first to York. In any case Anlaf won't know how old or young they are till he comes to take a look at them."

"We have it all worked out," said Edwin.

"The king will be relieved to know that," said Thorolf, thinking I wonder if he will trust these two and who they represent. A miller and a farmer, and who's really behind them? Would they change sides if it all goes wrong? "Where are you in this, Ivar?"

"My friend Eric Sigurdsson and I fight with Harald Edwinsson. We are good together in a fight."

"Yes, I knew his father. Long dead, I am sad to say. He would have been useful in the coming battles."

"I agree" said Grim. "He would have commanded the boats. He was good in a fight on water."

"Nearly as good as you, you old pirate," said Thorolf.

"But not as good as me, he couldn't swim."

Edwin and his wife couldn't stop laughing at this point.

"Grim, Edwin, send a messenger to me in Leicester if there is anything you need. Grim, I know you can write. I saw you doing it ten years ago. Edwin, if you can't, ask the monk or whatever he is, at that church to write.

If I am not there, they will know where to send it...... And Grim if we don't see each other again, don't fall in the water."

He went off in hurry, muttering something about being a day behind the king.

"Dad, why didn't you say you were to command the boats?"
"I wanted to see if he remembered and he did."
"How long do you think it will be before the invasion, Grim," said Edwin.
"Not before next summer, my friend. It will take Anlaf most of the good weather to sail around the north and west to east is the easy way. We'll have in the harvest and some of it milled before they get here. I think they may think they can count on stealing it and they won't want it until it is bagged. Advise your neighbours to look for places to hide their grain, just in case..... Hide their children too; they'll be looking for slaves. The forts will hold against the Scots if all else fails, but will not stop them crossing the Don. I don't see Anlaf moving too far from York and even if he wins the battle, Athelstan won't retreat too far, except into more of his forts. To go raiding they would have to split up the force no matter how big or small it is, and the king will attack again. I have seen most of the forts across the west of the country. They will hold also and so will the ones to the south. There will be a lot of hungry Scots and *wealas* looking for a meal. There isn't enough planted north of the Don to feed the people who live there in a bad year and they won't be feeling generous to invaders with too many hungry mouths, even if they are on their side. Really I don't think that many of them near the border support Anlaf. They have got used to peace."

"I wish I had travelled like you," said Edwin. "Moving out of the village always made me unsettled. I have been to Nottingham many times but I always find it noisy with all those people and more than one street. If I had, I think I might have a better understanding of the world. It's not the same going away to fight. You need to travel at a time of peace to understand the world. People are not the same in war."

"Well, know this, my friend, if you hear from people they have seen beacons along the Trent, then there is an invasion and you will have a few days to prepare. I think, however, there will be no surprises. If all the people from the north invade us at the same time, there are so many, we cannot fail to see them coming. The king has forts at Doncaster to delay them using the track way from the Humber and another old Roman one on Ryknield Street to your west, the one his aunt rebuilt. Disappear into the woods for a few weeks with the family and the food. Our problem in Knaith is we have nowhere to go, so we have to fight. Thorolf will get some defence organised for you and get a leader appointed. Fear not!"

"I'll really be glad when it's ended. Kings do bring you trouble."

On the way back to Knaith the following day Grim told Ivar of his plans.

"Listen well, my son! Anlaf is a mighty warrior and I fear if he loses the coming battle, it will not put him off another attempt to set up house in York. I think the King thinks that Anlaf may not invade us but I think he will. Anlaf wisely does not trust the Scots to defeat Athelstan. He does not believe they can, even though they have the most men. Constantine will come with his own forces the northern *wealas* who are his allies, the Cumbrian *wealas* and the Viking settlers, and then probably some Angles from Northumbria. Not as many of them as he may think, because the king has much support up north after his invasion of the Scots. For that reason Anlaf may have misjudged the desire of the people of York to have him as their king. The city may support him but people around it may not. He may not know this and he has not the time to find out. What we must do is deter him from an invasion east of the River Trent. Create a diversion and prevent them from using the river to skirt around the forts. They won't have enough ships to move the whole army even if he came with ships five times what he has and most of them are for sea-trading not war. We should make sure he knows we have the river and the marshes patrolled. Your mother is going to enlist the help of water fairies, although she doesn't know it yet."

"Mother will like that"

"Yes, she is always a woman of action when defending the home is concerned. We have some river boats on hand which are faster than any they will have. I will also take steps to bring all boats up river when they come so they can't steal them. Many boat owners don't know this yet either, but they and their boats will be safe with us. Now, you must go with Eric and he will look after you in the battle. You have good mail, and it won't be too warm in the late summer after the harvest so remember to wear your leather coat under it to make it more effective. You won't be too hot and your mother has made it specially to fit. Eric is older than you and so take his advice. Stay near him and listen for Lord Harald's orders."

"Dad, you don't think a lot of kings and lords!"

"No, I don't. Most of the time we can live without them and their taxation to fund their courts. I feel the same way about bishops and the Church."

"But you always are friendly to Harald Edwinsson."

"True, he is a bit different and his father was the same. He doesn't go to court or to church and he doesn't have a big house and hall. He behaves as a lord should in the perfect world. We do not have a perfect world. Besides his father gave us you to foster and you have brought us happiness, especially to your mother. If you were to marry who she wants, she'd be happier still."

"Dad, I can't marry that girl. She's boring and not a bit at all like mother. She's good around their farm and knows how to do all the domestic matters but she lacks a spark of life. Imagine what the children would be like."

Grim laughed to himself. He knew exactly what his son meant. He had delayed marriage for the same reasons and nearly too long. He was well past thirty and looking hard at forty when he met a girl who was out fishing in the marshes off the Humber. He was uncharacteristically lost and so was his pony. It was near dark, so he thought to settle down for the night and see what next day would bring. Spotting a fish trap, he thought of supper and no sooner had he opened it than an arrow fell to his left and another to his right.

"I'm lost and hungry," he shouted.

"Turn around and let me see you," said a voice from nowhere.

So he did and a girl appeared from between the trees out of a pool. A water fairy, he thought. No, I couldn't be so lucky.

"You are lost twenty paces from a track. Keep your hand off your knife and empty the trap slowly……."

He did so.

"……..Put it back in the river. Bring the fish and I might cook it for you. You don't look like a man who could cook."

"I'm a good cook; I can remember all my mother taught me."

"You have no wife then? You must be in need of one at your age."

"Have you a big sister in need of a husband then, child?" he asked.

"I like your wit," said the voice. "Life would never be boring with such a man as you. I have only met you for a few moments and already I like you. Bring your pony and follow me. There is our farm not far away. My name is Emma."

Grim arrived on a farm next to the marshes to find the girl's mother and her four sisters living there. Emma was the eldest at seventeen and certainly in charge. Her mother looked ill and was on a cot by the hearth. There was no sign of any men. One of the younger girls without orders took his pony to a barn. It was a cold night for a late April but there was a good fire in the hut and plenty of wood inside and out.

"Where is your father, Emma," he asked quietly?

"He died two years ago or at least we believe he did. The fishing boat never returned. There was no bad weather or storm. It was during summer. It may have been taken by thieves or raiders and then men killed or taken into slavery."

"This farm is quite large and you have many buildings, are there no men working here for you."

"We had two who worked for father. When Father did not return they tried to take it over with some of their friends but they did not expect me and Elfreda to fight them. They attacked mother and we killed three of them and wounded another. I shot two with my bow when she stabbed one with a *seax* when he tried to rape her. I shot another as they ran but it was a poor shot and only wounded him. For months I looked for a man with a limp." The other three never came back either. I often wondered if they had killed my father and the crew of the boat but the coroner declared them drowned at sea."

Your mother is very ill now," Grim whispered.

"My grandmother knows about herbs and healing and lives along the coast. She comes with my aunt from time to time and brings mother some medicine. It only eases the pains in her body and she has been like this for four winters. Granny would come to stay for longer but many people in the country rely on her. She is teaching me all she knows. I have taught myself never to go anywhere without my bow and knife."

"Is your Granny one of the *wealas?*" asked Grim cautiously.

"We have always had family amongst them."

Same thing thought Grim but no matter. Emma had organised this house well for someone who had been just more than a child when she had to take charge. She worked hard. Her hands were small and seemingly delicate but looked hard like a man's. Elfreda was cooking the fish.

Laughing Grim said, "I thought you were going to cook the fish."

"No, I'm watching you." Emma replied. "I don't know if I trust you yet."

Grim often recalled their meeting and resisted the temptation to keep telling Ivar over and over again. From that day he and Emma never looked back. They handfasted at Lammas just before her mother died and she moved to Knaith with her sisters who grew up to marry local men as they came to the age. Despite their best efforts no children came along and Ivar, the son of his friend, was fostered. The other children on the farm were seldom away from the door. Not a day passed when they were not happy when together and sad when apart.

Ivar called out. "Lost in thought again, Dad? Thinking about Mother?"

"How well we all know each other, Son," said Grim and began to think about the frightened little boy they had taken in. We made him happier than the Edwinssons.

He would have been part family, part servant. At least he is heir to five farms and a good name. Just as his real mother would have wanted. Not absolutely sure about his real father, he thought. He was a man really determined to be an outlaw, if ever a man was.

"Well, Ivar," said Grim firmly, "no real need to marry this girl despite her parents wealth and her undoubted abilities. The world is full of such prizes and besides both she and them would want you out of this coming battle. I am not sure that is something I want for you. A man must defend his land, his family and his country with some honour. We have a standing amongst the people of Lindsey and amongst the Danes.... and none of us have ever run from a fight. What's more our women never dissuade us..... It will be time to go and practice with sword and shield after we have had supper if we get home on time. We'll have to see how the river is running."

"Eric says never fight on an empty stomach but he would say that, wouldn't he? I used to really think he was my brother, the times he turned up for meals."

"He could have been. His father has been dead since he was a boy and I always promised I would look out for him. I was most surprised his mother married again. His step-father tried his best but Eric has always gone his own way, just like Sigurd his father. He won't get you killed, son, just don't do anything silly to get him killed. He has always been your friend."

"He is a very wise man, Dad, and full of surprises. People were all shocked at his intervention in that land dispute on behalf of his Tildi."

"She wasn't his Tildi at the time, son."

"She was a woman in need of a just man's help against a rascal. Her dead husband's brother wanted that which was not his but his nephew's. There was no reason why it should not have been retained by the widow.....and he wanted what came from her first marriage as well."

"I really thought they would get to blows over it."

"It would have been a way to resolve it but Eric knew he could find sufficient men to swear to the truth and men who were not threatened by the other party. Only when the uncle became threatening, did Harald Edwinsson agree they could fight if necessary. I do think Harald felt that the uncle should be satisfied with the moot's decision and not make threats. Harald is a good friend but not good to have as an enemy."

"Eric's reputation with the axe should be enough to sway most reasonable people, son."

The conversation fell silent and they walked on a little more at that.

CHAPTER 6

THE MEETING AT LEICESTER

Earl Thorolf felt he couldn't believe his luck at getting a free meal out of a Saxon and delivered in such a friendly way. Still, he thought, Grim is one of us but sometimes he gets too close to the Saxons. He has friends everywhere. Then he remembered, he was Athelstan's favourite Dane, although he didn't forget the King had really also brought the Danelaw back under his effective control. He wasn't Alfred's grandson for nothing. Thorolf could recall his own grandfather saying how they thought they were creating another Danish kingdom on the island of Britain. Still time, thought Thorolf, but not this year and not with this king. He's too good for us. His brother isn't quite so good and Thorolf laughed as he rode along. His four guards asked him to share the joke but he just made up a riddle to question their imagination. He went deeper and darkly into his imagination and a foreboding of something awful came over him he could not shake off.

They travelled for two days up and down of gently sloping ridges and the road became a little better as they reached the Fosse, the old Roman road. The Romans had cut this road through the rolling landscape. They cut down a lot of the woodland to make farms and now it has all re-grown, the king had told him. Thorolf thought, sometimes I agree with the king about all things Roman. What it must have been like to move this way when they were in charge. No wonder they nearly controlled the whole world. I wonder what went wrong for them and why don't we start rebuilding the roads?....... That Dunstan Edwinsson, the Saxon who reads all those books the monks have, says it's because they started to care more for their souls than this world and stopped being warriors. We Danes won't make that mistake, Christians or not, but I do detect the Saxons are getting a bit that way. Belief is one thing but letting the Church get too much power is something else. Let the priests deal with God as long as we can still swing a sword when we want.

Thorolf was letting his mind wander again all the time on this journey, unusual for him. He was brought out of his musings when one of his men shouted to him.

"Jarl Thorolf, a rider ahead!"

They had reached a hilltop and a point where they could see into some fields cut out of the forest. The rider just disappeared as he looked out to where he was. They had not seen anyone for about half a day. As they entered the trees about two hundred paces before where the rider had been, a voice rang out from some cover.

"Uncle Thorolf, we meet again and don't bother reaching for your sword."

Thorolf turned and laughed and laughed for the first time in days.

"Aylmer Hansson, what, for the love of Christ, are you doing here?"

"Christ has no part in this as neither of us are believers, you old Danish rascal. King Athelstan is to blame. You know him, your friend from Winchester. The man who's expecting the Roman legions to land and come to our aid.... Let's ride on together. I presume you are going to Leicester."

"Does he think the Romans are going to drive us out and your lot as well, leaving him with just the Welsh and the Scots to rule? Much good that may do him," said Thorolf and then laughing even louder...."They couldn't find a horse to fit you again. Is the one you are riding the largest in the kings stables? It looks as if it has six legs with you sat on it. Has anyone worked out how tall you are yet? It must be three ells. Where do you find clothes to fit you?"

"Uncle Thorolf, you are being kind again to me. My aunt in Evesham makes my clothes now you ask. You're trying to find out what I've been doing for the King before he tells you. Don't worry you'll find out fast enough and may live to regret the knowledge. We had better make haste to Leicester together. The next stretch of road is awful. If it rains the horses will never pass easily and we shall be down to walking. There's a village we can reach before nightfall, although I think sometimes I prefer to sleep in the forest. There are fewer lice under the moon and stars."

"We need food for the horses, lad, especially yours she looks a bit tired even though I know you'll have been resting and walking her."

"Both she and I have had a hard month. I might carry her the last mile into Leicester as a mark of my appreciation. She has been a very patient horse."

Aylmer got off and walked with her at Thorolf's side as they approached another hill.

"I've been doing this all the time," said Aylmer

"Couldn't you have gone to some lord for a change of mount?"

"I could, but just like you he would have been wondering what I was doing on behalf of the King. Nothing wrong with her a month's rest and some corn can't cure."

"Aylmer, these roads never get any better. The locals only throw earth and rocks in the worst bits. It would be easier on horses and travellers if they were rebuilt. Can't you and Dunstan persuade the King? He would listen to clever young men like you two. He'd see me as a tired, moaning old man." Thorolf's men couldn't stop laughing at this confession from their old war leader.

"The Romans used their soldiers to build them according to the books the monks keep," said Aylmer with some sadness. "Our soldiers only want to fight and destroy."

Aylmer Hansson went silent for sometime after that. Thorolf knew him and his family well, a descendant of the old Mercian royalty. A clever young man, but one who always seemed to be in thought about something. He and Dunstan were friends although Dunstan was a bit older and not very good with weapons. Aylmer always seemed to be good at everything he did. The King employed him as a map maker, amongst many other things. He could paint pictures of the land which when explained to people, they could understand. Athelstan was always sending him off somewhere and he always went alone, armed to the teeth with a long sword which he always carried on the horse with a shield showing a raven. He wore a langseax, a family heirloom which nearly no one carried these days, but it was easy to ride with, a short knife and of course the bow and arrows. Everything about him said *warrior* and Thorolf loved that. Thorolf was happy now he had met Aylmer.

It was the leather bag full of his writing materials which fascinated

Thorolf every time he saw it. He had seen it opened many times and had marvelled at the knowledge it contained. Thorolf could read script and could write a little as befitted an Earl. He could even speak and read a little Latin. As a commander of soldiers he knew how to set out a battlefield, but to get a picture of a large area of land. He wondered how such a young man could acquire the skill. He had heard of a few monks who could do it. Aylmer was no monk and not likely to become one. He was promised to wed a daughter of one of the lords of Mercia who, like many fathers, was waiting till the threat from the Scots had passed before he allowed a wedding. The king had arranged it and most people thought it a good match as the groom had prospects and the bride had land in her own right.

When the arrangements were made at one of the king's courts, Thorolf recalled Aylmer's observation that both the bride and the land were extremely beautiful. The bride was willing but the land might have to be fought for as it was on the border with Yorkshire. Thurstan, the bride's father began to realise his lanky son to be was not going to someone he could bully despite his youth. Thorolf decided that he would have this young man on his side if the political wind blew stronger in the direction of the Danelaw.

When they reached the village a few pennies bought some feed for the horses, a place by the fire and food with a couple of families for all six of them.

Speaking in the Danish dialect to Thorolf when his men were not present and he thought the Saxons wouldn't understand, Aylmer said.

"Whilst doing my work for the king, I visited the land Thurstan proposes to give as part of the dowry, although it really is not his but Helena's in her own right. Her mother's family still feel they have a claim on it and that they should have a choice in who marries her. One of the farmers told me this. Thurstan doesn't dare come to collect rents. His wife's family collect them and send the money to her when they feel like it which isn't very often. They are a bit of a Saxon island in a Danish sea. I think Thurstan is a bit in awe of these local Danes and I think Helena's uncles would like her to marry one of them. When we have sorted out the Scots and the seafarers, I may have to go and reason with them."

"You will be taking your sword to support your words of wisdom, I suppose," ventured Thorolf.

"Oh, indeed, I could not think of leaving it at home. The king's example of dealing with people on such a basis has never been lost on me. I'll take my shield as well for it befits a warrior.......... and I want them to know it's me who's coming."

I am certain they will know, thought Thorolf. I suspect this young man would leave a trail of blood, death and widows in Danish Mercia given one half of two chances.

"I will assist you in this" said Thorolf. "It could help bring our peoples together if we all start off understanding one another and what's at stake."

They fell asleep by the fire after that.

To the pleasant surprise of all, they didn't wake up itching in the morning and with a belly full of porridge and fresh bread and cheese in their bags, they set off for Leicester on what was still a dry day. The following night they slept in the open. Aylmer had shot some hare as they travelled, so they ate well with some greens he picked from the woodland. Thorolf's men were impressed and said they would travel with him any time. Thorolf began to understand how he survived on his missions for the king and how he did it secretly.

After another stop over they arrived in Leicester and went straight to the fort. The town was supposed to have a bishop but he ran away when the Danes came and never returned. Not even his successors decided to chance it either. Thorolf could never understand why, the place always seemed so full of Saxons despite being one of the Five Boroughs. Then he thought about what Dunstan Edwinsson said about the Romans. He felt saddened a little for Romans and Saxons.

The next day the King appeared and called a Council for the coming Sunday after the sacraments. On the Sunday Thorolf noticed the church was especially full but he didn't see Aylmer. Perhaps he's been earlier, he thought. No one suspected of paganism or heresy would get the king's favour but that bunch of Mercian kings did fear nothing and I bet he sleeps with that *langseax*. It looks less dangerous than some women I know and probably more comforting in places where he goes.

There were stools set out in the hall in the fort when he went in. Aylmer was at the front, looking down on everyone with the ever-present seax. I know why he carries it, thought Thorolf. You can draw one faster than a sword. It could give you an edge even in a time of surprise, no pun intended, he laughed to himself.

"My lords," he called out, "please take your seats; the king will soon be here. Earl Thorold, there is a seat for you at the front."

He said this with such a commanding voice everyone moved at once which was good as the King appeared a few moments later. You did not keep Athelstan waiting.

"My lords, dear friends" said Athelstan, "welcome to Leicester!... Always one of my favourite places.... I really must do something about getting the bishop to return, a place so important needs one."

All the Danes present tried not to laugh at this point, knowing their presence had scared away the last one.

He went on: "Before we debate the issues facing us, Aylmer Hansson will give us some information about the land on the borders of Mercia and Northumbria. We will need this to understand what choices we have."

Aylmer stood up and on a frame showed a map of the border which puzzled most people present until he began to explain.

"This curving and moving line is the River Don, it moves from the Sheffield fort and the hills north east to the Humber, the best anchorage on the coast. It's a broad river with marshes all along its length in many places. It narrows in others....Here are our other forts at Wincobank, Brunanburgh, Masborough, Sprotborough, Conisborough, Doncaster, two of them there, and then the marshes to the sea, all around the Humber. The other river, the Trent, runs almost north-south to Nottingham. We have the big fort at Lincoln east of the Trent and others south of this line at Worksop, Chesterfield and Mansfield. All of them are on the main tracks....... To the north of this defensive line there are forts at Leeds, Wakefield, Barnsley and Castleford which could be held by Anlaf's supporters nearer the time. They don't have a definite border like the Don. They are scattered but some are on river crossings. The major and most immediate obstacle to a passage north out of Mercia is the earthworks on the hills which look down on to the Don Valley.....They, however, would only be as useful as the force defending them. They stretch from Sheffield to the marshes in the Dirne Valley, about fourteen Roman miles..... But there are gaps and we control one at Wincobank, for example. We have Sprotborough and Conisborough at the northeast end also.......It could be difficult for us to cross over with a large force if opposed. The hillsides are steep but there are no palisades on the top of them unless the enemy come and build some..... Similarly an army coming the other way would have a problem with our forts, a more difficult one. We could harass their rear....... There are three major fords and some smaller across the Don and narrow paths through the marshes but an army takes time to cross rivers and similar obstacles. The last time the king went north there was no opposition and the army mainly used the

Brunanburgh and Ryknield Street crossing for the track up north to York. The river there is wide and shallow, passable in most reasonable and fair weather. The marshes are wide in most of this part of the Don Valley and many of the other crossings are only passable where an embankment has been made up to the river through a marsh. At most other places, the river is less shallow and at some, only passable when there has been no rain for a while. The enemy therefore only have a fairly narrow area over which they can invade if they come this way. Bear in mind to the northeast is more marsh next to the Humber where other rivers flow into it………. and then there are hills to the west of all this."

Aylmer stood aside and the King rose to speak.

"Depending on what time of year we are invaded and how much it has rained, the way south for the enemy is determined by these factors. We must decide if they come south this way what we should do. Do we wait behind our forts or do we go north and meet them? All this also supposes that they attack us from the York side of the hills and not from the west. We have our ships in the western sea, but they would be outnumbered even by what warships the enemy have. There is also no harbour except for the Mersey and the Dee rivers which we are using as a base. In the event of an invasion our fleet would have to put to sea for it would be of no use trapped in a harbour. The ships would have to attack the enemy trying to anchor in those estuaries and would only make it difficult for them rather than preventing them from coming………..Our only hope of success is to let the enemy come and defeat them on land. If this alliance is as great as it is expected, most of its force will have to march down from the land of the Scots and the Northern Welsh. Once it has set off, we could reasonably guess where it is coming to. I am assuming they will come to the east because our west is much better defended. We have more forts there, they are nearer together, larger and we have more local support. Jarl Anlaf wants York, so why should he not go there first to gather more support for himself. The Scots king's army would have an easier march east of the hills through country where they have more support also. I speak of the Northern Angles. The land around York is wide and flatter, they have more movement, and they can spread out and break up into bands of raiders. There is also more food from supporters. If they land in the west there is less room to move and less food. We could have them hemmed in by land and sea in the west. Anlaf and Constantine are not fools. They intend to defeat us with the largest army they can put together but it's only of use if they can put it together, and keep it together. They may not be able to do that in the west. I think they will choose the east."

He paused for a while and let what he had said sink in. He continued.

"Let us suppose they come and meet at York where after all Anlaf seeks to be the king. They can march down to the middle of Mercia through Brunanburgh, or they could try the Great North track at Doncaster or they could try the Lincoln route, crossing more rivers and marsh. To confuse us they could do a feint attack on any or all of them including a western invasion with a small force or a fleet.... I have made preparations to deal with such diversions......We cannot risk going north to meet them and be stuck on the wrong side of the higher part of the hills. We have to get them to join up, make a move and then we have to move to meet them.... It's going to have to be south of our forts. We don't have so many real fighting men that we can afford to divide them before the main battle. We have enough other men for garrisons and for forces on the flanks to deal with a diversion, but I want to maintain an effective main force to meet these invaders and destroy them at a place of my choice or even their choice if it's a good one for us as well. Be assured, I have a selection in mind wherever they come. I intend this battle to be the final one Constantine will regret. Think on my words and discuss for a while before we speak further."

The king went and sat in a corner of the hall and Aylmer offered to give more information about the country for those who had never been.

Thorolf spoke first and said he was always surprised how much forest and marsh there was north of the Don in comparison to the land south.

A man from Suffolk, Leofstan, added that it was the hills that surprised him, especially when he had to walk up them but it had been good practice for the visit to King Constantine, who seemed to have a kingdom of hills.

The conversation seemed to warm up a bit following this bit of humour and Theodred from Wilton brought the conversation back to tactics.

"The king wants us to look at his plans to see if we can spot, where they could go wrong. The major problem I see is that we have a range of hills running down the middle of this land which is an issue for a large army moving north to south who might have to move east-west at any time. It forces choice of movement initially one side or the other as the king has said, but not east to west or the other way, although the distance is shorter, if you know what I mean. I think we will not know until the last moment which side the attacking army will use, not until a substantial fleet anchors in the Humber will we know and then there is still the issue of a diversion. The matter is at least resolved in part by the need to keep a substantial force near Chester to watch over the Southern Welsh who I do not trust despite their words and treaties and offers of help to our king."

Wighelm of Surrey who was a bit battle hardened by age said "they can come which side they want, but that huge force they threaten us with, is going to be unwieldy. How can they control it? It could prove more a danger to their friends than us. Think how much it will eat? If they had to march it across those bogs north of Doncaster the front end would be arriving at the River Don whilst the back end was still having breakfast in Micklegate. No, they will pick a route where they can advance on a broad front quickly and use a lot of tracks."

Thorolf mischievously threw in a comment. "That's how we Danes invaded at the time of King Alfred."

Wighelm continued. "The seafarers always get their invasions in the right place. The witty Thorolf admits it to us."

The mention of his namesake prompted another Dane called Alfred to speak. "A time will have to come when the king cannot delay bringing the army together and it will have to stand and wait to see what Anlaf and Constantine decide to do. What would happen if it formed up in the east? Would they decide to attack us and then move to the west, or would they split up and force us to divide to deal with them? What we need to do is respond to them and if we are going to wait for them to invade us, make sure they know as little as possible of our movements. We need to know as much as possible about theirs. We must take some comfort in their force being so large, that they cannot hide it, however."

Athelstan got to his feet and thanked everyone for their thoughts so far.

He asked, "Do you think we could delay forming up the main army for as long as possible? We need to get in the harvest. They might have to delay invading till they get in theirs or have no food to bring with them or get from supporters. We in the south harvest earlier than they do........... Bishops, pray for a good summer next year."

"Only in the south, my lord," said Alfred.

Thorolf observed. "They could not be arriving before the middle of August at the earliest and the end of September at the latest, taking into account marching and sailing time. There might be so many they won't all arrive at the same time. It could take them a month to get together and then move. The longer they wait the hungrier they may get."

"One thing we cannot escape" said Athelstan "is bringing in that harvest of grain as well as all the other food. We are going to have to take some risks and as long as we don't take as many as the enemy, we may be the victors...........My good friends; I have heard your comments so far. There are many places where we can meet the enemy whichever way they come, but we must bring as many as possible to battle. Let us talk some more and particularly of the problems we face to organise our forces."

The discussions went on for a couple hours more and they broke up to return to their homes. Athelstan was left with Aylmer.

"Not married yet, my boy. I think it's time Thurstan changed his mind. I'll arrange it for you. You need a winter of rest before the plans we need to make next spring. The lady is in the town with her father."

Two days later Aylmer married Helena much to her father's unhappiness but he could not put off the king allied to his wife and daughter. Her two older brothers agreed also. The king and Earl Thorolf stood by his side to witness. After the wedding Thorolf returned north but Aylmer and his bride went with Athelstan to Gloucester where he intended to spend part of the winter planning his campaign.

On his way back north from Leicester, Thorolf was more troubled. He knew what he had to do but he was worried about the situation next spring. He thought more and more in the darkness of the forests. I am getting past all this thinking. He concluded thought was something only the young should do. In maturity you need certainty and not constant questioning. In a village on the Fosseway he was settling down for the night by a fire when Dunstan Edwinsson walked in with his friend Denewulf, both were full of smiles.

"Last thing I need is two happy Saxons," he said. "What's making you two so cheerful? I can only sit in wonder and wait to hear."

"Wonder no longer, Uncle Thorolf," said Dunstan. "I am to wed Denewulf's cousin."

"And he is prepared to let you join his family. What sort of man is he to his relatives and to the poor girl? You'll bore her with your constant studies and conversation on history and religion.......... and poetry of course......... you must be the worst poet of this age. By the way your friend Aylmer has just wed. The king browbeat her father into allowing it."

"Two happy turns of fate to celebrate," said Denewulf. My cousin has admired Dunstan for a while, although I put it down to her being young and impressionable. She doesn't know the rascal like I do and how he has avoided matrimony as a man avoids a smelly dog." He laughed loudly at his own wit.

"If you two were not so happy I would discuss with you what has been said at Leicester. I'll wait till you are sober in the morning and ale is less clouding of your judgements. Just leave me in my misery to get some sleep. I am a man with much on his mind. Go and sleep in a ditch if you can't be quiet."

They took his advice at face value and left the hut to sleep in a store. The family at the other side of the fire looked relieved as well.

Next morning Thorolf and his four men sat quietly at the fire with the family having porridge. The pair walked in and sat down.

Dunstan spoke. "Dene's going home now. He can't bear serious conversation. He says he's too young and it should be the haven of the aged................"

Perhaps he's right, thought Thorolf. Dunstan looked pensive for a moment and spoke. "Thorolf, I am going to have to lead my father's men in the coming war and I am no warrior. The old man is dying, they say, and I must take over soon as the head of the family with the title. I think he's just tired and ill myself."

"Dunstan, you can lead men to a battle and not draw a sword. However, you had better learn how to stay alive for your family and your new wife's sake. You wander over all this land with a sword I have never seen you draw. I have always presumed you knew how to use it. You are seldom in the company of others, so you do not fear attack. You are thought of as a brave man by many people."

"Oh, I can use a sword in one to one combat to some extent. Father made sure of that if only for me to protect mother when she goes on her pilgrimages. Besides it goes with my rank."

"Fear not, my boy, I know a warrior who can teach you a few things you need to know about a battlefield, Harald Edwinsson, a Danish namesake. He is everything the king says he is. The leader of a bunch of berserks and his personal guard are some of the best Danish warriors. Before we march out against the enemy, I shall arrange for you to stay with him. He'll teach you about tactics and organising men for battle as well. Your father's men will not see you make any mistakes. Do bit of practising yourself meanwhile!.......But let me tell you what the king has said."

Thorolf told Dunstan about what happened. At the end of it, Dunstan said. "You must remind the king that I am familiar with the land north of the Don and have visited there several times with my mother on her pilgrimages. She goes to a shrine the Britons built near the Wincobank fort. We have distant relatives somewhere near."

"The king greatly values you, Dunstan; I'll make sure he knows. Your friend Aylmer knows the land also as I have said. You are two mysterious young men. You seem to have so much on your minds, you let life by pass you. He must be twenty five and you are near to thirty. Both of you should have been husbands and fathers long ago.... I hope you both survive this war for I am sure it will be bloody. We shall not hold off the enemy without a great loss of our own and I am so sad to think of this, even I who have seen a lot of war. I wish only the old men to die. Old men's dreams are surely the cause of war."

"I fear you are right, Thorolf, but I believe I am not destined to die in this war. I am almost not brave enough."

"Dunstan, as many cowards die in war as brave men but they do not do so out of choice."

"Thorolf, I shall visit my new cousin Harald to see how he may teach me the ways of war."

At that they all parted as friends. Thorolf was left brooding with his thoughts of impending battles. Dunstan was light-hearted and headed for Nottingham.

CHAPTER 7

UNMASKING A SPY

"Callum, Callum Dubh," shouted Moray. "Don't be so grumpy. You and I are on the same side here, remember!"

"I am not sure that you and your painted witch and her fairy shapeshifter are on anyone's side but your own. I watch the fairy listening at every chance she gets. No one else seems to notice."

"Or care," said Moray?

"Indeed, or care? Don't you realise we can't win against the Saxons in a pitched battle. War is changing...... It's not raids and skirmishing any more. They fight in formation like the Romans and your lot only defeated the Romans when they were at the end of their supply lines."

"We forced them to divide their armies, so we could meet them in small groups with our own small forces according to our legends. We had our backs to the sea, Callum. If we aren't careful, Athelstan or the next king from the south will do the same with us again. We'll lose, if we don't take that battle south to him. If not now we'll have to later."

"Moray, you and I nearly think alike in terms of how this business may end. It's what's happening on the way!"

"We have to make Athelstan divide his forces, get him nervous and confused. We can get enough men to force him to strengthen garrisons he'll never use and when we meet him, defeat him by numbers. We have to ignore the forts and defended places. We'll be at the end of our supply lines and our strength could be sapped. You must make sure King Constantine gets enough food together."

"What for?... The country is rich enough down south, they say."

"Callum, you are nothing but a pirate at heart. We are going to be looking for friends, not making enemies. Anlaf wants to be king in the south."

"His new subjects can feed their liberators then!"

"Callum Dubh, I can't believe I hear you say this."

"Moray, I was joking. I know you to be right. The macNeill sense of humour comes out once again. But tell me how much of this have you thought through and where do you all fit in? There's a lot of wood and water between you and this bunch of Saxons."

"Do you think so? Athelstan nearly came to our door to beg his bread the last time he came north. The road seemed easy enough and his resolve was great.... His resolve is still is great. He is following the Romans. Only death will part this man from his ideas and then he'll pull strings in heaven."

"Moray, I didn't know you were a believer in such dreams."

"You know what I mean!"

"Sadly, I do and I know it will be difficult to make him go away... and all those who follow after him. But, we should talk more, and with the king. The other Callum at this court seems to have taken over this venture. We should do something about him but we can't talk here. There's more than just your fairy child who listens in corners. If I were on the bare top of a hill, I'd swear she was there."

"Callum, she's no child but almost a woman. I married my wife at her age with a babe on the way."

"She ought to keep her years a secret around here. Some of the young princes fancy that every woman should be theirs. They draw the line at your *Cailleach*, however. .....Lets meet later for a more serious discussion, Moray. I'll speak to the king for you."

Callum walked off thinking, who's running this country? It's not me. Moray would like a chance to revive Pictish fortunes, but doesn't want to be king at least, or can't be. It's got to be my namesake. The Saxons walked by his lands and never attacked. He claimed it's because he rallied his forces in time. Athelstan would have walked through them like he did with all the others. I wonder if anyone else has wondered about all this; and Callum's knowledge of the Danelaw. Is he just well educated? Callum Dubh knew that he was. He could speak Latin and had been schooled by monks. He could read and write well. He was said to own some books. Only the church and kings had books. He had been a third son never expected to inherit until the other two died fighting in some silly local battle with the northern *Sasseneach*. They were folk who'd be more on our side given a chance. He went off in despair, looking for some food.

Moray wandered in the opposite direction, looking for Brollachan. He felt responsible for her since her idiot brother took over their *Clan*. Definitely a young man who would go out and get you killed for no reason, and now the country is full of them, all dressing it up in past glories. Moray hadn't brought him in his retinue. There would have been too many fights with the Scotti and everyone else. He was saving him for a battlefield where he could do everyone a favour and die. The lad even botched his own father's murder, doing it himself in a country full of men who would murder for a pot of ale. All the brains in that family were rescued by the sister. He stood and looked around Dunnottar, thinking she's too good at hiding for me to find her, Brigid taught her well. She wouldn't stand on a windy hill top anyway.

She found him moments later. "I watched you with Callum Dubh. You are making him a friend."

"He was never an enemy but I think he is on our side. He is getting us a private talk with the king. I really want to speak to you about your presence here. Watch out for the young men. Remember your dedication to bring us victory. The younger princes are beginning to notice you. You are not so scrawny to pass for a boy. I have seen you and Brigid practice with your swords and shields. You are not a child anymore."

"I thought we went somewhere secluded."

"You're not the only person in this camp who takes a look around from time to time. Just be careful. I would hate for you to have to kill someone important defending your body. Fortunately when you go out, most of this place is dead drunk. Constantine does know what we intend to do in the battles. I think he secretly approves but I am unsure of what some of the others think. The churchmen oppose it, of course, but they are not seeking to revive past glories. Let's go for some food. There always seem to be lots of it around here."

Later Brollachan thought about Moray's words. She, Brigid and Brigid's sister Sine had caused a bit of a stir in Dunnottar. Women were not usually so exalted amongst the Scots unless they were nobler than they. Brigid held high status amongst the Picti but her family history was almost unknown to others. Brollachan was the only surviving daughter of a clan chief and if her two brothers died, she would be leader. She understood her older brother's jealousy and kept out his way as much as she could. He was not expected to live long. He was too rash in battle and with his followers' women. One would get really jealous and his luck would run out. Rory wasn't even a good swordsman. Only his guard kept him alive in the skirmishes in which he always seemed to be fighting.

She wasn't impressed by most men she had met. They always got off to a bad start assuming she was younger than she was. Brigid always advised her to find herself a warrior and a survivor. A man who can fight, will live long enough to become rich and provide for his children, she would say. Brollachan decided to follow the advice. Brigid had buried four men so she knew the problem. She wasn't even forty. Every time she had a new man she had more power, however.

Both Brigid and Moray were worried about her because of her brother. He was planning to take nearly all of their *clan* south to this battle and most seeming willing to go, some women included. A few even planned to fight although they did no training for it. When they had spoken of it, none of the three women expected anyone from the clan to return, even if the northern allies were victorious. Rory would expect them to settle in the south if it took his fancy. Moray didn't think he'd survive a real battle. Many of Rory's followers wouldn't either. He openly boasted he was going to charge the Saxon battle lines. He was definitely in the camp of the king's sons with their plans to lay out a field and issue a challenge. Moray knew himself to be no great fighter but he had lived a few decent years by learning when to run away, and he always advised his men to learn the same tactics. Brollachan laughed every time she thought of Moray, brave but not foolhardy. A pity he was well over twice her age with a wife. She liked a man with intelligence.

The visitors' camps were outside the fortress next to the woodland and a stream which poured out of the hills. The Picts had chosen the furthest from the gatehouse. Moray didn't feel too comfortable with Constantine or his forces. He felt his hand drifting to his sword at the mention of the king's name. Brollachan didn't worry about this and liked to walk in the woods, lost in thought some might have said. Really she was in touch with nature and felt every change in its tunes. Brigid had found a clearing near to a pool for weapons practice and worship of the Great Goddess. They had built a shrine there as they washed in the pool before they began and when they had finished. No one but them ever seemed to go there. Brollachan hated one thing in people more than anything, and that was being dirty. At the convent she had been one of the few who would willingly take a bath. She had heard Roman soldiers did it every day. It was said to be one reason why they had been victorious over most of the world. When they stopped doing it and went around dirty, they lost their empire. She didn't like being dirty and took a bath or a wash every two or three days, even in winter if she could. She hated dirty people nearly as much as she hated the nuns at the convent, and not just because some of them beat her for being late for prayers all the time. It was their lack of respect for her country and her people's way of life. They insisted everyone was renamed, and she was called Anne after the Saviour's grandmother. Only Sister Magdalena the gardener and healer understood her and took her under her wing. When she left she took the risk of saying goodbye. Magdalena understood and didn't betray her.

After the meal Moray and Brigid went to the other Pictish leaders for a discussion on what might happen next. Brollachan and Sine, Brigid's younger sister wandered off to the woods to where they had hidden their weapons. The summer evening was still warm despite the portents of rain from the west. Sine talked too much for Brollachan but she could fight, if she wanted, and was good to be with for practice. All the way up the valley to the clearing, she talked about everything. Brollachan began to realise how desperately unhappy Sine had been in her life.

"I feel so happy now I've come with you and Brigid. My husband's death has lifted a burden from me but I've become a nobody once again. His brother is looking for me a husband amongst his warriors, and I am going to have difficulty in saying no, as I've no one to support me. He won't do it for ever. The only thing that seems to stop anyone coming forward is that I'm still suspected of murdering Donal. Everyone knew how much I hated him, everyone except him, of course. None of them dare say. They won't take the risk or my brother will ask too many questions of them. They hated Donal nearly as much as I did. They still haven't worked out why I was never pregnant, the numbers of times he boasted of raping me, the unwilling wife. I had to do it, Brollachan. He was beginning to guess I was using one of Brigid's potions to prevent conceiving."

"You really did it then!"

"I put something in his food to blur his sight and addle his brain before he set out on his horse one morning. He rode the horse too fast, I think. When they found him he was raving about being chased by wolves. He tried to ride the horse over a cliff one of his men said, but the horse pulled up and he fell off and broke his shoulder and some other bones against a rock. He raved for about two hours before he died. I don't think they tried too hard to save his life, but he screamed and ranted in agony all the time. I was glad when I heard that. They said he went on about people trying to kill him but never mentioned me once."

Brollachan's attention wandered thinking how unusually quiet it was except for an occasional bird noise. In a gap in Sine's next polemic on what her elder sister should do with her latest man who everyone assumed was Moray, she silenced her.

"We're being followed or there's a trap, Sine!"

Sine transformed from a gossip into a wildcat and they moved into cover. They listened for a while.

A young man's voice said, "I can't hear them, we've lost them, I told you all to keep up and move faster."

"They'd have heard us if we got any nearer," said another.

"That's it then, let's go back home for some more ale," another muttered.

"No let's go on, they're only going up the valley, we can trap them up there or when they come back. Are you sure they run around naked in the spring?"

"Yes, that's where I saw them from the other side of the valley," said the first voice.

"You couldn't, it's too far and anyhow what are we going to do if the older woman comes, she's fearsome."

"We'll have her as well," someone joked, noisily. "But I want a piss first."

Brollachan and Sine were absolutely still as this conversation passed by. They watched five young men from Constantine's entourage, including one they thought was a grandson. They had swords and knives. None had armour, helmets or shields.

"Shall we go back and tell Brigid and Moray," said Sine?

Brollachan whispered. "No, not likely, they can't do anything. They can't go to the king and in the meanwhile these five will discover our sacred space and desecrate it. They will also come looking for us again as they will know we spotted them. I have heard them all before planning what they will do in the war against the Saxons. I think they plan more rape and thieving than fighting, despite their talk. We aren't safe around here now. We are going to have to kill them."

"We can't kill a king's grandson....... The others don't matter."

"Yes, we can. They won't have told their friends about this or there would be more of them. They obviously wanted us for themselves. Let's get ready and do it quietly. The real problem is getting rid of the evidence. We shall have to take the bodies further up into the hills. I once went up there and there are some places where we can hide them. They'll be discovered in the end and we'll be suspected..... But if there is no proof. They just might not believe we are match for five men."

"You know, Brollachan, we ought to find out what else is being planned. I know you think I talk too much. While you are busy listening, I talk to them all and they tell me things as well. I think these five are getting jealous of their older brothers and the attention they have had from me. Before we kill the grandson we can get him to talk about what he knows. An older woman knows how to get things out of a younger man. I've buried one husband, you know. I hated him but I could get him to tell me anything or do anything for me. Not bad for twenty two. What I suggest we do is separate him off the other four. It'll be dusk soon. We can follow them until then and make our move. We should leave them where we kill them and take all that's valuable. People will think the locals killed them for the loot. These men aren't popular around here."

"We could get them to split up with a distraction. It's important that the grandson doesn't see us kill the others. What's his name by the way?"

"No idea, is it important? Sometimes I think you have a heart of gold, Brollachan. Let's go and get ready. We can leave our clothes near that bend in the stream. We'll need to find them in the dark."

Further up the valley Gavin the king's grandson decided he should pull rank and take charge of what was becoming chaos and argument. Lachlan, who had led them up here, clearly had no idea where he was. Gavin was at least sure of the way back home, down the hill. He was all for going home but the others wanted to move on further up the hillside.

"We have either lost them or they've seen us and hidden. No one knows we have gone out. They might get suspicious if they notice we are gone and send a search party. Grandad will have us whipped if we are found out."

"Well, he won't," said Lachlan. "When we find them, we get rid of the evidence. The locals around here kill, rob and rape all the time. That's what the priests tell me. It's a country full of sinners."

Everyone except Gavin laughed loudly at this. "Right" he said, "that will have give us away, we might as well all go home. Every shepherd between here and the Clyde will have heard that noise."

As they turned, a shadowy figure moved between the trees, higher up the valley.

"There's one, she's naked as well, after her," shouted Andrew.

The four of them ran into the trees leaving Gavin walking behind shouting, "come back, it could be a trap."

They disappeared. Gavin stopped in the clearing and drew his sword and dagger.

In the trees Sine ran a short distance until the clearing couldn't be seen and turned to make sure they were following. When they were nearer, she showed herself again and waited before she moved into some closer cover. The four ran after her as she ran slower. She ran past the waiting Brollachan, followed by the four youths. Two arrows from her picked off the last two through, who were panting some distance behind the others. Brollachan ran by them and finished them off with a knife she took from her first victim. She removed the arrows and ran after the others.

Sine had stopped by some rocks and was facing the other two. As they advanced, she disappeared into a gap and slipped out the other side.

"Where did she go, Andrew?" said Michael.

"Not far" said Sine from behind them. Brollachan appeared at her side and shot the pair. Sine ran back down the valley towards the clearing where Gavin was standing in fear. Both looked on in powerless amazement as a naked Brollachan finished them off without a word. She took all that was valuable and disappeared into the rocks.

Gavin had remained motionless expecting his friends to return as it got darker. The animal sounds changed and he thought now he was by himself. The must have gone further up into the hills. Soon it would be dark, and they would hardly find their way back. He saw two fires suddenly start up a short distance away and heard drumming or at least he thought it was. He walked towards them as a moth drawn to a flame. Sat between the two fires was Sine. She stood up and said; "welcome to the son of a king."

Gavin went on guard and looked at her as the drumming continued. Too much ale and fear were taking its toll on him.

"Where are my friends" he stuttered?

"There is no one here. Only the sons of kings may pass the way between the fires."

"Who are you? What are you?

A naked Sine emerged into the firelight and then stepped back again into the shadows. Gavin moved forward to the fires relaxing his guard when he saw she had no weapons.

"Stop" she said. "You are moving between worlds in this place. Everything of the other world you should leave behind."

The sun had finally set and the night was moonless. Gavin stood motionless, not knowing what to do. For what seemed too long he stood there and Sine moved away a little further from the space between the fires.

"Wait, wait, please wait," he whined and then dropped his weapons and removed his clothes to walk between the fires.

Sine walked up and held him tightly and said "tell me what you want for the future and I will predict whether it can be yours but first you shall lie here with me as payment for my wisdom."

Sine pulled him to the earth and lay on her back. She pulled him inside her. She rolled over on him and the tension of the last hour was suddenly released in him as her body moved everywhere over his. All this time the drum beats had continued. After a few moments he began to speak.

"We are going to the land of the Saxons and I want to be a hero. We have been promised we may go there as boys and return as men. Everything there will be ours. We can have all the women, drink and food we want. We can have the land and live as kings. We shall be so many that no one can oppose us, not even King Athelstan who has won so many battles."

"Is it King Athelstan who has promised you this in his own country or your grandfather, King Constantine?"

"My grandfather is a coward who cannot decide whether he should go or stay at home in his dotage. We have a chance to deliver the Dublin Vikings who are everyone's enemy into the hands of King Athelstan, who will defeat and kill them. If we stand aside from the battle, Athelstan will allow us to stay or to go home as we will."

"He has promised this?"

"Red Callum has told us in secret this is what he has agreed to do provided we attack the Vikings and do not attack the Saxons. He has not told this to my grandfather as he would not agree. Constantine only wants vengeance on the Saxons. Callum has agreed a plan with my father and uncles."

"Red Callum will not get Athelstan to keep his bargain in this matter, young prince, I will tell you this. A traitor deals only with a traitor. Only death lies in wait for the young men of this country as it has done tonight. Your companions are dead and you will suffer their same fate if you fight the Saxons."

"How do you mean?" Gavin mumbled in fear. "My friends, dead?"

"As you walked up this valley, the birds overheard your conversation and came to tell me, their mistress. Their bodies lie in the woods and the rocks. My worshippers have killed them. I am the Mistress of the Wildwood."

Gavin got up and ran between the fires, looking for his sword and dagger. He had not seen Brollachan remove them. He looked about in the firelight. Sine put out the fires as fast as she could and disappeared into the trees.

"Sine, we should let him live and see what happens." Brollachan said. "No one will believe him if he tells what really happened. I've robbed the bodies and left them scattered. I've hidden everything a peasant would steal. Let's chase him up the hill on to the moor. Once he is lost, we can return to the camp."

Sine nodded and they watched Gavin panic and run deeper into the woods away from the camp. They beat the drum and their shields and watched him run deeper. They ran down the hill as fast as they could to pick up their clothes. They made their way stealthily into the camp, unseen by their own guards and settled down for the night.

Next morning Brigid came late to their tent, complaining of too much ale, mead and wine.

"I am getting too old to stay up till dawn drinking with men. I must look like I've been running with wolves all night."

Brollachan offered her some water with herbs to make her feel better but Sine just looked envious.

"I'll go in your place next time, Brigid," she muttered under her breath. "And not mix the drinks unless it's with a man."

Later a couple of riders came into the camp and spoke to Moray who called everyone together and said.

"Five young men, including the king's grandson Gavin, went out last night from the fort and haven't returned. The guard saw them leave and they haven't been found in the usual places. They do make a habit of it but usually return by now. Search parties have gone out. They couldn't be here, and we know that and no one left camp at all according to our guard."

One of the riders said "the king has frequently ordered there should be no wandering around after dark. There are many thieves in the area, especially up on the moorlands. You should all remain in this camp until we discover what's happened to the boys."

When they left Moray went to Sine and Brollachan. "Tell me what happened. I know you left camp unseen last night. Brigid always makes a point of doing it that way."

Sine looked innocently at him but Brollachan spoke. "Lord Moray, we wouldn't lie to you or at least I wouldn't. We went out and the boys followed us. I heard them coming and we hid. We heard them planning to rape and then kill us. We killed the four and let Constantine's grandson live after Sine had got information from him."

Sine told Moray what she had done. Moray faced the dilemma of believing her but worried for the consequences.

"No one will believe him. They'll think he dreamt it," she said.

"No, they will believe him provided that he doesn't say what he told you. He daren't tell the King that bit and no one around here dare let him, you silly girl. As for you Brollachan, you obviously enjoy killing."

"I was doing what Brigid always says I should if my body is threatened. It's alright for Sine; she can have any man she wants. She makes them all envious. Anyway, we know who the traitor is. Tell Callum Dubh, they'll find the boy alive probably still drunk. He's up on the moor, we chased him there. The shepherds will bring him back."

"Don't tell anyone else, not even Brigid." said Moray. "Let's see how the situation develops."

Later that day a message came to Moray from Constantine saying all the five bodies had been found either in the valley or on the moor. His soldiers had caught three men from a nearby village burying two of the bodies. His grandson had been found naked at the foot of a cliff, clearly where they had thrown his body after robbing it. The court was to go into mourning for five days and all discussions on the war were suspended until it was over. Moray thought to himself, I think the Saxons haven't suspended talking about the reception they have waiting for us. All this fuss about five noble youths who set out on a mission to rape two women. If only the church knew, well, it would make no difference. It's like real life, he thought. The relatively innocent are punished and the guilty go free. To be on the safe side he ought to send home the little murderess, but if anyone did have suspicions, it would confirm them.

The following morning it was too late. He was called to King Constantine who confronted him with a story which another youth had repeated about what Gavin and the others had been planning. Moray didn't deny that Brigid and her two companions often went up the valley into the woods to practice with their weapons and carry out rituals. He just stated this had nothing to do with the murders of the five youths as they had already caught the guilty. Brigid he could swear for and the other two were in camp as far as he knew. He would question his own guards and the king's own in the area would have seen them when they had left or on their return. The king's men had already said they had seen nothing. The men they had caught would only admit to robbing the bodies, despite being tortured all night. They had not got the swords or knives the youths carried. Nothing was found of what Gavin was wearing or his sword and knife. The guard commander thought there might be two gangs and the one they caught were just picking up what the first didn't want. Robbery was common in the area. Constantine decided to hang the three who were caught in the act and had all the nearby villages searched. Nothing was found.

Moray decided Sine and Brollachan had to stay in their camp. Many of the Scots were getting suspicious and making threats. The monks were going around declaring them witches as well. Moray couldn't wait for the dust to settle and get back to discussing the war. Now he knew with reasonable certainty Red Callum was double dealing but how to prove it. Perhaps he could not prove it at all.

CHAPTER 8

DECISION DAYS AT DUNNOTAR

Black Callum had no stomach for the fripperies around funerals, a young prince or not. He knew Constantine could hardly remember which one he was, having the benefit of so much royal fodder to marry off in alliances. After the news was received of Gavin's death and when one of his gang who didn't go, said what they were planning, the king nearly went into a frenzy. He went on to Callum at some length, especially when he heard Moray wanted an audience with him over the preparations for war.

"What's Moray going to say, and everyone else who's here, if they think their women are not safe at my court? Athelstan would never be accused of taking a blind eye to anything like this. He'd hang them like that awful aunt of his did with any kind of dissent and double dealing. You could have guaranteed had they been successful in raping and killing those girls; that Brigid woman would have had some revenge on us all, and being a king doesn't save you from women like her. You don't think those girls did it, do you, Callum? The boy said they'd seen them practice with weapons. Do you think they are any good? Are they going to be any good in a battle?"

Callum tried to get a word in edgeways but Constantine carried on.

"Callum, my court is full of traitors. They side with my enemies. They have no vision to build up a strong kingdom to defend ourselves against these new Romans. Even the Saxons on our borders are on our side. Can we ask more of them? I know what Moray means when he says to you about Athelstan's real intentions being to conquer us where the Romans failed. They'll never let go now they know they can just walk up north to us any time they want. They've got the Church and the Franks on their side. They even use my money to pay mercenaries to fight me. Those treacherous Danes! Anlaf's no better, he'll do a deal with Athelstan and they'll divide up my kingdom."

Callum could see his king on the verge of tears and understood why. Athelstan is too smart for us all because he knows all about what we doing, he thought. Every time we change our mind he seems to know why. Constantine went on.

"You know I've misjudged Moray. I thought him a traitor, but he wants me to be King of North Britain, I can see that."

"I have to stop you there, my lord," said Callum firmly. "I am not sure of Moray. I wonder if he says one thing but thinks another to see what reaction there is. I think he knows more of the death of your grandson than he tells us. You would have thought that on hearing of a plan to rape and murder three of his women, he would have stormed in here demanding justice for the plotters of the evil deed, or issued a challenge to them. Do the Picts hatch plots to rape and murder every day? They certainly may not stop at murder. They know everything happening around here. That little fairy listens in corners and the young woman gets the men to talk to her about anything she wants when they lie between her legs. They fawn over her like there isn't another one like her in the north."

"Perhaps he's considering my family's feelings at this time. I hardly knew the lad but he was one of mine, Callum."

"My Lord, if we aren't careful, he'll be labelled a rapist and a murderer, even though he never succeeded. Some are already saying the young men will get out of hand when we go south and turn away support for us."

"What does Moray think to all this, Callum?"

"He's told me no one saw the girls leave camp last night and Brigid was with him and his men. I have questioned our guards and no one saw them leave the camp. They saw our boys move out still drinking and they joked about finding a virgin. Moray also told me he thinks Red Callum is not on our side."

"This gets worse," whined Constantine. "We shall have to get a grip on the whole situation. Who's in charge in my country and who's going to run the invasion? I want you and Moray to meet me where and when no one can overhear, not even his little spy. We need some examples made here. I shall tell the lords that their sons must not plan crimes against people under my protection. I shall expect to hear that any who were involved get a whipping for not coming out with it. They should have told someone, it debases our hospitality. It's resulted in five deaths we could do without. When this funeral is over, we will have a council......... and *I* will tell them how the invasion will take place. Moray and everyone else will keep their spies at home, or no matter how young or pretty they are, they'll hang or be sold into slavery. But I want to hear Moray about Red Callum. Organise all this for me, Callum Dubh."

"My Lord, it shall be done and right now...... Athelstan won't be worrying about funerals despite his piety."

For the duration of the mourning of his grandson Constantine had ordered all formal banquets to cease despite the numbers of delegations at his court. Callum Dubh used this as an opportunity for him and Moray to dine with the king next afternoon in a hut near to the kitchens and had his men quietly watch the outside.

When the servants were dismissed Constantine said, "Moray, if you believe yourself a loyal subject of mine, tell me all you know about what is happening with this war we're planning, and about the death of my grandson. If there is anything to tell on that last matter, I promise you as your lord if you are honest, there will be no consequences. Callum Dubh knows me as a man who does not break promises to honourable men. I am only devious with rogues and traitors."

"Lord Constantine," said Moray "you have no shortage of those hereabouts. People constantly plot to divert you from your plans. Can I say that I may seem to be one because I am unsure of what your plans are? I will tell you what I know of the death of your grandson first. The two women, Sine and Brollachan killed his four companions because they overheard them planning to rape and kill them. They spared your grandson because they heard him try to get the others to go home. They did trick him into believing Sine was a spirit of the woodland. He told her that Red Callum and your sons, his father and uncles, were plotting to do an agreement with Athelstan to defeat the Vikings and the others, to secure his claim to Cumbria and Bambrugh. Red Callum has met either Athelstan or his agents. They say after he gave the information, they chased the boy up on to the moor and returned to camp."

Constantine went into a rage almost choking on his food. "You brought two murderesses into my court!"

"A court where rape and murder are taught at an early age? Did they never think some women are capable of defending themselves? We have to hope if we are going to war that you have better warriors, King Constantine."

He went on to repeat the events in the forest and what the boy had said as Sine had told him. The king went quiet and then said carry on.

"The information the girl obtained indicated that your sons are planning a deal to deliver Anlaf to Athelstan. The boy didn't know any more details except that, and he has been overhearing conversations, I suspect. I can see why it's appealing to your sons. They can see how it prevents a lot of bloodshed among our peoples in the short term. In the long term it just leaves us open to attack without allies. If Athelstan gets proper control of Cumbria and the northern Saxons, either he or his brother will be visiting us again demanding more tribute............ People say the Romans left no real impact on Britain. They did, they left ideas of empire, just as they did everywhere else they went in the west. They say their empire still exists in the east."

Constantine went quiet for a while and drank his ale. He'd forbidden wine as part of the mourning, except for mass.

"Moray, Callum, I have counted on my sons too much. One of them has waited too long for my seat. They are starting to act as if I am not here. I've been king over thirty five years and will go a bit longer with God's help, for few men seem on my side."

Callum who had hardly spoke or moved said. "Let's clear up the issue of Sine and the fairy. Moray has to send them home."

Moray looked a bit relieved to hear this and more still when Constantine agreed.

"There'll be no more temptation," he observed. "But tell me, Moray, do they all behave like this. Did that scrawny child really kill four young men who had been training in war with some of my best warriors?"

"My lord, she's fifteen or sixteen and very much a woman. They would have noticed that when she took off her clothes. We've got many more like her amongst Brigid's priestesses. She has to remain a virgin for the magic to work on the battlefield. It's the promise of victory for many of our warriors."

"But Moray, do you believe it," said Callum?

"I believe the idea works for us if we get the rest right on the day. And by that, I mean the tactics"

Constantine had calmed down considerably and asked Moray what he thought they should do against the Saxons.

"Lord King, we should take one main force south after he has dispersed some of his forces chasing the smaller ones we send earlier into Mercia. We should pick the battlefield and make him come to us. Unless we defeat the Saxons, they will keep coming back for a little bit more. The monks taught me most of the soldiers the Romans had in northern Britain were Saxons when they abandoned the place. The Romans trained them to fight as groups and not the individual combat, which we are all so fond of. Unless we can meet them on the same basis, we will not have a chance. We have to get organised to do that."

Constantine fell silent again but spoke after a while. "It's too late to change the way we fight. We'll have to win by strength of numbers. Dear God, we are proposing to take enough. We had better make sure only the fighters go. Extra mouths to feed will do us no good at all. We had better make sure everyone sticks to a plan as well."

"We don't have a plan," Callum said.

"We will over the next few days because I shall make one as your king. In the meantime I want twenty of your men we can trust before nightfall. Go and organise them now for me. Moray can stay here and tell me about the witches."

"What shall I tell them and why not your own?"

"Tell them not to talk about it now or ever, or their blood will be shed as well as that they might be spilling on my behalf."

Callum said no more and left carrying a piece of chicken.

Moray began. "My people believe that the Great Queen chooses who will live and die and her priestesses should be present to lead the battle. They do not expect to live but to die as warriors equal to men. They expect to be present at the front of the battle calling on the Great Queen, Mhor Rioghain. If nothing else it might frighten the enemy. Something has got to frighten those Saxons. We've fought the local ones often enough to know they are not invincible."

Constantine nodded agreement, thinking here is a man I have overlooked as he isn't exactly one of my own people but he's as convinced we should defend this land as anyone I know. "Continue, Lord Moray."

"We should use the women for skirmishing with other lightly-armed men, and the men in formation in armour should follow them. They want to fight naked so they'll be lightly armed. But I digress, we should make sure we have enough troops to stand and fight the Saxon and not run. No one seems to have enough or the correct sort of armour, and the Saxons have lots of it."

Constantine said "we can't make any more, we don't have the metal. What we have most soldiers have inherited. They are too rich down in the south of this island. No wonder they have a lot of it. Athelstan stopped all trade in metal with us a long time ago."

Moray laughed. "There is a great truth, my lord, and some of us get too envious of them. We need to get amongst that wealth but defeat their army first, and then take their money. We need to arrive with the Viking fleet and then leave as soon as possible. I suspect Red Callum has been telling your sons they can easily break through the line of forts. Of course they can, they won't fight then, it's getting back which could be difficult if Athelstan re-enforces them and they come out and form another army. We have to bring him to a battle and ignore taking the forts, even if they are weak, because we don't know what they are really like."

Callum Dubh came back in. "The men are ready, my lord…. And it's got dark early."

"Get your sword Callum and come with me. Stay away from this, Moray. You and yours could be in enough trouble as it is. Put your camp on alert. Walk quietly away from here."

Moray went off thinking something has put life in this old man, has he been pushed too far by events?

Constantine like an old fox took the macNeills and arrested his three eldest sons who he knew were most likely to be the ring leaders. He sent his own men to arrest the others and before midnight they were all safe out of sight of their own supporters. One or two of them were caught trying to leave Dunnotar. By morning the tale was out as a sufficient number of confessions had been extracted and Constantine confronted his family.

They were all herded into the main hall at the fort and Constantine addressed them. They were all tired and hungry and to remind them who was in charge, they had to stand.

"Traitors, bandits, cow stealers, scum of the earth, how dare you treat a father like this. Don't deny a thing, your worms have been dug from the earth and confessed. You have been dealing with my enemy. Small wonder he considers he can march his killers and murderers into our land without opposition, take our gold and burn our houses without resistance……… You plan to throw away our last chance to redeem our honour and defeat this Saxon Athelstan and his servile Danes and Franks. For what? For gold and silver! Has your father not provided you with enough riches in this poor country? Now you will be like dogs and feed on scraps until you learn gratitude. Look out into the yard. Your slaves are hanging there instead of yourselves."

At this point one of them broke down and confessed and implicated all the others. Constantine walked over and hit him several times with his stick calling him a traitor to his brothers as well as his father, spineless, and a disgrace to the family. Realising he was young Gavin's father, he called him the sire of a rapist and a murderer of children. He then called the bishop and told him the funeral was off and to throw the body in the pit with all the recent dead who included the three hanged peasants. Gavin's mother wailed at this point and Constantine went over and gave her a few blows with his stick.

"Ungrateful children! The hours your mothers spent in labour are now fruitless. You will all make amends. Get your armies away from their ale and out of their houses to practice with the sword. We are going to defeat the warrior of the age and get back our honour. Donal, you worm, you have a special task. You are going to Dublin with a message for Red Callum."

At this point he stuck a dagger through Donal's hand, pinning it to the floor on which he was grovelling.

"When you have the courage to remove it, take it to Dublin and push it through his heart in front of Anlaf. Show the world we mean business. Come back with the deed undone and you are a dead man and your wife and family follow you to God."

Constantine walked about and cursed a bit more kicking the hapless sons while their wives and children and the rest of the court watched.

"Out, out, the lot of you! The cook house is closed for you. Your dinner's going to the poor at the church door. Beg your bread in the country."

He drew his sword and beat them with the flat of the blade. They all ran off and Constantine went to rest in a chair to recover his breath.

Callum Dubh watched all the events with interest and wondered if Constantine had gone too far, even though he enjoyed every moment. Donal was still lying there so he went over pulled out the knife from his hand and the boarded floor. He picked him off the ground. The king had got up and gone by then.

"Donal, my prince, do as he says. This land does not love traitors. There is too much bitterness against the *Sassenaech* for you to have any choice. If your father does not kill you, I will myself."

"Callum, you are right. He'll hang us all if we don't do what he says."

"Donal, he'll hang the ones he loves. If he doesn't love you, it will be worse."

Callum went off to find his dinner and seek out Moray in just that order. Politics makes you hungry, he thought on entering the hall, picking up a bowl of stew.

"Sweet God, not mutton again," he shouted at the cook, who blanked him totally.

He sat down and looked around. Wisely Moray and his followers were not dining in public today. From listening to conversations he assessed some bad feeling against the Picts. No one was saying they murdered the five boys but the confusion around what the boys intended and what happened to them, was becoming an issue. Some were saying the peasants were put up to the deeds by the women. Words such as witches and fairies were being used. The conversations were so interesting Callum had a second bowl of stew, so he could listen without arousing too much suspicion. He thought a third would be too much, and in any case he had work to do.

He went first to his men and told them to be ready for a fight at a few moments notice. Then he went to the king who he found moping in a corner, exhausted from his tirade against his family.

"Lord Constantine, there is a lot of muttering and plotting in the town. I am going to tell Moray to send the two young women away at once before someone is able to organise more murders. They won't even be safe even inside the fort."

"Callum, that's a good idea. Have I done the right thing by my sons? They clearly have no respect for me."

"They thought you had no plan. They see you as being without diplomacy in your dealings with Athelstan. They're frightened of dying on a battlefield down south."

"They are right to feel that way. That evil Saxon and his legions have eyes and ears everywhere and they will be back here soon if we don't do something, Callum."

"My lord, Moray thinks we have a long term problem with them. Athelstan he believes is rebuilding Rome in Britain and he and his successors will not rest until it is done. The only solution is to keep fighting them and to take the battle to them. Didn't he say that to you? Didn't he mention changing tactics?"

"He did and I agree with him but we don't have the time or money to change how we fight now. We just have to do it with numbers. We ought to go and sit in York with Anlaf and negotiate but we are past talking peace. Even I cannot change that. Too many of the allies want a fight and plunder. It may be our undoing if we lose. We have to cross the river between the eastern forts and defeat him. My plan shall be to get the whole of the army over that river form up and wait for an attack. Once we are over, he cannot ignore us......he has to attack and if we are set out over a large enough area......... he has the smaller force and should be weaker. We have to keep the best of our army together. The poorer elements can go raiding as a diversion. We must take and hold those fords even if we cannot get control of the forts protecting them."

"Lord King, that sounds like Red Callum's plan. Can you trust it?"

"It's his plan sure enough but he isn't the only one who knows about the land around the River Don. Every wool trader and salt pedlar can walk by and see what's built. I don't doubt he takes Saxon gold but he doesn't decide what happens on the day of the battle. We have to prepare and meet the Saxons. I despair of controlling large numbers and feeding them, Callum, but we shall have to try. We can double bluff the Saxons. Once they learn their spy is dead, they might think we won't stick to his plan."

"My lord, we should all talk about this in detail. We have all to know what Callum said and what he planned in more detail. Your sons must speak about what he said to them. Fetch Donal, and tell him to return with Callum, so we can question him. Don't have him murdered."

"No, Callum. It would be showing too much weakness at time I should be seen to strong. He's a dead man and its time my Donal learnt that wanting to be a king involves hard decisions like killing your friends and your family. Athelstan knew that at an early age and so did I................ Enough of planning, until we meet in council. Time for more thought."

Constantine still looked miserable, so Callum continued to sit and talk to him well into the night. As he walked back to his camp with a couple of his guard, he thought long and hard about what he had learnt. He sat up all night thinking about the future and wondered if this battle with the Saxons is not going to be a good one to miss. But how to stay away, without being thought a coward, or breaking an oath? It's got to be a doomed venture, everyone agrees on one thing, and one thing only, and that is we are doing it the wrong way. Then, they want to follow a plan the enemy knows about. The Western Isles began to beckon macNeill.

CHAPTER 9

GUDRUN'S PREDICTION

From the looks on her grandchildren's faces Gudrun knew something was afoot about the invasion. Sitric was her only surviving son and he was now risking the end of the family with this ill-thought venture with the Scots. The Saxons had killed her husband and two other sons and he was giving them a chance to finish off him with the rest of her family. She was not going to allow this. She had many allies in Dublin, both Viking and Irish, and she was going to use them now. The details of what had been decided; she would get these out of Guthric in a few days time. Siward would give an inkling and Guthric would flesh it up. For her to influence events, however, was another matter. She needed to look into the future for that and in a week there was a full moon.

Gudrun had put together her sisters with great care. Women who would talk about many matters spoke of nothing they did amongst themselves. Her greatest treasure was Bronagh. She spotted her immediately the girl turned up with Hemming. The fear and desperation deep in her eyes went unnoticed by the men around the camp. They only saw her as aloof and under Hemming's protection. Within days Gudrun had her under her wing and to her surprise she found belief in Christianity was less than nominal. She knew very little and seemed never to have been in a church except for baptism. Gudrun thought this strange for an Irish girl. She knew the traditional Celtic practices and the stories which Gudrun knew. When Hemming was absent they would spend hours in conversation. Sitric approved because he thought it kept his mother out of his affairs. He had been in for a surprise on many occasions. Gudrun was proud of her clever son. He could think of everything but only the women in the family could *see* everything.

Four years ago she had sent out Bronagh with one of the local girls, Keeva, to find a place down river as near to the sea as possible and to do so without being followed. They found an island in the marshes only properly accessible at low tide unless you were prepared to wade through deep water and they had been using it ever since. They were once nearly discovered when Bronagh was followed by a drunken Viking. Unknown to them all, Hemming had taught her how to use a short knife which she carried everywhere with her. He was still alive when they buried him in the bog although Bronagh had cut out his tongue so his screams before the burial couldn't be heard. Odin and Freya heard her song even clearer that night, and Gudrun knew from here on, this was a woman she could trust. The others since, had learned to fear her. She could take over from Gudrun if anything happened.

Secretly Gudrun hoped they could have an offering on this coming moon as she and Bronagh made preparations. They had only been followed once in four years and it was as if most of the men knew what had happened to their fellow and had the sense not to interfere again. Neither Sitric nor Anlaf ever raised it with her, nor was Bronagh ever questioned. Bronagh said Hemming never questioned her on the matter, except to say the man had disappeared without trace, but he was like his chief, he would speak carefully on important matters. He was not one for too much idle chatter. He also never questioned about where she went with Gudrun.....Gudrun knew her son chose his close followers wisely.

Within two days of his instructions from Sitric, Hemming and his party were on their way and without Bronagh. She was pregnant. The plans for the journey had been in place a while in Hemming's head and knew she would have to remain behind once it was certain. It would be something to hold over her family at the other end of the road and speed was of the essence getting there. They had been expecting confirmation of the pregnancy for a couple of weeks and Bronagh was relieved Hemming was staying behind whenever the expedition set off for the north.

On the night of the full moon as always, Gudrun seemed to be full of energy for a woman past her seventy years. She knew she couldn't risk a pony for even part of the journey. Slipping out in the late summer shadows with her two maids, Edith and Gytha was the only answer. Bronagh, Keeva and the others, Sive, Ciara, and Eachna were waiting out in the woods. Gudrun's granddaughter Margareta and Sigrid her friend would be already there. She had the nine she wanted. She seldom felt happier.

The journey to the island was easy in the half light. Bronagh and Keeva stayed back to watch the path. Gudrun had taken advantage of Bronagh's handiness with a knife to suggest she train the others. Now they all carried one.

Bronagh had detected uneasiness in Dublin, once it became certain that Anlaf was going to ally himself with Constantine for the attack on the Saxons. She remembered her own people how they optimistically looked forward to war on the outside, but their inner thoughts, they kept as quiet as possible. Keeva lived with one of Anlaf's personal guard and knew everything going on there just by listening. She often observed she learnt more by staying silent than asking questions, as loose talk was everywhere. She sometimes had a bit of difficulty with the Viking's language and because she couldn't speak it too well, some people thought she couldn't understand it. Bronagh had learnt it well enough from Hemming who was a good and patient teacher. It was a labour of love to him and Gudrun had helped a lot. She had taught Hemming better Irish and a lot about the country and people, he never knew before. The two women were the same age and they often talked about what might happen in the event of war, the Irish trying to recover Dublin, the death of their men, children etc. Both had been coming to the conclusion that at twenty it was better to live for this moment, even though a difficult time might be coming.

Keeva had another problem related to the excessive attention she was receiving from the ambassador from the Scots, the man known as Red Callum. She kept out of his way which was difficult in such a small place like Dublin. She had told Hakon but he laughed saying the man was a windbag in this as everything else about him, but he would watch him. If things looked especially dangerous he would speak to King Anlaf, and Red Callum was like this with all the women he met. Gudrun had advised her to follow her instincts in this and if she felt he was around her, to get as far from him as possible. Gudrun thought Callum was more a spy than an ambassador but who was he spying for, she wondered. She suspected the Saxons.

Hiding in the bushes on the outside of the fort, the conversation between Bronagh and Keeva came around to this again.

"Bron, I've felt him around today, everywhere I have been. Hakon's not been at home and I have felt unsafe. Most of the men in this place think he is some sort of hero who's going to lead them to a fortune. I know your man thinks he's going to lead them to their deaths……. You are glad he's not going, aren't you?"

"How did you know that?"

"Bron, all the men at the fort think to be left behind is the worst that can happen to them. Both Viking and Irish feel the same way but this isn't going to be a raid is it?"

"No, it isn't and I have a bad feeling about it and Gudrun is going to tell us something tonight we perhaps already know. Some of the men know this too but are more scared of being thought a coward than dying in battle. The Oslacssons are an exception. They don't mind being thought of as cowards and if anyone dares voice it, they kill them. Most men around here have fallen under Red Callum's spell. He must wonder why the women don't feel the same way. I have only ever seen him from a distance and he has never spoken to me."

"But you rarely go into the fort and he hardly goes outside I've noticed."

"Well, Keeva, today must be an exception because he's coming this way, I think. I have red hair myself and if you want to be unnoticed, you cover it up. He's got a couple of the *Jarl's* nephews with him, I think. Let's just step back deeper into these bushes."

Callum and the two boys walked nearer to the path and stopped. "Did you lads say this path leads down into the marshes?"

"We used to go fishing down there next to the river until we had to start training for war. You have to walk a long way and not walk off the main path. There are a lot of small ones running off south down to the riverbank. Just keep on till you get your feet wet."

"Thanks, Lachlan," said Callum, "and that's the way you saw the old lady going?"

"She takes all the girls down that way quite often but they won't go too far. Granny Gudrun must be seventy if a day; sometimes it seems she can hardly walk. What do you want to know for?"

"Never you mind, young Stigand, the bits of silver I gave you, are to stop you worrying about this. Don't tell anyone, this is our secret. There could even be more for you later. Go back to the fort now and leave me to deal with this. Tell no one, you hear me!"

Callum walked past the two women and stopped as if to listen. He then moved on at a run. When he had gone Bronagh whispered. "He is going to spy on us. He'll have to go to the end of the path where they will be waiting for us and we can't get around him to warn them."

"Bron, we don't have to. All we have to do is stop him from coming back. The girls will be ready and waiting quietly for us. They will be waiting to wade across to the island and just off the path. If he makes as much noise as he has done so far, they'll hear him coming and know something's wrong. He won't expect us behind him."

" Keev,I don't think he is much of a warrior……… but he has got his sword."

Callum ran till he was a bit breathless and had still found nothing. He had passed four or five narrow paths and when the main path went downhill he could see the bay and the marshes. He could make out an island, even though it was getting dark. He then fell over a tree root and twisted his ankle. The cry of pain seemed to echo around the quiet woods despite the noise of the waves nearby breaking over some rocks.

"I'll have to go back" he said out loud, "when the pain goes away a little."

He had not seen Eachna watching the path and she came nearer to see what was happening. She ran off to Gudrun.

"Well, it's not his lucky day whoever he is, my children," said Gudrun. "If he has been following us, a man with a sword is what we want. Let us hope our sisters saw him. Let us go and see. A warrior would be a good sacrifice. Let us hope he can be brave and die slowly."

Bronagh and Keeva waited in the bushes near to Callum who was limping a little and was breaking up a stick to help him walk. Gudrun and the sisters appeared. He did not see them, as he was making too much noise. He looked up and for a moment, didn't know how to take in seven naked young women appearing out of the shadows. Only Gudrun's voice brought him around as she appeared from another direction.

"Lord Callum, have you come to join us sitting out on this night of the full moon?"

Callum's instinct was to say no and he would not take part in such heathen practices. They didn't know that in his early life he had been considering becoming a priest. The family needed him to return when his two elder brothers had died in a fight over some land with the Saxons. Callum had resolved that would never happen to him.

"Lady, if you are seeking knowledge, I would be glad to take part," he said, trying not to think of the contrast between her aged body and those of her young followers.

"Do you come of your own freewill?"

"I come of my own choice," he said.

"Draw your sword and follow us," said Gudrun. This put him at ease for a moment and gave enough time for distraction and for Sigrid to hit him over the head. Whilst he was stunned the rest jumped over him, cut off his clothes, removed his boots and weapons, tied him up and gagged him before he had time to come around properly.

Bronagh and Keeva appeared. Keeva whispered to Gudrun. "He bribed the two of the King's nephews to tell we had come this way."

"Don't worry about them," said Gudrun. "I can deal with them if they are the two which keep mooning over Margareta. It does prove that some people know we come this way. Drag him down to the island, girls. Get a fire going to burn his clothes. You two come with me for a moment."

When the others had dragged Callum away to the marsh, Gudrun looked sternly at them. "You did the right thing to follow him so he couldn't escape. The last time this happened there was just the three of us. Now we have seven very young girls who may not be too happy about killing him the way we are going to do it. They all know men and women die cruelly in wars, the risk of being raped, dying in childbed and I know they are all still virgins. We have to let him cry out as we kill him and they are going to have to take part."

"Gudrun" said Bronagh, "I think only you and I in our coven have ever killed anyone and you know that Viking was not my first. I had to defend myself at home on many occasions. Keeva feels he has threatened her and she can't wait to start on him."

"That's right," said Keeva. "All the girls need is a reason. They are only just past childhood. Edith's the oldest at seventeen and Sigrid's only just fourteen. Old enough to marry and have children, I know, but not to be sensible about it."

"I had no choice at that age," said Gudrun.

"That was because your family nominally converted to Christianity and women become chattels. In Ireland we are more civilised," said Keeva. "I think I should tell them he is an evil man who is sending their fathers and brothers to their deaths against the Saxons. They should make him suffer till he confesses, and then we can finish him at the right time."

Gudrun laughed, "I thought I would only ever hear Bronagh speak such words, Keeva. She has had a hard life until Hemming came to her rescue, but you, I remember how much we all loved you as a child. Your parents when they were alive doted on you. You were their only daughter."

"I can see what life has left me being taken from me by this man and the others he influences and I feel so miserable. What I shall do to him, I want to do to them."

"You had better explain all this to the others while Gudrun and I hang him in the tree," said Bronagh. "The moon is rising, we must begin soon. Bring the drums and take my clothes. I'll cut some willows for them to beat him."

Keeva went off and spoke to the girls. They listened intently to what she said about the misfortune that Red Callum was going to bring on their families. She reminded them about what Gudrun wanted to do and how his slow death was going to help her talk to Odin and Freya and look into the future. He was to be her way to knowledge on what the future held for the people of Dublin. No one was going to hold them accountable for tonight's work, and Gudrun would make sure of that. They had to play their part and then watch what she and Bron are doing. He was to die three times.

They were all silent except for Sigrid. She couldn't wait to start and confessed he had shown some interest in her and she hadn't known what to do. Her mother and father had not been much help. Her mother had even wondered if there was anything serious on his part, and could they arrange a marriage.

Gudrun and Bronagh were less light-hearted.

"Gudrun, how are we going to explain away his death if any of the girls talk or *Jarl* Anlaf enquires too deeply?"

"Easily, child, when I tell Sitric what happened. Anlaf can't do without him. Your Hemming is holding this place while they are away. In public we deny everything. Besides I feel the hands of Odin and Freya guiding these events for a reason. I need to *see* what's happening here. Let's worry about all this afterwards. We need visions."

"Let's hang the man in the tree then."

They hung the screaming and cursing Callum upside down in a tree. He was still stunned a little from Sigrid's bang on the head and half-drowned from being pulled to the island by the girls. The cold water had brought him round and he was beginning to guess his fate. The girls returned and began to dance around him with Keeva encouraging them to beat him. Bronagh and Keeva were drumming as Gudrun prepared for her trance. Sigrid particularly began to enjoy hurting him and taunted him for his past interest in her by showing him her body. After a period of agony Callum began to go unconscious and Bronagh stopped them. They all sat and waited for Gudrun. She seemed ages and returned after a while, looking particularly ill and tired in the firelight.

Bronagh looked at her and decided to take charge. "Cut him down, bring him round, its time and get the stones."

When he was cut down and pushed in the water, she and Keeva strangled him and cut his throat with the blood spurting all over everyone. He was nearly when dead they all pushed his body under the water, holding it down with the stones. The younger girls went ecstatic. Blood and water was over everyone but Gudrun.

Gudrun began to speak and they all went quiet. The younger girls moved away a little.

"All I have seen is blood and the end of life for many of us in Dublin. This venture will see the end of what we have. King Athelstan will be victorious now but Anlaf will live and have to wait his time, then he will succeed when that king is dead. This man is only the first of the Scots to die. They will perish in their thousands with all their allies including ourselves. We will never be strong in this place again. There will be universal mourning amongst the Christians."

She fainted as usual when she related her visions and was out for a long time.

"Margareta, get everyone together, we have to get her back home," said Bronagh. "She's getting too old for this."

"Bron, who can we tell about this?" Keeva asked.

"No one, Keeva. Only Gudrun can speak and the girls will stay quiet. We must make sure they stay silent or we are all doomed. The Christians are getting too powerful around here. They won't like what's happening."

"Bron, an ambassador will be missed. His own king will want an explanation."

"We have to trust Gudrun. Now we all need a wash, hair as well. I've got blood all over my head."

They carried her home and put her in bed and threatened the remainder of the servants that no one was to know what happened, or when during the night they returned.

The following afternoon there was general consternation in the camp. Red Callum was missing and Anlaf wanted to talk to him. Sitric always had a bad feeling after a full moon and went to speak to his mother. He came straight to the point.

"Any number of people saw Red Callum walk out of the gates towards the woods. Will anyone find the body? I know he must have met you and your ladies."

"No" said Gudrun. "He won't be found."

"That's a relief. What did Odin reveal?"

"The expedition is doomed but Anlaf will return and triumph when Athelstan is dead. Many will be slain next year. Stay at home, son!"

"I cannot, Mother."

"Then be careful. Not only are the Saxons treacherous, they are good fighters."

She turned over and went back to sleep again.

Sitric wondered how he was going to tell Anlaf about any of this. He hoped he would find words at the time. As for what he should do in the battle, he had better find some way to stay out of it. If his men were split up, he would have none to lead as a warband. He would not have to appear a coward. The Oslacssons were never frightened, just cautious on occasion. History had taught Sitric taking risks could result in your death. The memory of his father's unnecessary death was never far from his mind.

CHAPTER 10

THE NEW SCOTS AMBASSADOR

Anlaf was worried when a messenger came to say that Constantine was sending one of his sons to Dublin. The message arrived on the very day after Red Callum disappeared. He thought the man's a bit of a mystery anyway. The fellow appeared out of the blue with a small group of Scots who he sent home almost at once leaving just himself to talk to Anlaf. Almost as if the man was not going back. Perhaps he has slipped away to spy on the Saxons. No, he reasoned, there must be another explanation. After two days of hearing speculation by nearly everyone at his court except Sitric Oslacsson, he thought he had better ask him what he thought and he would do it now. He'd go to his house.

Sitric Oslacsson and his men lived near the wharf and their ships like real seafarers and Anlaf was always impressed by that. No easy, soft life for them. Their camp was extensive but not grand. It was defensible as well, from within and without. Oh, for a dozen more like Sitric, he mused.

His arrival near the wharf had not gone unnoticed and Sitric was at the gate to meet him.

"Welcome, *Jarl* Anlaf."

"Greetings, Sitric." He was about to inquire after the health of his mother but he saw her at the door of a hut with a strikingly beautiful Irish woman. Not a slave that one, he thought.

"Sitric, I want to know what you think about this Scot disappearing so strangely"

"Let's talk in private, *Jarl*. Dismiss your guards."

They walked into the main house.

"Tell me what you think happened, Sitric."

"I'll do better. I know what happened. He interrupted mother and her ladies while they were sitting out and they sacrificed him to Odin and Freya."

"Why didn't you come and tell me," said Anlaf, almost dying of fright?

"What, with everyone in earshot? It's not something you can announce in public any more, like a wedding."

Anlaf looked for a moment as if he was about to burst with anger but calmed and said. "What did Odin say? She has told you?"

"Yes, you will not defeat the Saxons with the help of the Scots and the *wealas*. You will triumph after Athelstan's death by your own efforts."

"Is that all? Still, what more is there to say? That would be enough for most men. Would it not, Sitric?"

"She did say men will die in their thousands but that doesn't surprise me, taking account of how the Saxons are preparing. She said we would lose Dublin."

"Sitric, these are Odin's warnings. What we do now is up to us. Have you prepared our defence here? Who else knows of the prediction?"

"There is only you, me, mother, Bronagh and Keeva, two Irish girls. Bronagh lives with Hemming who I am leaving here in charge of the town. He's gone recruiting allies for us amongst her people. Keeva lives with one of your guard. Their silence can be relied on. There were some younger girls but they didn't hear the prophesy. They were too busy killing Callum."

"Sitric, I shall never be easy again when I see more than two women with their heads together," Anlaf said with a laugh. "All this has brought to me my worst fears about the expedition. This Scots king has let revenge carry away reason. He thinks he can substitute brute force for politics. He does not for all his years know what Athelstan and we knew as young men, that they run side by side and a sensible man chooses peace and trade before war and theft."

"What will you say to Constantine's son?"

"I will tell him that Callum went off to Chester to spy on the Saxons. I presume the port is still open to trade?"

"It was a month ago."

"Tell your mother to make sure all her ladies stay quiet about everything. I know we can count on her. I have a suspicion the children of some of our friends are involved here without their knowledge. It perhaps should stay that way. Be at my side when this Scot arrives, I hope he causes less trouble than the last one..... Sitric, I am content now I know what's happened. Let's hope not too many Christians guess the man's fate"

He left chuckling to himself.

Two weeks later the speculation had not died down but a rather crestfallen Scottish prince appeared with only a handful of followers. So few, like the other one that the Dubliners couldn't believe he was really a prince. Some ventured to say perhaps the Scots were not really sending ambassadors and princes, just adventurers to fool us.

"Prince Donal" he announced himself.

"Welcome, dear friend and brother," said Anlaf and then he introduced his men and one or two of the ladies in an effort to distract him. Gudrun and Bronagh were introduced. Anlaf had decided he wanted them there to hear what the Scots had to say as if he expected them to divine the truth from the lies he thought to hear.

The prince came straight to the point in a shaky voice and full of fear.

"Some events at my father's court have proved that our ambassador to you, Red Callum macAnnan is a traitor and dealing with the Saxons."

Anlaf looked dropped on and looked at Sitric who spoke.

"Prince Donal, you unfortunately confirm our suspicions and we are grateful that on discovering this, that your father should despatch a son with the news and the apology. We take this as an indication of the high regard he has for us as his allies...."

Donal began to look relieved.

".......Please convey to him our gratitude and respect for the swift action he has taken. Take also our apology for Red Callum has disappeared and we do not yet know where. We suspect he has gone to the Saxons."

Regaining some confidence Donal said quietly. "This disappearance must be proof of his guilt."

"Indeed," said Anlaf with a smile. "But now we must take advantage of your presence to finalise more details of our venture next year. We can do

this with confidence now that the Saxons will not be listening to us………
But first a feast tomorrow in your honour when you are rested."

"Let us all look forward to success" said Sitric. "We have not yet made any firm plans the traitor could have taken away to King Athelstan."

During the meal Donal was seated to the right of Anlaf. On his right was Sitric but opposite him were Gudrun and Bronagh. Donal could not take his eyes from her to the point it became embarrassing.

Bronagh knew she was attractive but since the day Anlaf had seen her, the requests to appear at the court had been constant. The pregnancy was making her bloom but no one except for Gudrun and Keeva knew about it for certain.

"Prince Donal, you have a wound on your right hand," she said.

Donal nearly said his father had stabbed him. He thought the better of it but made the mistake of making up something neither she nor Gudrun believed. Gudrun's eyes said it all to Anlaf and Sitric.

Sitric made it worse by saying Bronagh was handfasted to one of his chief men who was away recruiting soldiers for the invasion. Donal was wondering whether she was being offered to him but realised not. He certainly wasn't risking an involvement with a Viking's woman. His wife was expecting him to return as soon as he had despatched Red Callum. He had not told Anlaf this. He was, however, beginning to feel uncomfortable in Dublin and he had only been there for two days. The place had a feel of a battle camp without an immediate battle to fight. All the men wore their swords even at a feast. The women laughed too much. Only the bishops looked remotely sour-faced. The lower orders seemed to be having too much of a good time irrespective of what was happening on the high table. There was too much ale, it was too strong and the Scots including himself were drinking too much of it. They hadn't even started on the mead.

When the food was eaten, Anlaf proposed a toast. "To our ally King Constantine of the Scots. We pledge him our support." All the Dubliners, Viking and Irish, resounded the words.

"To you King Anlaf," replied Prince Donal. "May your life be long and prosperous!"

He sat down before he fell down.

Anlaf was beginning to tire of the title, king. He was beginning to see Sitric's point of view and that of many of his other men, that only the fawning courtiers and not the soldiers were using the title.

Donal was expecting the feast to last well into the night and wondering how he would survive but fairly early Anlaf wished him a goodnight and the high table dispersed, leaving the rest to carry on.

The following morning Hakon Eriksson came to him with information on what he had heard in private the previous night.

"*Jarl*, Keeva and I sat with a couple of the Scots and they told us many interesting things about events at King Constantine's court. The king suspected his sons of being in league with Red Callum to make a peace with King Athelstan to avoid a battle. They were planning to ally with the Saxons to get control of the north of the country held by the Angles. The Scots would get the country of the *wealas* and the Sassenaech as they call them, the border areas. Constantine and his supporters who want revenge on the Saxons have prevented this. They are confidant the people on the border will support them anyway and want Constantine as their king."

Anlaf sat quietly and let the storm brew in his head. Who can keep track of all this, he thought. Events conspire in Athelstan's favour. Prophesy or not, how can I ever beat him.

"Carry on, my good soldier," he said. "You and Keeva are loyal to me."

"The son of one of his earls confessed the information and others volunteered when found out. Prince Donal was one of the conspirators and was sent here to kill Red Callum. Perhaps he found out and it's what's made him flee the city............"

Gudrun's choice of ladies cannot be faulted thought Anlaf. She hasn't even told her man the fate of Callum. Perhaps he doesn't know the rest either.

"…..The wound on his hand is where Constantine pinned his hand to the floor with a knife and told him to bring it here to kill Red Callum."

Anlaf stopped getting angry and began to laugh. He walked over to a chest and took out a box. He took two gold rings out of it.

"Your rewards! A king could not have better supporters than you and your lady for this work. A *Jarl* like me is doubly blessed. Go now and talk some more to the Scots."

When he had gone Anlaf laughed, cried and got angry again. He shouted to a servant outside. "Fetch me Sitric Oslacsson. He is to come immediately."

Sitric strolled in casually. "*Jarl* Anlaf, you once used to send for me urgently when we needed to kill someone."

"We were younger then, Sitric and we have learnt more sense since, but we may need to do exactly that."

"Not the Scots prince? I would cheerfully do it now if you wanted."

"Has your mother been reading runes again?" Anlaf chuckled. "It's on my mind."

"We cannot keep killing ambassadors, *Jarl* Anlaf. People will think we are uncivilised, although they might make allowances if they were all Scots who we murdered. I could smell treachery the moment he walked off his ship. Well, he did not so much walk as shuffle in fear."

"He might well do that," said Anlaf and told him what Hakon and Keeva had discovered.

"*Jarl*, we cannot allow such a man to return and go boasting around Greater Britain that he hoodwinked you. This will not make you King of York. It could result in all our certain deaths, even at a time when our lives are looking in danger of being lost due to the treachery of friends. Unlike Callum, he can't die here. On the sea would be a good place when he returns to his father. To ensure no one suspects us more than they normally might, we shall have to make sure that some of his party remain behind to say he set off in good order."

"You can work something and tell me later, just like you did when we were younger."

Sitric went back to Anlaf in the afternoon and they had a walk out in the sunshine.

"Unusually sunny for the time of year," said Sitric as they passed by some ladies.

"People will start suspecting we are plotting something," said Anlaf with a smile, "you are being uncharacteristically friendly. Be your usual self and scowl at people."

"I am one of the friendliest in the world to my friends," protested Sitric, but not too much. "What we must do is not get too many more people involved with this. My man Hemming will return soon with some Irish warriors.... and he's going to pick ones who can fight, not ones who pretend after a drink or two. Bronagh's family are helping in this......."

Ah the lovely Bronagh was bound to come into this sometime, thought Anlaf.

"......and we could use them as they don't know he's a Scots prince. If your man Hakon leads them, he can identify Donal and do the deed. There are some Scots traders due to arrive to buy slaves next week. They will want to return before the weather changes up north. They will suggest the prince returns, even if we don't advise him."

"Arrange it, Sitric. We had better go through the motions of planning a campaign."

"Not so! Someone who remains behind who we can trust should carry our plans to King Constantine. We can still beat the Saxons. We have had Odin's warning and we have discovered the treachery. Athelstan still has time to make mistakes. What we must do is put our ships together and arrange to pick up some of Constantine's armies. No wonder he suffers from traitors with so many around him."

"You are wise as usual, Sitric."

"One last thing, just to ensure his survival, young Hakon should remain here. Hemming needs all he can trust and no one involved in the death of the prince, should go to the Scots king."

"Arrange it all, my good friend!"

Sitric walked back to his huts and saw Bronagh and Keeva looking into the water. Strange, I have never noticed those two together before. I thought I saw most important things around here. They can be the eyes and hears for their men. I am happy with that and walked on.

The two women were lost in thought. Keeva spoke first. "We seem to have survived as murderesses, Bron."

"There are events unfolding and we are only playing a small part. Gudrun sees it all. Not just in her dreams, her age and experience tell her things we have yet to learn. We should not worry too much. The *Jarl* has rewarded you and Hakon and I suspect he may know the part you played in Red Callum's death. It's a sign he approves. The main danger is if he wants us to do it again."

"If we have to do it to stay alive, then we must, but there were too many involved the last time. One of those little girls will talk. I am certain."

"We tell no one, not even our men. Only Gudrun has the right to speak of it."

"Sitric was watching us as well. He's like his mother, he sees everything. Let's move elsewhere."

Sitric found Hakon teaching some boys the use of a shield. A good fighter, he thought, he understands the need to stay alive. When the lesson was over he went to speak to him and explained the plan. Hakon laughed, particularly about staying behind in Dublin. He did say he wouldn't tell

Keeva until nearer the time. He was enjoying her fussing because she thought she might lose him. Sitric said Anlaf would actually announce it formally and probably soon so as not to create suspicion. They parted on the basis that Hakon would get more instructions on Hemming's return.

The more Sitric thought about it, he wondered if the information leaked about Prince Donal had been done deliberately to see what they would do. Donal obviously had no part in this but he thought he might try a double bluff. It might be a way to encourage him to leave. He decided to seek him out whilst everything was fresh in his mind. He saw him sat on his ship at the wharves and walked over.

"Prince Donal, you are not packing up to leave already?"

"I'm not really an ambassador, I'm a messenger," he said wistfully.

"Well, that's true," said Sitric, "but our invasion plans should be conveyed by someone important. We need to work on them with speed so you can take them back to you father to consider over the winter. There is much to do and little time before the weather changes, and the northeast winds are not good for a return journey. We have someone who can write Latin for the details but it's really important that you are able to convey the spirit of the ideas."

This made Donal uncomfortable and he said, "I have brought Kenneth macAllan with me who understands matters of war in much better ways. He had better be there to hear what you have to say......."

Strange he didn't introduce him yesterday if he's so important, thought Sitric or is he his father's man sent to watch his son.

"......he'll remember it better than me. He's quite a warrior."

"I must meet him, Prince Donal."

Donal pointed out Kenneth who was sitting on the bankside talking with some of the Irish.

"Was he at the feast the other night, I didn't see him?"

"No, he was getting over being sea sick. He's no sailor."

Donal called him over and Sitric could tell instantly he was not Donal's man. He also wasn't the man who told what had happened to Donal. Here was a prince not short of enemies, even in such a small party as came with him. Sitric introduced himself and explained about the plans Anlaf was to send to Constantine. Kenneth was less than impressed, observing his King would be making his own and all Earl Anlaf was required to do, was lead the armies on the day of the battle. All the Vikings had to do was turn up with their ships and men. He then went off, muttering something about getting back his appetite.

Sitric thought, I like this man. We can deal with him. He won't interfere when we murder the prince and even if he suspects us, he won't tell his king. No wonder Donal is frightened of his own shadow with him around. Then he thought, perhaps Constantine has ordered his own son's death, after he was to kill Red Callum. He made his farewells to Donal and saw Bronagh and Keeva returning. He went up to them and asked Keeva to discreetly show him the man she and Hakon questioned last night. Keeva was surprised he knew about their information, although Bronagh was not. Even Anlaf was unaware Bronagh knew, but Sitric understood they would have told each other and his mother. He had to make sure they didn't know the next part of the plans.

He decided to speak to Kenneth again when he could, on the basis he might be a better way to deal with Constantine. He would tell Anlaf what he had discovered. He now had to wait for Hemming. He came back five days later.

Sitric was always happy with what Hemming could do and how he did it. He had set off by sea but returned overland to everyone's surprise. He had left Sitric's sons to return by sea with the Irish they had recruited. Nothing Hemming did was predictable to anybody but him.

"Gave the lads a command," he said to Sitric. "The winds weren't too good for an immediate start by sea either."

Sitric explained what he wanted doing. In ten days Prince Donal was to return with a ship of Scots merchants before the weather worsened. The remainder of the Scots were to stay with their ship until the plans were finalised. One of the Scots was grumbling, the king's warrior macAllan. The prince couldn't wait to set off. Hemming and Hakon were to go to meet Sitric's sons as far as the world was concerned. In reality they were to meet the ships with Guthric and Siward. Hakon was to take the Irish and kill the Scots and rob the ship. They were to let a couple of the meaner members of the crew survive to tell the tale and let Irish pirates get the blame.

Hemming spent one night at home and went off with another crew. Fortunately he met the ship with the boys a day up the coast and returned before the Scots left. Hakon was a relatively insignificant character around Dublin, whereas Hemming was known by all and his return with the boys was noted by all.

Donal was keeping to his friends or to the Vikings, carefully avoiding Kenneth, especially at night as if he suspected something. He looked relieved to be aboard the merchant ship and macAllan looked as if his plans were going wrong. Sitric took him aside and came to the point.

"Kenneth, my new friend, I do not think it a good idea for you to kill your master's son here in Dublin. Can't you wait till you get home? Two ambassadors lost from one place would get us an undeserved reputation."

Kenneth laughed so loud the whole quayside turned around but whispered to Sitric.

"The world knows what a set of murderers you are in this town. I accept your advice. It will have to be at home now or on the battlefield, or may be there'll be a storm to sink the ship."

He walked off laughing some more.

"He suspects us," said Hemming. "But I think he will stay silent."

Eight days later almost in sight of the friendly coast of Cumbria the ship carrying the prince met a Scots ship and a battle ensued in which he was killed. Some distance away the battle was observed by Hakon with Hemming and his crew. They sailed up when the Scottish ship sailed away in time to pull one of the merchants out of the water before he froze to death. Hemming set sail for Dublin wondering what to make of it all. He hadn't told the Irish the details only suggested they do a bit of piracy as they were near to the Saxons coast. When they arrived he went to see Sitric and they went to Anlaf with the merchant who explained it all. Anlaf sent for Kenneth.

"Your countrymen do not draw a line at murdering honest merchants and royal princes doing their duty to their country" said Anlaf. "What can I say to his father when we meet?"

Kenneth snorted. "Try telling him his son was a rogue and a traitor to his cause. He may agree with you."

"You arranged this, macAllan," said Anlaf. "It's a wonder you didn't try to implicate us in this."

"You've implicated yourselves. You had a ship passing just at the right time to rescue a witness. If he'd drowned, who would have been the wiser?"

"Everyone would have blamed us," said Sitric, "and you would have encouraged them. We don't normally murder Scots but I am beginning to think I need the practice."

"A man should be careful of his friends as well as his enemies," said Anlaf.

"I agree" said Kenneth. "Tell me what really happened to Red Callum."

Sitric told the story.

"By the Gods of our fathers" said Kenneth, "Constantine will laugh when he hears that. Bands of women have been running around Dunnottar killing men. Well, two girls managed to kill five young men one night because they followed them to some sort of women's ritual. The story has got out of hand, of course."

Kenneth told the storey of Brollachan and Sine.

"Last I heard before we left, the boys' relatives were out for revenge but I think they will be disappointed. We are getting out of practice at real war. Men have to drink a barrel of ale before they find their courage in the bottom of it."

"You know, Kenneth" said Hemming, "you are so philosophical, and could pass for a Seafarer on a good day. I hope your king is taking you south to die fighting King Athelstan, because if you turn up here in Dublin when I am in charge, you will die at once so I may sleep safe in my bed at night."

Kenneth laughed. "It is always a pleasure to see such wisdom in a young man. You may live many years keeping to such practices. How do you think I have lived so long?"

CHAPTER 11

THE JOURNEY TO THE HILLS

Brigid and Moray decided to send home Sine and Brollachan. The king's instructions seemed final and there was nowhere near they could hide them in safety. Moray put a guard of ten men together with instructions to move off as soon as they could pack and off they went.

Brigid sent them off with their weapons which she had recovered from their secret camp. She expected an attack and thought at least they would fight well if attacked, but she never voiced her worries. She watched them move out and thought at least they travel light. Most of Dunnotar seemed to turn out to watch them go as if some spy had found out about the move or had the crowd just guessed. With her aristocratic nose in the air, Bridget correctly dismissed most of them as peasants who had been listening to the priests denounce her sisters as murderers. All they did was murmur and look downcast as usual. She did not fail to identify the better dressed in the crowd who had come with a purpose. Watching them slink away, she ran to Moray.

"There's a plot for revenge, Moray. What can we do?"

"Not much beyond what I have already. The men we have hidden in the hills have been told what's happening and will be setting out to meet them. We only have to hope they meet before anything happens. It will be dark soon and I suspect the Scots won't know the track so well at night, whereas we do. Young Hamish knows not to stop till he reaches his comrades. Constantine will be in even a worse temper when the reports of more deaths reach him. I think I'll speak to Callum macNeill about it.

Callum was worried after Moray repeated Brigid's suspicions.

"They will be well organised if they plan to take on your men and the two girls. They must have the numbers or are they planning to leave them alone and attack your camp. You have sent nearly half your men with them."

"We didn't bring too many. A man should be safe in his king's protection" said Moray not mentioning his reserves hidden in the safety of the hills.

"I'll re-enforce your camp with some of my men and speak to the king. You have kept to his orders but this country is getting to be one where nobody obeys the king anymore and we are planning a war."

Callum went off to arrange both matters.

Moray walked out of the fort just to see a larger crowd gathering near to his camp and all his men on guard. The father of one of the dead boys was haranguing them from horseback. Moray held back next to a hut and at the right time, ran out and hit the horse across the face with his sword. The horse reared and deposited the rider at Moray's feet before any of his men had time to help him. With Moray's sword at his neck the man fell silent and his men held back.

"Come forward, anyone who wants to die today with his lord?" said Moray. Looking at the man, he said. "Send them home and you can live or you can be first to die. Make your choice swiftly!"

"The filthy Pict won't dare kill a cousin of the king," the man shouted as his last words. Moray's sword cut his neck so that blood spurted out in a fountain over the crowd. Moray ran at his men and despatched two before any of the others had chance to draw a sword. His own men charged the crowd followed by Bridget with a staff. The Scots retreated, leaving a dozen dead who had resisted and a few more wounded. Most of the crowd had run away once Moray had knocked the man off the horse. He hadn't quite died when the fight was over. He was still gasping as Bridget walked over and strangled him.

"This will encourage the others" she observed calmly.

One of the wounded shouted at her. "Our clan will avenge all this."

"Who's going to lead them? You'd never think your king was planning a war with the enthusiasm you have for fighting his allies. Let's see how good you are against the Saxons and the Danes." She was about to draw her knife and finish him off when Moray stopped her.

"MacNeill's men are coming to help us" he said.

They appeared but had Callum and the King following behind. Constantine looked at Brigid. "Death follows you everywhere, woman!" he said.

"It will be waiting for us all in the land of the Saxons unless your men stop trying to murder us. Do you want an army or just a rabble" Brigid replied?

Callum intervened. "This is your king, Brigid."

"He doesn't do much to protect his subjects from his family. Does he know they are following the girls?"

Constantine fumed some more. "Does no one obey me in this country? They think I'm an old man. There's always someone looking for my throne." He went over and kicked his cousin's body. "He's only a second cousin. He always did make more of our family connection than he should. You may have saved me the trouble of doing it myself, Moray."

Moray began to feel relieved thinking he might survive the day as Constantine's own guard were appearing and the king was getting a bit better-humoured.

Constantine looked at Brigid. "You're supposed to be a healer. Do something for the wounded. Don't finish them off. I can tell what you are thinking. I'll send a party of riders to protect your people. The rest of you, take the bodies away. Callum, Moray and the others, stay in this camp. You are not forgiven yet. I'm just thinking about it."

Hamish and Brollachan thought they would have to face a fight sooner or later after the crowd gathered. They just needed to choose the ground. On leaving Dunnotar they headed for the forest as fast as they could without wearing out the horses and then dismounted to hide. Not long after they left the main track and had hidden the horses, a party of twenty or so riders passed them, speeding northwest into the hills. They decided to follow carefully and at a distance. Their pursuers had to slow down when their horses began to tire. They had kept off the main track and were about to rejoin it when the king's horsemen appeared and rode by them.

"Re-enforcements or help for us, Broll" said Hamish?

"I don't trust them in any case, whichever side they are on. You and I should shadow them and everyone else stay in hiding. We can't move safely back on the track until its dark."

"I'll tell everyone. Let's creep back into the trees."

Back in the hiding place deep in the woods, everyone was relieved to stay hidden until dawn. The lights at Dunnotar were being lit.

"We haven't come very far," said Sine, tucking herself into a blanket.

Hamish and Brollachan went off without the horses and after a while heard voices in disagreement. They moved a bit nearer to catch the conversation. The Scots, who originally followed them, were mad with anger to know their lord had been killed by the Picts and that the king had sent his own men to stop them avenging the death of his grandson. They now had two deaths to deal with.

The king's officer ordered that they all should return to camp but found his own men had began to wonder about these deaths. The general view began to form that the Picts needed teaching a lesson, especially the women. The officer was sent back to Dunnotar to tell the king they were going to find the Picts and kill them as soon as it was light. The king wouldn't hang them all over a few Picts.

"There's about fifty of them, Hamish and too many for us to take on. We have to watch out for our own coming out of the hills. Let us watch the Scots and send a messenger on to our people. The rest of the men and Sine should go on cautiously but off the track. Sine's no good in a real fight. They can set off and skirt this lot before dawn. We can follow behind and catch them in between us. I cannot see how we can escape a fight or they will follow us all the way to the northern sea."

"You think of everything, Broll, but we had better be ready to hit them hard and with surprise. Better to make sure none we attack escape if we can. To give us a chance to contact the others we ought to try and delay them. They'll move slowly anyway and they'll be noisy."

"Hamish, you go back and organise the move and I will see you and them back here after dawn. I'll go into the woods to the west and light a fire. They'll see the smoke in the morning and think it's us. When they see it's not they might return to the main track, thinking they are following us. Tell whoever goes with Sine to leave a few clues."

Hamish left leaving Brollachan to plan. She had all night and watched while the Scots argued whether or not to move or rest for the night. The condition of the horses of the newcomers decided for them and they settled down around the fires without posting a guard. Brollachan ran off to start her fire further up a little valley. She followed a track for a while till she could look down to where the Scots were camped and then moved off it.

Near a hilltop she came across a ruined hut and decided to shelter in it from the wind. She settled down for a sleep under some old hay.

The early dawn cold woke her but she felt better for the sleep and quickly set a fire going covering it with damp hay and grass. She ran back down the hill. It was still not light and the Scots had not stirred. She thought she might creep in and loosen some of the horses but one of the Scots got up to relieve himself. Then one more got up and they began to talk. Someone appeared to assume he was in charge issued orders and was contradicted by another. The sun began to appear and the rest of the men began to waken. The night's sleep had seemingly caused some thought and first one and then another talked of returning to Dunnottar. After a while and more light in the sky, a group of about ten had decided to leave. Then someone noticed the smoke.

"They're up that valley having breakfast, thinking we'd ride by in the night."

"Don't be foolish, that's a farmer or a shepherd up there," said another.

"No, it isn't! No one lives up there anymore. I once went hunting there. Someone has lit a fire. There is a track and it turn off northwest."

"The Picts aren't so stupid as to light a fire with all that smoke."

"Of course they are. They're Picts. All they have done is cause trouble!"

"Let's ride up and see."

"They will hear us coming."

"It will be too late when they do."

Someone trying to assume command said "how do we know it's not a trap?"

"What, with ten men and two women?"

A man saddling his horse shouted "we are wasting time" and about a dozen ran to their horses and set off with him up the valley. After more argument another twenty or so followed. Brollachan watched the rest mount up and ride back towards Dunnottar, leaving her watching their camp and all they had left behind. It occurred to her now they would comeback fairly quickly and went to meet Hamish.

Meanwhile the Scots had reached the hut and realised they had been distracted by the fire and all they had done was make the horses sweaty. After a period of accusation and order and counter order, they rode back quickly down the hill. Their overnight camp was deserted and they decided to follow the track to the hills. The remainder of comrades had decided that this was all becoming a waste of time as well as dangerous. They had packed up and gone back to Dunnottar. Hamish and Brollachan watched the others return from behind some rocks.

After the smaller band returned to Dunnottar, those intending to go on, seemed to get better organised. One man they didn't know took charge and ordered three to remain behind to take up the camp and follow the others with the pack ponies. Within the time it took for them to pick up their personal gear, they were ready to move and beginning to look organised to Hamish, as if all the dissenters had now left and the ones keen on revenge remained.

"Broll, we'll wait until they have gone over the hill and we'll get these three," he whispered.

She nodded with a smile, taking out a couple of arrows.

The main party went off at a fast trot and when they could no longer see or hear them, they came out of cover. Hamish crept up on the man nearest to them. Brollachan let off two arrows at the others some distance away and one man fell dead. The other only wounded, ran to help his comrade who had time to draw his sword and fight Hamish. Both were shouting by this time. A third arrow from Brollachan despatched the unwounded Scot and Hamish finished off the other.

The shouting had carried further than they thought and four more riders came back down the track. Brollachan kept calm and shot down two of them before they reached her and Hamish. One turned his horse and rode back to his comrades. The other rode on, crashing into Hamish as his horse tumbled. When the rider was on the ground, she ran up to him with her sword and stabbed him. Hamish was unconscious and she dragged him into some cover out of sight of the camp. She saw a loose horse and went to get it just as the rest of the Scots were returning.

"One of the women," someone shouted.

She hopped on it and rode back down the track to Dunnottar.

She stopped to see she was being followed only by a couple of Scots and feared the worst for Hamish if they found him. A couple more appeared and she decided to ride on. They followed and so she rode into the forest. She led them around in a circle away from Dunnottar hoping to confuse them. It worked when they stopped to argue that was happening and that they should either go to Dunnottar after her or go back to the others.

Brollachan circled them and rode to look for Hamish.

At their camp most of the Scots had decided to move on to the hills and had left two men to wait for the others to come back. She watched the two for a while to make sure there were no more. Just four arrows left. No room for mistakes, she thought if they spot me. Leaving the horse she carefully walked to where she had left Hamish. She arrived to find him cold. He had died without her, and all she could do was cry to think he died alone. He had never regained consciousness, she could tell that as he had not moved.

A stick cracked and she turned to see the two Scots running towards her. She managed to shoot off one arrow which wounded the more athletic one and he fell over. She was just able to draw her sword and dodge the other.

"You'll do no good with that toy," he said.

"Try me" said Brollachan with a sweet smile.

His comrade was trying to stand despite losing blood. He was crawling behind her. To his friend's surprise she ran over and stabbed him.

"We shall not have to worry where he is," she said and moved a couple of paces nearer to him.

This unnerved the Scot and he nervously swung his sword between his hands. Brollachan moved towards him as if death suddenly did not matter to her any more, tears welling up in her eyes and rage on her face. He turned and ran, pursued by her in the direction of the Scots overnight camp right into four of his companions. Brollachan had seen them in time and returned to Hamish. She took the rested horse and put his body over the saddle and quietly led it deeper into the forest. She found a clearing in a small valley and collected branches, built a fire and put his body on it. She kissed him goodbye and lit the fire.

The four Scots were so surprised to see their comrade one of them nearly ran him through with a spear in his surprise.

"There's that mad girl chasing me out there. She's killed Fergal. We were to wait to bring you up the track. We'd better go. She'll be waiting to kill us."

"We are going nowhere," said one of the others. "She's run us around the forest and run you out of it. We'll be the laughing stock of all the country if we go back without her dead. She's killed a handful of us already and we can't risk anymore."

His three friends agreed. A flask of whiskey came out and after a few swigs and a rest with some food; they were all determined to find Brollachan. They saw smoke in the distance.

"Another trap? Not this time," said Struan. "I am tired of all this panic. Of course it is but we shall set it. I am taking charge of you lot. We can't be defeated by a girl and when we capture her, I'm having her first before we kill her. Follow me."

And they did.

Brollachan had watched Hamish's body begin to burn and cried and cried. She had hoped when the war was over they would become lovers. Now a bit of her future was gone. He had always looked to her and cared for her since they had come to Constantine's court. She was going to get revenge for his death. She took the horse and rode off in the direction of where they had left their own, well hidden from the Scots. It was a short distance and with her good sense of direction she was there quickly. When she arrived she felt almost on the point of collapse. She found some food and hurriedly ate it but couldn't keep open her eyes. It was well into the afternoon when she woke and looked around. The three horses were still hobbled and grazing as she had left them. She took them for a drink in the little stream nearby and bathed herself. The early autumn was still warm and she left off her clothes whilst she sat and thought what to do next. She ate some more food, feeling she was going to need all her strength to take her revenge. In a bag on Hamish's horse she found some of his personal things which she swore to keep. She put the remaining food and her clothes in it. On her own pony she put his sword and her bow and arrows. On his she put her sword which was smaller and made of bronze, thinking this may not be the best weapon to have today. Her own pony would be swifter and more sure footed in the forest and could go places a larger animal could not. Brollachan was light for any animal to carry but her own pony knew her ways and was straining to go. Off she went riding her own and leading the others in the direction of the smoke from Hamish's funeral pyre.

Brollachan thought they have probably been looking for me around there and since they haven't found me, are widening their search. She found a small clearing next to a cliff face to hide the horses and rode the pony up into the trees. Sitting quietly on Eachna she began to listen and feel what was on the wind passing through the trees on to her naked body. She heard the birds as the silence was disturbed and watched them fly around. Suddenly she felt the way to go and without a word or direction, Eachna her pony went that way.

Struan and his men had gone to the fire and seen Hamish in the flames.

The effect of the whiskey was falling off and a couple of them were feeling fearful. They had been a roundabout route and had spent time watching and listening. Nothing was heard or seen so eventually they decided to go more directly to the fire.

"She's burnt his body and gone. What is she a Viking? I'd didn't think the Picts went in for this. They are never what they seem to be. She won't be far away if he was her man. I thought she was supposed to be a virgin. He was her lover," said Struan.

The man who had escaped her who was called Ronan said he had seen her weeping over him and expected she wanted revenge.

"I'm surprised we haven't had arrows coming out of the trees," he said.

"She's used them all or she's gone," said Struan. "There's horse tracks going north over there. We'll follow them. She could have gone after our lads or her comrades."

"It's another trap, Struan" said Ronan.

"You all thought this fire was one and it isn't. You lot are frightened of a girl. The Saxons are really going to make you wet yourselves. If you are going south that is."

They all moved off carefully with Struan tracking until they came to the path across the valley Brollachan had followed. The tracks became less easy to follow although she had not been careful to disguise her way. She had regretted this afterwards when she was considering what to do. However, she thought she would retrace her steps carefully just to see if they were so foolish as to follow her directly. The trees were thickest in the valley bottom but she could look down on to the path from a ridge. Just as she reached the ridge she saw them bunched together about to climb up the opposite side of the valley.

The night was drawing in and she thought she would come up behind them at dusk. By then she hoped they would be convinced she was gone and she returned to collect the other horses. It was getting cool and she put on her cloak. Riding across the valley she had almost reached where she thought they would be when she stopped to look and listen. Tying up the horses she went ahead to investigate something she thought she saw in the half light on the main track to the northern hills. By the time she reached the place there were lights and she could hear voices arguing.

She worked out that the larger force of the Scots had decided to come back to look for their comrades and had been waiting there the best part of the day.

"You've let them escape," Struan was shouting.

Another voice was screaming, "You've been riding up and down getting everyone killed. What's the king going to say and do? At least if we had got them, the people would support us. They'll take the side of the Picts now."

"We'll get after them at first light. They won't be too far down the road."

Brollachan returned to the horses and took them around to the north side of where they were camped and waited for dark. She tied up Hamish's horse, took the other with Eachna and moved slowly and quietly down towards the camp. Through the firelight she could see the men moving about but no one really on guard. She let the horse go and it went with a fast trot down the track to the camp. The noise made the Scots reach for weapons but they relaxed when they saw it was a loose horse. Brollachan had followed but stopped short in some cover. The horse trotted up to the fire and when a few men gathered round it wondering whose it was, she fired off her remaining arrows.

Without command Eachna turned and quietly trotted into the darkness. They picked up Hamish's horse and galloped off north to the hills. No one followed.

In the camp there were more dead and wounded Scots.

"We've been led into a trap again by Struan and his half-wits," a voice was shouting. "There's more than just the one girl he's chasing round the woods. The king is sure to hang us all now just for being stupid. I'm going back home in the morning."

"This is too much death over two women. Your clan chief and all his men couldn't match that Moray. He did the talking while Moray did the killing, just like you talk, Struan. You're just a windbag and you've got my brother killed now. When my clan chief gets to know what's happened, he'll have the king hang you."

The arguments went on into the night and in the morning the band split between those intent on revenge and the others who went back to face King Constantine's uncertain mercy.

CHAPTER 12

BROLLACHAN'S RIDE

Brollachan was expecting the Scots to follow her but no one mounted and rode into the darkness. After picking up Hamish's horse she only rode a short way till she saw a good place to camp for the night. She was getting tired and so were the horse and her pony. She risked a fire but put it out once she was warm and her food cooked and then she went to sleep.

Next morning she finished off the food and mentally took stock of all she had and what she had to do. She must get more arrows. The Scots had plenty but they would be on their guard. Should she ride hard for her friends to warn them, but they knew they were being followed? She could not get out her mind the death of Hamish and every consequence it had for her. She had her later life planned with the home and babies, a good man of her choosing, once this battle was over and she came home. She could not help but think that after the battle if she didn't die in it, there would be no homecoming or any happiness. They would lose and end their lives as slaves to the Saxons. The Scots treated them no better and now she was going to extract some personal revenge for the death of the man she had wanted.

She sat in thought for a while and took off the clothes she had put on to stay warm overnight and set out to look for the Scots. They would find out what a Pictish warrior princess could really do. She put on her knife and Hamish's sword and hooked the bronze shield to Eachna's saddle. Everything else went on to the other horse. Poor thing she thought I don't know her name, she just came out of the king's stable. Hamish was too poor to have his own horse. Eachna was a present to Brollachan from Brigid when she returned to the clan. She is so wonderful, Brollachan thought, the best grey pony in the north.

Brollachan trotted the two beasts at speed along the path which was only just wide enough for one. The horse was on a long rope behind Eachna. She looked ahead and concentrated on the sounds and feelings of the forest. No human life appeared present but she did not let that lull her into any false sense of security. The Scots were somewhere on the parallel main track, although she knew there was a broad diversion.

Revenge was on her mind. Suddenly she felt the forest change. No bird sang and it was a little colder. There was a scream and she stopped, tied up the horse and let Eachna move on at a slow walk.

In a clearing by the track a group of people were hanging a naked girl from a tree branch. Brollachan watched and planned. There were another group of men around a fire with burning sticks. As some of them set off towards the girl with the sticks she charged. Two women and all but three of the men ran away. One of the men threw a spear at her as she rode by and it fell short. She turned Eachna and picked it up from the ground in time to ram it in the back of a man trying to string a bow. The man, who threw the spear, ran at her with a sword. Eachna ran at the man and Brollachan hit him full on with her shield. He fell over and she jumped off and stabbed him. The other ran at her with a spear in one hand and an axe in the other. She threw the other man's sword at him, catching him on the hip and then followed through with her own.

Eachna came back and stood near her whilst she ran over and cut down the girl.

"What's happening to you," she asked. "We had better go before they come back."

"Go where" said the girl? "This is my home. These are my family and neighbours," and began to cry.

The three men were not dead and when the nearest one made a noise, the girl brought herself together and went over to him. He was the last one to attack Brollachan and was clutching his abdomen.

"All the gold in the world will do you no good now, uncle. The only thing you can share now with your friends is pain in Hell for your evil deeds. You have died for nothing because my father had nothing. Did you really think if we had money, we would live here and starve all winter? Look at me; do I look fat like the daughter of a rich man?"

The other two men were groaning and the one Brollachan had stabbed was trying to get up. The girl went over to him and said the same about gold. The other was just lying there groaning and shivering, near to death.

Brollachan looked at the girl and realised why the others had run from her. It was more than fear, they looked like twins. The girl studied her and came to the same conclusion.

"You're my sister," she mumbled.

"We could be, I see why they ran," said Brollachan. "My name is Brollachan."

"That's a name from the northern hills. I am Ceara. I lived here with my father until he died at Easter. My uncle came to claim his goods and the farm. He believed father had some money as he had been south as a soldier when he was younger. The neighbours believed it too. They were going to burn me until I told them where it was hidden. He hadn't any or he would have spent it on medicines for mother when she was ill. She died three winters ago."

"I wondered what was happening. You can't stay here. Your neighbours will kill you now. Why not come with me to my people in the hills? Some are going with King Constantine to fight the Saxons but most will stay behind and carry on as nothing were happening. I think you have nowhere else to go."

"That's true and I don't have a lot to take and they have run off with my best dress as well."

"I have a spare horse for you to ride if you want to put everything together."

They went to collect the horse and walked over to the collection of huts nearby. Ceara went into one and came out with a couple of baskets and some bags of food she put on Hamish's horse. Brollachan had already been to the clearing and picked up the arrows and the other weapons lying around. Ceara's uncle's sword was a good one and she put that on the horse. She took the spear out of the dying man which was the better of the two. The other had a crack in the shaft. The spare weapons she threw in the hut.

"Ceara, if there is nothing else, we should set fire to all this."

"If we burn the huts and the barns they'll die in the winter."

"They were going to kill you after they burnt you."

"I know but I am not like them. Father taught me better. Did your father not teach you how to be good?"

"No" said Brollachan, "he was a murderer himself and so he was murdered by my brother to become Clan Chief."

"Perhaps I should not go to your people and take my chance here. They appear to be very evil."

"Well, your neighbours are coming out of the woods, what do you think?

The five men and two women had found their courage and we coming armed with a variety of axes and other tools. A handful of children similarly armed were behind them. They had the man she had stabbed with them although he was struggling to move. Instinctively Brollachan took an arrow and shot at him. She missed but hit one of the other men, and then shot him with a second arrow. They all ran out of arrow shot.

Ceara mounted the horse as Brollachan held her, mumbling, "I can't ride."

There was a cooking fire nearby and Brollachan picked up a broom as a torch and went round all the huts and a couple of barns. The weather had been dry for over a week and they went up while the owners watched menacingly. She hopped on Eachna and led the horse and Ceara into the forest once the fire had took hold.

"Brollachan, I want to stop and put on my clothes. I'm cold and hungry. I haven't eaten for two days."

"We can do that when we are at a safe distance from the valley. We can even have a fire."

She had taken some more food from one of the huts and Ceara had brought some pots and a griddle in her baskets. They stopped by a stream and gave the animals a chance to rest and eat. They ate a hurried meal themselves.

Ceara was having a sort out of what she had hurriedly packed. "Not much for a life just starting," she said.

"How old are you," said Brollachan.

"Fourteen."

"Two years younger than me but you have the sound of someone years older."

"I was an only child and I spent a lot of time with mother. I think she had been in a convent. She knew lots of things."

"I lived in a convent once and all we did was pray and starve."

"Well, we starved here for some of the time."

Brollachan fell silent and then went for a bathe in the stream despite the cold. Ceara joined her but not for long. She came out and sat under a blanket.

"Why are you not wearing a dress, Brollachan?"

"When I am a warrior, I do not wear any clothes as preparation for the battle with the Saxons."

She told her then the long story of her life as a hostage, sent to a convent for safe keeping, her escape and training as a warrior and how she was going to fight on the battlefield against the Saxons. Then she explained what had happened over the last week and finished with her resolve to get revenge for Hamish.

"I have stopped you from doing this," said Ceara. "You should be following them."

"There is plenty of time. The living need help as well as the dead. I couldn't leave you there hanging in a tree."

"I watched you fight. You were better than all those three men. My uncle has been a soldier, but I think not a very good one."

"I train a lot and I am faster. I also think quicker and I am thinking now we should move. The fire has been lit for long enough to draw attention to us. I think that we will pack up and move into the trees up there to see if we have attracted attention before we move on. We will know then we are not followed."

Ceara had some energy return and packed up quickly. She didn't put on her clothes.

"I'm going to ride like you; it's easier astride the horse. He's a bit big for me. It's a good job you were leading him."

They went up in to the trees and this time Brollachan was careful to leave no trace. They watched the track while they told each other more about their lives. Ceara as a child had lived in the country of the Angles and could still speak some of their language. In fact she thought her grandmother on her mother's side came from the Angles.

Brollachan talked about Hamish and cried a bit more, until she sensed some movement in the valley. Ceara had the sense to stay silent and to feel something in her had changed. They had left the fire burning as bait and sure enough a handful of men ran out of the woods to it.

"One of them is Logan my neighbour" whispered Ceara.

When they brought out the horses and five more men, Brollachan recognised one horse from the party which had followed them. The colour pattern was unusual, almost all brown on one side, almost all white on the other.

"We'll stay here until they pass us up to the head of the valley. They might get suspicious there are no tracks. We had better watch them and then avoid them. Is there another path north west?"

Ceara shook her head. "It's all trees and rocky ground up on that ridge. Logan knows it as well as I do."

They watched for a while as Logan stood and looked around himself in all directions. He pointed up into the trees, almost at them, as if to say up there, that's where they are. The others just mounted up and rode up the track and left him shouting at them, perhaps because they took the horse he came on leaving him to walk home.

"It seems to me, Ceara, they will travel up the hill for a while find nothing and return to look where he has suggested. I have killed some of their friends as revenge for Hamish and they want me. We had better move."

"Not yet, Brollachan. Look down there."

Two riders had returned with the party's food and cooking gear and were starting to set up camp. Logan stayed after an initial argument with them.

"That is it, then Ceara. We move and fast. They are going up the valley and they will return this way in daylight. They could pass us at night but they won't take that risk. We'll just go back in the direction from which we came and burn the rest of the place if we have to."

"No, I can't even go near it now. Where else can we go?"

"We need to go and join my people in the hills but while these men are seeking me and your neighbours are after you, we are not safe around here. I feel the need to kill some more of them. I shall sleep easier at night and feel revenged for Hamish. If I read the situation correctly at the king's fort, the more of them I kill, the more dishonoured the rest will be………. and the more likely he is to have them hanged."

She explained what had happened after the prince and his young men had followed her and Sine. Ceara was appalled at the event and the consequences, and went very quiet for a while as they watched the three men in the valley. She spoke after a while.

"Brollachan, I think my parents sheltered me from the world in this valley but my father's death and uncle's visit has shown me what an evil place it can be. I thought my neighbours might have supported me but the thought of money turned their heads. Take me with you and teach me how to fight. A woman by herself is going to need to know about fighting."

"We can do this once we are back at our camp in the hills. I didn't start to learn seriously until your age. However, we left your home in a hurry. Is there nothing we need to save from there?

"If we can find him, there is a boy who lived with us until my uncle and his friends drove him out. If they didn't kill him, he might be living nearby. He tried to help me, so they might have killed him."

"We can ask the neighbours. We'll camp near the houses tonight. They have probably started to rebuild them. The smoke is still rising in the direction of Dunnottar. The fort will be lit up tonight and we can make our way in that direction but we had better be gone from here. I have a plan for our three friends down there."

Brollachan explained she proposed basically to approach them along the stream and Ceara was to wait with Eachna and the horse in the trees. Brollachan would call Eachna if she was in trouble and the sight of Ceara would distract the men. Eachna would run towards the fight and Brollachan. The horse would remain tied to Eachna and Ceara was to wave her uncle's sword. They would do it now.

Brollachan set Ceara and the animals in position and moved along the stream. She knew where the three were but couldn't see them from the stream bed which was in fairly open land. It had once been cleared but was filling up again with trees through lack of use as grazing. Emerging from the stream bed into some bushes she saw two of the men some distance apart. Two clear shots she thought and not too far. Two shots did it and the two men fell but were not dead. The third was Logan who now was nowhere to be seen. He had seen his comrades fall and had the sense to stay hidden, even though they were crying out in pain for his help. Brollachan made her way back to Ceara.

"Can you see that Logan," she whispered?

"He's behind the large rocks to the left of the stream. He came out but ran back in there."

"We'll wait and when he comes out we ride at him."

They waited and nothing happened and it began to get darker. Suddenly some of the Scots returned down the track and the rest came out of the trees near to where the two girls were hiding.

"We stay here. If we move now they will hear us," said Brollachan.

They watched but couldn't hear what was happening. The two wounded Scots pointed in the direction of the rocks and two of the men rode over.

They stopped short and called over to the rest. They then pulled out a body, Logan's. Even at such a distance the girls could see in failing light, the head was part severed and there was blood over the rest of the body.

"Time to move" said Brollachan and she turned Eachna and the horse into the trees and walked them quietly into the deeper forest. No one followed and they walked quietly on for some time. She spoke after a while.

"Someone has had the same idea as us and was watching those three. I wonder if he saw us."

"It could be Keir; he was good with an axe. He could cut and carve with one."

"Was he the boy" said Brollachan?

Ceara nodded and they moved on to near the burning farm. It was dark and they could see Dunnottar's lights in the far distance. They hid the animals and the gear and went down the hill for a look. In the light of a camp fire they could see the three men, two women and the children, who had survived. They had already rigged up a shelter for the night.

Ceara was starting to shiver and they went back to their hiding place and dressed. They ate some cold food and settled down for the night. Brollachan had forgotten how tired she was.

She woke in the morning to find a man with an axe sat by a tree opposite them.

"Keir" she said.

"That's me" he replied. "I followed you last night after you watched the farmers. I had been following Logan and the others. I watched you rescue Ceara. I was about to help but you are too good for me with that sword and a bow. You might have mistaken me for an enemy."

"You move around too quietly for me" said Brollachan, "but you are welcome to have some food."

"I was trying to get a horse to follow you. I have nothing around here and I can't go to Dunnottar. The king's constable wants my neck for stealing food."

Ceara was sleeping through all this and woke when Brollachan prodded her. She flung her arms around Keir who was a bit surprised. They had breakfast and Keir explained he had been sent off by her uncle with death threats and warned not to return. Keir had kept the axe handy and none of the three men took the risk to attack him although they clearly had it in mind. He saw the horseman arrive and Logan go off with them and he thought that he would follow as close as he could be running through the trees which was nearer to where they eventually stopped than the track. He had been fine for food as he helped himself to a sheep and some oatmeal when they weren't looking. He thought some of the children may have spotted him on one occasion. Ceara told him what had happened to her and Brollachan.

"We need to get around this valley and away from these men; I recognise some of them from Dunnottar. They aren't the King's men; they're from one of the *clans* from the south."

Suddenly they could hear some shouting down in the valley and Keir said he would go and take a look and listen while they got ready to move. After a long while and Ceara getting worried, he returned.

"They have brought back Logan's body and the two you wounded or at least three of them have. The rest must be in the upper valley. If they take the very high ground, it's nearly treeless and they will spot us if we go that way," he said. "They must really set on getting their revenge on you. They have left two spare horses there. I watched them ride off back up the valley as well."

"You have the makings of a good fighter," said Brollachan. "You look for everything. Can you use a sword as well as that axe?"

"No, it's a rich man's weapon. Have you any idea how much one costs? I have an idea of what to do. I could soon learn."

"You can have my uncle's," said Ceara. "It's too heavy and long for me; I could never learn to use such a weapon. Brollachan's bronze sword is fine for me. It's much smaller and I can wield it easily, although it's heavy for its size."

"We have to go and steal you a horse and I want to finish off those two men. Our leader Moray always says; never leave anyone alive who will come looking for revenge. So, since you two are feeling as bloodthirsty as I am, let's just ride in and get the horses. We take all three. This is the plan and Ceara can use my sword."

Brollachan explained they would ride in and Keir would get the horses and a saddle. She would deal with any opposition and Ceara would just have to look threatening to the women and children if they intervened. She should stay on the horse and when he was ready, Keir should lead off her horse and the others. If she could, Brollachan would find the two men.

It all worked well to a point. Keir caught a horse and saddled it before any of the farmers realised what was happening. They had tied them to a fence but the two others got loose and ran off into the forest. Then the people heard the noise. The three farmers and the two wounded men, who were obviously much better, picked up their weapons. They had armed the farmers with spears and told them not to throw them. One ran at Ceara but Brollachan shot him in the arm. Ceara's horse shied and she was on the ground. The rest ran to her. Brollachan and Keir had to rescue her. Brollachan shot off more arrows, wounding the two soldiers again. The farmers ran away. Brollachan caught the horse and Ceara scrambled back on. They rode off up the track where the main party had gone and then doubled back into the forest in the direction of Dunnottar.

"They'll catch the horse and find the others," said Keir.

"We need a hiding place and I think I know where," said Brollachan. "Somewhere they have been and won't look again. We can hide our tracks in theirs. The main track to the hills we set out on, is just up here out of the trees and I know an abandoned hut which they have already searched. They won't look at it again."

They got to the hut where she had spent the night before Hamish died. They followed a roundabout route hoping no one was tracking them. Keir lit a fire when it was dark and they ate. He put it out and they went to sleep. The horses munched on the old hay. Ceara slept with Keir at the back of the hut but seemed to be in tears most of the night. Brollachan slept by the door but awoke very early and made her plans.

They ate a cold breakfast and Brollachan decided they should take the risk to follow the main track carefully which they did for the whole day. At night they moved off it and set off again in the morning. At midday they had rested the horses and were about to set off when Keir heard a horse. A loose horse came down the track and joined them. It still had its saddle. They waited a while and another followed. Both were lathered and had been running for some time. Pity they can't talk thought Brollachan. Keir had been leading Ceara on her horse and so Brollachan led the other two when they decide to set off at an even more careful pace. As it began to get dark they found a couple of bodies on the track.

"Both Scots from Dunnottar, I think" said Brollachan. "Something is happening around here and we don't want to run across it in the dark."

One of the bodies had a quiver with some arrows and she removed them, thinking the other weapons have been taken by someone, why not the arrows? They moved back down the track and then off it.

"No fire tonight" she said.

Next morning they moved off even more carefully and in mid morning came across the remains of the Scots who had been following them. They had clearly been lying in wait but had been surprised. The attack was complete and no other bodies but the Scots were visible. All the weapons had gone also.

With some relief Brollachan said. "This is my people who have been here."

Ceara and Keir winced and after a while Ceara spoke. "My father used to tell me about things like this which when he was a soldier. I thought he made it up to scare me, but now I know different."

Out of the ground five figures appeared with bows. Brollachan called out and they rested them. One of them men spoke to her in a language Keir understood as Pictish and responded.

"Keir, you are full of surprises" said Brollachan.

"I learnt it from my grandmother but have not used it for a while. There has been no one who speaks it around here for many years."

One of the men said they were waiting for them to come along and decided to search for them. Sine had told them what was happening and they came down the track. Everyone was to go to the hills as soon as possible. They did not feel safe so near to the coast. The main party was still hidden and they thought the two Scots who escaped might return from Dunnottar with some help. It was with some relief they were told they were dead and were lying on the track.

"We didn't injure them, so that's another mystery then" said another of the warriors. "Someone is shadowing us."

CHAPTER 13

THE GREEN MAN

Brollachan felt a bit of a shiver at the thought of someone wandering around the forest that she couldn't see, even though he, or even she, might be on her side. He or she didn't like the Scots whoever they were. They might not just like anyone wandering about their home, but she wondered who are they?

"I'll follow on once I settle this mystery. It could be Brigid or someone Lord Moray has sent.

With not another word she collected her gear and set off on foot with Eachna. She took only her bronze sword and shield, her iron knife, a blanket, and a little food. She told Ceara to give Hamish's sword to Sine.

Down the path she came to the place where she thought the Scots had been ambushed and looked around for tracks. Plenty of evidence for the attack but none of the attacker, she thought. Looking around she saw a place where all of the track running down the hill could be observed and walked carefully to it on a roundabout route through the forest. There was a small clearing nearby and she hobbled Eachna to give her a chance to eat. She packed her clothes on her pony and everything but her weapons and sat down to wait.

After sometime a quiet voice spoke in Pictish. "We knew you would return, sister, we have waited for you."

A man and three women stepped out of the forest, and they were all three armed with bronze swords, shields and spears. Brollachan had been tattooed as part of her initiation on return to her clan but almost all of their four bodies were covered. One of the women carried a baby in a sling.

Brollachan had not heard their approach but she had sensed a change in the air and knew it must be friends. She stood up.

"Greetings, my own people" she whispered.

"Princess, follow us and bring your pony" said one of the women. "It is not far."

They went deep into the forest until they came to a tent in which there was an older woman with two children. She signalled Brollachan to sit next to a fire which was mainly charcoal and smokeless. She threw some herbs on it.

"I saw you being pursued by death around these woods. You did a wise, wise thing to chase it away yourself. While you chase it, it will never catch you. Your friends would not be so fortunate. I sent my son and his companions to help them. Many of us have lost the old ways of knowing when we are being followed or when someone waits to trap us. We live safely in this forest as we know these things. The birds and deer tell us who is visiting, who is welcome and who we must kill to stay alive. We will not be able to live here forever………. but it will be good while it lasts as we have everything."

Brollachan asked, "Are there more such as you?"

"A few more families are keeping the traditions alive. We meet for feasts during the seasons."

The woman went quiet for a while and spoke again.

"You are one of the warriors of our people, child. Your marks show you to be a royal princess. Beware no one persuades you to be sacrificed, whatever the circumstances. The future of our people is uncertain and it cannot be discerned by spilling royal blood as in our past. It is all now out of the hands of our Goddess. Her power is now in the river and the woodland and not in the houses and stone towers. Soon even this may pass from her. You must remember to go to her when you need help. You will come to little danger near water and wood wherever you go. Tonight we will go to our pool and see your future. Then you must go to face it…… Stay here until I call you."

She put more herbs on the fire and left.

Brollachan's head began to fill up as she sat there. She had feelings unknown so far in her life as it flashed in front of her. She was weeping again, something she could never recall doing since a small child. She missed Hamish most of all. When two women fetched here she went as if in a deep trance. The older woman was by a pool and all four sat there naked in the darkness with a chill wind blowing on them. None shivered.

Out of the pool came a figure with long dark hair carrying a sword and laughing.

"Welcome, little girl! You have already a taste for blood. You are my true servant. You have been killing for me, An Mhor Rioghain, and my ravens already are feasting wherever you pass..... Have no fear for you have my protection. Your life will be long but not in this land. Your children will be many but none will pass this way. Only a man, such as you are a woman, can be their father. He will be there with you on the battlefield and he will know you as me. The more blood you shed, the more he will love you. No powers on the earth will keep you from one another. Death will pass by you both as it takes in all those around you."

The image disappeared and Brollachan began to shake violently. The women pushed her into the pool and the cold water brought her round. She screamed as they tied her arms and legs and hung her on a tree branch over the pool. At last Brollachan shook with the cold and went into dreams as they burnt more herbs around her. Images of dead warriors on a distant battlefield went through her head, burning buildings, horses, screaming women and children and pain everywhere. She saw herself walking through all this crying out for more death and destruction. She fended off swords, dodged arrows, caught spears and threw them back, horses reared on seeing her and the looks of fear on the faces of men were something she could scarce comprehend. She saw a man limping to her defence again and again. He was wounded but he would not give up helping her.

She woke in the tent covered in mud and sweat, her body bleeding from a number of cuts. The old woman was looking on.

"When we cut you down, you fought us and ran off into the forest. We lost you for a while. We have never had such an experience. The Great Goddess is truly with you and we have one more thing we must do and that is mark you in her name on your belly where your children will grow. You must also stay until you properly recover."

Brollachan did not speak and nor did she cry out as the mark of the Goddess was made. She bathed in a nearby stream and the old woman treated her wounds.

Eachna had been glad of the rest and was full of life a couple of days later as they departed. The man walked with them to show the way, avoiding any farms and villages. He talked as they walked.

"What is this great battle" he asked, "and why do we fight in it so far from home?"

"Our people now are pledged by our princes to fight for King Constantine against the Saxons."

"No good can come of it. The only true path for us is to live in peace in the forest. It provides all for us, winter and summer. We men who live in it and know its ways, we know its lessons. We can dress like bushes and stalk a deer. If we do not kill too many, there will always be new ones. There is food growing in all seasons and we know where to gather it. We are safe in winter and free to wander in summer. Other people should envy us and we do not seek what is theirs."

"Your life is good" said Brollachan "but it is one we can all no longer have. Make the best of it, my friend. I shall remember your wise words."

She walked on with Eachna and they waved goodbye to him. He disappeared leaving just the memory of his face in the bushes as she had first seen him a few days earlier.

Brollachan looked on at the familiar mountains. Safety, she thought and smiled.

After a week of travel she was able to find her family home although she had not seen it for many years. It was still a fairly substantial collection of huts, surrounded by a ditch and a palisade. As she looked at it she noticed a few additions, a more substantial hut, a chapel and some recently built huts. She had thought about riding in as a warrior princess but she felt a pang of suspicion. She put on her clothes but kept her sword handy. She did not trust her brother or his men.

As she rode up to the gates, Sine ran out to her screaming a welcome that the whole place heard. Soon everyone had turned out including her brother and his priest. She rode up to them.

He spoke first as was the custom. "My name is Malcolm now as I have been baptised. My former name may not even be uttered in this place unless the speaker wants a beating. I am recommending everyone is now baptised before we set off on our journey south."

The priest chipped in to Malcolm's annoyance. "Only in this way will God look kindly on King Constantine's venture and give us a victory."

Malcolm continued "anyone who is not baptised will not go, sister."

"Brother, you already know I was baptised Anne at the convent......."

"Ah, the name of our Lord's grandmother," the priest chipped in again. "This is most fortuitous. Lord Malcolm, your sister will surely be a good example to all the unbelieving women in this place."

Brollachan smiled and said "I wouldn't count on that. I am going to fight the Saxons as a Pictish princess should do. You had best remember that, priest."

Malcolm and his men began to laugh. "She's put you in your place, Brother Gregory. But don't worry, I have husband in mind for her. You can bless her at her wedding."

Brollachan knew better than to argue with a man who she guessed when he wasn't drunk with power, was usually full of ale.

"Women choose their own husbands in this clan, brother. The best men usually get picked over quickly. Only a warrior will have to come looking for me."

The laughter fell off at this point and only a joke about lots of warriors in the camp eased the situation. Sine came out of the crowd with an offer of hospitality and off they went. Brollachan found Ceara and Keir were living with her as servants. Sine had reclaimed the hut which had been in her husband's family. It had been neglected and Keir was repairing it. Other people were starting to move back into the village as times were becoming a little more peaceful as King Constantine's rule began to be more effective. There was less of a need to be hidden away in forests or up on hilltops. The defences here wouldn't keep out a determined enemy unless properly manned. The place seemed less rowdy than in her father's time, except around her brother and his men. Sine already had her eye on one she said more than once. They all talked into the night about what had happened..... Brollachan did not mention her vision of the Goddess.

The next day her brother sent four of his men to fetch her. They marched her into to his presence with Sine tagging on behind.

"Anne, there are to be some changes in the way we all live now. I am in charge now and you are my sister and subject to my rule. You will go to the priest and take the sacrament and prepare yourself to marry. I have not properly decided who as yet. You were correct; no ordinary person should be marrying my sister, the sister of a clan chief and of a royal line. Only a loyal follower of the king and my friend should be eligible. I will give the choice some thought........By the way your friend there is marrying Curran.

He indicated one of the four men who had brought her to him.

There's no argument. You are dismissed."

Two of the men took her out and Sine looked sheepishly at her.

"I didn't argue as there was no point" said Brollachan. "You could have told me you were getting another man from my brother's warriors. You have wasted no time."

"Broll, you know I can't live without a man, of any sort. But it seems you have to marry them here if you want one. It must make them hard to get rid of. It's a good that a war is coming. I'm sure I'll get bored with him sooner than later."

Brollachan laughed. Sine was really no warrior. She could fight if she had to, but she would have been useful to seduce the Saxons. King Athelstan himself would have no chance against Sine. Brollachan wondered what she could do. She could only run back to the Green Man's camp but her brother might follow her, and it would spoil things for the people there. She could try and make it to Bridget and Moray at Dunnottar, but clearly if her brother went to the king, they would have to give her up. She would have to just hope something worked in her favour. She had the Great Goddess's prediction which gave her some hope.

Four weeks later a group of soldiers came to call and Brollachan knew this was the time.

"This is your husband Finlay macColl," said Malcolm. "You wanted a warrior, you have got one. He'll be leading one of the king's armies. The one we are going with."

"I know his reputation as a leader, all Dunnottar spoke of him" said Brollachan. "He can he use a sword on the battlefield better than most men. But what's happened to his wife or his he planning on having two?"

"My wife died of child-bed fever over the summer" said Finlay softly. "I have three children and a baby in need of a mother. I cannot grieve too long and ignore their needs."

He looked sad and Brollachan felt slightly sorry for him as he clearly had loved his wife and loved his children.

"Finlay, my brother Malcolm, I think, may have been less than honest with you. He has not told you my history and how I escaped from a convent. I have been training with Brigid the *Cailleach* to lead our warriors on the battlefield against the Saxons. I am suspected of killing some young men at Dunnottar, including one of the King's grandsons, and other men on my way here. I will admit to their deaths as they were trying to kill me and my people. Your king, and his family, will not welcome me at his court. You will not then truly welcome me in your bed, nor will your family want me as a daughter and a mother."

Brollachan took off her dress at this point and revealed all her markings including the one of the Great Queen.

Finlay looked at her in slight amazement and said, "You are an honest girl and your brother is a lying rogue. The only clearly true thing, he has said, is that you are a virgin. I would marry you for your own sake if you would have me, but unfortunately my family would reject you as the sister of this man, if for no other reason, when they hear of his deception. The other matters I could live with after we return from the war. They are not really so bad in these troubled times. However, it would be a poor start to a marriage and the joining of two clans if I were to marry into a family with such a man at its head........ One who cannot deal honestly with a man he is to call brother."

He turned and hit Malcolm so hard he fell against the hut wall and was stunned.

"Let's hope we can use some of your trickery against the Saxons. You seem to have been practising it well against your own people."

None of Malcolm's men moved or drew a sword. Not even the priest dare speak. Finlay went on.

"The king shall hear of this attempt to hoodwink me and my family. We have noble ancestry like yours and we are not to be disgraced. Your conduct on the battlefield had best be good, Rory, Malcolm, whatever you are? In fact a good death might save your name."

Turning to Brollachan he said "Princess, you are welcome at my house but unfortunately not as my wife. I am grieved on this for you are truly noble. I regret you are promised to the Goddess for I could love a woman like you."

"I'll kill her first" swore Malcolm.

"Have your chance, brother," said Brollachan. "Draw your sword and fight me in front of all these men."

Keir had brought her Hamish's sword.

"Here I have the sword of a good man, who I did hope to wed and who died protecting me...... Stand up and fight."

Malcolm stayed on the floor but two of Finlay's men picked him up, dragged him outside and put his sword in his hand as a crowd began to gather. Malcolm ordered his men to intervene but none dared move. Brollachan prodded him with her sword and he moved away. After some more insults from Finlay's men, he decided to fight but by then Brollachan had decided it was now or never. She realised if he lived, she would not. His men would do his bidding, once Finlay had left. A quick stab under his guard and it was all over except to behead him. She just took him by surprise and he was unprepared.

Finlay was aghast she killed him so quickly and then took his head. He asked what he should say to Constantine.

"Take him the head of a coward and he can put it with all the others at his court, including the ones still on men's shoulders" was her answer.

Brollachan immediately challenged her brother's men. None took it up except for Curran and a serious fight began. He was already wearing a stiff leather jerkin with some plating and had picked up his shield. She was still naked with just a sword but moved towards him. As he advanced towards her Sine came out of the crowd and put a spear in his back. As he stumbled, she cut his throat.

"There are some bonds greater than love or lust and need for a man" she said. "Broll, you saved my life once. He was a good fighter and he would have killed you to make himself master here. The men around here are looking for a real leader."

"Good" said Finlay. "They can have me as a war leader until their princess can find a prince brave enough to wed her. We can have no more fighting amongst ourselves when our king has an enemy to deal with…….. Come here, priest. …Brother Gregory, get these men something to swear on if they are Christian and something else if they are not. They will be no more bloodshed and treachery on their part. You can rule here, Princess."

"I do have another brother hidden somewhere unless Malcolm or the King has had him killed. Finlay, I am only sixteen. I cannot rule here. I do not want to. I must join my sisterhood. I am sworn to it. Get the king to appoint you to look after us. You are certainly a good man….. Or can you at least find someone for us?"

"If he isn't dead, I'll ask the king what he has done with your other brother. These men can swear an oath to him then….. But by God if they harm you or your friend here, Hell will seem a comfort after what I shall have in mind."

The crowd broke up and everyone went back into their huts or inside the hall. Sine went over to the men and told them to pick up Malcolm and Curran's bodies for burial.

"Don't bury Curran with his chief" she said. "Curran was a brave man and deserves not to lie with a coward."

She went inside to join Brollachan but only found Finlay and his men there.

"A man should be careful turning his back on you," said Finlay macColl and all his men laughed. "The Saxons had best watch out if you are going to fight."

"Lord macColl, I am no virgin and I am not going.....You are a man wanting a woman to run a house and take care of children. I can do that. I have been married before to Donald of the Red Hill. He fell off his horse and died last year but one. I joined with the *Cailleach* when his brothers wanted to find me a husband not of my choice. Brigid is my sister."

"I remember him and you were suspected of some part in his death, by witchcraft if nothing else."

"I did not love Donald, it's true, and he had no respect for me. I was forced to marry him. I will only love a man of my choice. My father was a chief influenced by the priests and he broke with our traditions. He married me to a warrior in name only. He was like Brollachan's brother, too fond of ale and the company of men. I only ever saw him in bed."

"So, you think to take on me and my four little ones. You don't seem too matronly to me."

"I am only twenty two," said Sine with a laugh. "I thought you might want a woman who still has some excitement to offer you. What is more, I think you didn't father four children looking into an ale cup."

Finlay's men laughed at this point and one spoke out.

"Lord Finlay, if you don't take this woman back home with us, I certainly will. She's got more fire than many I know......... but I'd keep an eye on her."

"Angus, you had better do that and take her if she'll have you." He walked out the door at that point and called out for Anne.

Sine looked over Angus. "I'll give you a try, if you agree, for a year and a day in our tradition. None of this wedded for life unless it works well. I have my land and goods and I can share but not give away."

Finlay's men cheered at this and Angus agreed.

Finlay found Brollachan tending Eachna. She turned to face him.

"Call me Brollachan," she said earnestly.

"Your friend made me a proposal, and I nearly accepted. It is just that the need for a mother is greater than that for a wife in my household at the moment. Neither of you really need to start off a marriage with four children and a husband leaving for an uncertain future."

"You need a cosy widow, Lord Finlay. There'll be lots around when this battle with the Saxons is over. If you come home, you'll be able to have your pick. More than one if you want, as our ancestors did. So make sure you do."

"Lady Brollachan, I fought the Saxons when they visited us last year. King Athelstan is not to be considered lightly. He has many good commanders with experience of battle and we have but few. I do not count stealing cattle off our neighbours the Angles, the Welsh and the Cumbrians as battle experience. For someone so young, you have wisdom beyond your years. Do you know all these things because you have had a vision?"

"I have had a vision.... but I have heard the words of Lord Moray and Lord macNeill on the state of our preparation."

"I know macNeill's views. He may have the choice to stay away. I do not."

"Then tread carefully in Angleland, Finlay. Come home to your children. The Great Queen has told me I shall not return here. My life shall be elsewhere."

"I am glad you are not going to die, Brollachan. I am over twice your age and have learned to love life in the Glens. I hope to carry on for a few more years."

"I hope you may, but not with Sine. She would only bring you unhappiness in the end."

"One of my men was impressed with her but that isn't difficult in his case. What his mother may think, we can only guess if they have decided to join.... You know your friend well?"

"I think she tires easily of whatever company she keeps, so avoid her, Finlay."

They walked back into the camp at that. Brollachan already was regretting she had not come together with Finlay macColl in better times. Good men are rare in good times and rarer still in bad, she thought. Why are the best always so much older than me? Hamish was so different.

CHAPTER 14

THE BATTLE ON THE RIVERS

For some months Grim the Miller had been planning what he would do when the invasion came. He knew on land that the Lincolnshire flank was reasonably well garrisoned as much as it needed to be. No one thought that on the east side of the river that there would be a large scale attack. A raid, perhaps, that a small force could counter was the worst they could expect. He already had a spy system set up to watch any fleet which used the Humber. He had his wife's relatives who fished in it, all on his side, but not necessarily the king's as they often reminded him. Just before the winter he had informed Earl Thorolf of the outline of his plan and Thorolf had let him know that King Athelstan approved. The small fleet of river craft he put together would make using and crossing the Trent hazardous for a good part of its tidal reaches and the marshes where it came to the Humber. This force could prevent a local raid or make it difficult for the enemy to escape after a battle. If the enemy fleet tried to sail up the river, they could stall it.

Grim had joked about river fairies and all winter had made his plans. He loved the marshlands around the Trent and the Humber he had wandered as a child. They had a comforting, secure feeling to them. He felt at home there. It came as no surprise to him to have found a wife in them.

"I should have looked there years ago," he said to his friends proudly when he turned up with Emma. "Such a magical place can only produce wondrous women."

When spring had come he sent Emma to talk to her family accompanied by his usual generosity to them. The result was what he expected. The first sign of a fleet and the fishermen would send word and then, so not to arouse too much suspicion, the women would watch the enemies' boats. Wilfred Egbertsson, the local commander wanted as many people as possible withdrawn from any area near to the invasion when it started, but nothing was to be destroyed. Only large boats were to be moved immediately as Grim had suggested very early on. No river craft were to fall into the hands of the enemy, nor any horses, ponies or carts. It went without saying that all cattle, sheep, goats and grain were to be removed to beyond the invaders reach.

Meanwhile Grim got his force organised with their riverboats, men who could fight and row, a bit older than the ones who were to march off, but ones who knew how to drop an oar and step into another boat. He put a couple of boats full of boys with bows and instructions not to do anything but fire into the enemies ships when he signalled. All the boats were light and fast once the cargo decks were taken out and extra oars put in. It was going to be his last battle as a warrior and he was going to be remembered. Peace and trade were definitely to be his watchwords after all this went away.

Things went better than he expected. On the north bank of the Humber a system of beacons had been set up by Anlaf's supporters to signal his fleet's arrival. Word of it had got to Emma's relatives, as it had to everyone who fished the area. Grim heard they were near before they arrived. He had time to travel north to watch the first ships appear, and then to organise the movement of the boats on the south side. It took more than a week and a half for any real numbers of Anlaf's ships and those of the Scots to arrive. No attempt was made to make a passage up the Trent or land on the south side. They sailed as far as the Ouse and many went up to York or so it seemed to Grim. The rest just beached on the north bank of the Ouse and the Humber, all in the drier parts of the marshes. Grim observed all this and sent messages to the King by a system of horsemen.

Athelstan was grateful to know all this but it left him pondering. He voiced his concerns to Thorolf.

"Listen to what I think and give me your thoughts. Anlaf looks as if he is going to York to see whether he really has any support there and in the lands around. He's going to check he has no opposition at his back before he moves south or is he going to just settle in there and let the Scots move on us? Ships are still arriving and therefore he hasn't got all his army. He must be collecting food and local support as well. He can't wait for too long as the food will run out. What we need to decide is whether or not he is going to come south to us, or do we have to cross the Don and go to him? This Brunanburgh information we have, could just be a ruse on someone's part. One thing is certain if we have to go to him, we cannot wait for too long. If we attack before all his army are there, we could have a decisive victory or find they just run away north. We have to get them all on one battlefield and kill them in my thinking. I think we just have to wait and see what they do. They appear to be moving inland and are not going for Lincoln and a move down the east coast supported by their fleet. I do not think they have decided yet as their whole force are not here and certainly not all their leaders. While we are south of our forts, they are in the same dilemma. Concentrate our army around the north of Nottingham and wait for information, I think. We have Grim and Wilfred to our east if they do send a small force to see what is there. We can oppose it and put them off without moving the main army. I know that Grim is waiting for a chance to attack them on water whether on the Trent or the Humber. Wilfred has more men than he ever expected to bring together, so he could oppose another small force if it landed. What worries me is they might march all the way west and avoid the Don Valley forts. But they must know our western forts are stronger and we have enough forces there as well as our fleet. God knows, we have caught enough of their spies. They must know also they have the least support in the west. They won't march west of the hills. It will be too late in the year and they will be too hungry by then. No, they will concentrate in the east and try to use Ryknield Street to move south, so we might as well wait for them there, but we have to let them cross the Don as one force and not let them divide. The crossing at the brown fort must be held to force them to come over where we can meet them in a tight little corner. The crossings at Roderham have the marshes and the river to the south, we have the high ground. There are the Dirne marshes to the north. Let them commit themselves and we'll move in. We'll put a plan together for the move from near Nottingham as the situation develops. What are your thoughts, Thorolf?"

"Lord Athelstan, you know the last thing I want is to go chasing Northmen around the Five Boroughs. We need to tempt the enemy over in our own time. We ought to cause diversions to tempt them. I agree with your conclusions but we must not be inactive. We must let them think they have the initiative while they fall into our trap. We should tempt them to cross at the brown fort but not allow them over. We must make sure it is strong and let them waste their strength. We should give Grim a free hand to raid their fleet but give the impression we are stronger than we are. He should start while they are still weak and let them think they have made the right decision to anchor or beach away from the south bank of the Humber and the Trent. They should know that area is dangerous for them. At the same time we must get a larger force at the fort. We should carry a raid across the Don on horseback. Perhaps, even two or three. Not on the people but on any of the enemy who set up there. It will tell us if they are not going to move as well. Our spies in the area will tell us but if we raid as well, and take prisoners, they will think we have no spies and everyone is their friend."

"Thorolf, you are the best of men. You understand me but know my weakness. I was almost numbed by the thoughts of inactivity. I will issue all the orders. Let us show Constantine and Anlaf we are here."

When he had gone Athelstan thought for a while. They are much too clever these Danes. I can't make up my mind whether I am really glad they are on my side, even though Thorolf is such a good friend and has been so many years. The security of the border is almost totally in their hands. Even the Angles are on their side. God, how I hate the land being called after them! Still it could be worse. It could be Daneland.... Thorolf would like that, and his brother would, and Ericsson, and that Grim. He's more a pirate than a miller. How many millers have you ever met who raise armies and fleets out of nowhere?

"Don't be a silly boy" said his aunts voice. "You are still king and in charge. Forget the Angles, the Danes and the wealas."

"But I want them to be Romans, Auntie. I want the country to be Britannia. Anyway the *wealas* at least are nearly all on my side and I can trust them. The Danes and the Angles are working against me. Their language is awful and none of them bother to learn Latin. They are too busy making money and not building an empire. They are getting too rich. No wonder the Scots and the Northmen want to come and steal it. They should be giving money to their king to defend them."

"Athelstan, they do. You tax them enough. They would complain more if there weren't every greedy pirate knocking on our door and you weren't keeping the rascals at bay. The Eastern Romans have the right idea with pirates and invaders. They kill them or sell them into slavery to the Moors."

"Auntie, I couldn't sell Christians to the unbelievers."

"Silly boy! Why not? Everyone else does! It's a wonder anyone is left in Ireland now the Vikings are there."

"They are sinners and apostates in Byzantium and Dublin is full of pirates. God will deliver them all into the hands of the Moors for the evil they do. The Moors will convert their churches into their temples……. and I am a Christian king, and Britannia will never fall to the forces of evil while I rule."

"Athelstan, try not to be a complete bigot as well as a king," said Auntie.

After this period of introspection he carried on talking tactics with Thorolf.

Grim was happy to receive Athelstan's agreement to what he was going to do anyway. He was glad for the money which came with the orders. He rode off with Emma for another look at the Humber without going too deep into the marshes. There was a stiff offshore wind and he could see some boats anchored just off the north bank waiting for a change of wind and tide to sail up the river.

"As soon as we can, we'll have a visit over there," he said.

"Grim, you had better go before the wind changes and our rowers lose the advantage. Shall I send the fairies out for a look?" Emma said this as if it were her personal challenge.

"Good idea, as long as they don't get too near and arouse suspicion. We don't want the Scots and whoever else they have with them associating a visit from fisher folk with an attack."

Emma's cousin Maria's youngest daughter Mabyn with three friends set out to check their fish traps, keeping a safe distance from the ships. Their skin boat bobbed over the waves and seemed very little affected by the tides and currents in comparison to larger seagoing wooden boats. They paddled the full length of the waiting boats, keeping to the south bank, seeming to arouse no suspicion. However, the sight of them proved too tempting for one captain who raised his sail and anchor and tried to sail over to them.

"No rowed warships then in this lot" said Mabyn to her friends.

The ship had to turn and crashed into a couple more at anchor. Suddenly a Northmen's ship appeared with rowers from the back of them to investigate the chaos. The captain barked out orders to the other ships to remain at anchor and inquired what was happening.

"A gang of fisherwomen on the south bank" was the reply.

The warship turned and rowed in their direction. The girls paddled for the marshes and shallow water. They had a narrow escape as it grounded on a sandbank when it came nearly upon them. The captain shouted over to them not to be afraid in something like Saxon. Despite her knowledge of the language, Mabyn replied in Welsh.

"We are only fishing. We are poor people."

"What's she say" said the captain?

"She's one of the *wealas*" called out a member of the crew. "Shall I talk to her? I can speak some of the language."

"Go on then, ask them to come over, ask where they are from and where the Saxons are?"

He shouted over the invitation and the questions.

Mabyn replied in Welsh. "The Saxons are in Lincoln and Nottingham up the river."

"What river" he asked?

"The river" replied Mabyn with a straight face.

"They only seem to know one river" he said to the captain. "Do you know where the towns are?"

"South of here, that must be where the river goes. Ask how many they are?

He did but the only reply he got was many of them with horses.

The captain said. "They are only the locals, they probably only listen to rumours. They won't know any more."

"We'll give you some silver as a reward if you come over here," the crewman shouted.

Mabyn replied "Don't be silly, if the Saxons find us with silver they'll steal it and kill us after they've raped us."

"Just like you want to" shouted one of her friends.

"No, we've come to settle, you can be our wives" came the reply.

"Don't believe you" shouted Mabyn and they paddled off deeper into the marshes and away from the ship. Leaving it settled on the sandbank,

Mabyn reported back to Grim. "I said what you told me when they challenged us. We had a narrow escape." She related what happened.

Grim rode along the coast to look at the ship. Despite the rise and fall of the tide it was still stuck. Nice vessel, we could pick up that ship, he thought and rode back to make his plans.

Two days later with no change in the wind, his little fleet rowed out into the Humber under cover of the early morning darkness. The tide was going out and little effort was needed by the crews. Grim could see a few more ships had arrived from the numbers Mabyn had counted. The northwest wind was stronger if anything and he could see the ship still on the sandbank with only a few of the crew remaining.

"On the way back, that is ours" he said and laughed very loudly, which was uncharacteristic of Grim the Miller. "Not many of their warships in this lot."

The captain and most of the crew had been taken off the longship by another one which had just arrived and he was taken up to York with the information to Anlaf. The new captain was sceptical about the information from a bunch of half-naked women who seemed smart enough to keep out of their grasp. He wanted to remain behind to guard the fleet until the wind had changed, but the prospect of his leader not having the information seemed to worry him more than the information being useless or a ruse.

The new captain Stigand went with his colleague Knut to see Anlaf and both put their points of view.

"Stig," said Anlaf, "you did right to bring Knut and your assessment of the danger to the fleet is correct while they cannot sail to safety or beach. Sail back down as fast as you can. Leave now, waste no time and rescue Knut's ship and he can pay you the salvage dues. He should have had more sense, sailing after women in strange waters. The damn country is full of women if that is all that is on your mind, Knut. Bear in mind these are now our people. We have come to lead, not to conquer and rape. Go back to Ireland if that is all you can do, but you'll go without your crew and your ship….. I think the information you got out of those girls is actually accurate from what we know from other sources. The locals around here are frightened of everyone and with good reason. The Saxons and the Danes have stolen everything worth having from them over the last years. They live on the margins of the country. We could make allies of them if we try…….. You can redeem yourself by going back to your crew and finding your man who speaks their language and making contact with them again…. and peacefully this time. I want you to go for more information about what's happening in the east of the country up the rivers which flow from the south. I want to know where the men are. Why are they not out fishing?"

"I'll do that" said Knut. "Is there a small river boat I can use to get through the marshes? Those girls were in some sort of skin boat like the Irish use."

"I haven't seen any of those around here but the people who support us by the river might have something similar. Ask peaceably for the use and take somebody as a guide. Reward them. Make friends. Not everything can be taken by the sword, you great oaf!............Sweet Freya, what would your father have thought of your lack of brains?"

The reference to Freya had made Bishop Wulfstan wince. He was present in the hall and listening avidly to all the conversation. He had been looking forward to Anlaf coming but had now for a moment just wondered. Anlaf had seen his expressions.

"Stop worrying, Bishop, it's the way we speak" he said quietly.

Grim felt his plan was moving into action. His eleven boats moved along quietly with all the crews saving their energy. It was just light enough for them to see what they wanted in the late summer mists. His nine boats full of the old fighters each attacked a boat. The sea-going boats had a higher freeboard and so they threw over bundles of burning dried reeds dosed with pitch, fired arrows and cut the anchor ropes. The ships were full of men and some women, he noticed. Grim never dismissed the part women played in anything and thought, are they just camp followers or do they have a purpose here, we do not know yet?

The whole fleet woke and his two ships of boy archers were rowed in between them at speed, shooting arrows. After his men had attacked two ships or so each, he gave the signal to withdraw. The element of surprise which was key to the success of the attack was now gone. They withdrew past the burning ships firing on them again at crews trying to douse the fires. Once the over-enthusiastic boys had returned, he took two crews and his own over to the stranded longship, sending home the others out of the way. The guarding crew were awake and ready for them. Grim was the first to leap on board as he believed in leading an attack at the front. As always he took a couple of short spears to throw ahead of him. The method never failed him and his crew followed. The other two boats secured the ship and towed it off the sandbank even as the fighting was continuing. The twenty or so Northmen were not any easy target and Grim had known this. It took the fighters from the crews of all three boats to subdue them and then five of his men were killed and many were wounded. None of the Vikings surrendered and Grim wasn't giving them the chance anyway. They threw the bodies overboard and Grim's men rowed away the ship with his original three river boats up to the mouth of the Trent just in time to be observed by Stigand Wynstansson and his men.

Stigand was not prepared for what happened next. He expected them to turn up the mouth of the river he could see from the south and make their escape, but at a signal from a man steering Knut's ship, they all turned towards his. The mist was just clearing and he could see the ships burning further along the Humber. Hrolf his steersman said in panic.

"Three boats of Saxons can't have done all that, Stig, and refloated Knut's warship."

"Well, they are all we can see. If there were more, they'd be coming to attack us as well. ....Raise the sail, we'll make a run for the other ships...... every man to an oar."

By this time Grim's little navy were ahead of them and turning to face them with his new ship in the middle and the others spaced out at a spears throw between.

"Get ready to run up to that ship and grapple" he shouted, "and cut down the sail."

Stigand had begun to wish he had not unloaded the Scots' soldiers he had brought south. He had a feeling he was going to need them now. He had seen he was not outnumbered but felt somehow at a disadvantage. He thought his ship was about to speed through when suddenly one of the smaller boats turned and his ship rammed into it. It stopped nearly dead in the water and Hrolf had no time to steer round it. The crew of the other three were then all over his ship. A wizened old man at the prow of Knut's ship threw two spears at him and missed, so he thought. He turned to see Hrolf dying behind him and realised he wasn't the target. The steering oar was all over the place.

Neither Stigand nor his crew had put on all of their armour as they were not expecting battle. Despite a brave resistance, Grim's men slaughtered them all except for Stigand and a few others who jumped overboard and swam for the shore avoiding the arrows.

"Home now, dear friends," shouted Grim. "If we meet any more, we shall have no crew to take their ships home."

Guthric Wadasson commanding one of the other boats shouted over. "Shall we finish off the rest, Grim? We can catch them in the water."

"No, let them go and spread some panic in York."

True to Grim's prediction, a change in the wind and another fast ship arriving meant the news was with Anlaf in hardly a day. Anlaf was now in no doubt of what he had been saying to everyone, the east of the country is well defended and there is no point in dividing our forces to attack it.

Straight down the middle, keep to the original plan. We can do another feint on the flanks to keep them guessing. We don't want Athelstan moving soldiers over to attack our main force. Knut Ragnarsson's information was correct. We have enough troops to meet the Saxons in any case."

Constantine arrived a few days later and agreed with him. They made plans for the army to move south to Brunanburgh and cross the Don using that crossing and the two or three others they had located downriver. The king did have some difficulty in believing three boatloads of Saxons had done all the damage. Not until he did find out there were more who had gone before Stigand had arrived, did he begin to understand, and issued orders for guardships in the estuary.

"They are obviously able to disappear into the marshes but we have no time to root them out at the moment," he observed. "Plenty of time later!"

Grim in the meantime had sailed his little fleet to a safe haven and hidden all the boats. The two ships he moved upriver. When Grim recounted their exploits, Harald Edwinsson decided it was the best story he had ever heard and didn't care if it was true or not. He was going to repeat it to anyone who would listen. He had Dunstan Edwinsson, a Saxon and no relation, staying with him as King Athelstan's messenger who was to take back details of all the forces. Dunstan was a poet and he threatened to immortalise Grim in verse for eternity.

"Just tell the king what we are doing for him" said Grim, "and that his plan to confuse the enemy may be working. Now we have two big ships it could work even better. We could sail them out on the open sea or catch the Scots coming up the river. Don't dramatise it either. We were just lucky and they were stupid or inexperienced."

Dunstan was suitably chastened by an old warrior and went off for some weapon practice with Eric Sigurdsson. He was always prepared to agree he was more a poet than a fighter and knew heroic verse was never going to keep him alive in the coming battle, but he had to lead his father's men. Harald had been giving him advice on this as well.

Grim and Harald went off to plan another attack.

"We won't get away so easy next time, Harald."

"Perhaps, you should follow up quickly before they have time to set too many guards on the rivers and the banks. We should certainly watch out for a counter-attack and for spies."

"We have our water fairies watching for them. They must have reasoned that we are a strong force and now we have their two warships, even stronger.

We have to try to make ourselves seem stronger still. I think I would like to set bait for a trap which is so obvious they would not dare fall for it. So then, we don't have to worry about not having the forces to spring it and it won't surprise them when we don't. They will just think we are not letting go."

"We need more luck and them to make more mistakes, Grim."

"I am going to take another small boat down the river and see what happens. There is bound to be a lost ship, separated from the others, overloaded, leaking, inexperienced crew. They must have picked up everyone they could find with pretence of seamanship."

"From what your men say there has been no pretence of fighting. It's all been real. About a quarter of your men aren't fit to set out again. At least you kept the lads out of any danger. I have to say I thought that a good idea, wisely handled, but I would have dreaded it getting out of control. We can't do it again on sea or land. They'll be ready for us."

"I learnt it from the Scots actually."

"When did you ever fight the Scotti?"

"I have never fought against the Scots until today, Harald. I fought with them about forty years ago."

"I don't think I dare ask," said Harald Edwinsson, thinking he had known all there was to know about Grim. It made him wonder, what was his own father doing at the time with Grim? He did not know about that either.

Grim made his plans to set off with some picked men in one boat on another foray to the Humber marshes. "We'll look at what's going off around the mouth of the River Don. It will mean a trip up the Ouse for a short way and we'll have to be careful. There will be a lot of ships on the river and it's much narrower than the Humber. Get ready for an escape into the marshes."

"Grim, if we are going to do that, we are in the wrong boat. This might be the lightest we have but we can't lift it by ourselves or extract it if it gets stuck" said his cousin Orm Cuthbertsson.

"Orm, I am glad to see not everyone sleeps when I issue my orders or does not question them except in a proper manner. You are correct.....and we are only going down river in this boat. We are going to borrow some lighter fishing boats from Emma's relatives. Then when, the Scots see us, we'll look like fishermen and not soldiers."

Harald Edwinsson and Dunstan, who had returned with Eric, laughed at all this.

Eric said, "Uncle Grim, you are getting too sensitive as you get older. Everyone knows that in the past there has been no better sea-raider and pirate on the Northern Ocean."

"You rascal, you can starve the next time you come to my house. I have never stolen anything on the seas."

"No, you stole all your money on land," said Harald. "I begin to believe my father taught you all you know when seafaring. A man, who uses sword and spear like you, did not learn it guarding altars in churches."

"You taught me all I know in the use of those weapons," said Eric.

"It's why he prefers an axe" said Orm.

"I do not know," said Grim, "why I bother going to war with such rogues as you. It's a good job my wife and son love me. I would want for love and affection with you lot."

"Fear not, good Grim," said Dunstan. "Your king seems to love you for all your efforts defending his realm. I think he will love you even more when he hears what I shall report. He has great respect for men of long years who can still fight. This war has brought forward many such as you. We can only hope we beardless boys can live as long as you."

"By Odin," said Harald, "you bear the name Edwinsson well and have a way with words, Dunstan. Grim will be making you a partner in his mill if you praise him some more."

"Leave the young man alone, his words are like music to me," said Grim. "Sadly, we must go and do a bit more killing on behalf of his king. Make sure he can use his weapons a little better. Poetry is fine but it won't keep the Scots at home or him alive. Look to the shield, Eric teach him well..... Remember what your Uncle Grim taught you."

Later Grim and his crew of twenty rowed off down river in the September sunshine. He checked each of the beacons as they passed, all covered and dry with a boy or a girl watching. As they drifted along at rest he issued more orders.

"We do not know what we shall see down here but we are going to divide up into three smaller boats. Four of you will also remain behind with this one. They will be enough to sail and row it away from any enemy. I am going to arrange for the relatives to help you if necessary. The rest of us will not take our armour. We are going to raid and run. Burn not battle. We do not need any temptation to stand and fight. We might have to swim for it as well, and I picked you all because I know you can swim. Sword, axes, spears, shields and helmets, all we are going to need, and bows, of course. No boys to help us today."

"The north west wind is back," someone chipped in.

"This can only help us. Some ship will be struggling to get up the Ouse from the Humber," continued Grim. "I really want to check if they are sailing up the Don. This voyage can be a success even if we don't get into a fight."

They sailed on and left the boat hidden during darkness with the relatives. In the early morning light they set off again westward in their three boats and paddled on the fringes of the marshes. To the north they could see so many ships they couldn't count them. That poet will never believe this, thought Grim. No one spotted them and by late afternoon they had arrived at the junction of the Don and the Ouse. They turned south but met no one. During darkness they slept after a cold meal. In the morning they still saw no signs of life. Later in the morning they saw smoke on an island in the marshes. Grim took his boat to investigate.

As he expected the inhabitants had gone by the time they arrived. He couldn't see them anywhere, called out, waited and decided to leave. He hung up a small bag of flour as a gift next to the door of a hut and they all left the island. They paddled on up river until mid-afternoon when Grim ordered a turn around. They rested and let the current take them slowly down river with the change of the tide. When they neared they island where they had left the flour, a small boat came out of the trees with three men and a boy on board. Grim steered his own boat over to them and halted within hailing distance, when he saw them take up their bows.

"Who are you, Saxon," shouted one of the men?

"No Saxon but the miller of Knaith, Grim the Dane."

"Thanks for the flour, but what's your business?"

"I'm looking for ships coming out of the Humber."

"There was one sailed up the river yesterday but we could tell it was lost. It was full of people, all well armed. It nearly grounded a couple of times. We thought we might have some salvage out of it, if it were abandoned."

"I think you and I could speak a similar language if we tried very hard," said Grim. "I could persuade them to abandon it for you."

"And what's your reward, Master Grim the Miller?"

"I need to deter people from coming to my mill when they don't intend to pay for the corn. I can be generous with it if I do not have too many friends. Could this ship be rowed?"

"No, it was big with a high deck and a large sail. It went at quite a speed in this wind but it will get stuck further up if it doesn't turn round and drift down again with the current. It was full of painted people and some were women with swords and shields."

Damn such a mystery, thought Grim. I'll let the King know and he can work out what's going off. Constantine has got the Picts involved.

"Should we go up river and catch it in the shallows or wait," questioned Grim?

"Go up river," the man answered. "We can bring sixty men but we have few real weapons, only bows and knives..... a few spears."

"Not a problem, if you have plenty of arrows, we can do the close quarter stuff. They won't put on their armour unless they expect a fight. We must surprise them. If we paddle up over night we could catch them in the dark. How quickly can you get your men?"

A signal brought ten boats out of the cover of the marshes.

I am getting old and soft in the head thought Grim. I let him talk me into ease and I didn't see them.

"Let's go," said Grim. "Can you send out a scout boat?"

They paddled until nearly night fall and the scout boat returned to say they had spotted the ship, anchored and waiting for a wind change. It was pointing down river. The occupants were on the bank, cooking a meal of sorts and they had guards out. Grim decided to go for a look with Owain the leader of the river people and one of the scouts. He counted over a hundred including ten women. Not good odds he thought.... They were all crammed into that vessel. No wonder they got off at first chance.

Owain spoke first. "Grim we don't have enough men to take on that lot. The women look like warriors to me as well. They might not have armour but they all walk about with their swords and spears as if they are expecting us. I know we can see the fires from a long way but they are not frightened to be here. Let's take another look in better daylight."

They went off for some food. Grim's crew shared their food and were about to wait for daylight when Owain made a suggestion.

"Why don't you and your men and the better armed of us, do a faint attack in the night. While they are busy dealing with what they could think is a large force on land, we'll attack from the river and steal the ship. They won't get any fewer before daylight."

"Well," said Grim, "this is the only plan we have, so I agree, we'll do it. Twenty five should be enough. Anymore and we'll get lost in the dark.

When you hear us attack, move in but we'll do it while there is a bit of light."

"We can be in position by moonrise and it's up to you then, Grim, but, take a few more men and spread them out. Take forty."

Grim agreed.

CHAPTER 15

THE JOURNEY UP THE RIVER DON

Brollachan found it amazing that anyone should be seasick. Sailing was so exciting and she was particularly surprised that Bridget was so affected. She had enjoyed the journey around the north of Britain to Dunnotar, despite the constant rough seas and was glad to see Brigid again for the journey south. Moray had disappeared into the north. Since she had left with Sine, he had found himself constantly having to defend his people and this had resulted in many deaths amongst the Scots. In the end King Constantine sent him home as his Scottish followers would not let rest their desire for vengeance. Not even Black Callum could protect him and Constantine did not want his death. Another Pictish Earl had stepped in as their spokesman and things began to quieten over the winter. She was frightened that if she re-appeared the trouble would begin again. Sine was to marry again and with a man of her own choice not her brother-in-law's and so she was not there to cause trouble. Ceara and Keir had remained behind as servants to Sine, deeply in love themselves. Hamish was dead and she felt without a friend until she returned to Brigid.

During the winter Brollachan had gone over to the west coast as she didn't trust her dead brother's men despite their pledges. She had an aunt who lived near to the High Mountain and she wished to say farewell to her.

She left her pony Eachna with a family on the coast who took her in when she left her aunt to look in vain for her mother. In the late spring she found a place on one of King Anlaf's ships when it called nearby to pick up soldiers for the invasion. The captain had been originally reluctant to bring her but the men accompanying her from her aunt's camp, testified to her skill as a warrior, despite her youth. During the whole of her stay in the west, she had not been able to locate her mother or receive any certain news about her. No one had seen her for ten years.

Brollachan found the winter had changed Brigid. The constant pressure of life at Dunnotar had aged her in almost a year. Brollachan was revitalised after her adventures, her visit home and to her family in the west. She was ready to do her part. She was relieved when she met Brigid again and was invited aboard the ship she had been allocated. It was a merchant ship with a crew from the east of the country but the crew were not the most experienced. The captain and owner, Brude had not planned to sail and his original crew had dispersed. Most of the new ones had no experience of a long sea voyage and had only fished coastal waters. When they finally set sail, they lagged behind the main fleet and found themselves sailing with other stragglers. The ship had been particularly poorly provisioned and almost immediately food was short. It improved a bit when they picked up thirty Angle warriors who were better supplied and prepared to share. Brollachan was never used to eating too well and it never really bothered her. People also seemed to have forgotten about her killing of the young men the previous year. War fever had taken over King Constantine's land.

Bridget also had grown a bit fat on the King's bounty at Dunnottar and Brollachan noticed the change to her appearance. She seemed less imposing than before. The only saving grace to the journey was that the majority of the hundred or so people on board were so seasick for the most of the voyage, they didn't want to eat. The vessel itself was quite seaworthy, had the crew been able to handle it. At the first stop three of the originals deserted and the passengers had to help out. Four men were lost overboard almost immediately. The ship could not be turned or slowed to pick up the people who fell overboard, so they drowned. They made the Humber with difficulty and escaped the attention of Baltic pirates by hugging the coast. The beacons provided by Anlaf's supporters and a warship at the mouth of the river guided them in. The crew were not able to steer the ship properly and tack against a prevailing wind. They were pushed against the south bank and eventually confused the Don with the Ouse it flowed into.

Everywhere looked the same to them. They had seldom seen such large tracts of marsh which added to the confusion.

After sailing easily up the Don the captain began to realise his mistake, stopped and turned the ship but could make no headway except to drift with the current. The passengers and crew were so tired that he decided to halt overnight and go in search of some food. Supplies had run out a few days before as they entered the Humber.

Ever the resourceful, Brollachan had taken her bow, and gone hunting with another girl, Ida. There were woods and fields just off the flooded river. It was unnerving. There was no one about but many empty huts could be seen. Ida was from the south and had an Angle-Scots ancestry and spoke Gaelic, Welsh and Anglic. Brollachan thought she would be useful to know and Ida was glad to go looking for some food. Brollachan was not sure why Ida had joined with Brigid.

Brollachan shot a couple of ducks almost immediately. She had adapted some arrows for hunting birds. She skinned one as Ida lit a fire and they roasted it immediately before any thought of returning to camp. They roasted and ate the second one.

"Ida, I don't like the absence of people in this place. King Constantine said they would welcome us and I don't see any one on the farms we have been near," she said.

"Perhaps we should go up to the farms. I can speak a form of the language. The amount of smoke from our camp by the river is going to attract some attention soon anyway. It's comforting to know there are enough to defend us," said Ida.

"Well, that would depend on how many were attacking. Most of us haven't eaten properly for weeks and are still seasick. You and I have been fine. We were too excited to be ill."

"Broll, let's go and have a look at that collection of huts over there. I am sure something moved. We can move in carefully from some cover."

They moved into the trees and walked carefully to the huts. Ida had her sword ready and Brollachan a couple of arrows. The huts had not been abandoned for more than a couple of nights. They were just about to leave when Ida heard movement in the woods, so they remained hidden in a cowshed. About twenty men came into view and walked through the huts silently. The girls noticed they were well armed but without armour. They watched as they moved into some woods near the river.

"They are going to attack us" said Ida. "How do they think they'll do it with so few?"

"They are probably not the only ones but I don't see any more. We'll try to sneak around them in the dark."

They found the remains of a loaf and a piece of cheese in the hut next door and ate it. It was still fresh.

"I could live here, Ida," said Brollachan. "You can live well even as a scavenger, in a land like this."

"I always have understood why the Northmen have wanted it" said Ida. "There's always a lot of food here. Think how much fish we caught in the river. We would have caught more if we had had the proper lines."

They watched the men form up in the woods in two groups and then noticed there were more on either side of them.

"This seems strange to me," said Ida, "the new ones seem to be watching the first lot more than our camp. We can't get around them and there still isn't enough to tackle our men. They'll put their armour on at night, those that have it. All of the Angles have some. They were taking it off the ship as I left them. Perhaps we had better stay here and see what happens."

Brollachan didn't like the idea but didn't say anything. She thought I'll get a few arrows and a plan ready, just in case I can do something.

The moon rose just before dark and the men moved forward quietly. The two groups either side did the same and they all moved towards the river bank. The Angles and the Picts from the ship had prepared for an attack by this time and were already moving out to meet what they thought was the main body of the attackers. The forces met and the attackers instantly gave way followed by the Angles and Picts. Then Brollachan and Ida watched a strange thing. The other two groups came up and the first group split. At the same time there was some chaos on the bank next to the ship. The Angles and Picts moved carefully back as at the same time the attackers began to fight amongst themselves. It had got so dark by now the girls could see little beyond the fight in the woodland. They took advantage of the noise to move out of the farm into some more cover with a couple of old cloaks they had found and decided to settle down for the night. A small group of men managed to extricate themselves from the fight and run in the upriver direction. The remainder did not follow.

Next morning they made their way carefully around the wood noticing that there were a handful of bodies visible. They turned in the direction of their camp but couldn't see the ship's mast. Until they saw everyone on the bankside, they thought they had been abandoned.

"A feint attack while they stole the ship" said Brigid.

"A bit more" said Ida, "they attacked each other. There's a handful dead in that wood. Ten or so more moved up river, the rest went down river. Looks like falling out of friends to me."

"Did our side kill anyone," said Brollachan?

Ida repeated her question in Anglic and their leader shook his head. "We had better get out of here before they return, but where can we go? There's something strange happening here."

Grim the Miller was taking stock of the situation. He had lost six men and had two wounded quite badly. Only nine including him were capable of a fight. They could not rescue their boats. The treacherous marsh dwellers had those. All they could do was walk back to the Trent and home, carrying the wounded through the marshes. No point in going to the Doncaster forts, even though they were quite near. Emma's folk were too far way and on a more difficult track through the deeper marshes and a wider river to cross. Home to his lovely Emma, and by the most direct eastern route was his only choice. Once home he would plan his revenge on Owain and his men. Neither Anlaf nor Athelstan would list Owain amongst their friends. Grim would come back with Ivar and Eric and his survivors. It wouldn't need many of them. Once we have dealt with the Scots, he thought. Athelstan would be glad of some help dealing with the traitors, but then he thought, stealing a Scots ship puts Owain on Athelstan's side. We'll just have to make it a private matter, one of honour. Once Athelstan has gone, he won't worry about stolen ships. I've got two warships and I'll get the other one.

Back at the riverbank the answer to the Angle's question came soon enough. The ship sailed back down the river. It seemed out of control and was followed by four boats being rowed and paddled frantically to the sound of order and counter-order.

The Anglian warriors needed no orders, they ran for their armour and the Picts were galvanised by Brollachan who began to fire arrows at the men struggling to bring the sail on the ship under control. A handful of the Picts were already in the water engaging the occupants of the nearest boat who thought they were safe. Within moments they had control of it and pulled it to the bank. The Angles in their armour filled it and were in pursuit of the rest. Other archers had come to help Brollachan and the men on the ship lost control of it under the hail of arrows. The ship grounded on the opposite bank. Brigid, Brollachan and Ida swam over to it through the fight taking place mid-stream. The unarmoured Britons were not faring well despite other boats appearing to support them. Archers firing from cover on the bank were picking off the rowers and paddlers who were forced to withdraw and leave their comrades to be slaughtered. On the ship the remaining crew did not expect three women to appear out of the river. They had been hiding out of arrowshot. Ida despatched two with her sword at where they were hidden. Brollachan killed another just by hurling arrows at him which she found on board. Bridget nearly got hit by a spear but it was thrown too quickly and had to get into a sword-fight with the thrower. Brollachan picked up the spear and killed the man as he was trying to jump over board. One man escaped to the bank and ran off into the marshes.

The proper crew of the ship swam over and took control. They steered it to the other bank and people began to walk up river to it. The Angles had captured another two boats. Berwin, their leader took charge.

"Back on board for all of us and down river as fast as we can. Watch out for another attack. The wind is against us again. Can we tow the ship? We'll split up the armoured warriors between the ship and the boats. Let us leave here as soon as we can."

When they were all on board, Berwin stationed Brollachan with her bow at the stern of the big ship. "Keep a lookout" he said. "They might just as well try to sneak up on us from the rear as head-on might be too dangerous. They've already had a taste of our arrows."

She got into conversation with Brigid. "This is the nearest I have ever been to a real battle. Those without armour or shields didn't stand a chance, not even those Saxons last night. They were experienced warriors. They knew how to pull out of a fight without losing men. They knew not to face armoured men. What's a big battle against the Saxons going to be like? Magic will make no difference."

Brigid dismissed her thoughts. "Weight of numbers and our inspiration will win the day for us. Not all Saxons have armour. The ones last night had none despite being sent to attack us. Those Britons just got greedy. Don't they know we are the same people, on the same side?"

"No, they are just thieves, looking out for plunder. We keep meeting lots of those on our side," said Brollachan.

Brollachan got a bit moody and didn't speak any more. Brigid went dreamy, thinking about food and the lack of it. She was also thinking she had not done very well as a fighter in the little battle for the ship. She was too fat and had not practiced enough.

Grim the Miller had been looking for a place to cross the river or find a boat. They were all tired and hungry and the wounded were getting worse. All the houses had been abandoned. He thought, the king didn't order this along the Don. What's happening here? He heard some shouting and took Orm his cousin to investigate. They watched the fight over the ship and the Britons retreating.

Orm snorted and said. "We'll say goodbye to that prize, cousin, but not to revenge I think."

"The revenge will be sweeter still, dear friend. I hope Owain has survived all this. I would hold it truly against the Scots, if they have cheated me of revenge. They can have York and the rest of the world but not my revenge for our dead comrades. We had better watch out for women on the battlefield, even if it only a skirmish at the bottom of the lane. Don't they have enough men to fight from among the Gaels? I thought my dear Emma was useful in a fight but those three who clambered on board that tub; they really knew what a fight was about. By the Gods I do feel old at this time."

"Let's go home and fight another day, my old comrade," said Orm.

Berwin's prediction of the voyage back to the Ouse was true. They passed Owain's camp and some men followed, firing arrows at them. Everyone sat tight behind their shields, except for a few selected archers who returned some shots. They were pursued nearly to the evening. Reaching a small island they stopped for the night keeping a sharp watch. Hardly anyone slept, hunger keeping them awake.

The following day they made the Ouse and met a ship sailing down from York which directed them to the north bank to wait for orders. They managed to catch a few fish and beg some flour and dried meat off an adjoining ship. One of the Angles took a captured river boat and sailed with a couple of others to the marshes where he picked some plants. They tasted good when cooked and seemed in endless supply. They sat on the ship for another three days and a message to move came from the king. The Scots and the Picts landed in the marshes. They went one way and the Angles another, taking the captured river boats. The crew stayed with the ship although only seven had survived, not enough to manage it at sea.

"Brollachan," said Brigid when they had sat down on the land. "I have a thought that the Angles will change sides. It's something Ida has said also. It would not surprise me if she went with them. Athelstan's gold and the desire to be with kith and kin can be strong in any people."

"I have thought that also despite their promise to fight with us. They have lived to the south of us for many generations, so the nuns taught me."

"They have not always lived in peace with the Scots or the Britons. They could do better with their own from around here. Perhaps they don't believe we can beat the Saxons."

"Brigid, I have never fought in a war but after I left Dunnottar, I had to fight for my life. I get the feeling there is no unity in this army. The Northmen and the Scots look down on us and the Irish. They have food and we are hungry. They have all the best weapons and armour."

"We have weapons and we don't need armour. We fight naked because we frighten the enemy and our determination will carry us through the battle."

"Brigid, what can we get out of this battle? After it's over, win or lose, there is nothing for us. How will we get back home? Who will welcome us here? We will be someone's slaves either way without our men to defend us......... and if they are all dead……?

"Brollachan, you are irritating. You're like Moray, you think too much for your own good. Look what happened to him. The best leader we have gets sent back into the hills, leaving us at the mercy of the Scots."

"That's what I mean. We'll be sent to die in this battle and all we have been working for, will be pointless."

Brigid picked up a spear and hit Brollachan with the shaft several times bruising her and drawing blood.

"I am in charge" she screamed. "Don't anyone forget it and don't argue with me again."

One of the other girls, Mairie went to Brollachan and tended her wounds.

"Broll, I'm frightened and want to go home."

Brollachan looked at her and thought, dear Mother, she's only a baby. She can hardly be fourteen. Why have we brought her? No, she's older, older than me. She was already at the convent with the older girls when they imprisoned me there. She's just worn out and weepy like the rest of us. I've seen her practice with her sword as well. She's been permanently seasick. I can't remember when last she ate or slept properly on the ship."

"Don't worry, Mairie, Brigid's just hungry and worried for us all. I've had a worse beating than this from nuns when I wouldn't say my prayers….. But she'd better not do it again, I think."

"I can't face food till I get my feet properly on land, Broll, and I can't sleep either. I just have a premonition of death all the time. I just want someone to take me somewhere safe."

"Preferably a big strong man," joked Brollachan? "One who could make you forget there is anything else in the all world ....but a warm bed and him."

"Broll, are you still a virgin?"

"Unfortunately, I am. The Scots killed Hamish, Lord Moray's man. The man I wanted. If he would have had me, I would have given up all this, the way I feel now."

"I'm so tired and sick all the time. I can't stomach food. I couldn't fight those Britons by the river, "said Mairie. "I used to be quite healthy despite life in that convent."

Both she and Brollachan burst into tears and Brigid saw them, thinking she had been the cause.

Brigid came over and apologised but Brollachan just repeated all her questions and then Bridget shared some of her worries.

"When Moray left the other earls just decided to go along with what the king wanted. Callum macNeill was on our side but the rest of the Scots were mad with hate. It began to get worse when the warriors came back from the hills with the stories about being attacked, traps, treacherous peasants and all kinds of made up tales. Constantine was in no mood for lies and had anyone whipped who repeated them, calling the perpetrators a bunch of cowards. They vented their anger on Moray. Constantine missed his presence as well. Only Black Callum and Moray had a real grasp of the situation and neither of them is here."

"Where's macNeill now, asked Brollachan?

"He fell out as well with the king's family, so he took his men away. The king's sons have started to re-assert their influence, but they can't escape the fight. I am sorry I have not told you all this before. I really wish you had stayed in the hills. You may be right, we shall all die."

"But why bring us now," said Broll?

"The men would not fight unless all the women came."

"Brigid, you could have made them see different."

"No, I couldn't. You don't understand how disadvantaged our men feel now the take- over by the Scots is near complete. People are ceasing to speak our language as well."

"I think if you had talked to me about this before we set out, I would have stayed behind and joined Moray. I could have gone to what my brother has left behind. He and his followers will not see it again. The people will need me. Whatever way this battle goes, and more than ever, I think it will do us no good, I should make my way home, if I can."

She began to tell Brigid about her vision of the Goddess but she moved away when a Northman ship came near. When it pulled alongside the bank, the commander shouted for Brigid. She returned and ordered all the women to pack up their sacks and transfer on board with her. Brollachan tried to dodge away but Brigid came to fetch her. Mairie looked terrified at moving off land again. They sailed in the direction of York.

Brigid questioned her again about her vision of the Goddess and where she had heard it. Brollachan's story made her unhappy, especially the prediction. She told her not to tell anyone.

Brollachan was indignant. She had kept the revelation to herself till now as she had not felt the need to share it until she could get time with Brigid to fully explain what had happened. Brigid had realised what the men had said about being attacked was true. It had been Brollachan and Hamish and the allies they had picked up on the way. All on the king's doorstep. No wonder the court was so irate. Constantine had dismissed them as a bunch of drunken cowards. Some of them were, but the information was true. Brollachan was definitely going to be an asset in the battle, if only she could get her there. We still have some fight in us, she thought if it is only in our young people.

Brigid took some comfort in the Brollachan's younger brother being back with the clan. He was at least young enough to have no fear, although he had been kept out of the way and had had little opportunity to develop as a warrior. He was at least no coward unlike the one Brollachan had killed. Strangely, he didn't want his sister with him in the battle. All the men talked about what she did in the hills and were prepared to follow her. He would have no problem taking them forward with his sister present. He was, however, going to get Mairie instead and he was happy with that. She was a distant relative of the king, a macAlpin, one of the last surviving direct line, and a woman through whom a man could claim a kingdom. Brigid thought, Constantine is hoping she never returns. I had better watch that he doesn't allow her to meet with an accident after the battle if she survives. The consequences of us losing this battle could be terrible but for some, winning will be the same. Moray and Brollachan are sounding right, she thought, and wondered, why she had never seen it. She had been blinded by the prospect of a revival of Pictish power against the Scots. It was not going to be and she let herself shed a few careful tears.

After a hard journey Grim reached Knaith and left the two wounded men with Emma. He took everyone else back to Harald's camp next to the Fossdyke.

"We can't have victory every day," said Harald, stoically.

"Defeat comes usually through the action of traitors," said Grim and told the full story. "Although I must confess I let vanity and my desire for another ship, carry away my reason."

Dunstan took it all in and said he would relate it to the king. He knew Athelstan would not be pleased to hear how his allies were treated.

Two days later a messenger came ordering the troops making up the main army to assemble west of the Trent near Mansfield.

"Grim, go and plot your revenge" said Harald, "and leave us all a share. If we are successful in this battle, we may need some diversion when it is over. There will be no lack of swordplay soon, I am sure, but practice is always good when war is over."

"You bloodthirsty lot," said Dunstan. "Peace is not for you, I see."

"We can have no peace without honour," said Grim, "Besides if the Don valley ceases to be such a wide border and is open for trade and use by more river craft, a bunch of pirates will not help the king's peace."

"I never thought of you as a great supporter of my king, He will be pleased to know how much you have the interests of his realm at heart. But he will not like to hear about piracy, theft and murder. I am sure he will agree with what you are doing"

"He's not a great supporter of the king," said Harald. "The grain and flour trade is what he loves."

"How well you know me," said Grim with a smile. "But you'll come along for the fight!"

"Nothing can keep me from it, save death or a better offer," said Harald.

Eric Sigurdsson had done quite a good job teaching Dunstan the better use of a sword and shield, enough to keep him alive, if he didn't get too adventurous. He did quietly speak with one or two of his men to make sure they did not let him get into too much danger. After all he was only required to lead his father's men, not to go out and die with them. One of them, Edmund, his second-in-command, told Eric, the king required him to eventually become an ambassador and Dunstan's father Edwin had already given him instructions to look after him. Fortunately Dunstan had no ambitions to be a warrior. Poetry and history were what he really enjoyed. He was already writing about the King's life, concentrating on the wars and battles. He was leaving the piety to the monks. However, another one told Eric and Harald that his father's only worry was his lack of urgency to marry and provide the family with an heir. He was nearly thirty but his lack of a martial way of life, had put off most potential fathers in law, and he was always going somewhere for the king or studying. However, his high status as one of Athelstan's circle of friends had finally persuaded one to give his consent recently. The girl seemed keen also as she found him a clever man, both amusing and interesting. Most of her family thought her strange.

Dunstan was wondering whether he ought to volunteer his sword for this revenge raid but realised it was nearly a family matter when he looked at the blood connections. He volunteered his pen to write the history of it.

Grim bellowed with laughter. "For a Saxon you are a good fellow. Here are me and mine just wanting a bit of revenge and you will make us immortal. Write it well and make it scan well for the skalds to speak. Let people remember Grim the Miller suffered no treachery without he revenged it. Perhaps then they will remember not to trifle with honest men, not even with a humble miller."

"When were you ever just a miller and when were you humble? You were a pirate and a robber with my father," said Harald.

"Yes, but only when we were young and had no more sense. Money and goods were difficult to come by honestly in those days. Your father was the first of us to understand why we must change. Ivar's true father never did. We must all not only observe the law now but deal with lawbreakers. …….. and they are not a great distance from our homes either. It only took us just over a day and a night to walk back to Knaith carrying our wounded."

"Justice or not, revenge, if it is" said Harald, "I will help you, Grim, for the friendship you gave my father, but I would much rather see justice. There are clearly some men in that village who are thieves and some who are honest. We must separate them and their families. If we go around killing wantonly, it would be dishonourable. I think Dunstan should come with us as someone impartial to ensure the king knows we are not lawbreakers but men genuinely seeking justice."

Dunstan was quite relieved to be invited as he was intending to write about the deed. He was a little concerned that the people were some of the last remaining *Wealas* in the area and told everyone so. He observed the king saw himself as king of all peoples, as his grandfather had been……… and he expected to see justice done for them all. Dunstan felt that living in marshes was not the best place to make a living. The king thought that he should particularly care for the *wealas*. They had suffered much.

Grim grumbled and observed his grandfather had lived in the marshes of Denmark.

"Look what a pirate, he was," said Eric. "Nothing was safe on sea or land when he was about and you are only just a bit better. I can't think why Auntie Emma married you!"

"Well, I couldn't pass up the chance of her. She is so beautiful. She had land and stock also. Beautiful sisters to marry off to my friends………. and she could shoot a bow better than most men I know. I fell in love with her almost from the moment she nearly put an arrow through me for stealing her fish."

"There you go again," said Dunstan. "You were stealing fish off a poor hungry girl who was only defending herself."

"Don't you start, you grinning poet! Write my history and make her sound the most noble woman in the world or she'll be the death of all of us. She is good with a knife and an axe as well……… and I have taught her to use a sword."

"You haven't seen her throw a spear either. A miller's wife will tend to be a strong woman, lifting bags of flour. She can cast a spear farther than her husband and some say with greater accuracy," said Harald quietly.

"Who's said that," shouted Grim? "Is it Ivar? He's always sticking up for his mother."

"We should hold a contest. There's not too much to do till this war starts. It would be good practice. We could open the contest to Emma. She would probably take the prizes," said Harald.

Grim fumed and went off to talk to Orm who he claimed had a better view of life than any of them….except for Dunstan who wasn't bad for a Saxon.

"Dunstan, you'll get a share in the flour trade before you are much older," said Harald. "Already you have made a friend for life."

Dunstan began to think about this and what he should report to the king. Morale amongst his Danish allies was high despite the setbacks of a minor skirmish. All garrisons were in place. There was still a force left on the river. The king need not worry about his Danish allies in this fight…….. But should he learn to trust them afterwards?

CHAPTER 16

NORTH OF THE DON

Aylmer Hansson sat under a tree and looked out into the warm summer rain and the clouds over the northern hills. He wondered why all this water didn't fill the hole in his heart. It could rain twelve months, he thought and it would not fill that hole. He sat back and thought of the last year or so of his life and the pain he now felt.

It had all began so well. The wedding was held in Leicester in September. They spent a pleasant few days together with Helena's family before they set off to Gloucester, and then the happy times spent over the winter at Athelstan's court in Winchester. The joyful news of a baby came and how much pleasure it brought to everyone, especially the king, who said he would take the child for baptism and stand as a witness. Then the two tragedies of a premature and stillbirth and the death of the mother with childbed fever. "Oh, how I love you both" he called out to the wind blowing the rain up from Gloucester where they lay, to Yorkshire. "I can feel you so near."

For months now he had been a man in another world but one who knew he would never die until he had suffered more pain in this life. So he volunteered to the king to come to Yorkshire to find out what was happening north of The Don. Athelstan at first would not agree but Aylmer reminded him that this is what he was always going to do when the invasion came. Athelstan agreed at once, realising he had no choice but let him go. So here he was dressed like a local farmer offering to sell sheep to the invaders. Helena would not have recognised her handsome and normally tidy husband. He was dirty and looked ten years older. His beard was long and he had not washed for some time. He even stooped. Her loss was the cause of all this, not his attempts at disguise, however convincing. People from amongst the invaders, who saw him, had no thought of what he was before.

He had concluded a deal with one of the Northern Welsh lords and delivered forty sheep. The deal had made his name known and other commanders had approached him for animals. They had not realised the complexity of the arrangements he had made. Farmers in the hills had not wanted to sell to the invaders, but some of the king's gold to buy their silence and guarantees of innocence for the future, had brought them into the plot. He was only promising small numbers and the price was high, and they had to guarantee safe passage for him and a couple of shepherds. They thought he was really a farmer who was dealing with them on the basis he supported Anlaf for king in York. He persuaded the Welsh that once one or two farmers would sell, the rest would follow. This happened of its own accord once deals had been struck. No extra gold was necessary. He managed also to get two messages out to the king through some relatives of Dunstan, whose lands had been pillaged already by the invaders. Anyone suspected of being a supporter of Athelstan was in for a rough time.

Aylmer did wonder how long before he would be challenged for what he was doing and envy of the money he was getting. He'd left all his weapons and armour behind and had just the old *langseax*, a knife and a staff. On a visit to the northern allies' camp, a drunken Viking challenged him in front of a Scots chief to show what he could do with the *langseax*, and had already drawn his axe and was waving it at Aylmer and everyone else. Unlike his friend Dunstan, Aylmer had generally no qualms about killing a man, especially the enemy of his king. He felt it had no choice but to draw it quickly and despatch the man and take the consequences. It paid off. The man's companions all drunk themselves, laughed. The Scots officer said he understood he had to defend himself. Aylmer or Thorkil, as he called himself there, thanked him for his support. The heat went out of the situation but Aylmer decided not to be so forward in future. He even said he wouldn't come back with any more sheep as it was too dangerous to be challenged even in what appeared to be jest. The Viking commander asked him to bring more sheep and they would forget the incident as the man was not known for his bravery, except when drunk and no one would seek vengeance. The Scots asked him to stay to eat with them, and that was when he began to wonder at what he saw.

He noticed some young women carrying weapons. Aylmer was puzzled and forgot his grief a little, more interested in the phenomena than the women themselves. His Welsh was not too bad and so he inquired about them, as many of the Scots spoke that language and not Saxon. A Clan chief immediately picked up on his skill with the language and so he said his grandmother was one of the *wealas*. Many still lived around here, more than people thought, especially in the hills as the Saxons, and then the Danes, had taken the best land. The man then told him, they were Picts from the very far north and they believed the presence on the battlefield of these women, would bring them victory as it had done in past times. Only women who were from the nobility were allowed to fight and they also had to be virgins, or so it was said. Their men guarded them jealously and some of the women were good with their weapons. He was not the only one to have beaten a drunken Viking to drawing a sword or swinging an axe. One or two women had defended themselves more than adequately. The chief went on to say how the Church was very much against women on the battlefield and had declared God would not grant them victory if the vessels of sin, the descendants of Eve, were there to fight. He thought that was taking things a little too far.

Aylmer laughed genuinely at this thinking of his beautiful Helena. He could not imagine a scrap of sin in her, despite what her father had said to him when she had died. Only a wilful and vengeful god would have taken her from him and killed their child. The chief went on to say again he thought the Churchmen were talking rubbish and that they were going to need all the help they could get against Athelstan. He was personally worried they had been allowed to travel so far into Angleland without a battle or even a skirmish. King Constantine had done the same up north two years ago when the Saxons invaded. He could not understand why King Athelstan appeared to be making the same mistake of not fighting an invader. It had to be a trap. They were all in danger of starving and there was no sign of Athelstan's army coming to fight or large amounts of food being available.

Aylmer made no comment thinking this is how the king has planned it. They think he's not coming. Of course he is. The shock will be terrible when they meet our army. He came out of his shell a little and said.

"We farmers do not have too much to sell. It will soon be gone. We will have to think of next year's stock to breed or we all will starve."

A Viking and clearly one of Anlaf's men appeared and said in Gaelic. "They are King Anlaf's people; they cannot give everything just to die of starvation. He will be king of nowhere, the king of a wasteland, if everyone is dead."

Someone translated for him and Aylmer spoke warmly to the man in Welsh and said. "There is no law north of The Don now, we need a strong ruler to kill the outlaws and keep us all safe. We struggle all the time against thieves and murderers. A man's safety depends on how fast he can draw a knife or strike out with a staff. He cannot guarantee the safety of his wife and children. If King Anlaf can bring peace, people will support him, but he must not tax us unjustly."

"My name is Sitric Oslacsson, Thorkil," said the man in Saxon. "I'll take you to *Jarl* Anlaf."

Aylmer didn't pick him up on that, thinking he is testing me and he asked. "Why should a king need to speak to a farmer?"

"My *Jarl* is a man of the people. Come and meet him," said Sitric repeating himself.

"I am only a farmer and I can't see what he would want to know of me. You are certainly someone important and can take me to him. I shall have to speak honestly to him about how we see things around here."

"Speak as you find, my friend" said Sitric. "He's not far away, just over there, on the hill by those trees. That is his tent..... Come on! You've had your food."

Once they were away from the rest near some trees where no one was really close, out came the *langseax* and Sitric was the next of his line to die by a Saxon's blade, just as his father had done. He had been taken by surprise. No one saw the deed or moved towards them. Aylmer moved into the trees carrying the body still upright, and began to walk deeper into them. No one had seen him. No one followed or so he thought. Anlaf Godfricsson is in York, not here, he mused.

"The Welsh talked about it, Sitric," he said to the body, as he hid him in some brambles. "Since I arrived today they've complained about nothing else except his absence and the lack of food. They are real soldiers and complain all the time."

He walked for a while but was suddenly conscious of being watched. He walked on and turned back. A shadowy small figure appeared, walking carefully and quietly. One of those women, she guards this Sitric? Surely not! Aylmer grabbed her and held her throat. She muttered something in a language he could not comprehend.

"Speak Welsh" he said. "Or something we can all understand."

In Welsh far worse than his she said. "The seafarer was going to kill you."

"You're not very clever, even I knew that, but why should he want to kill a poor farmer like me?"

"You are not a farmer. You can't fool a Pictish princess, you Saxon dumpling. I heard you talking to the others."

"I fooled most of them it seems and I can fool you and I can kill you. You are my prisoner with a knife at your back... and why are you protecting a Viking?"

"I am not. His men are plotting against my kind. They are going to kill us or sell us into slavery to the Moors like they do with the Irish."

"I was thinking that you had all come here to kill us and steal our land and our sheep. Suddenly I find you are really stealing and selling each other. You are good to each other, especially the seafarers. They are the kindest of all."

"You are not clever" she said. "They want to use Yorkshire to take over the rest of the country."

"Oh, I am very clever. All the really smart people around here think I am a spy and so I had better go home to my farm."

"What about me?"

"You are coming so you don't bring them after me..... I don't want to kill you. Two people in a day are enough for a poor man. You can look after my sheep and cook. We could use another servant on the farm."

"You should stop pretending you are a farmer. I was brought up on a farm after my parents died. Then my family sent me to a nunnery, hoping they would rear me alive and we had to work on a farm there. You are not at all like a farmer."

"Girl, if you want to live, princess or not, you had best believe I am a farmer."

"Stop this, you are really frightening me. First the seafarers want to kill us and now you, people who are like us. Why can't you just let us go home?"

She burst into tears. Aylmer dragged her as far from the Scots' camp as he could and then deeper into the woods. It began to get dark and it was clear no one had followed, although he could hear that Sitric's body had been discovered. Time to move further on he thought and dragged her into a narrow valley with no paths. He tied her hands to her feet and hid her in some bushes. She made no sounds but a low weeping. About the middle of the night he wrapped her in his cloak and let her sleep. He sat and listened. No one came near.

About sunrise she was awake with eyes till full of tears. She was about to speak but he gagged her and tied her to a fallen branch.

"A farmer always carries a bit of rope. Always comes in handy," he said and walked away.

He returned mid morning and undid her gag.

"There's no one around here and no one to steal food from. We shall have to go hungry for a while. I have been back to your camp or as near as I dare.... It's chaos. That Sitric must have been someone important, just like he claimed. It's strange no one has followed us. We must have left a trail at the speed we moved. I was much more careful on the way back."

"For a farmer you are very concerned about what is happening."

"A farmer needs to get home and the short way is blocked by you invaders. We will have to go the long way round..... But not until I have had some sleep."

By the late afternoon Aylmer was awake. He looked at the girl who had fallen asleep again. He went over and untied her. She got up and squatted next to a tree.

"Don't Saxon women have bodily functions. You've kept me tied up all night and morning and I've dirtied my clothes, you oaf."

"Don't dare run off or you are dead," he said sternly, ignoring her insults. "You can tell me what's happening. Can't you speak any Saxon or Anglic?"

Quite proudly she said. "No, I have never met any Saxons or Angles until I came south with the army but I know my own language, and Gaelic, some Welsh and some Latin. A peasant like you would have only heard that mumbled at you in church. I only know some Welsh because the sisters spoke it when the abbess wasn't listening."

"Why aren't you carrying weapons like those other women from the north?"

"I haven't completed my training and initiation yet. The Scots don't let us carry them around all the time but soon it will make no difference. The camp is running out of food. We are going to move soon to invade the Saxons south of a river somewhere. I thought we were already in their land."

Aylmer smiled to himself. The king has worked out all this, well in advance. He needs nothing more from me. I just need to get home alive.

"I want to go home just like you" she said. "Can't you take me back to my people or let me go?"

"If I let you go around here, you'll die. If your so-called friends don't catch you, my countrymen will once the army has gone. King Constantine is not welcome here and nor anyone who has been brought with his army."

She cried some more. "I said to my friend Brollachan on the ship south that we would all die. The army is getting too hungry to fight. None of us have had a proper meal in weeks. The Scots and the Welsh keep the best for themselves while we steal and scavenge."

Aylmer smiled. "It will be dark in a while and we can move but first I have something to show you…………"

He pulled her towards a tree and took out of it a hare and some roots.

"……When no one can see the smoke we will have a fire."

"Perhaps you are a farmer after all. Do you have a wife and family" she said kindly?

"No, I have none now. They are dead" he said as his eyes filled with tears.

She stood looking at him not knowing what to do but weep.

"You are a kind man, I think. War makes beasts of us all. I do not think you want to harm me."

They both continued with their tears.

When the smoke couldn't be seen because of the dark, they moved on into some better cover to hide the flames. During the wait for the food they talked some more. She told him her name was Mairie, and the abbess had given that name to her when she was baptised. She could hardly remember what her parents had called her, and neither her uncles and brothers or their wives, would tell it to her, although she really saw little of them. She knew they were all distant relatives of King Constantine's family, the macAlpins, and she was the only girl in the family. She had run away with her friend Brollachan as she was tired of being starved and beaten in the convent, even though she was considered a royal hostage. The abbess was also talking to her brothers about getting her a husband, when she was not taking to convent life. She asked him about himself and he decided to tell her the truth, much against his better judgement. Both were in tears again and she put her arms around him this time.

Aylmer let the girl eat most of the baked hare and roots. She looked so tiny and scrawny. Tears always cured his hunger anyway, or so he had noticed. He had put out the fire when the meal was cooked and they ate in the dark. She fell asleep and he put her on top of the dead fire for warmth inside his cloak. Then he fell asleep.

About the middle of the night she woke him up.
"I can hear horses, Aylmer."
He listened carefully. "About four or five" he whispered. Then he heard voices at the top of the hill, all trying to talk quietly. They passed along the hilltop in conversation. He could hear it was the Northumbrian dialect when they stopped, and the man in command spoke.
"We're too late. That Saxon will be long gone from around here and why ever the Scots think he's taken that missing girl I cannot think. The Vikings have had her like they took the other two. They had better own up to it and give her back, or show the body. That Scottish witch is really mad this time as well. This one really is a child, she says."
"I can't think why they brought those women. Only a handful can fight. The rest are just decoration."
"It's their religion. They are not Christians like us."
"It won't do them any good in a battle."
They moved off then. Aylmer and Mairie moved across the track and the hillside. The trees were thinning out. He had not realised how near they were to the moorlands. They had better make some good speed, he thought but not move around in the day across all the open spaces in the hills. Someone would spot them and he could not tell friend from foe. When it became light they hid by a stream and Aylmer decided to have a bath and wash some of his clothes.
"If I don't have to be a farmer, I'm not going to smell like one" he said.
When he was washed Mairie had produced a little bag containing a short knife, scissors and needles and thread and insisted on cutting his hair and beard. How did I miss that bag? She had it well concealed, he thought.
"You don't look very old now, how old are you Aylmer, twenty five?"
He nodded and asked her age. He reminded her not to lie. Hiding the truth was what he did and she shouldn't follow his bad example.
"I don't know how old I am, Aylmer, probably seventeen or eighteen. I know I am old enough for children. I have bled every month for a long time and the abbess was wanting rid of me and my friend Brollachan. We caused trouble all the time for her.... I want to go somewhere safe. This place reminds me of the northern mountains which I'll never see again. I see now you have really been kind to me and told me the truth. You truly are a good

man. Your wife was very lucky to even be with you a short while. She could have got a man who doesn't miss her or mourn her baby. I cannot go back to the army. I know that, the first patrol I meet will kill me after they've raped me. Take me somewhere I can be safe."

"I will" he said. "Our king wants us all to be honourable men as he believes the Romans were when they ruled Britannia. I do not believe it was entirely true, but to want to do so is a noble intention and our king is not just the greatest warrior, he also has hopes for peace and justice."

Aylmer suddenly realised he had started to speak Latin when he talked about Athelstan.

Mairie started to smile. "You are not a farmer at all. Why did you pretend so much? You speak Latin very well. Did you learn it in a monastery?"

"I did in part but it was really from my friend's mother. Dunstan's mother is extraordinarily pious. I have never studied for the church, but I have been taught by it. They have books full of knowledge, which I know how to use. I shall have men to lead in the future but my father is still alive to lead them to this battle, while I work directly for the king. After the coming battle who knows what there will be to do……….Will you promise to stay here while I search for some food? Please don't run off."

"I will stay, Aylmer, I may even have a bath with you not there to watch. I'll have to have to wash my clothes as well. I told you I was tied up for so long I dirtied myself….. Find me something nice to eat and I'll forgive you."

When he was in search of food he began to think of Helena and what her father Earl Thurstan had said to him at her death. Then, for the first time he seemed to warm to Aylmer and speak kindly to him.

"My son, I did not want this marriage so soon, not because you are not a good man. The king I know holds you so very high in his regard, and I have always. I was concerned my daughter did not love you as a wife should love and respect her husband. She was so very taken by the position you have at the king's court and appeared to not be considering you. She did not of course know you personally very well before you married, but knew a lot of you from myself and her brothers. You have a very good future and are from a noble family. Descendants of the kings of Mercia have a great and noble ancestry. Our king has so many great hopes for you and I know you are of such a strong character, you will not disappoint him. I was worried you would be disappointed by my daughter, but this will not happen now she is buried with your child. Your love for her was there for all to see, except perhaps, for her."

Thurstan said no more. He was known by all for his few words and he shared Aylmer's tears for many hours.

Now some months later Aylmer reflected on this again. He thought to himself, I have met lots of women, but I only know a few of them very well and did never have feelings for any, the way I felt for Helena. Perhaps this is because I never decided to marry before. War forces decisions on people when you look broadly at its consequences. Two years ago I never considered this when invading the Scots and Welsh with the king's army. War was an adventure to me then. Now it is all pain and grief as it has been throughout time. Helena was my way to forget what I knew was real. Did I see her as my comfort in a cruel world? Poor Helena, I think I did, she knew nothing of what I have done, or am doing now. Oh, but how I loved her!

He found himself sat again crying and looking out into an abandoned farm. The trees were starting to grow back on the land which generations had struggled to clear. The king is right again, he thought. The Wasteland is returning as there is no strong government in these places. People have no desire to live and work here. They live in fear all the time. He carefully walked over to the hut. Abandoned for four or five years, he thought, and he picked up a hoe with a broken handle. The blade was still serviceable. I could use that. Nothing else remained of use. He looked around and dug up a few roots and found a couple of hares in the traps he had set the day before. He watched for a while before he moved out of the area.

There appeared no one about as he returned to Mairie. She was sat almost in the same spot he had left her but looking cleaner. She had washed some of her clothes also.

"Food" she said softly. "How do you do it, Aylmer? You always do what you say."

"I am pleased you agree with that, as I want to move out of here for somewhere safer. From the hilltop we can still see the camp you came from in the distance. I want to go somewhere we can have a fire for longer without someone seeing the blaze or smelling the smoke. We can have fire to keep us warm then. I am sure some rain is on the way.......... We need somewhere to shelter. "

"You wrapped me in your cloak last night and put me on the embers. You were cold yourself but you never complained. Don't you see me as your enemy?"

"I did not become a soldier to make war on women and children. I know they suffer greatly in war."

"My people have a long tradition of women warriors. Some of us still worship the Mhor Rioghain, the Great Goddess of life and death, the Great Queen. Her name is our battle cry. We are going to charge at you Saxons shouting that name and die for her."

"Little one, I think that would be certain to happen. The Welsh do not think you make good soldiers."

"Our men who follow us are….. Or they would be with full stomachs and better leaders."

"Mairie, you seem like a child sometimes to me, but when you speak of serious matters, you are clearer in your thoughts than many much older women I know………. I think it is because you lived in a convent as a child. I have met others who are the same. They have a childhood of only work, learning and prayer…………. But you cannot return to that life or to your own country…. Choose another name and make another life."

"How can I choose another name?"

"Very easily……How do you see yourself? What do you want to become? ….I see that you are small with dark hair. Although you are quite tall really for a woman, most people are small to me…….. but I do not know what you can be in this land. Only the future will show you. And what did your parents call you?"

"Aylmer, you must take me with you to your people. What will they see? The same as you, a small dark girl? A child like that would be called Kyra in my land."

"I like that name, Kyra it shall be, but let's move from here ……..or neither of us may have a future."

They moved on until it started to get dark and were further into the hills. Aylmer found another valley with some overhanging rocks. He built a fire under them when it was dark in a place enclosed to keep in the heat. He cut some branches which gave some cover just before the rain fell. After some food Kyra felt much happier and fell asleep for a while. Aylmer sat and watched the fire and the rain. She woke when the moon was up and the rain had stopped."

"You have done it again, Aylmer. You have wrapped me in your cloak while you sit and shiver."

"The fire has kept me warm."

"Aylmer, what are you going to do with me?"

This caught him off guard for a moment and suddenly he thought.

"Auntie Edith, she will take care of you. She did look after me for many years when I was studying. She does things like that. She's buried three husbands."

He fired out a few thoughts. Kyra looked puzzled. He went on.

"Edith lives in a collection of huts with her servants near Evesham. She was a one of the King's Aunt's ladies at her court, although Lady Ethelfreda has been dead for nearly twenty years. Because of three husbands she has a lot of land and rents. You'll get the best of care, but she is not conventional or religious. Monks and nuns keep clear of her. She often says she is looking forward to meeting the Devil to say how grateful she is for her three husbands. She keeps the only house I have known since mother died. Father moves around a lot with his second wife. My half brothers live with their mother's family or with her and father. Edith is my mother's sister not my father's."

"So, I would see you a lot."

Aylmer was a little startled by the way she said that and how she looked at him in the firelight.

"Poor Kyra, it is much too early for me to be looking for another wife and you look too young to be looking for a husband, even though you are not. Auntie Edith will be a mother to you for a while and we do not know about our futures. You will be safe. Edith taught me how to shoot a bow. She never travels without one...... The king's officers can never entirely keep the roads clear of outlaws. Lady Ethelfreda gave short shrift to outlaws and traitors when she ran Mercia for King Edward. Edith is so nearly like his aunt and I think it is the reason the king likes her. He was raised by his aunt also."

"I will be happy with her if you are there" said Kyra. "She sounds a very good lady."

"Ah, she is not, she gets drunk, is bad tempered and keeps a lover, just like a lot of men..... She will look after you for me. She will be your mother and life will never be quiet or boring. It was never for me. Sometimes I was glad to go to the monastery for a few days rest from auntie."

Kyra laughed and said "I think you are sending me there because you care for people. What will she think of me as a foreigner and from the enemy?.........."

Kyra took off her clothes at this point and in the firelight showed him the patterns on her body.

"…...These are signs of a Pictish Princess and of my dedication to the Great Queen. What will she think?"

"The old rascal will wonder why she never had any. We are descendants of the Mercian kings. Our family is similarly noble."

"Aylmer, I really want to be with you."

"I know, Kyra, but this cannot be for a while. You are so young and perhaps do not yet know your mind. You haven't seen much of life. We have known each other only two days and have been thrown together by war. Lets us at least decide to get to know each other much better, although I have to say I have spent more time with you than I did with Helena before we married."

He did not tell her what Thurstan had said nor how this had been on his mind for a while. Aylmer was a little disappointed that Helena might not have loved him the same way as he loved her, but they were two different people. She was interested in his knowledge, but never had any understanding of it. She could read and write a little, but that was all expected of a lady in her position. She felt she had made a good marriage to a man of rank. He was in love with a beautiful young woman and he decided he would be grateful for that. He felt that on reflection, there was something that may have been lacking in the relationship which would have only unravelled in the future. He looked at Kyra standing naked in front of him. She was starting to shiver.

"Put on your clothes and sit next to me, Kyra."

He put his cloak around her again and held her. When she had stopped shivering, he kissed her and held her tighter still. She started to cry and after a while she looked at him.

"Aylmer, I don't why I followed you out of that camp. I know I just need to escape. I had a feeling death was following me around and now I feel there is a life I can have. Don't be angry with me because I feel happy and have found a man I want. There have been lots of men around me all my life and none of them have been like you. They have been boastful and shallow. Worse still, they would have been uncaring of me and the other women in our country. Our country traditionally valued women but this changed with the coming of the Scots and the Christians. We have lost our position as the foundation of life in the land."

"Kyra, this land is no better. There are just people who remember how life should be lived when men and women choose to live together in a better way. I know the next time I marry; it must be more on a more equal basis. Rank is not the only matter to consider, nor is the beauty of the woman."

"You are a clever man and I believe you think you learnt it from Auntie Edith."

"I learnt much from her but tell me, can you read and write?"

"I had no choice but to learn in the convent. They thought I would eventually become a nun when I was put there. I was never expected to leave it and it was intended to be my prison. My family did not want me to come out and be a burden to them or run the risk of a claim on the land. If I married, they wanted it to be to someone without any power to have a claim on the titles or their part of the country."

"What else did you learn there?"

"Aylmer, I learnt it was no life for a woman........"

"Shhhh!... I can hear something" he said quietly. One thing he had begun to admire about the girl was how she could move quietly. She listened also. "Let's move very slowly, pick up everything."

They moved on to behind some more rocks where they could see their previous camp. Just as they reached them, the moon came from behind a cloud and lit up four figures, moving not very carefully up the valley. After a few moments all four went to the fire behind the rocks.

"I thought there was someone here. I could smell the smoke. He's heard us and moved."

"It's that Saxon farmer who killed the Viking."

"No, he'll have got home by now. This is someone who's deserted like us. He's thought we are looking for him. We ought to try and join forces to get home, he might know the way."

They found the wood Aylmer had gathered for the night and stoked up the fire so much it crackled.

"Someone will see that!"

"The army is moving on tomorrow, they won't bother about us. Let's get warm and get some sleep."

Aylmer and Kyra moved into some better cover away from them and talked.

"They are Angles" said Aylmer, "and deserters from the Scots Army. I could hear them speak. They are lost and should be going north as we go south. If we move too fast, they will hear us as we heard them. We'll let them go by us in the morning."

As soon as it was light one of the soldiers got up and walked to the top of the hill and ran back very quickly to his friends and shouted.

"There's smoke and a farm over the top of this hill. We could try it for food. There's sheep in a pen."

One soldier a bit better dressed than the others spoke out. "Not so fast, we don't know how many men are there. They could be well armed…. Beck you stay here and keep the fire going and put on the porridge as it's all we seem to have. The three of us will sneak up to the farm and see what we can beg or steal."

Aylmer listened to all this carefully and signalled Kyra to stay quiet and under cover. When the three had gone he moved over to where Beck was sat cooking porridge without a care in the world. Some moments later he returned to Kyra, the pot of porridge, a griddle, a cloak and a couple of blankets with a bag to carry everything. He also had a sword, a knife and a short spear.

"We'll be a bit warmer tonight and a bit better armed in case of trouble," he whispered. "Let us move on now to the south."

They followed the trees up the other side of the valley from the Angles, keeping off the moorland, and in the trees.

CHAPTER 17

THE JOURNEY SOUTH TO MERCIA

When Aylmer and Kyra had reached the top of the hill, they were able to see across to the farm. About a dozen people, men and women, armed with a variety of tools, and a spear or two, had the three Angles surrounded but could do little as they were behind their shields. They were trying desperately to extract themselves from the farmers. One man, standing aside waiting his chance, had a bow and a handful of arrows.

"We must move quickly away from here, little Kyra. The cloak is for you, although it's a bit long. Take this knife…… I don't think you are planning to harm me. I'll carry the rest. We'll eat the porridge as we go."

Kyra didn't dare ask what had happened to the man in the valley.

They made the best pace they could across the moorland, keeping off the horizons and stopping for the occasional look around. Aylmer thought Kyra looked weak after a long period of near-starvation and didn't want to rush her, although she didn't complain. The rain was holding off and but there was still a lot of low cloud hanging low over the hills, giving them some cover as they made their way. He was worried about the lack of food. He saw nothing he could catch and while they did have lots of blackberries and bilberries, there was little else of substance. As the day wore on and was drawing to a close, he spotted a flock of sheep. Strange there are no shepherds, he thought. They must be hiding.

As they moved around the flock, a handful of people appeared and collected up as many of the sheep as they could. Aylmer prayed; please leave me just a little one. He signalled Kyra to hide and he followed the herd. A few younger animals, missed by the shepherds were following and he helped himself to just a small one, hoping they wouldn't miss it. He returned to a beaming Kyra.

"A sheltered place and some dry wood is what we need to find now," he said with a smile.

"It's the first time I have seen you properly smile," said Kyra…. "By the way, I know you don't like killing people either, Aylmer."

They moved on in silence until they came to a pool. Aylmer butchered the lamb, washed it and buried the uneatable remains while Kyra collected wood. They moved on and it was nearly dark before Aylmer found somewhere he thought safe, by a stream with a waterfall. They had moved nearly into a wooded valley.

"The falling water will hide any noise we make," he said.

Kyra had said very little all day and was looking tired. She looked a lot better when she had eaten some food.

"Kyra, you look like you have not eaten well in months."

"Not since I left the north. I was seasick for most of the journey and there was very little to eat on the ship. There was not too much when we landed but I have felt a lot better over the last two days, and I have had more sleep. The camp was always noisy and I never felt safe there."

"You are still like a child, and you need regular food and sleep."

She looked at him fiercely.

"No, I am not a child. I told you, I bleed like a woman, I feel what a woman feels and I am sure they had someone to marry me. I was brought south to do what a woman of my rank must do in a war…….. And don't you understand how I feel about you?"

"Yes, I do and I have thought about it all day, as we have walked over these hills. Would you have me forget my wife and child so soon?"

"No, you will not forget them. No one ever forgets anyone they truly love but they can never come back to you. I am here, wanting you so desperately and I don't know how I can hold on to you. You'll leave me with your mad aunt and forget me, because you see me as a child……….I'm a woman whatever age I am, and women like me marry and have children all over this island.... Most don't even bother marrying in the way that you and your wife were married. Only rich and powerful ones marry as you did. She brought you land, I think..... Until recently a woman like me would have brought a man a small kingdom in the north. He might have been ruler of the people but the land would have been mine to pass to my daughter."

"Kyra, I have said before you speak like a woman and not a child, and today is no different. You should understand I am a man who is concerned about you. This war seems to have brought us together in the worst of circumstances. Only our meeting seems to have been good to me so far. Since my wife died I have had much to resolve in my mind. Her father spoke to me after her death, saying he did not believe she truly loved me, just my position in the king's army, the country and as the heir to my father. He hoped she would love me better when she knew me better. I think he was trying to tell me, he did not believe that had happened, not even after all the time we were together. Earl Thurstan is a good man who always speaks honestly, I have always known that, and he never concealed his opposition to the marriage taking place until the war was over. I think perhaps then it may never have done so. King Athelstan knew this when he hurried it along. He wanted to see me happy and settled. The marriage was also a political one to join two families...... None of this eases the pain I feel."

"Aylmer, I think it is me who can ease your pain. We are both tired out now, let us talk again in the morning. We shall at least have a warmer night and I hope those Angles didn't have too many lice....... You need to think a little more."

She rolled herself into her new cloak and a blanket and was asleep very quickly, leaving Aylmer to watch the fire for a while.

The sun was up a long time when Kyra finally woke. The smell of more lamb for breakfast filled her head. Aylmer was keeping it warm in the embers.

"This is a good spot but we'll move out for the day and come back at night. We both need a day's rest before we start out for the border. I think I know where I am. We can head directly south and make contact with any of the forts at Sheffield, Brunanburgh or Wincobank, or with some friends I have who farm near to them."

"Brunanburgh, I heard the men in the camp talk about Brunanburgh. They want us to fight the battle there." She yawned and snuggled down in her cloak and blanket, thinking to herself, this is the warmest I have been all the summer.

The king is correct again thought Aylmer. This war goes according to his plan. If only I could get to him to confirm it. He won't have moved north yet and we won't get there by rushing. He had slept briefly but well. Then he had gone up to the hill top and seen the camp fires to the east. They have moved he thought. They have moved a stage nearer. We shall have to be careful. They will have patrols out along the border. They will, if they are smart, anyway.

"Kyra, it's not safe here any longer in the daytime." He said to her as she woke.

She stood up and packed her cloak and blanket. They ate and then moved to somewhere higher where they had a better view around. They could see the smoke from the camp fires.

"That army is so large," said Kyra. "It doesn't need to hide. I think King Constantine wants your king to attack him."

Hmmm! I think he will not be disappointed, thought Aylmer. It's perhaps as well I am not the only person who has been watching this army. I am sure the king is well supplied with information on its movements.

They sat quietly for some hours and had some cold meat at midday.

"Aylmer, I don't think I have ever eaten as much lamb in one day and it tastes so nice. I suppose we shall be eating it tonight as well."

"I left some baking under embers of the fire. It will be done nicely if it is safe to return. There seems no one around here. That army would scare anyone from these hills. What I don't understand is why no one from it is foraging."

"What is there to eat around here, Aylmer? It's all in the valleys over there. King Constantine did bring some food from York as well, although we saw little of it. Look......some riders!"

Across a near hilltop were several horsemen on a track they had crossed over the day before. Aylmer had said to Kyra he thought it was the one to Manchester. The men had come from that direction. They were heading to where the camp had been for the last few days, not where it was now even though the riders stopped briefly and looked in its direction. Aylmer thought, that's why they don't come here, their riders pass it all the time. They know everyone has left. He began to feel a little safer. But he thought I am going to have to start concentrating on what's around me and not little lovely Kyra. I should have spotted those men first. He realised he spent the last hours looking at her, but trying not to let her know it.

When the riders had gone they moved just in case they had been spotted and went down into the edge of the next valley. He foraged for some roots and she collected up some dry wood. They found a sunny spot by the stream. The late summer sun was warm and Kyra fell asleep. She woke up to find Aylmer having a wash in a pool. Now or never she thought, and took off her clothes and leapt in with him.

To her surprise he took her hand and then held her to him. She kissed him and told him it was alright. She'd make everything better for him and take some of the pain away. They lay together in the water as she washed herself. They got out of the pool when she started to shiver, and then she lay on her back in the sun.

"Aylmer, I'm all yours, come to me now or whenever you want. Don't be in pain when I can take it away. Come and love me but you'll have to show me what to do."

She put her arms around him and held him. He just kissed and kissed her, every bit he could possibly find which he could hold still as she moved around him. He entered her as she screamed in pain but much to the relief of both of them. A mix of pain and passion caused her to just lie there clinging to him as he moved inside her. When it was over for both of them, they just lay there for a while.

"Oh Aylmer, I really needed you and you needed me. I felt the pain leaving you. You can have me as often as you want, if you are just so kind to me. I've been wanting you all day. I have never had such feelings, I've found most men repulsive."

Suddenly Aylmer looked at her differently. He noticed the long hair, larger breasts as she leaned forward to him and a different look on her face. She didn't look a child any more to him. He took hold of her again as they made love in the sunshine, much more gently for both of them this time.

When it was over she looked at him and said, "I'm really sore but I enjoyed it all the time."

He looked at the blood on her legs and lifted her back into the stream to gently wash it off.

"Aylmer, we must remember this place. If we have a child after today, we must bring it here. I know I am in my most fertile time. We women in the north learn about these things, usually so we can avoid having babies. Even the unmarried are taught this…… but I want to have your baby. I can never go home now. I have to make my way in this land. Even if you don't want me, your family may not turn away your child and its mother."

"Indeed they would not and nor would I. Just do not ask me to say words of love I cannot be sure of meaning."

He kissed her again and wrapped her in her cloak. She fell asleep.

It was evening when she woke. Aylmer was dressed and ready to move. She dressed and off they went. Aylmer went off and dug up the baked lamb and they moved to another place nearby to eat it. They slept in each other's arms that night although Aylmer woke up before dawn as he usually did and listened, more voices. He woke Kyra very quietly and they listened.

"Whoever they were, they were here last night and gone today. They haven't come back to spy on us," someone said loudly in Welsh.

"It's got to be the Saxons spying, all the locals have moved out. There are two of them, one is a boy. Look at the small boot marks."

There were ten of them and they went off down into the valley. Aylmer looked at Kyra. "Welsh" he said. "They are patrolling. We will move a bit deeper into the hills once it is safe to move."

About mid morning they moved on and walked all day, eating more of the lamb.

Kyra said with a laugh. "Do you always eat so well out spying for your king?"

"No, I don't" Aylmer replied with an almost straight face, "and I don't get anyone to sleep with at night. I miss eating cheese when I have to live like this. People who help me always have cheese waiting for me when I have been away. I always take some when I travel."

"I shall have to remember that."

Speaking of memory, thought Aylmer, this girl will be the death of us both if I don't keep a better watch.

They walked on until it was early evening and Aylmer whispered to her.

"Over this valley on the next hilltop is a farm where I have stayed many times but we must approach it carefully if there are soldiers massing on the border. My friends may have been forced to abandon it. They walked on as the sun sank a little lower and they sat watching the farmstead. There were noises inside it but Aylmer couldn't make out what it was. He suddenly became aware of someone near to them and he drew his seax.

"Lord Aylmer, its Wilfred."

"What's happening, lad" he said to a boy of about fourteen or fifteen who appeared out of some bushes very quietly and crawled up to his side to look at the farm?

"Osbert, Ecbert and I are left to watch the farm. Everyone else has moved deeper into the hills to Bradfield. The hill tops around the Don are full of Vikings. They came over the hills, but not without warning. They make a lot of noise, do Vikings. They never learnt their warcraft from you. I have remembered everything you taught me."

"Well, you came up on us very quietly and if I had known that everyone was at Bradfield, I would have gone straight there. We almost passed it, this morning."

"There are about two score Vikings and Irish in the farm. They moved in just after midday and are settling down for the night. Ecbert went to count them. I have taught him all you taught me."

The two other boys had appeared quietly, nearly out of nowhere. Aylmer instantly recognised lanky Ecbert.

"Ecbert, what else were they doing," asked Aylmer?

"They were wrecking everything as if searching for wealth we don't have" said Ecbert rather dryly. "We had time to move everything out ...and our neighbours as well."

"We are watching the main track and if they move down it, we shall follow them and report back to Grandad by the backways," chipped in Osbert. "There are more of us around between here and Bradfield."

The three of them looked at Kyra without any finding the courage to ask about her.

"This is Kyra. She doesn't speak our language," said Aylmer, thinking what else he could say. "She's from the far north and helped me escape the Vikings. She can speak Welsh if you have learnt any."

None of them admitted they had and looked disappointed.

"Lads, I need to look what's happening on the Don near the forts" said Aylmer.

"We can tell you," said Ecbert. "The invaders are camped the full length of the valley. Their numbers increase all the time. Some days ago I carried a message of yours to the fort commander at Wincobank to pass on to the king. It's not safe to go near it now. We watched the lot over there at the farm walk up the hill. They are from the soldiers camped outside. They haven't taken Wincobank or Sheffield and I don't even think they have tried yet. They are massing around Brunanburgh. We can take you for a look at Wincobank if you want."

Aylmer agreed and all five of them moved to a hill Wilfred had indicated to the south of the farm. From the camp fire smoke, he realised it would not be safe to pass in daylight and not without problems at night. The track to the fort passed east of the hill and ten horsemen suddenly came up it at speed and rode up to the farm. There was a great commotion for some time. Then they all dismounted and went inside the enclosure, taking their horses with them. A couple of extra fires were lit as they all settled down for the night. He thought they have got themselves a nice little fort as an outpost. The farm is quite defensible. Old Oswulf knew what he was doing when he put the place together and there's not a lot of chance to sneak up to it. He looked at the whole area for a while as it began to get dark.

"We have moved our camp every night just as you taught me," Wilfred whispered. "These two think it is daft but Grandad put me in charge, so they have to obey me."

"Where do we stay tonight then," asked Aylmer?

"A little hollow, just over that hill to the west! It could be safe to have a fire and cook there."

Off they went and Aylmer produced the last of the cooked lamb for warming up and the lads had some bread and cheese left to Aylmer's great joy. They had one person watching in shifts all night and put out the fire.

In the morning they moved out to look at the farm just in time to watch the Vikings noisily split up in to two groups. All but one of the horsemen and all but a handful of the infantry marched off to the north. The remainder went back inside the farm except for the horseman. He was obviously going back to the enemy watching Wincobank.

"Quick, down to the track, if he goes that way we have him, string your bows, my lads," said Aylmer.

It was almost too easy. The rider just walked his horse along and Wilfred shot him as he passed by. He fell off the horse without a sound. Kyra ran over and captured it. The lads moved the body and removed the weapons.

The sword is yours, Wilfred. I have seen you practice with your grandfather's. Kyra, can you use the bow? Ecbert, the knife is better than the one you carry and the jacket will fit you. Osbert, the cloak will keep you much warmer at night this winter. Is everyone happy with the spoils?"

They all nodded except for Kyra who didn't understand. Aylmer had not used a language she spoke, so he asked her again in Latin. She nodded.

Back in cover Aylmer asked the four of them how they felt about an attack on the farm. They could probably crawl up to it by way of the ditch Ecbert had used, if the occupants weren't watching. He would walk up to the gate with the Viking's shield when they were in position and get them to come out. The occupants all seemed to be the Irish who Anlaf had recruited with a couple of his own men mixed in. He was going to use Kyra as bait if she would agree. Once they were out, the boys were to fire at them, and at the same time he would pass Kyra the bow. Ecbert thought they could get near to the farm if necessary and could get a decent shot at the front gate quite easily. To add to the effect why didn't he lead Kyra on the horse? They agreed on the plan and Kyra said she would ride the horse over any of the Vikings who ran from the fight so they didn't escape.

Aylmer and Kyra watched as the boys got in place and waited. They walked up slowly and Aylmer called out to the farm in something resembling Norse. Five men ran out one at a time surprised to see someone with a woman. The boys on Wilfred's instruction shot the last three immediately, Aylmer killed the first with the spear. The last one ran only to be shot by Ecbert who also ran forward and finished off the two wounded. Wilfred in the meantime was the first to enter the farm and looked around.

"We've missed one" he called out. "There's another one in here, I know it."

Kyra dismounted and undid the girth on the horse and then gave Aylmer a knowing look. She moved away from the animal and took Aylmer to one side.

"I didn't understand. Did he say there's another? I think so too. Watch if he tries to ride off."

After a few moments a man ran out of the barn and tried to mount the horse by grabbing the saddle and it fell on the ground. Wilfred was instantly between him and the gate with his new sword in hand. The man drew his but Kyra had already picked up a throwing axe, a *francisca*, and threw it at the man, killing him instantly.

"The boy didn't realise he was a Fianna. You call them berserkers. He would have killed Wilfred. All these three are too brave for their own good....... Aylmer, don't lead them to their deaths. The ones they killed were just farmers like themselves."

She had spoken in Welsh not Latin and Ecbert appeared to know what she had said.

"You can understand me" she screamed at him. "You've been pretending you can't speak anything but Saxon."

"These are dangerous times. You have to be sure of people before you take them into your kith and kin," Ecbert said firmly. You've come south with people trying to kill us. Lord Aylmer might trust you but we can make up our own minds. In these borderlands you have to be careful. You saved Wilfred's life and he is my friend........ I shall be your friend for that. You are correct to say we are just farmers who know a bit about fighting. Enough we hope to stay alive and grow old."

"Ecbert, you have lots of talents we do not know", Aylmer observed quietly. "And I know where you learnt your Welsh. I know where your mother was born, and not far from mine as it happens. I should have suspected."

Aylmer reflected. I am beginning to overlook and forget things. What's this girl doing to me? Surely she isn't on my mind so much.

Ecbert looked pensive. "We should collect up these weapons and take them to Bradfield by the backways. When those Vikings get there, our people will need them... and us to fight with them."

Osbert who really was still just a boy said, if they put them on the horse, he would ride with them and tell the people they were coming. Aylmer jumped into action.

"Collect everything, make bundles. Ecbert, can you ride? The rest of us will follow them down the track. Can you come back then with a couple more men or boys with bows? Fit people who can run away once we have attacked."

Ecbert was about to say, send Osbert, I want to stay and fight, when he guessed Aylmer's plan. He packed the horse and was gone saying he would meet them later down the track. Wilfred held him up long enough to say, don't wind the horse.

"He'll be gone to about the middle or late into the afternoon," said Wilfred. "By that time we should have caught up with the enemy. They won't move too fast as they don't exactly know where they are going except they will be following the track. We have left a few surprises for them on the way. Grandad expected to be followed and knew he couldn't hide the passage of so many people.

"We had better be careful that we don't walk into one of Oswulf's traps. I have seen him in a fight when I was much younger. One or two Danes regretted crossing your grandfather's path in the days of King Edward. He takes no prisoners."

Taking what food and equipment they wanted from the camp and hiding the rest they moved out leaving the bodies where they fell as a warning. They walked nearly in silence until Wilfred asked Aylmer about Kyra.

"She can fight like a man" he said. "Where and how did she learn?"

"I am not sure. I have not seen her kill anyone until today, even when we came across other enemy, but she has never had any weapons till now.

She followed me as I escaped the enemy's camp, and I took her prisoner as I didn't want to kill her. One of the Viking commanders had me identified as a spy and was going to kill me….. But I killed him first. She watched me hide the body."

"I am grateful she killed the Irish warrior. He was better than me but I thought if I held him up, one of you had a chance with an arrow in his back. His shield was facing me until he dropped it. Hold on to your shield is what Grandad Oswulf always says. If all else fails you can hit someone with it."

"In this next fight we need no shields. We are going to shoot and run away before they get too close. Make them frightened to turn their backs."

"Ecbert said she told you not to get us killed."

"He's a mystery, your friend Ecbert."

"He is to all of us but our mothers are friends. He is also brave."

CHAPTER 18

THE WAY TO BRADFIELD

As they walked cautiously along the track, they came across a couple of dead horses peppered with arrows. *Oswulf doesn't mean anyone to escape whatever trap he has prepared*, thought Aylmer. *I hope he's taken account of numbers but he'll know how many by now.*

Later in the afternoon they heard noises ahead and hid in the trees. Sometime after, Ecbert appeared on a horse, pursued by a couple of Vikings. Aylmer let him ride by and leapt out to hit the first horse across the head with a spear. It threw the rider nearly at Wilfred's feet and he had a chance with his new sword. The other rider turned his horse in time to avoid the same fate as his companion. Kyra shot at him, bringing him off.

"Hide the bodies, grab the horses and the weapons in case there are more," ordered Aylmer.

Ecbert returned. "Oswulf told me to draw them off. A few too many for us but we have killed three and wounded one. We ran away at that but they followed for a while, until I diverted them."

"Oswulf is trying to hold them off with boys like you?" Aylmer stumbled with his words.

Wilfred looked sheepish and said. "Most of the fighting men are in the forts. At Bradfield we have the young, the old, women and children."

Aylmer explained this to Kyra. She looked stern for a moment and asked in Welsh how many of the Vikings were left to fight? Ecbert tried to count but the numbers he couldn't tally.

"Thirty seven and one wounded........They only have five horses left," said Osbert in full possession of the facts. "We haven't lost anyone yet and won't if we run away all the time."

"For twelve, he's clever" said Wilfred. "I want to find Grandad. He's too old to wander the woods by himself looking for Vikings. He needs me with him now Dad's died."

They walked carefully on leading the horses. Oswulf appeared as if from nowhere with four other boys and looked at Aylmer as he grabbed him warmly.

"The Valkyries haven't taken you yet, you old hero," Aylmer whispered.

"My boy, they have not taken you either, but before these next days come to an end, we may have to offer them the chance."

"Then let us do so and show these lads how to fight. Tell me what is happening at Bradfield."

Oswulf explained that he and his neighbours had moved all their stock and families there, thinking they would be safe after a mixed army of Northmen, Irish and some Cumbrians had arrived near Wincobank. They had only expected enemy from the direction of York. An enemy, which would not come too far out of the valleys or so they thought. They decided to move at last moment and had the enclosure at their summer pasture defended by old men and boys but with few good weapons until Aylmer had sent some. They only had spears, knifes and bows and four swords until then. All the best had gone with the fighting men to the forts. At the end of it all he said.

"We can't hold them off forever and next time they will expect us."

"Why don't we follow them up to the gates at Bradfield and then have them trapped. If we can get rid of their horses they will have to run after us after every attack. Then we will just run away and return when they give up" suggested Aylmer cautiously.

"Some trap when we are the bait all the time" said Ecbert.

"Best sort" said Oswulf. "You boys have no experience of war and its risks. Attack and run. We have no armour like the Vikings. They'll send the Irish after us as they can run faster and they don't have much in the way of armour. It was three Irish we killed. They had no shields either. What's the girl going to do while we do all this? Watch the horses."

Aylmer translated for Kyra who became angry and said. "Tell him I have killed two men today and he need not worry about me. Without this dress I can run, and I shall remove it for the battle. We can tie up the horses or let them run loose."

A fifth boy appeared and said the Vikings were making a camp for the night but had sent some men up the track in this direction, about ten in number, five on horses and all moving slowly. Ecbert took the two bodies and the three horses some distance away into the woods. They all hid and watched as the ten men, all well armed and armoured Vikings, came and followed the tracks of the horses. Ecbert had by now taken all three horses deeper into the woods and Oswulf signalled one of the boys to go after him to move them further. The men stopped where the fight had been to look at the traces of blood and where the tracks went.

"Only three horses and riders went that way, they must have followed the boy."

"Whose blood is all this then, his or Magnus' and Erik's? Something is not right here."

"Simple, they caught him, he got away wounded and they followed. Let's follow them."

"Do you think we are all crazy just wandering into this forest? If they had caught him they would be back by now. They were stupid to chase him if they hadn't. He's led them into a trap and we are probably in it now. We had one with those archers back there."

"They ran off fast enough when we chased them."

"After they killed three of the Irish!"

"We are going back to camp and as I am in charge, we are doing this," said one of the horsemen, "before anything else happens. Our comrades are dead or lost. These woods will be full of Saxons."

A general mutter of agreement came from the soldiers but as they turned for home and relaxed their guard, three flights of arrows came their way. Then nothing, as their attackers fled into the forest.

"Stop," shouted the officer as four men ran off the track, "behind shields!" He looked at two men dead and two wounded. Four horses had arrows in them and were trying to run off in pain. Then something awful came into his head. Some of the arrows were ones used by the Irish they had left behind. When all was clear and quiet, he collected some to take back to camp.

He led his men quickly down the track, thinking we are being followed by Saxons who have attacked the farm, killed the Irish and taken the weapons. They couldn't be warriors or they would have attacked openly and finished the job. It's just the farmers. We'll be safe if we stick together. Back at the camp, Brand Collsson, the commander was disappointed and grumbled at him, but doubled the night guard just in case. The Irish became irritable when they realised their comrades may be dead and that didn't make Brand any happier.

Aylmer thought it would be more dangerous than it was worth for another attack so they all withdrew to a safer place where Oswulf had food hidden. He and Aylmer talked long into the night and at first light he left for Bradfield with details of the plan.

Kyra would not go with him, despite Aylmer pleading with her to go somewhere safe.

"You said you had not completed your training as a warrior," he reminded her.

"I am trained as a warrior but not as a priestess. That is why I don't have all the markings. I have not enjoyed killing today but I will do it to protect you, and to prove to your people what I can do. And now I do not think the Great Queen will want me to die as I am not a virgin. Besides what is safe with thirty Seafarers trying to break down the doors?"

Aylmer gave up and issued his orders to the boys.

"We move quickly all the time. Hit and run. All our food and gear we hide and go back for. Wilfred knows where we can make a camp near the farmstead. When they are outside it, half of us attack, the other half covers the retreat, first half run on, stop and cover the second half's retreat until the enemy give up. They can't come at us with too many horses any more but if we have to scatter, come together where Wilfred takes us. Wilfred, your four will shoot first. Ecbert, Osbert, Kyra and Edwin will be with me, the rest with you and you are in charge. No heroics, three flights and run, just like we did with Oswulf.... Ecbert take care of Osbert and Edwin. I have a feeling Kyra will do what she likes."

"We all think that" said Ecbert with a laugh for once.

Aylmer was impressed by Wilfred's hideaway. Not easy to find unless he took you there. They left the horses in another hollow nearby and got ready. Kyra, as she said, removed her dress. Aylmer suggested she cut it shorter but she refused saying it was the only one she had and didn't want to spoil it for wearing afterwards. It had come all the way from the north with her. The boys didn't know which way to look even though they all had sisters. He realised again that she was quite tall for a woman when he saw her pick up a shield and an axe. Her sword didn't trail on the floor and she was taller than all the boys except for Wilfred and Ecbert.

"Can you run with the shield" asked Aylmer?

"I am leaving it to pick up as we move back, in case we have to stand and fight" came her reply.

They watched the farm from the cover of the woods and watched as the Northmen and Irish came up the hill. They had the wounded stumbling behind and they sat down as the rest looked at the defences and the men behind them. Oswulf as always, had done well in the time he had. His defenders now had all the weapons from the last encounter and were waving the shields at the Vikings which had previously been their comrades.

Brand Collsson looked at the gate and ordered his men to form into a square with shields to the sides and above. Clever, thought Aylmer. This is a defence against our arrows. We shall have to try something else. Then he realised Kyra had gone. He watched as she crept up on the wounded and killed them all. Collsson saw all this and so did his men. The last line broke off and ran toward her, despite his orders to maintain ranks. She stood her ground and some more of the Irish ran to help their comrades. The square broke up for a moment and so everyone shot at it from both the farm and Aylmer's band. Aylmer and the boys ran nearer and shot more arrows, as Oswulf and ten of his old men and boys came out of the farm. The close range and lack of armour took its toll on the Irish and even some of the Northmen were wounded. Collsson got his men into a circle as more people came out of the farm with forks and billhooks, both men and women. A stalemate was reached with the Vikings being unable to get out, despite being better armed and the Saxons unable to get in, despite having the larger numbers.

Not all the Vikings had made it into the circle due to wounds and Kyra had gone around and killed most of them herself. The cost had been heavy for the Saxons also. Oswulf had got everyone with bows on the outside waiting for the Vikings to break and run. They were starting to move carefully away from the farm. An attempt to rush them had resulted in two Saxons being killed but the resulting arrows had killed three of the Northerners.

Kyra ran up to Aylmer and shouted "drive oxen at them."

He shouted to the women to get them out of the field and they drove them between the two rows of Saxons at their enemy. Kyra was following behind to press home the attack. She had given her bow to one of the boys from the farm and he was following her with the women who were prodding the oxen.

The charge had the desired effect to break up the wall of shields, despite the oxen being prodded from the front with spears. They eventually ran through the shields crazed with pain, trampling some men on the way. The constant arrows and numbers of attackers took its toll on the Vikings who became fewer and fewer. Oswulf's old warriors did their best but gradually they were worn down and had to rest. Another stalemate was reached.

Wilfred and Ecbert had gone to fetch the horses and had found where the Vikings had hidden their last horse and two other wounded ones.

"We can do the same with horses" they shouted and drove them at the Vikings. The horses ran around them and not at them. The shields didn't break but the men behind them were becoming more uncomfortable.

"Keep the horses running" shouted Oswulf. "Everyone stand firm!"

He got the boys and girls to fetch a cart which was loaded with hay. They pushed it up a slope, lit the hay and steered to the shield circle. No one moved until it hit them.

"Charge" shouted Oswulf and everyone did as the circle broke.

The Vikings did what they were good at in hand to hand fighting and despite numbers they killed more of the Saxons, both men and women, but were eventually split up and none surrendered. Aylmer was in the thick of the fighting acting as if he knew nothing could kill him now. Kyra had brought her shield and was running with it at any of the Irish or Viking to knock them over for the others to stab.

When it was nearly over, only Brand Collsson and two more were left back to back standing in and amongst dead friend and foe. The Saxon wounded had been taken away.

"We had best all die here, dear friends," he said to his men, "or we shall only hear folk say we were defeated by a bunch of farmers, women and children. There is no honour on this battlefield and no escape. We have killed too many of their kith and kin to expect to walk away with mercy."

All this had become too much for Kyra. "Follow me, Ecbert and when I throw this axe and one raises his shield, shoot under it quickly and have an arrow to follow."

"I wondered why you have carried that axe all morning and not used it. You were saving it for now. You are in luck, as I have only two arrows left," and he laughed.

Kyra screamed and ran out of the outer circle and threw the axe to fall from above on to the men. As they raised their shields, Ecbert fired his two arrows and wounded two Vikings in the legs. Without prompting four women followed up the arrows and they all crashed into the men. Kyra ran into Collsson's back with her shield and pushed him over with more surprise then weight. A girl about her age knocked off his helmet with an adze and another stabbed him through his mail.

"Farmers, I knew they would be my death from the day I set foot in Ireland," he said as Ecbert finished him off with a sword.

"I shall never look at girls again without a sense of fear," said Ecbert. He looked at the two girls who had wounded Collsson. "Audrey, Cristina, you always seemed so quiet."

He walked away and they followed him in tears as they looked around at the dead and wounded.

An older lady walked out of the enclosure and called to everyone.

"Take all the children and young people away from this."

Aylmer who was wounded with a number of sword cuts limped up to her.

"My son," she said! "I knew you would not desert us when we needed you."

"Mother Hilda, it is good to see you whenever we meet," he replied as he hugged her. "Perhaps better times may come our way."

"I do not think so but we do not forget each other," she said

Kyra ran up to him in tears and Hilda held them both.

"Oswulf has told me about this young lady warrior. I did not believe him until now. His mind has been known to drift of late. Mine has also been wandering... But all is well now you are here."

They spent the rest of the afternoon collecting what was lying around after the fight and burying the dead of both sides. The wounded were in Hilda's care with help from the other women. Seven of the men and four boys had been killed and five wounded. Most distressing to Hilda was the death of three women and two girls.

"We are too used to peace" she said to the other women. "If I think about it deeply, there would have been many more dead, had we not defended ourselves. They would have killed more of us and taken our children for slaves. Since King Alfred's time when I was born, there has been safety for us in these hills and valleys. All peoples have lived in peace. This was not so for my grandmother."

Kyra was relatively unscathed by the fight as she had kept on the move, remembering all she had been taught. All the young women had discovered

Ecbert could speak Welsh and had taken him to her to ask about where she was from and why she was fighting. She explained she had been the only sister of a Pictish noble family but when her mother died she was put in a convent to prevent her marrying. Her older brothers were looking to find her an inconsequential husband who could have no claim on the land. Noble women could chose husbands who could then become the *Clan* leader but only if he was equally noble. Now men just passed the titles to their sons. There had been a history of women fighting, but a bishop from the Scots, Adomnan, and got everyone to agree not to do it. The Scots took over after that, but there were still some who kept to the old ways, and they were a refuge for her when she ran away from the convent. She had learnt to fight and was becoming a priestess of the Great Queen, Mhor Rioghain, who controls life and death. She was going to fight, and most likely die, with her warriors on the battlefield but had been fearful of the treachery of the Scots and the Vikings. They were going to have a king in York but sell us as slaves when the battle was over. This is what she suspected.

All the girls thought this was exciting and wanted her to teach them how to fight properly. Ecbert listened intently to all this and with wisdom beyond his years, said, he thought they would have lost today if the women had not come to support the men. He thought that they might have to fight again to defend the farm, and he would train them. They disagreed and wanted Kyra to be their leader. He went off in a temper, leaving them without a translator. Audrey fetched him back, telling him he was a hero.

Meanwhile Aylmer was talking with Oswulf.

"They will come looking for their friends. We can take the weapons, hide the bodies, ride out on the horses to keep a watch, but it won't stop them."

"Aylmer, only the start of the battle will divert them. They want to get into Mercia proper. They are still coming over the hills in small numbers. I am having the trackways watched, but like you I can get no message to the king. Why they never came in one force, I do not know. It is like they have no leader or a poor one."

"We must either move or defend ourselves here. Even after the battle whichever side triumphs, it will not be safe for weeks until they have gone or become in charge. The only place to go from here is into the woods or moorlands and I do not like the idea of that now winter is none too far away. Many of the women and children would not survive........we should defend ourselves here as long as we can."

Oswulf agreed and said he would work out the details. Aylmer thought of all the help and advice his adopted father had given him down the years. This crisis had given him a new lease on life.

Hilda was talking with Kyra once the wounded were tended. Kyra had asked about Aylmer.

"His mother died and he became my son. I was his wet nurse. She was too ill to feed him for months when he was born. I had only daughters, she had one son. He was a joy to both of us. He just stayed with Oswulf and me until he was twelve from the age of five when she died. We lived south of here then......Oh, how we all loved him as a child. His step-mother has produced two sons but he is still the heir. He acts nobly like a lord, they are dogs in comparison, and they walk around in fear of him. One of them got drunk and challenged him. He did nothing but the king found out and threatened to execute the man and his brother if anything further took place. Athelstan is a king who does what he says and Aylmer is the same. There are many dead men in Angleland who had cause to regret crossing King Athelstan. Some of them did not die well. The king can also be cruel, which is something he has copied from his Aunt Ethelfreda. She suffered no traitors and outlaws to wander Mercia boasting of their deeds. If your King Constantine knows nothing of this land, it is because either no one is prepared to tell him.....or they are too scared and not without a reason."

Kyra thought on these words of Hilda's.

Hilda went on. "I can tell you love my Aylmer. That is fine. His step-mother would not welcome you as a daughter but I will. You risked your life for my people in these hills. It is strange for a woman to fight but we are now to live in strange times.

We are only safe while a king is strong. When he is weak, the wolves will come. Only men like Aylmer and my old Oswulf keep the country safe for the king to rule justly.....Oh I am so tired, child."

Kyra gave her a kiss and went to find Aylmer. Wilfred had returned with her clothes and people had stopped staring at her. On her way to find him a very young girl had appeared with Ecbert who translated what she had to say.

"This dress was my sister's. She died in the fight. I know she would want you to have it. She handfasted in it and only wore it on special days. Her husband is in the fort in Sheffield and does not know she is dead. It is mine now to give away or wear but I would only wear it and cry for her. My mother also would cry if I wore it."

"Thank you" said Kyra, "We all fought to protect you from men who do not care whether you live or die."

"If you are Lord Aylmer's wife, you must take care of him. He came back to rescue us."

She ran off at that leaving Kyra in tears and Ecbert not knowing what to say for once.

"Ecbert, we had best teach the people here to fight." She went off to find Aylmer.

CHAPTER 19

THE WAY SOUTH TO WAR

When he arrived at the camp Anlaf could not contain his anger. He screamed at his men.

"You all stood by while some Saxon peasant murdered Sitric Oslacsson! Did no one see it? What have you done to find the man? Can't someone tell me what Sitric was doing walking around camp with the man? What's all this about a woman disappearing at the same time? Tell me!"

No one could. The Scots and Welsh involved with the sheep sales had moved on south with Constantine and Owen of Strathclyde. It had become a mystery but the more Anlaf thought about it, perhaps not. Sitric was making arrangements with the Saxon over something. Perhaps it was their escape if something went wrong. They had a falling out. Anlaf had found out the Saxon had killed one of Sitric's berserks when he was challenged and expertly by all accounts. Clearly the man, whoever he was, was no ordinary farmer. He called for Ragnold and Stigand, Sitric's two elder sons to explain what they knew, but was irritated when he they told him they knew nothing. Their father had just left their camp and walked over to talk to the Scots about getting hold of some more sheep. Anlaf was irritated further when he found out they had revenged themselves on the two shepherds accompanying this mysterious man without questioning them.

"They protested their innocence" said Stigand with a laugh, "but it didn't save them."

"You are fools, they might have been telling the truth. Some Saxon has walked in this camp and fooled you all and his cover was a farmer. He even came with some real farmers and for a small amount of money and saving their lives, you could have found out about him."

When they had gone, before he took his sword to them, he wailed in desperation.

"Athelstan has outsmarted us all once more. How many times did that man come? No one guessed he was a spy? My loyal Sitric spotted him at once. Why am I surrounded by fools all the time? Athelstan has all the clever men and I have lost my best!"

He burst into tears for the loss of his friend.

The next few days didn't get better for him either. His nephew Hakon has disobeyed his orders. He was moving his men from the west of the hills from outside the Saxon fort at Manchester. The message just came and there was no explanation. They hadn't been attacked by the garrison and they should have had plenty of food. His message said he was heading for the Don Valley to meet up with the Scots and the Welsh. Surely Constantine hadn't sent for him? Odin's prophecy, thought Anlaf. Things are starting to go wrong for us. It's a good job I have got everyone moved south out of York except for a garrison. I am going to need every man. I can spare someone to tell that fool of a nephew of mine to stay where he is by the River Don until he receives orders.

Constantine was a lot happier now he had a battle to fight. He had most of his army under reliable commanders and his sons were here.... where he could keep an eye on them at long last. They had begun to behave themselves a little better when they heard about the death of their brother who had been to Dublin, knowing that their father had probably ordered it, despite his denials. Sending Kenneth macAllan with him did make it a bit obvious, even though he managed to be in Dublin when the deed was done. Kenneth was good at arranging these events for their father. Having people murdered while he was elsewhere was Kenneth's claim to fame.

Constantine was much happier still being with Owen of Strathclyde. He never felt intimidated by Constantine even though he knew one day the Scots would take over his declining country. Better them than the Angles, was his view. At least we are near- relatives as peoples, he thought. The Angles for centuries had been chipping away at Strathclyde, even some of his own people were starting to speak their language as well as Welsh. Strathclyde had suffered from Athelstan's raiders, more than the rest of the country. Owen liked Constantine also. They had an agreement that with Athelstan out of the way, Owen would get a freer hand in Cumbria and help against some of the Angles who were sat on the fence waiting to see how this campaign was going. Very few had brought their swords or their sons. Lots were deserting.

As soon as possible Constantine had wisely moved his army a bit further south. They had moved to within two days march of the fords on the River Don and he was waiting for Anlaf. There was a bit more food available than where they had been. The ground there was beginning to be fouled by the numbers of men he had brought. He managed to get his men to control the shares of food a little better. All he had to do was wait for Anlaf, and near the Northumbrian forts, seemed a good and a safe place in case the Saxons crossed the Don. After all they had been that way before two years ago. But strange, no sign of Athelstan and his spies came back with no information. The cowards won't go far enough south, he mused. Can't say I blame them. Athelstan doesn't welcome spies and traitors. His men seem to be able to sniff them out. I seem to live with a handful of them, even the family. I don't care how many of them die in this battle. They had better die well or I'll do the deed myself. I'll do it for the Irish and the Vikings if they don't behave as well, and as for the pagan prophesy they keep repeating about Anlaf losing the battle but still being king in York, I'll hang the next one of them who repeats that to my face, even if its Anlaf himself.

With a few days to go to the middle of September Anlaf had moved south and it was now or never, he said. The Three Kings as Anlaf liked to call them, had a joint meeting which was ruined by the news that Hakon, Anlaf's nephew had tried to take control of the ford at Brunanburgh and had failed, losing a large number of his men to the Saxon defenders. A surprise attack had failed. The defenders had anticipated the action and had met the attack by the ford. More Saxons had been waiting in the bushes to support the fort's garrison. The survivors reported more re-enforcements still arriving as they were forced to leave.

"Athelstan is nearby," said Anlaf. "We have to cross the river and bring him to a battle. We can use the other fords which don't have forts. To save face we had better take Brunanburgh, although all surprise is now gone. Owen, your Cumbrians and Strathclyders are good soldiers. They could do it."

Owen grumbled. "Your nephew has lost us the surprise and closed off one door for us into Mercia. He can do it ... and he could try leading from the front this time like a warrior should.............But I can't see the point. If we cross over our soldiers, there's another river between them and the rest of you, I know this even if you don't. We might have a lot of men but it serves no purpose to split them. We have no idea how many men Athelstan has or where they are. One thing is certain if we all cross over, he has to meet us. The longer we stay here, the hungrier we can get."

Anlaf looked darkly at him but said nothing.

Ah, thought Constantine, Owen gives as good as he gets from this damned Viking, King of Nowhere, Earl of an Ale-can..... That's unfair he thought on reflection, Anlaf is quite temperate. His reputation as a fighter seems a little tested at the moment. His choice of leaders is poor. Most of mine are at least trustworthy, probably because they aren't my awful family. However did I come by such sons? Thank God I'm getting too old to have any more. I hope they die honourably. People could praise me for having brave boys when history is written. Perhaps I had just better pay the monks and tell them what I want to read..... Read, it's so long since I read anything, I've forgotten how. He allowed himself a smile and so much so, all the others in the room wondered what the old fox was thinking, and believed it could be nothing to their advantage.

Anlaf thought the old man is more senile than ever. It's all these family worries and he's let his dog Owen off the leash to savage me. I think I'll solve my family problems by disposing of Hakon if the Saxons don't oblige me. Oh, Sitric. I could do with you here to see though all this bluff and bluster.... Odin, lead me south to a battle. There's no wonder the prophecy is of defeat. It's the allies. If I wasn't here, I couldn't be defeated. I should have stayed in York, fulfilled the prophecy and let these fools deal with Athelstan.............. Too late now though.

They decided to march south in two days towards Brunanburgh and cross using the other fords in the Don valley between there and the Saxon fort at Conisborough.

Athelstan's agents immediately spotted the preparations for a move and within a few days he knew of the plans. His own army was ready for a complete move in one day. The northern allies as an army took nearly a week to reach the hills above the Don. Their scouts went to look at the fords and a small force attacked the fort at Masborough only to be met with arrows. Hakon in the meantime hovered on the opposite bank from Brunanburgh telling himself to attack as a diversion when the Saxons appear. The Saxons were quietly re-enforcing it with more troops to back up the garrison. They could just be seen from the hills across the valley by those who bothered to look.

Athelstan slowly moved his men nearer to The Don at pace he hoped would not tire them. It was allowing his enemies time to cross the river.

The voice in his head said to him. "Let them come, move slowly. They will have a river and your forts behind them to the north, a river to their west and then the hills, and then to the east more forts and marshes. They have your men to the south, a trap of their own making.

"The best sort, Athelstan, my boy," said Auntie, "and it's all of your making to everyone else looking on."

"With a little help from God, of course! We mustn't leave out God as his church is paying for some of it," Athelstan reminded her.

Ethelfreda took this reference to the church as time to remind him they were getting too powerful and, if he didn't do something to curb their power, another king would have to do so. He ought to go down in history as the one who did it.

"Auntie," he shouted! "You can't conduct a war against heresy and sin and curb the power of the church at the same time. No one will understand."

He started to cry and remembered Juliana who came to him in his dreams to comfort him. He fell asleep in tears, dreaming of what might have been. They could have been a king and queen of a new Roman Britain, like Arthur and Gwenhyfar.

Juliana looked like a Roman from the south. She looked like the paintings of saints he had seen in the churches, like St. Helena, mother of Emperor Constantine who had been born in Eboracum when York was a centre of civilisation and not coveted by some Viking pirate. I would have moved my capital to there and lived with Juliana, he mused. Auntie thought it was never her real name, just one she used to impress me. I'm not sure Auntie liked her but they were always kind to each other. Oh so long ago now and not a day has gone by without I have missed them both. What a much better king I would have been, had both of them lived, kinder perhaps and even a little less intolerant.

Athelstan left his bed the next day in a better temper having dreamt of Juliana. The desire for battle was inspiring him also. He decided to move his main army a couple of days march nearer the River Don and re-enforced Brunanburgh again, thinking they might have another attempt to take it for reasons of prestige. They went round most of Britain telling their supporters it was the place to meet and they haven't even set foot inside it. They never will either. I'll feed the best soldiers I can find into the land around it. We don't want raiders slipping past it either. Athelstan began to laugh so much, he began to ache.

Later that day he passed a little wooden chapel next to a farm. He rode over with his guard and enquired of a girl milking some cows, if there was a priest.

"He's abandoned us, my lord," she said. "As soon as those fires appeared on the other side of The Don, he said he was going on a pilgrimage."

"Give me his name, child. His next pilgrimage he will take swinging from the end of a rope. His prayers will be for the Devil to take his soul quickly."

Athelstan went into the chapel and knelt by the altar to pray.

Lord God, omnipotent King of Kings and Lord of Lords in whose hands all victory lies and all war is ground out, please let your hand strengthen my heart, that in your virtue, hands and strength, I might fight much better and act courageously so that my enemies might fall in my sight before me and might fall as Goliath did in the face of your boy David and as did the people of Pharaoh before Moses in the Red Sea. And just as the Philistines fell before the people of Israel and Amalech before Moses and the Canaanites before Joshua, so may my enemies fall under my feet, and may they come together against me on one road and flee from me along seven and may God wear out their arms and shatter their spears and may they melt away in my sight like wax before a fire so that all the peoples of the Earth might know that it was because the name of our Lord Jesus Christ was invoked upon me and may your name be magnified O Lord amongst my enemies, O lord God of Israel.

Athelstan walked out of the chapel to where a crowd had gathered.

"Not many men here present." He said to a woman with three children.

"Most are in the forts, my Lord, but one or two have remained to hide the grain and take us into the woods, but only if the Scots get any nearer," she replied.

"Don't worry, I just intend them to get wet feet and pass one way over the river. They won't get a chance to visit this pretty little chapel you have here. What was the priest's name? Not even the Church will save a man running from my people. I may give you all a treat and bring him back to hang here."

All the villagers looked happy at that suggestion.

The northern allies decided also on a move to just behind the earthworks on the hills north of the Don. It was fairer to say Constantine decided. He had had enough of waiting and Owen supported him. Anlaf didn't argue. He had become fatalistic about the battle ever since Sitric had come with his mother's prophesy and one or two others she received in the subsequent weeks. She had gone back to where the body of Red Callum lay on a number of occasions. Sometimes she told Sitric what she saw. Other times not, and the two girls who went with her kept silent. The old lady became very sad and seemed to be declining. Sitric had said he didn't expect to find her alive when he returned. Anlaf was worried about these prophesies. Christianity never sat easy with him. It didn't say enough to a warrior.

He was now about to come into his element but one thing out of all things worried him the most. He found he was dividing up his own forces in an effort to put some backbone into some of his allies. They seemed to lack direction and never seemed to practice with weapons or formations. They were counting on numbers and not skill. Their weapons were quite poor quality and there was less armour than he thought. None of them seem to know how to fight in a formation. There was no way even of passing orders, except to the most royal or noble commanders. Certainly no initiative was allowed at the bottom of the command chain, even if one existed. He could only hope his chain of command could put some order into them and fit them into a plan. Anlaf feared most of all the inertia. A good-sized part of the army was formed up north of the Don, but there was still significant numbers of Scots and Welsh which formed the larger part of the army, still arriving after just hanging around at the rear. Constantine and Owen had lacked enthusiasm for marching out. They just wanted to consolidate their hold on the old earthworks, the crossings and surround the forts. He couldn't help feeling they were dancing to Athelstan's tune. The Roman names they used Constantius and Eugenius didn't impress him either. He thought they were pretentious and got them into Athelstan's way of delusional thinking.

It came as no surprise when a reconnaissance in strength of his own to the south met up with the Saxons and the soldiers had difficulty extracting themselves from the fight. He was not convinced they were the main army despite the battering his men received. After killing most of this force and running them back towards The Don, the Saxons had marched off in the direction of their stone fort, Brunanburgh, according to his commander, Toolig. It was even less surprise when a report of the main Saxon army was brought to him at last. They were on the move, slowly and carefully.

"They're moving at last" he screamed at his commanders. "They're a day's march from us and now they let us find out. We're in a trap, you'll see."

Neither Hakon nor Anlaf had been able to encircle Brunanburgh. They could not find a way across the marshes or the river. No one could be found who knew a path of a ford and when they tried to send out spies, they never returned unless to report bad news. It was almost as if Athelstan allowed this. Once again larger forces were met with an outright attack by the Saxons and Frankish mercenaries who clearly knew the pathways. The main Saxon army, however, did not appear.

He's coming now, thought Anlaf. We can have the battle but we had better find some space. As fast as he tried to get the army to spread out from the fords, when they did cross, the slower they moved. Suddenly the Saxons appeared from nowhere and had his army encircled and with their backs to the river, even though they had clearly fewer men. From his horse Anlaf looked up at the hills and the valleys running away from The Don. He could see long lines of armoured soldiers. All moving slowly, all disciplined and quiet, all behind their shields. His own army seemed suddenly galvanised into action. They formed up to meet the Saxons as far from the river as they could...but without actually engaging them.

"Thank God we don't have to fight with our feet in the river," he said to Toolig.

He watched. Clearly the Saxons seemed in no hurry but they were carefully forming a line around his army which seemed to stretch for miles with few gaps in it. Depth did not seem to worry them. They have a reserve somewhere, he thought. These few can't be all he has. Athelstan is waiting to see where we try to break through. He was correct up to a point. The Saxon lines thickened in places but not too much as men appeared from over the crest of the slopes.

Athelstan and Thurstan with one or two of other commanders sat on the hills watching all this.

"My lord, get younger men to look for me. My eyes are getting worse," said Thurstan.

"Don't worry, my friend, we do not need to see what we already know. We have them trapped but may not have enough men to spring the trap. We are getting thin in places. We had best attack now and squeeze them in a little tighter."

Everyone laughed at this but moved off to put into action the King's previous orders. Earl Thurstan moved off last to pick up his men and join them with Dunstan Edwinsson's to go to capture the ford at Roderham whenever the opportunity arose. The king would give the order.

"Before you move, Thurstan, I have had no reports from Aylmer for some time now. Were it any other man, I would fear he had been taken? I do not believe he has let grief cloud his judgements. As soon as I hear anything I will let you and his father know."

Thurstan said nothing but rode off with a sad expression, still thinking of his daughter, Helena.

The Scots and their allies had not properly formed up before the Saxons attacked from both flanks and pressed it home, squeezing then into a box. They had a downhill advantage over most of the area and then the main attack began. The advantage of numbers began to work in the allies favour and in the north eastern part of the battlefield, they forced back the Saxons. This didn't work in the south where they held on. What in Athelstan's plan was a small square box in which he was going to trap them became nearly a larger triangle as his enemies advanced.

"Nothing else for it," he said to Thorolf. "One hard blood-stained slog ahead for us all!.... Across from that hilltop in the south, and cut right through them. Cut off the lot who are making their way up the hill. Split the battlefield! We'll fight two battles in one place but only we shall live to tell this tale."

Anlaf was panicking. Half the battle had gone from his control. The Cumbrians and some Scots had successfully attacked the Saxons who fell back. They were just pursuing success too far and leaving the middle of the force stretched. The Saxons had retreated further without a clear reason, as far as he could tell, and then others attacked in the middle cutting off the over confident Cumbrians.

"Great Odin," he shouted! "It's hardly the end of the morning and already your prophesy has come true."

He looked at the hills and saw thick layers of his own side hemmed in by narrow lines of Saxons and Danes. The banners of their commanders were all over. Horsemen were everywhere passing messages. A group of men on horses were watching from a hilltop.

"Athelstan, I can see you, you devil," he shouted. "Have you bloodied your sword yet?"

More men were crossing the river and he issued orders for them to be sent to different parts of the battle. All they did was stand behind the others. No one moved but the Saxons who seemed to advance a score of paces at a time, were killing more of his men on the way. Everyone on his side seemed struck by the enormity of death until it seemed they could take no more and sporadic counter-attacks began without any coordination. They were interspersed with periods of inertia in which the Saxons, regrouped and attacked again. Anlaf watched all this in horror.

CHAPTER 20

ON THE BATTLEFIELD

Eric Sigurdsson and Ivar Grimsson were taking a rest at the front of the shield wall. Some little time had passed since the Scots and the Picts facing them had attacked and then been repulsed leaving many dead. Even the wounded had time to crawl back down the gentle slope to their comrades. Harald Edwinsson, their commander had ordered "rest shields" and was standing with them. They were looking at the enemy down in the valleys and across to the ridges north of the river.

"Lord Harald, where does the man come from who is riding that horse" said Eric. "He can't ride, he's got no armour and he's no idea how to fight from horseback. I'm no expert on fighting from horses, but even a child would know, you needed a long sword or spear for use in the saddle."

Harald observed wryly, "he's a Pict. They aren't much on armour, they think it restricts their movement and most are so poor they can't afford any. That one's not much on horses either. He ought to have stolen something useful on his way here. They're all looking a big hungry and lack energy…… Perhaps they should have had the horse for breakfast?"

"Well he's irritating me and Ivar and we'd like a go at him and take the horse. Didn't you say the King wants all horses captured?"

"He does and in a while we are going to move the line forward about five score paces. Those archers are beginning to be a nuisance. They've brought every child with a bow they can find and they're shooting at us from behind their line. I think they've put their worst troops here, but a lot of them. There is more for us to kill. When I give the word, you two divert the attention of the rest by attacking that horseman. Then our line will move around you. But watch out, as there are one or two of Earl Anlaf's men in there and they might catch on what's happening. Work out between you, how you'll do it."

Harald went up the line telling everyone to get ready. He'd seen the line was curving inwards a little at his part. Can't have the Saxons thinking we Danes are a bunch of slackers, he thought. They don't trust us at the best of times and thought back to his last meeting with the King at that village near Worksop. Fine words from Athelstan but at least he always did what he said. In many cases it meant bringing his army to your door, if you didn't agree with him. The men were impressed by him as a fighter even though his fellow Danish commanders were unsure how long it would last. Their conclusion was, as long as he's alive, his side is the one to be on. It was not only his organisation that was good. It was nearly as good as his money. Where did it all come from?

Harald decided what he could learn from this Saxon, was better organisation. Especially learn from the sayings of that Aunt of his, and he talked about her all the time. Harald's grandfather had met her and he was a man who didn't fear a lot. King Alfred didn't worry him too much but the man's daughter put the fear of death into him....... A Valkyrie, he'd say!.... A chooser of the slain, and if you're very lucky she'll miss you. Ethelred of Mercia can keep her. She had those eyes which missed nothing. When Ethelred died a number of notables began to panic when some wit observed, she was looking for another husband. Harald remembered the chaos, and the literal meaning of *Valkyrie* made him smile. A *Valkyrie* will have her work to do before this day has passed, he mused. There will be many slain to chose on this hillside.

Back in the shield wall, Ivar suggested he diverted the horseman while Eric went and got him with his axe.

"I don't know why you don't invest in a new sword, a man of your means and new found wealth. You can use one as well as any man I know."

"What do you mean? You know a forester like me is famous for swinging an axe, and I am the best there is. A sword as well in a battle would get in the way. I'd carry too much weight. The Picts and Scots may be stupid enough to come south and fight us but they haven't got everything wrong. Mobility in battle is important."

Ivar went on. "You've got your family one at home and it's made in the old fashioned way. Your grandad brought it with him in the boat. It doesn't look impressive but I'd trust it more than some I've seen. It's better than some new ones."

"Yes, I know it's a good one but I've left it with Tildi. She might need it if we don't beat this lot today. She knows how to use it, so does her lad."

"So, when are you and her going to handfast then? You know, stand in front of the village. Tell everyone you are a pair. State rights of inheritance etc. Have a feast. Loads of ale and mead……and food."

"She's a bit reluctant. She's buried two husbands already at twenty eight and she's worried about number three in these times."

Eric raised his shield to stop an arrow.

Ivar thought, perhaps she has her point, no pun intended. We are going to have to get at those stupid children with bows. Are the enemy so desperate for men? Athelstan at least told us to leave the next generation at home. He's not too bad for a Saxon.

"Eric, you're living in her house. If you survive today, do the honourable thing. Persuade her!"

"I will because she'll want the next baby's father to be acknowledged!"

"You kept that a secret, you rascal!"

Harald came just in time to hear that. "Eric, you rogue! Why didn't you tell us?"

"We are not absolutely sure, the baby hasn't quickened yet, according to the wisewoman. Matilda knows enough about these things herself anyway. She's had two live ones."

Harald had heard enough of this and said sternly.

"Eric, you are a good fighter and now for another reason I don't want you throwing your life away in battle against this bunch of amateurs. They've no business coming cattle stealing so far from their home. They ought to steal from a nearer neighbour or from each other. Can you save yourself long enough to see your child? Can you stay alive long enough to fight against our real enemies next time round?"

"Good advice, Lord Harald" enjoined Ivar.

"Same goes for you, young Ivar, and Eric, remember Matilda is a kinswoman of my wife. They are an unusual family, and we'll be related through them."

"Even though we'd be family, I could still be your forester? I like it in the woods. It's peaceful"

"Yes and get ready, the fool on the horse is here again. In your own time, everyone else is waiting."

Ivar ran out to challenge the horseman. A cheer went up from the Scots and the Picts which set everyone on edge and they got ready on the Danish side. The man rode up to Ivar, battered his sword on Ivar's shield but couldn't steer the horse. Ivar turned, ran and tripped. The horseman turned the animal in his direction as he scrambled on the ground. As it reached Ivar, the horse trampled him, but Eric appeared and with a spear pushed the rider off the horse, then took his axe with the usual consequences of such an expert as Eric Sigurdsson.

Ivar was back on his feet fast enough to ram Eric's spear through the back of a Viking who had rushed out, trying to rescue the rider. Ivar thought, this is strange to lose your own life for an idiot's.

Harald Edwinsson and his men had charged their hundred paces at this time and the impact of armoured warriors on the rows of unarmoured Scots and Picts was instant. The surprise enabled the three front rows to break through whilst the two rear rows cleaned up. The Edwinssons had a history of not taking prisoners in any case, and were more than happy to oblige King Athelstan in his orders to that effect. Harald knew his neighbouring commanders felt the same. In his heart Harald wished they could have all stayed at home. The enemy were too surprised or too frightened to run in some cases and were cut down were they stood. The success led to a wholesale movement along the whole of the Danish battle lines a little further down the gentle slope towards the River Don.

The complete line began to move. Earl Thorolf or *Jarl* Thorolf as his men preferred, gave the signal once he saw the break. His brother Egil standing nearby with his men shouted, "Now, let us justify our famous names, let us give the scalds more deeds to put in their poetry to delight the men who cannot be here today. Some new swordplay, my friends! Onward! Only Death waits us!"

Thorolf thought, my younger brother is anxious to die once again A man with such enthusiasm will never survive a battle with a real enemy. He'd never fight the Saxons on that basis. Some "ceorl" with a long axe would slip out of the shield wall and it would all be over, just like it was for that horseman.

He wasn't surprised when King Athelstan rode up either.

"Thorolf, your lads are doing good service today. That movement was just the right time. Now it's time for me to go and set the example of a King from the front of this battle. We don't want to lose this momentum and I can see they are starting to re-enforce around that original push. You keep an eye on the wider area for me. The battle's scattered but we've got it under control in most places."

"My Lord Athelstan, take care, Harald Edwinsson and his berserks from out east started all this movement. I hope they can sustain it..... Don't let them get you killed."

Athelstan and his guard rode towards the fight and Thorolf sat on his horse and watched. We picked the right side today, he thought. He'd be in difficulty if we'd stayed at home or been on the other side, but I have no doubt he would have found a solution to that. Where does he get his ideas from and where does all the money come from for us and to pay the Franks? This is not the day to be fighting the Saxons.

Riding down the hill Athelstan saw a man tying a horse to the body of a northerner.

"Hold on to this animal a bit longer for me," he said with a broad Danish accent. "You wanted it so much; you can keep it for me. Just don't run off with it again or I shall be cross."

"What's your next move, Dane," said Athelstan with a slight amount of humour.

Ivar looked at him suspiciously, having seen the king before and he recognised the banners and the guard. He thought had better be careful what he said. He knew Athelstan could understand and speak well the language of Danish part of his rule.

"It seems a long time since I have killed someone, my Lord, and I need to return this spear to my friend Eric. He dropped it in preference to an axe to deal with the horse thief. He's always telling me never to throw a spear in case someone throws it back at you, or drop it in case you need something to lean on..... A bit more bloodletting is now required to make the day go well."

Athelstan thought Thorolf was right. Berserks everyone, it's living away from civilisation, God and the influence of Rome, and on the other side of the Trent that does it.

"Shall we all go and do this then?" He said to his guard.

They all dismounted.

Ivar limped after Athelstan and his guard, weighed down with all his gear and two spears. This didn't impede his progress and Athelstan politely enquired if he was wounded.

"That horse trod on me. I can't go home and say, I left the fight because a horse trod on me. Its fine, nothing broken, just bruised, it was only a small horse."

Everyone in the king's guard laughed at that observation. Athelstan thought again he was glad they were on his side but reminded himself to keep a watch on his new found friends, as often as he had when they had been his old enemies.

The sight of the King's banner at the battle had the effect Athelstan knew it would. The Danes got a bit more impetus and the enemy got a bit more worried. The Viking commander had done a good job rallying his motley forces and was holding on as best he could. Athelstan and his personal guard of eighty made a difference and especially the King himself. He'd arrived in time to plug the holes in a widening front line. Eric was there swinging his axe but looked a bit tired.

"Ivar, I'd given you up for lost. Have you found a buyer for the horse? Ah, you've brought my spear, how considerate? Here's me and mine, with only an axe and shield in the whole world, holding back the enemies of Angleland."

Standing a few paces from Eric, Athelstan thought I'll bet they are all like this. The berserk is referring to Angleland as well. Doesn't he know I intend to be king of Britain, the new Rome?

Ivar slung him the spear and said, "I could see you have taken on more dinner than you can eat again, so I brought the King to help out. It's his damn country after all!"

"Why are you limping? You're not feigning injury again as an excuse to leave the battle." Eric said this whilst sticking the spear in some hapless Scot, causing it to break and thinking, you can't beat an axe on a battlefield.

Ivar hit another one with his shield. The man was completely stunned for a moment and Ivar hit him again shouting to Eric.

"Look at you, I bring you a spear all this way and the first thing you do is break it."

Athelstan stabbed the Scot with his sword.

"We work well together, Dane!" He called to Ivar. "You clearly enjoy a battle."

Then Athelstan broke his sword on a northern warrior's shield. A Viking had decided to go down in history as the man who killed King Athelstan and had run at him. The King brought his own shield around with such force the man was stunned and for the second time that day Ivar put a spear in the back of a Viking and shouted.

"Take my sword, Lord Athelstan."

Athelstan was taken aback by this as they were in some difficulty and the line was looking a bit shaky, but he grabbed it eagerly. Ivar seemed undefended but for his shield, having had no time to extract the spear. He was being attacked by two Picts but to the King's surprise pulled out a langseax, which looked a bit battered with age. Ivar pushed it in to one of the enemy while another chopped at him with a sword, totally surprised at the lack of effect on his armour. Ivar used his own shield and pushed over the other one, kicking him in the face with his good leg. He fell over then and the man crawled on top of him, putting his hands around his throat and knocking off his helmet. Eric watched all this with interest and seeing the man had no weapons in his hand and seemed almost childlike, casually kicked him off Ivar. He ran off before Eric had chance to have a go with the axe.

While this was going on Earl Thorolf brought some more men to support the king and the pressure on the line eased. Athelstan was able to step back out of the battle.

"Have you stopped killing today, Dane?" said the king to Eric as they both gasped for breath.

"I had not realised you had brought us here today to kill women, Lord Athelstan. For that is what was just trying to strangle my friend. Men aren't that shape and when she ran away, men don't run like that. The shape of their bodies and the way they move give it away. She had longer hair than most men have, even those from the north."

"Woman or not, she almost killed me" said Ivar, croaking. "First a horse, then a woman and she could use a sword." He picked it up and found it a bit lighter than he expected. He compared it to the one carried by the other Scot who was clearly a man. "Much lighter" he remarked. "This is a smaller sword, Eric. It's very well made; a bit light for cutting, better for stabbing. My ribs hurt where she tried to cut through the mail."

Damn them all, thought Athelstan. How can God forgive them for bringing women and boys to such a battle? However, it will make no difference. They'll die like the rest when we catch them. I'll give the order so there's no doubt. I'll let Him deal with forgiveness.

Athelstan returned Ivar his sword. "A family weapon, I think. I am grateful for it at a time like this and for your service. May you both live much longer! What are your names?"

"Eric Sigurdsson and Ivar Grimsson," said Ivar

"Ivar, I have met your father speaking for the Danes and he has done good work for me on the Trent. I am pleased you are all on my side. Good fortune till we meet again."

Athelstan then got back on his horse and rode forward with Thorolf to where the battle was moving. He thought them two forthright young men, no real respect for kings but what could you expect from men only two generations from being pirates. At least they were not cowards!

Harald Edwinsson ran up to Eric and Ivar. "A break from the battle, we're in reserve for a while or what's left of us is. Why are you limping, Ivar, a wound?"

"No, the horse trod on him," said Eric with a beaming smile.

"I said, be careful. But at least there's a funny side to everything. I suppose if we aren't careful, today will be remembered as the day Ivar was trodden by a horse. People will forget there was a battle…….. What are those marks and scratches on your face? Have you been fighting with a woman?"

Both Ivar and Eric looked at one another, thinking this will take too long to explain.

In another part of the battle Dunstan Edwinsson watched in an equal amount of horror and amazement as before him his father's men were dying one by one as they pressed home their attacks. He had promised his father, that although he thought himself no warrior, he would not run from the battle. He kept to his word and was grateful for all the training with the shield Eric Sigurdsson had given him. It had kept him alive. Dunstan managed to be at the front with his soldiers without actually killing anyone. Whilst he was there they followed. In a break in the conflict Earl Thorolf brought him some re-enforcements and off went the killing machine once again. Gradually they pressed home the attacks until Athelstan called a halt to movement at just before midday. He moved men around the battlefield.

The king appeared to show support his men.

"Just thought I would see how things are here, Dunstan. The Danish branch of your family, were my last call," he said with a laugh.

Dunstan's men thought this funny also, but all he could think about was how many men he had lost and how Eric and Ivar were doing.

"Cheer up, boy," said Athelstan. "This entertainment can't go on much longer. I had to get off the horse back there. There were so many bodies, she wouldn't walk over them. Thankfully most of them were not ours."

Dunstan listened in silence, holding back his tears for all his own men back there.

Then Athelstan drew his new sword. His guard followed.

"Come on, I'll show you what a king can do against his enemies."

As one they all moved to follow and the rest of the Saxon commanders ordered a move as the battle began again. Dunstan suddenly forgot his tears, didn't feel sick any more, took out his sword and walked next to his king. One of his men, Edmund, picked up his helmet and reminded him to put it on.

"Lord Dunstan, we can't lose you now the battles nearly over. If you die, no one will tell the story."

"Quite right, "said Athelstan. "Just make sure you make out me and your man Edmund as the heroes of the battle or I'll die Britannia's forgotten king."

Britannia! Britannia! Oh much better name than Angleland thought Athelstan. Everyone can feel a bit of it is theirs. I don't mind ruling the *wealas*, the Danes, the Scotti not even the Irish, or the Vikings but they had all better realise who is king of this island. They'll know it after this battle, especially when they count the dead. They'll know it if they come back for revenge, because I shall be waiting for them. I shall let just a few escape …… enough to frighten those who had the sense to stay at home. Athelstan had already thought it out in Leicester and his men had agreed. We don't pursue them too far north of the Don but we do kill all we find on the south and east side of it. Even as he stood he could just make out men still crossing over the river in small numbers and more coming down the hills in the distance, banners flying.

His Aunt's voice still shouted at him. "Don't spare your enemies; keep up the momentum in the battle!"

Seeing the king's banner, the Saxons surged forward making the gap between the northern army and the river narrower still and closing up the gaps and thinner parts of their own line. Steadily they moved down hill towards the river until a fairly wide but narrow battlefield was created on the riverbank. The northern army was getting hemmed in with only back across the Don as a place to move. Anlaf's Vikings were preventing retreat and some fighting was taking place with their allies. At the same time the Saxons slowly pressed home their advantage of better weapons, armour and tactics. Dunstan and Thurstan's men were now despatched to capture and hold the ford next to the footbridge. It was almost all over by this part of river. The northern army was scattered along its full length. Hundreds had drowned or were killed trying to re-cross and the survivors were being hunted down. The afternoon saw the Saxons in control of all the fords and the village of Roderham.

Some time earlier both Eric and Ivar had walked slowly to sit with their comrades next to a hedge. Ivar had recovered the horse and tied it there. Both sat down and started to tremble.

"Ivar, I'm glad I'm not the only one affected like this. Have some of Tildi's fruit bread, she said save it for a rest during the battle. It's got honey and dried fruit in it!"

"She obviously expects you to live then."

Both sat in silence watching everyone come and sit together. Harald went around to count his men. He'd started off with three hundred and four. He did his own troop and his other troop commanders reported. He stood up to speak after a few moments.

"Lads, we have twenty seven dead and sixty one wounded, only a handful seriously... Ivar Horsetrodden............!"

This caused laughter and laughter and laughter. Ivar thought it was never going to stop, even on such a baleful day.

"Ivar, I want you to remain with the wounded here until the healers get here. I have sent for them. When any men are fit enough to move, take them somewhere safe. We are going for a long walk, and don't even suggest you'll come on the horse! I need someone to be in charge here who is reasonably fit. Give the horse to the healers; they'll need it more than us. Keep an eye on everyone here, keep them safe, and watch the battle! The rest of us are going to have a look at the fort which seems to be the centre of all this bother... and we are going to have to be quick. The enemy are trying to force a passage across the Ryknield Street ford thinking they can get to our rear. They haven't noticed the other river in the way, the one that joins the Don. One of the locals has shown Jarl Thorolf a ford over that one, so we are going to re-enforce the fort at Brunanburgh."

The mention of the name caused a stir around Harald's men. Most had never seen a large stone building or a real fortification. Some said they'd be a bit scared about going in because of the history with the Romans. Strange spirits might lurk there and they couldn't understand the King's interest in these things. Harald went on.

"We have a serious challenge this time. It's the Dublin Vikings, the Irish and the Cumbrian Welsh. The Saxons and the Franks have held them as long as they can and they need some real fighters to help out. All we need to do is stand by the water's edge and kill them. We do not let them on to the bank. Get ready to move! We need to be there quickly...... Eric Sigurdsson to me!"

"Eric, I want you to command my troop while I deal with the battle, the king's order puts me in charge. We need to give the Saxons and Franks a rest while we keep the ford covered from the land. The Saxons in the fort are all old soldiers and some boys and they can keep the arrows flying. The crossing is under the walls. The real battle is on the bank. Jarl Thorolf thinks the whole thing is a diversion and doesn't want hundreds of us there away from the real battle. They have tried to cross twice some days ago but the fort guard and the Franks turned them back. They seem to be wasting men for nothing unless they have something in mind. The king seems to think they might want to attack Nottingham with a small force but knows the defences on the way would stop them."

"These people are a mystery to me, Lord Harald, they seem to have so many men but do nothing with them."

"You'll be pleased to know the Saxons are getting the worst of it on the far northeast side. That where both sides are concentrating the forces. Jarl Thorolf has said the King is there and neither side is giving way. King Constantine and Owen of Strathclyde are there he thinks. The two fords down near that village enabled them to cross most of their army but none too quickly. They wouldn't have got them over the Trent as quickly or so safely. I think many of the Scots we saw today swam over."

"I wish I knew what they held against us," Ivar said to his comrades as the others marched off, leaving him with his first command in the charge of the wounded. Oh well, he thought, at least it's a start but I'd better rest this leg sometime. He hobbled around and looked at everyone. Most of his friends were in worse condition than him. He thought many will be fine once their bleeding has stopped. If only mother was here, she'd know what to do. She'd get things organised, everything would be well. He sat wondering about his real mother. He could only remember her being very tearful and thin. She rejected him as he reminded her of his father, so he was told later. Emma was different. She was warm and cuddled him all the time as she did with everyone else. His new aunties and their babies were constantly her concern. All the workers and their families were always in her thoughts and still she devoted so much time to him. Children with their real mothers had envied him.

She'll be on edge all the time I am away as if Grim hadn't taught me well in the ways of war. I must bring something home to her if it is only my experience to make me a better son. This is a real war, not like chasing a few pirates and bandits with Dad and Lord Harald. He looked at his wounded comrades and thought many of their injuries are due to arrows. They were just standing there in the line. Those boys at the rear of the Scots were more effective than we thought. No wonder Dad filled those boats with boys when he attacked that fleet in the Humber. Uncle Orm thought it was a waste of resources. Dad takes some bettering when it comes to a fight despite his age..... Odin and Freya! I'm so tired.

The death of one more of his comrades from a spear wound brought him round. Thurig just slipped away and he had hardly noticed. He was too lost in his own thoughts. Poor Thurig, a wife and two little orphans to care for, Mother Emma. They only live a morning's walk from us. Emma will go as soon as she knows. He got up, closed Thurig's eyes and put all his weapons together to take home for his son. I wonder how many more she will be caring for when this is all done. She needs a helper. I must find myself a wife like her to help her, and not a woman who freezes at the sight of blood and sickness. Not many about, even dad was well past thirty before he met mother.

He walked slowly around everyone else lying in a row. Many had been bandaged by comrades and a few moments rest had been a help to stop the blood flow in some cases. He started to clean up some wounds as Emma had instructed and one or two more of the lightly wounded began to help him. He realised Harald was only taking the absolutely fit men with him to Brunanburgh. He could have insisted that some of his men here go with him. Harald might have thought they had done enough in a fight not entirely theirs, especially the twenty eight dead. As their lord, Harald would be thinking of the future, and how he was to care for the widows and orphans, explain to the mothers and fathers. Grim his father didn't have too much time for lords but always made an exception in Harald's case. Grim knew he would never throw lives away, and not the son and stepson of his own father's best friends. Despite this, Ivar resolved he was going to fight again in this battle, and Brunanburgh was going to be the place.

CHAPTER 21

HAKON ATTACKS BRUNANBURGH

Anlaf's orders to his nephew had been quite specific..... Land in Cumbria, pick up the allies and march down to the Mercian border and threaten the forts. They are too strong for you to take by storm, just keep the enemy tied down in them. When I send you the orders, join up with the men I shall land from the Mersey. You then support the southern Welsh to attack Mercia.

Only Anlaf and his brother Lachlan really thought Hakon would follow those orders to anything like the letter. This applied also to the advice on trying to make friends and get support in western Yorkshire.

When Sitric Oslacsson heard Anlaf had ordered this without referring the idea to his chiefs, he was enraged. For one of the few times in his life, he fell out with his *Jarl*. He was so mad even his mother Gudrun could not calm him. She even hid his sword and thought about drugging his food. Eventually he calmed and went to see Anlaf who was a bit defensive and blamed his brother.

"You should send me, Jarl Anlaf. I know what to do. Hakon will just sit there with good men we could use elsewhere while the Saxons laugh at him. You know we can hardly move without the Saxons gain advantage. Hakon knows nothing of making friends or tactics. He's just a young fighter."

"I know, Sitric, and we need him to cause trouble on that border."

"He only needs a tenth of the men you are sending with to make trouble. All those men have to be fed, housed and amused. The locals won't support him. The Saxons will wait their chance to kill him at worst or defeat his force at best. Your brother will lose his only son. The Cumbrians will feel their men are being wasted for nothing."

"Sitric, as long as he is there he is a threat."

"He's more of a threat to us and our plan, Jarl Anlaf! Change your mind. Let him stay here instead of my man Hemming....... Hemming knows how to keep half a country of Saxons entertained...... and with a hundred men."

"No, what Hemming does here is more important to me and I have told him so. Holding Dublin is almost as important to me as taking York and being King of Northumbria. We have nowhere without Dublin if all fails. Hemming is not wild. His father was a cool man... and reliable... and a good friend to you. I am not changing the plans. We have your mother's prophesy about York. All we have to do is not lose sight of what we really want."

Sitric gave up, thinking families will be the death of us all with what we do for them.

Hakon and his band of warriors thought this is the beginning of his fame and only pretended to listen to his uncle. He was secretly plotting a path to glory. After listening to Callum the Red talk about the area of North Mercia and what spoils could be obtained for a conqueror, he only had one goal in mind..........Brunanburgh. The last thing the Saxons would expect was a force the size he was taking to march over the hills and walk into it. He reasoned they would not have the defences really manned until they knew King Anlaf was landing in the Humber.

Athelstan in the meantime gave much thought to Brunanburgh. Aunt Ethelfreda's words about forts on river crossings were seldom out of his head, and here he had the major crossing east of the hills, in and out of Mercia. The fort she had personally supervised rebuilding. He constantly promised her not a single invader would set foot in it and her voice in his head constantly reminded him.

"Athelstan you need a good man in charge there...... .A fighter not just a defender........ A lot of men, remember the size of it.......station some on the outside to the flanks of the ford......some horsemen for watching the area around.....bowmen to cover the ford from the walls, old men and the young....and Athelstan, plenty of food. Men fight better on a full stomach when behind a wall, as well as in the field."

Athelstan never interrupted his aunt when she spoke and always listened carefully. Ethelfreda knew about a fight and more than a few Danes in Mercia knew it. Ah, he thought, not King Alfred's daughter for nothing.

Over a few months Athelstan put the plan into action. Wulfmaer Stigandsson was made commander with orders to defend fort and ford. Wulfmaer needed no telling it had to be to the death. Athelstan knew he would never have to face him with an admission of failure. Wulfmaer made a list and Athelstan made sure he had what was on it and as a declaration of his faith in him, added the Frankish mercenaries. His friend Henrig's only surviving son Karl was in command of them. By the passing of Lammas AD937 they were lying in wait, although to anyone passing by along the balk to the fort and the ford from the south, they might not have guessed. There were a few extra hands at the harvest in the surrounding villages.

Wulfmaer very early on had suggested to Athelstan that the Wincobank fort was strengthened.

"My Lord, if we are to defend the crossing we need the area watched to make sure we receive no surprises. The best point around is Wincobank. A man can see for good distances from it in all directions. Wincobank can see also Sheffield, Masborough, with Sprotborough and Conisborough at a pinch, but from Brunanburgh we see nothing but the top of Wincobank Hill and those old earthworks running up to the Dearne River. We can get signals the enemy are coming from that hill top and so we do not need watch ourselves. Furthermore the attack could come from either side of the river. We might need a useful force on the other bank to irritate the enemy from time to time."

Athelstan loved Wulfmaer's thoroughness. He thought of everything and it was how he had stayed alive for so long.

"Ah, how true, Wulfmaer! Much depends on this ford holding. They will have to use the other inferior and difficult crossings. Wincobank has an unreliable water supply but we can work out something. It won't fall. They won't work out how important it is until too late. As it is north of the river they won't bother with it, I suspect. To arouse no suspicions, they will not reply to any signal, and none will be sent until the enemy are identified. They can also signal which direction the enemy come from."

"I will have scouts out in all directions in any case. Brunanburgh will be defended to the last drop of the enemy's blood, my lord."

Athelstan loved that comment and kept repeating it weeks later to anyone who would listen.

Word came to Athelstan about a week after Lammas that the Vikings and the Cumbrians had moved south out of their hills. Many kings would have despaired but Athelstan couldn't believe his luck.

"How much of a diversion his this" he asked his council? "The news is the force is too big for a raid but not large enough for an invasion. Large enough to worry us... if we were not expecting it. They won't get much support from the people. Anlaf's support is east of the hills. Besides they have only put Anlaf's nephew in charge. He's not twenty yet and has had no real battle experience besides cow stealing from the Irish.... and they say he's none too good at that."

Everyone laughed at this observation of young Hakon.

"My lord, you were famous by that age and had fought with Count Henri in Britain and all over the Frankish lands," ventured Bishop Odo.

Henric laughed. "We fought in some real fights on land and sea. No mercy given by either side. The fate of land at stake just like now. Anlaf has sent this boy to irritate us and to get some battle experience. Let us refuse to fight him and provoke him into doing something stupid. If we can get him to camp permanently somewhere, his men will go off to raid. We can pick them off handfuls at a time and use far fewer men than he has."

"We'll do all of that without weakening our defences or our main force. We'll watch him with patience for a while at first" said the King. "We should try some ruse to detach the Cumbrians. I am not happy about fighting them. They should be my people."

"I believe" said the Bishop many of them are still pagans and unbelievers despite the church's attempts to convert them."

"I think they follow the Irish church" said the King.... "We must ensure the heresy is stamped out, Good Bishop, without killing too many. This boy leading them may be a Christian but he is a heretic. We shall not mourn his death, especially as he intends no good for our people. We shall watch him my friends. He's bound to put a foot wrong. Impetuous youth always does. Did we not Henric?"

"It does concern me," said Henric "who he may have with him as an adviser. Anlaf surely does not send a boy such a distance in total charge. My own son is very wise and competent for his years but he has Alain de Briscourt with him in the field."

"Alain's reputation as a commander is well known but has he not retired like you, Count Henric," asked Thorolf? "He's reaching the age to deserve it."

"Death is our retirement" said Henric with a laugh. "Just like it will be for you, old friend."

"No prophesies please, war is too serious," Thorolf replied, laughing also.

"Come, not so downhearted" said the king. "If this young man of Anlaf's had the sense to go home, we would ignore his fate. We'd let him be, but as it is, let's get down to making sure he does not do us any more harm than he will, just by being over here and looking enviously at the walls of Chester."

Wulfmaer had everything in place to his satisfaction. Even the Franks on horses he liked. They ran about carrying messages and scouting to the west of Sheffield. He was not disappointed when a band of them returned one day and said the Vikings are coming. Athelstan had effectively made him commander of all three forts, Brunanburgh, Wincobank and Sheffield. He rode out to have a look at them. He was nearly tempted to empty the forts of men and meet them in a pitched battle. Winning wasn't the issue, it was where their stragglers go afterwards. Wulfmaer wanted them in a place where they could go nowhere without an obstacle at their back. Another fort or the main Scots Army, he didn't mind as long as they didn't escape someone's wrath. He could quite imagine the look on Anlaf's face if Brunanburgh wasn't taken and his nephew gave him the count of the dead. These wouldn't be only his Cumbrian allies; they would be Anlaf's own men. What Wulfmaer didn't want, was them to come south of Sheffield. He needed them north of the river.

Hakon was having a bad war. Once out of Cumbria, everything was going wrong. The locals had all but vanished up into the hills or the marshes with their food and women. There were no towns or forts till they reached Manchester and even he could see new defences. Attempts to parlay with the defenders only resulted in arrows and accurate ones at that.

They got a similar response at Chester and he decided they should camp outside it on a more permanent basis, taking account of his uncle's orders. Because of the size of their force the cordon around the town was never complete and men still passed in and out, especially by the River Dee to the Saxon fleet stationed there. What was even worse, every day a few men were picked off by the Saxons appearing from nowhere. They were running out of food and the general consensus amongst the real warriors Anlaf sent, was that they would have to find some more soon. The only place they knew was with the main army, east of the hills. There was no sign either of the Southern Welsh or the promised fleet from Dublin.

"Right," said Hakon. "We stay here, we starve eventually, and we don't share the main action. Why don't we stop trying to divert the Saxons, because clearly we are not succeeding, and just move east and take Brunanburgh? Uncle Anlaf in his plans never mentioned anyone doing that. There's so many spies around, I am certain King Athelstan would know he intended to bypass it if it had been in his plans. There probably isn't much of a garrison. I am sure Uncle Anlaf was just going to cross the ford and ignore it. Let us just walk in and take it over."

"They'll never expect us if we do it before the main army arrives. We know our armies have the most men and we are stretching their reserves. Let us do it quickly then," said one of his warband. "Who here has ever laid siege to a fort?"

"No one" said Hakon. "This is the problem. This is a stone fort as well."

One of the older men in the expedition, Erik the Short, so called because of his height, spoke out. "This is foolish unless we have ladders to get over the wall or machines to break it down. We could have done that here if we had them, instead of sitting here for a week. We have made no impact on what happening over those walls in Chester."

"If as we suppose, Brunanburgh is smaller, we can contain the garrison and hold the ford for the main army if all else fails," said Hakon. "We are already doing that here, except no main army is coming here. Brunanburgh is a fort, this is a whole town and better defended than my uncle could imagine."

"If we plan this we must not let them think that's what we are doing," said Erik. "We must not lose sight of capturing that ford or it's all a waste of time."

They went back via Manchester quite slowly and then rushed across to Sheffield as fast as possible trying to find a route which would get them south of the town. They failed when they followed all the easy routes. It only made their presence known well in advance, although they did not realise at the time.

As Wulfmaer suspected they were spotted from Wincobank, as they tried to avoid Sheffield and its two rivers by passing to the north using an easier crossing when they should have chosen the difficult one to the south. Constant harassment from the south by Wulfmaer's men also drove the Vikings to the north. Eventually Hakon got all his men together and in place on the northern side of the Don opposite Brunanburgh with Wincobank to his rear, not realising he was in a trap set by Wulfmaer.

Hakon sent across a small party to try him out when his men finally reached the ford. Wulfmaer sent men from the fort to drive them back across the Don, keeping his main force hidden in the trees and the marsh. The Vikings took it as a signal to bring over their main force into his trap. His main force came from undercover, wiped out the reconnaissance and then prevented the main force from leaving the river once Hakon had committed them all and seemingly forced the Saxons back. Once he knew he had them all in his grasp, Wulfmaer, let them on the bank, brought in more of his reserves and began the long hard fight to destroy Hakon's little army, despite being outnumbered by them.

After two hours the Vikings retreated or what was left of them did, as Wulfmaer's men had encircled them before the gates of Brunanburgh. He was dying of his wounds inside the fort by this time having done his duty to his king. He appointed Charles de Tours as commander of the fort and the ford and with Alain de Briscourt's advice the defence was consolidated. A message was sent to Athelstan who wept for Wulfmaer like a brother. Then he sent a couple of hundred Saxons to re-enforce them before the next attack.

Athelstan thought it unlikely there would be another attack until the main northern army came nearer. They were two or three days march away or even a week but he took no chances.

Hakon was left with almost no effective command at all and was lucky to escape with his life. He was nearly cut off on the south bank of the Don. Back on the north side he counted his forces and decided he had better try to get some more out of his uncle and organise another attack. A day or so later an advance guard of the main army came up and Hakon told the commander his version of what happened. He wasn't interested in an attack with such limited men but when more of his own side came up to the river, they decided to try again.

This time they had less success as the Saxons and the Franks didn't let them leave the water. The garrison managed to kill a lot of them but never let them get a serious hold on the bank. Hakon withdrew all the forces as the new commander had got himself killed trying to break out from the bank side.

A message from Anlaf and King Owen of Strathclyde put an end to more adventures until the day the main army had crossed over by the other fords north of Rykneild Street. Anlaf decided not to risk another attack on

Brunanburgh despite Hakon pleading face to face with his uncle how easy it would be with more men.

"It's a trap, Hakon, and they have sprung it twice and you have survived. They won't let us get away so easy a third time."

"Uncle, we need to take this ford. It's the best way across that river, and we have been telling everyone to meet there..... And we are not even attacking it. We have all these men."

"You can have three hundred more men, now get out of my sight" said Anlaf, "or I'll do what the Saxons couldn't."

Hakon went off to fetch the men when more Welsh approached him to volunteer. They were southern Welsh and had been drawn into the conflict by the idea of crossing the border and linking up with their countrymen.

Idwal ap Kynon was their leader. Hakon had heard of him as a fighter and was more than happy to talk about a joint attack.

"Idwal, I think my uncle and King Constantine are too concerned with an easy crossing of the Don. They have gone around Britain telling everyone to meet at Brunanburgh and not one of us is going to set a foot in it."

"Hakon, your uncle is a warrior of experience. We have learnt now we have reached it, that Brunanburgh is surrounded in many places by marsh. It's dry around the fort and the hill at the back but if you want to go south on Ryknield Street, you get your feet wet again. The track is fine for a few carts but not an army. The big army needs to cross over and be on dry land as soon as it can. However, we want to go south to incite our people to rise up against King Athelstan and not take part in the big battle. There are enough men to defeat ten armies of Saxons in these islands if they could all bother to come together at the right time."

"We need to put our forces together and attack the same time as the kings invade."

"No, we need to let the battle start and wait while they think we are not bothering. You have bravely tried twice without the best numbers. Let's start collecting men and while the Saxons are pre-occupied with the main fight, we assemble under cover and then attack."

"Do you think, Idwal, there are more who would want to join us?"

"I can find some more Cumbrians and some more countrymen of mine. I just need time today. The main attack may be tomorrow"

"We can meet in the woods where the Salt Road meets the hill top and we could walk down unseen to the river."

"Hakon, you are thinking like a soldier."

CHAPTER 22

THE PICTS ATTACK

Brollachan was on the north side of the river on the morning the Saxons appeared. The women had been ordered by Constantine to stay there. The priests had prevailed and Anlaf didn't want the men distracted. War was too serious to allow women to fight, he had said to Brigid, Her reply had been, all we are good for is to get raped and murdered. She cursed him not to live long enough to enjoy his victory and had to be dragged from Constantine's council. She was not allowed back for some time. Anlaf sank deeper into depression after this, Gudrun's prediction never out of his mind. A curse from another witch to add to it now, he thought.

As the Pictish soldiers had moved out many of the women had slipped in with them, planning to emerge on the battlefield. Brollachan had not been able. She and Brigid were under guard by her brother's men. Her youngest brother was now clan leader and he was more of a Scot than the one she had killed. Fortunately even fewer of the Clan had followed him than planned to come south with Malcolm. He had taken the name Andrew and had the saint's Saltire on his personal banner. She had not seen him since they were small children and had not realised he was her twin. Many of the clan had wanted her to remain behind, hoping he would die and she would become leader. At the time she had not realised this wisdom of this thinking.

Their meeting up north had been frosty enough but by the time they had met again near Brunanburgh, Brollachan was feeling murderous. Andrew was aware of Malcolm's fate but seemed intent on goading his sister into the same course of action. He thought himself a better warrior and wanted the world to know, he would avenge his older brother. In the camp two of his men went too far in challenging her and were seriously wounded. Brigid had prevented her from killing them. No one bothered to challenge her after that and Andrew left her alone but in seclusion with the rest of the women.

Andrew formed up his men as part of the larger Scots army with the other Pict chiefs. The women were scattered in the ranks and dressed as men. Brollachan had attracted a few followers who formed her personal guard. As the invasion progressed her clan had become divided between those who supported her brother and the dissatisfied who just wanted to go home. She wanted to fight and was generally resentful of the men she saw as cowards gathering around her. She was mindful of the Great Goddess's prediction that she was not going to return and felt she could only remain here and fight in the battle. Andrew made an initial mistake of dividing up his men with himself commanding a larger part and letting the smaller part go off with Guthric, a Viking and the son of Sitric Oslacsson, one of Anlaf's supporters. The young man strutted about trying to look murderous and probably is, thought Brollachan. He's not got the discipline for a real fight. But he's dangerous and so are the men with him. More to us than the Saxons and she said this to the men with her.

The two groups eventually stood side by side on the battlefield. Andrew had been given a horse by King Anlaf while at York and never lost an opportunity to ride around on it wherever he was. The day of the battle was no exception and he irritated the Vikings by drawing attention to himself. At the first real clash with the enemy, a couple of Danish berserks ran out of their ranks and killed him and the Viking, Magnus Howerdsson. Anlaf had volunteered him to be his adviser. Magnus's men were irritated that their chief had thrown his life away over Andrew's stupidity but took control immediately when the Danes attacked. The Picts fought bravely but were demoralised by the loss of their chief. To make matters worse King Athelstan appeared and led an attack on them. The sight of his banner at that point caused a retreat eventually by all, Scots, Picts and Vikings, despite some initial hard fighting.

Guthric with Brollachan's help managed to rally their part of the force but he was resentful, most especially at her offer to lead a charge. His men pressured him to agreement when his instinct was to conserve his men and look for a more careful use of his forces. The Saxons were putting more pressure on the line when he relented. Brollachan removed her clothes and led the charge of both Picts and Vikings. The Saxons were not taken by surprise. They closed ranks and took the impact. They then continued their slow forward march towards the river. Guthric extracted what was left of his men and left the Picts to die.

"Dear God," said Guthric to his men. "Are all these people moonstruck? You lot are as bad. Whatever did you think we were going to do?.......... Stand your ground here and wait for the survivors to return. That crazy girl will be the end of us all, Pictish princess or not. She can swing a sword and throw a spear but that's all."

"I can't believe this is happening, Guthric," said one of his men. "Why don't they just step back from the battle line."

"The fools believe they can win while she's there. Even the ones who were ready to go home are joining in," he replied. "No one move.........we'll die fast enough today without being as eager as them.

The Vikings looked on while most of Guthric's first command was reduced to next to nothing. A handful of the Picts at last dragged Brollachan away from the lines of Saxons, leaving the rest dead and wounded.

"Cowards" she screamed at the Vikings several times!

"What's she saying, Guthric," asked Coll Collsson.

"Don't know exactly, my friend, but I think she is angry we did not stay to die with her," he replied.

"Guthric, have you noticed that as this battle has gone on, we get no further away from that river and that our friends around us are getting pushed back towards it. This mad woman and her men have temporarily halted them here, but the Saxons are on the move all over these hillsides."

"Right, move back as everyone else moves, don't get left behind. Bring the Picts as well. They may be daft but it's no reason to leave them to the Saxons."

Seeing Guthric leaving the battlefield was too much for Brollachan. When they had walked nearly to the river, she picked up a discarded spear and pushed it into his back.

"Die, like the coward you are, with your face looking for your home," she screamed at him.

"Coll," said Guthric! "Granny told me to be wary of women on the battlefield. Get revenge for me. Kill them all! Make the girl die slowly. Don't tell Dad we were retreating."

He started to cough blood and groan as Coll removed his helmet. Then life just drained from him.

The Vikings and the Picts began to fight and though the Vikings were outnumbered, they were saved by their armour and shields. Brollachan, pursued by some Vikings, ran off into the marshes, observed from a distance by Brigid. Fighting had broken out at many parts of the riverbank as the Scots and Picts retreated and the Vikings tried to stop them. She could do nothing to rescue her.

Brigid saw an opportunity to rally the army around her and was able to organise it to fight off Anlaf's men and make sure the ford was defended. More of the army were crossing from the northern side. They looked at the battered men who were standing leaderless except for Brigid and walked past them in the direction of the battle. An officer recognised Brigid and ran to her.

"What's happening? I could see you fighting the Irish. They've joined the Saxons. I knew Athelstan's gold would be too much for them. Anlaf's been taking it all the time. The rumours about him staying in York and prophesies to keep are all true."

"He is here, I've seen him" said Brigid. "His men are killing ours and attacking the women. Once a Viking, always a Viking." That will stir up trouble, she thought.

He ran back to his men and halted them. Then they moved in the direction of a group of Vikings and Irish, forming up to try another assault on the men trying to re-cross at the ford.

"Had enough of killing today or is it easier to kill your friends rather than your king's enemies," he called over to them. "You can come and try us now if you like or you can move towards the Saxons and show us how it's done."

They looked a bit puzzled until someone sorted out the translation. They moved back towards the riverbank.

"That's it, let's have them" shouted Brigid, as the Scots attacked.

Dunstan Edwinsson observed some of this, not knowing what to make of it. He decided instead to concentrate on the amount of men still crossing over and really re-enforcing the Scots. How are we going to deal with these numbers? Our own forces are stretched now the battlefield is splitting up, he thought. From the Saxon rear Earl Thurstan came with more men.

"King's been saving us for this! Got orders to take that ford, stop 'em crossing. Easier than fighting them once they've crossed," he called to Dunstan.

"Why not, I'm getting used to this battle. Come on then," he shouted to his men! "Follow me to the river. I need a drink!"

"My Lord, remember it's not ale only water" said some wit in the ranks."

"I don't care, it would taste like wine."

"We'll make it the same colour," muttered Thurstan. "This much I do know."

On they went.

Brigid had watched the battle all day and had realised that the ford at Roderham was key to getting support for Constantine's beleaguered army. When she had recovered the leadership of the Picts, she had initially resolved to hold it with her battered force to allow the men to keeping coming over. She had let her hatred of the Vikings distract her. It was too late. Again the Saxons had spotted a weakness in the northern allies' plans. Not only had they guessed the strategy but now they were guessing the tactics, even as the battle unfolded. The Saxons just concentrated their forces on taking the ford and the footbridge. It just happened. She watched from a distance whilst the Scots fought the Vikings. The Scots still crossing were not aware what was happening as the Saxons smashed into them. The Saxons formed up on the bank and around the ford and waited for the Scots reaction.

Brigid looked at them. Only three rows but all standing calm, all behind shields, two commanders banners in the middle. Everything about the arrangement said, come here to die! Brigid had a sudden vision of death, but not of her own. She watched as the Scots army became aware the Saxons had broken through them again. The men at the rear were showing the first signs of panic. The Saxons looked too good. In places they just stood a couple of paces on higher ground, a slight advantage for a man with a spear. A couple of Scots moving close to try them out were met with arrows. Men had stopped trying to cross over. The ford was deep, no room to fight in the water. I've lost us the battle, she thought............ Then she thought, me, and all the other idiots and went off to look for Brollachan.

Brollachan ran on into the marshes and hid under a holly bush. She let five Vikings pass and surprised another two following. One she killed by surprise but the other fought long enough for him to shout to his colleagues over the noise of battle. Suddenly she was on the run again and away from the marsh before she had time to finish him. There must be more of our men out here, she reasoned. She was breathless, had some cuts and bruising, and was feeling very hungry and very heady due to the berries she had eaten. There was a small spring nearby and she almost fell into it, noticing that it was also a shrine.

Meanwhile Brigid had decided the day was lost as more of the Scots were moving back to the river. As the ford was denied to them, they were trying to cross where it was deeper. Many couldn't swim and were drowning. She grabbed a sword off a dying Scot and went up river, following the marshes and the river in the direction she knew to be Brunanburgh. The tracks of her pursuers were clear although she thought Broll will be leaving little trace. The only obvious sign was a dead Viking and a trail of blood from another which she followed out of desperation, having no other clues. Two voices alerted her to trouble ahead. The wounded man and a comrade were talking. She leapt on them taking both by surprise and killed the unwounded man, the other fainted. As she was about to stab him, she looked into a clearing and there was Brollachan in a pool surrounded by four Vikings.

Brigid was about to intervene when a band of Saxons complete with a monk, all limped into view and attacked the Vikings. They left Brollachan in the pool and were attempting to talk to her, seemingly oblivious to all around them. She thought of making her way around to some trees to effect a rescue but some horsemen appeared and she decided to stay hidden. Two of the Vikings had escaped but not in her direction. Brollachan was speaking to the horsemen and in the end went off with the Saxons and their priest. Very strange, she thought, but I had better get back to the army. They didn't even take her weapons, another mystery.

CHAPTER 23

IVAR FINDS LOVE ON THE BATTLEFIELD

Ivar Grimsson was beginning to be better known as Ivar the Horsetrodden. A placid young man, he didn't mind such a name and Harald Edwinsson knew that. It had been obvious to any of his comrades in the battle that despite his injury, he had not shirked the worst of the fighting they had seen so far. One or two had grumbled about him lending his sword to a Saxon, even though it was a king in danger of being killed. Some said it was the first foolish thing he had ever done in his all life and this was a poor time to choose to do it. Although Ivar didn't know it, this had been the subject of much discussion on the march down the hill to Brunanburgh.

Ivar was left by Harald in charge of the wounded but fortunately six of the monks Bishop Odo had appointed to deal medical matters, arrived fairly quickly. Some of the men had been able to treat each others' minor wounds with what they carried. Ivar had gone around and helped a little. After short time Ivar and five of his fellows were considering they should to return to the fight but they didn't know where to go. Ivar had already decided on Brunanburgh. They were all feeling much better and none had wounds still bleeding. The monks were no help with detailed directions except a much younger monk with them, Brother Michael, said he knew the area and would take them down to the River Don. He thought that was where the battle was taking place from what had been said to the other healers. He wanted to go there to help with the casualties and asked to go with the Danes. He also claimed to know here the Roman fort was located on the river.

No one particularly objected, thinking it was a good idea to have him along to make the numbers up to seven, an auspicious number. This didn't please him and he grumbled about heathen practices and beliefs. Ivar's friend Seward told him not to be so miserable and in a battle you need all the help you can get.

As they walked down the hill to the marshes by the River Don with Ivar and the others, limping as best they could, Seward thought, what hidden talents Ivar had. He so seldom pushed himself forward in any matter and had recently lost chances for a good marriage. He could have been something beyond working with his stepfather in the mill near Torksey. His real father had been an outlaw, declared Wolfshead within a few years of Ivar's birth. Lord Edwin, Harald's father, and some local men had hunted him for weeks in the marshes but to no avail. His body was found later in the old Roman canal and the shock of it all eventually killed Ivar's mother. Edwin was saddened by the whole event and when Grim the Miller and his wife asked to adopt the child, the whole neighbourhood was glad. Edwin was considering bringing up the child in his own house, as he had been friends for many years with the child's real father. Lordship brought many difficulties for Edwin, but his worst was to pursue a friend to death. He regretted it up to his own death, although his position had given him no choice. At the time his own wife, Freda, had advised him to delegate the job but he could not, in case anyone thought him weak, and in dereliction of his duty as their lord.

People had said how different Ivar was from his real father and how much he was like Grim, who was known usually as Grim the Silent, a name he enjoyed, were the truth told. No one objected to his use of his stepfather's name and Grim was happy how his son had grown. When he wasn't silent, he would go on at great length about him. What a hard worker! Always up in the morning! Seldom grumbles! Loves his mother and her cooking!

Very early in his youth Harald Edwinsson recruited him for his personal warband. Edwin had taught him well in the duties of a son and a lord, and Harald was not disappointed today with his choices of men.

Seward tried to make conversation on the march with Brother Michael and managed to get a bit of information out him. He decided he wasn't bad for a Saxon and certainly had no fear of being killed in a battle, a useful talent on such a day as this. Michael wasn't his real name but the one he took entering the monastery ten years ago. He was happy today as his name was from his patron saint, the one dedicated to soldiers. His family owned land near Gloucester as socmen. He had had some education as a child and wanted more, so he took to the abbey in Gloucester. He said he could speak Latin, some of the Frankish language which he had learnt from a stay with them, and most of the dialects of Angles, Saxons and Danes. He could speak some Welsh and hoped to go and convert them to the true path. When Seward ventured to say he thought they were already Christians, Michael denounced them as heretics, sinners, apostates, unbelievers and several other names Seward and some of the others would never have thought of to call a fellow man. Out of a long list he described, their practice which seemed to irritate Michael most of all. It was monks and nuns being married and sharing the same seclusion.

This caused some laughter amongst the Danes and Thorkil observed at least they would never been short of little monks and little nuns to carry on after them. Michael didn't see the joke and sulked. As they walked down nearer to the river the noise of the battle became more apparent.

"Listen to me" said Ivar. "We don't know which side has their back to the river. Are our men holding a crossing to prevent the enemy passing back over? We don't know and I suggest we go a little more west to the river where we can move along it. If we run into the enemy by chance and they certainly outnumber us, Michael here will have his chance to find out if it's his Saint Peter who takes his spirit or a Valkyrie. The rest of us can escape into the marshes."

Michael grumbled more and called them heathens.

Unmoved by this compliment, Ivar continued. "Lord Harald said another river meets it so we can't go too far. Just be quiet. I can't run and I don't want to have to stand and fight by myself. A single file and Michael in the middle of us! Thorkil can hit him with his spear if he's noisy.

They moved about another few hundred paces to nearer to the river and some woodland when they heard voices. Ivar signalled to move forward quietly and even Michael began to tremble with fear. He clutched his bag of medicines and bandages even tighter and crossed himself every ten paces, not daring to utter a word. He looked at the grim look on Thorkil's face, uncertain who he feared the most and decided it was him at this moment……. and not God.

They moved forward through the trees and came out into a more open area with a pool fed by a spring, pouring out of a wall made in the hillside. Standing in the spring with her back to the wall, was a naked girl with a sword and shield fending off four laughing Norsemen. The four were having so much fun they didn't see the Danes till it was too late. The girl saw the Danes and lost her concentration only to be grabbed by one of the Norse, regaining it in time to push her sword into his leg.

Again that day, for the third time, Ivar put a spear into the back of an unwary northerner, the one holding on to her, thinking, don't these people know of the dangers of turning a back to the enemy. Two of the others turned and ran. The third met Seward's flying axe and Ivar thought, I wonder if he's been taking lessons from Eric. That was done most cleanly and he isn't even a forester. The two who ran, stopped and looked back wondering why they weren't followed, then ran on.

Thorkil remarked. "Those two will come back with their friends. The battle must be going their way if they can spare the time for rape."

"May be" said Oswin, "but she's on their side. Saxon and Danish women don't look like her?"

The seven had a chance to look at her. She was dark skinned, looked all skin and bone. She was obviously young but they couldn't tell her age as she was covered in blue paint and some tattoos, long swirly patterns and animals. Her hair had never been cut in all her life and it was matted. She was still holding a sword like she meant business with it, and Ivar remembered where he had seen one like it. It was the fight next to King Athelstan when a woman who tried to strangle him had dropped it. The one he had given to Eric. This was a bronze sword he was facing now, however, not steel.

"Well, Monk" said Seward. "You're the one with a talent for languages. Ask her where she's from, her name and what she's doing here besides come to kill us all?"

Michael was stuck for words for once and everyone else laughed, except the girl.

"She's a Pict" he said, forcing out the words.

Ivar looked menacing at him and then ordered everyone else to keep a watch out for the Vikings and their friends.

"You're very clever for a monk. Even we lads from east of the Trent, uncivilised Danes accused by you of heresy and sin, already know that much. Try to be nice to her, she's got a sword and can use it well I suspect."

Thorkil said with some humour, "She's obviously a water sprite or a fairy, perhaps even a Valkyrie come for the souls of these Northerners and they didn't realise. Look how they upset her!"

Ivar thought she can come for my soul if she wants, but glared again at Michael.

"Get on with it!.... We do have all day because I feel I can't walk another step and these lads are looking faint. We'll take a rest while you do it. Speak nicely to her. Not the usual way you monks speak to women."

Michael grumbled again. "You should have stayed in the camp. You're all too sick to fight. How long must you carry on this slaughter?"

Someone shouted, "There are horsemen coming."

Down the hill towards them came about thirty men on horses and they rode at them. They formed a quick line, ignoring the girl and Michael.

This isn't my day, thought Ivar. It's that Saxon King again. He'd spotted the banner and was relieved it was the Saxons.

Athelstan rode up to the line and looked at Ivar who looked sternly at him. He said with a laugh.

"This isn't my day, Dane. I keep meeting you and your friends having a rest from defeating my enemies. My gold not good enough for you! You've made an end to his two friends, kill the long haired boy in the water and I can find you a battle.... Get on with it quickly..... We need to water the horses."

"My Lord, we did not take you money to kill women, take another look at your boy!"

Athelstan looked again in the direction of the spring and began to feel faint for just a moment. Juliana, he thought. Juliana! Juliana! My lovely precious beautiful Juliana! He thought back over twenty years and a fight at sea off Marseilles and the silly young man who jumped in the water to rescue another drowning boy to only be surprised it was no boy. Here was Juliana again, long dark hair, dark eyes, dark skin, how was all this happening? His friends said they didn't know he could swim. He said it came in handy to rescue fair ladies from the water and his Auntie Ethelfreda had insisted he learn. Might be useful one day, she'd say. Only two women in his whole life! They understood him, not like the others. He got love from them both. When they were gone, he couldn't face getting close to anyone again. No political marriage for him either.…. He collected himself.

"Tell me what's happening, Monk? Who is the girl? Why are you all here?"

Michael stumbled towards him and stuttered, "My Lord, we came across some Northerners attacking this child. The Danes killed two and the other two ran away. All these men are wounded and couldn't run after them. They left the camp and the care of Brother Osbert to look for the battle at the fort."

"I can believe anything of Edwinsson's berserks" said the King, thinking also this monk has a peculiar view of children, especially ones carrying swords. "They look a bit worse for wear................ If you are a healer, do something for them."

All this time the girl was standing in the water at the ready behind her shield.

"Ivar Grimsson asked me to question her but I'm too frightened. I think she's a witch"

Athelstan laughed. Superstitious monks always did make him smile and he thought: They all walked around in fear of women and for all the wrong reasons. He had wondered how long it would be before he met young Grimsson again.

"Go on ask her what she's up to here and what's her name.....Don't hang about! The worst that can happen is that she'll kill you. We can tell the Bishop you died in battle," said Athelstan with his customary wit.

A voice behind him said, "I'll be able to see it for myself. Hurry up, young Michael! Don't disobey your king."

"I'm not" wailed Michael. "She'll kill me..... Or put a spell on me."

At this point Ivar pulled the spear out of the dead Viking and gave Michael a prod saying, "One of us will kill you, my friend. I used to dream of getting into conversations with water sprites on the banks of the Trent when I was a boy. Not a chance given to everyone."

Michael moved forward and asked her in Welsh where she was from and what she was doing. She stood there glaring at him. He asked her name but still no reply.

Thorkil joked, "Try Latin. You monks and nuns speak it all the time to each other!"

Everyone laughed at this except for Michael and the girl and so he said something to her.

To everyone's surprise she answered him. "Mhor Rioghain, Badb Catha, Neman!" She said something else in Latin which made the King and the Bishop laugh again. She told Michael what she would do to him if he came nearer.

"For a barbarian, her Latin is better than yours, Michael" said Bishop Odo. "She can only have learnt bad language like that from the northern heretics. You also asked her what she is, not who she is. You should have learnt better Latin in Gloucester."

Sweet Holy Christ! Athelstan thought. All the money Auntie spent on that abbey and they turn out monks like this one who can't speak Latin properly. However are we going to drive out heresy in these islands?

Bishop Odo intervened for a moment. "Lord Athelstan, you are needed elsewhere today, and not here arguing over a lost girl. You need to show yourself elsewhere to you men." But before he could say more a groaning came from the nearby trees and the four men of the bishops guard rode over, dragging out a Viking who was bleeding from a wound in his chest. Michael ran over and stopped the blood.

The Viking moaned "Devils, witches, fairies! The Scots brought them all down on the ships to curse us. God's not giving victory to us because of them. *Jarl* Anlaf was right."

Then despite Michael's best efforts he died. The bishop's guard produced another body, very much dead.

"Did you kill them, girl" asked Odo quietly in Latin?

"They were going to rape and then kill me. They killed our warriors who were with me and I managed to escape. They caught up with me here. I came to wash my wounds. It looks like a holy spring." She replied proudly.

"I believe it is," said the Bishop. "There is a statue of the Virgin in that niche in the wall behind you. You will find its water healing"

"I didn't mean holy to Christians. I meant to the Goddesses of the Land, you Saxon hypocrite. To the Great Queen and Brigid," said the girl, still behind her shield.

Listening to all this Athelstan thought, there isn't only a King of Britain needs to keep an eye on his friends in this world. I wonder how much the enemy have been falling out. I must speak with more of these women. They will know what is happening better than some men.

He shouted to Ivar. "Capture the girl, don't harm her and look out for any more. Bring them to me when you can. I want to ask them what's happening with their army."

He then rode off with his guard.

Bishop Odo asked Ivar his name, and then if he could return Michael to him in one piece as he had a future in the Church. He thought he would be wasted if he was murdered by Vikings or fairies and rode off laughing. Michael looked glumly at Ivar and asked what they were going to do. Ivar called everyone together. "It's dangerous in the open here. We need to get into cover…Back into the trees next to the marsh!" He was relieved everyone obeyed his commands. Harald Edwinsson would not exactly be happy if he got any more of his men killed, chasing girls about the battlefield.

The movement of everyone back to the River diverted the girl's attention and Michael asked her to follow. She moved to stab him but Ivar grabbed her, but not before she hacked at him a couple of times. She fainted and he carried her into cover, telling Michael to pick up the sword and shield. He dutifully did as he was told.

Seward thought another narrow escape for Ivar, but realised the bronze sword wasn't much good to hack at mail armour, fine for stabbing. The girl clearly had used it, the blade was covered in blood, he noticed, as Michael handed it over to him. Not a very sharp edge but a good point and quite heavy. The shield was beaten bronze also but not very large. She had fended off blows with it. It was battered.

Michael was tending her wounds which were numerous but mainly superficial. "She has not lost much blood but I think she's really hungry and tired. She hasn't eaten for days, I suspect. She's cold as well."

She began to come round, mumbling, "Mhor Rioghain, Babd Catha!" Ivar wrapped her in his cloak and she stopped shivering.

"Listen lads, this wasn't a good idea finding the battle. We are all suffering a bit and I don't think I can walk too far. My leg's getting worse. My ribs ache now where this girl whacked me. Harald's shoulder is bleeding again. We can all hear the battles getting nearer and we still don't know whose side is nearest to us. We should try to locate the ford to cross over to Brunanburgh to join up with everyone else."

All this, he said thinking. I'll get to Brunanburgh yet, see if I don't.

Thorkil said he would climb a tree and see if he could see the fort. He climbed one higher up the bank with Seward's help and came back excited. "I can see it. It's just over to the west but there's the river and a marsh between us and it. It's magical. Did the Romans really build it? It's in red stone."

When the girl had finally come round Michael was able to have a proper conversation in a mix of Latin and Welsh of which she could speak a little, it seemed. Neither were her native tongues. Ivar and the others had shared some food with her and after a while she began to talk through Michael, who could hardly translate fast enough.

Between the shaking in fear and the tears of relief, she said she had lived in the far north where her people had once been the rulers but were conquered by the Scots. They had been powerful but Viking raids had made them so weak they had to agree to join with the Scots and become

Christians. They had had to give up their horses to the Scots as well. This was all in the time of her great-great-grandfather or perhaps before. Her father was a chief of his *Clan* and had been forced to give her as a hostage as a child. She was sent to a convent. Her people weren't really Christian and when the chance came to take part in an attack on the Saxons, no one was prepared to fight unless women were allowed to go into battle as in the old days. The Scots agreed not realising that the Picts had to practice their old beliefs to do so.

She escaped from the convent and joined up with the women who had been secretly practising magic and training with weapons. Their custom was not to eat proper food before the battle, only a potion made from berries they had brought with them to give visions. However, the whole army was running out of food and the Scots had kept most of it for themselves. They hadn't anything left for after the battle either. She didn't think there would be many survivors anyway. The Scots and the Picts had been in some of the worst of the fighting. Many of the women had not been allowed to take part naked, so this spoilt the magic. In the end things were so bad they had to change their mind but it was too late. Their soldiers hadn't enough armour even though the Scots had promised them some, and men were just getting killed and wounded by the Saxons. She'd only just escaped from the battlefield when the Vikings had attacked her people to stop them retreating and tried to rape her. She wanted to know if she was safe with them.

Ivar assured her she would be safe if she stayed with them, but they were going to rejoin their comrades and fight with them. Their commander was an honourable man but he did not, however, like taking prisoners from the enemy. The king had commanded she and any other women they could find should be kept safe. He would obey the king when Ivar told Harald about this order.

She said she was still frightened and wanted to have her sword and shield. Ivar gave it her but she fainted again when she tried to lift them. Michael thought she had taken the potion before the battle and the effects were showing. He didn't like losing any of his patients, not even Danes and Picts, so could they all rest for a while and give the girl a chance for some sleep? He wanted to stitch up Harald's shoulder as well. Only Seward was looking anything like healthy so Ivar asked him to find a way over the river. Seward said he couldn't bear the thought of watching Michael stitch up a wound and went off to find a way to Brunanburgh.

The girl went into a deep sleep as Ivar watched over her for Michael. She came round occasionally mumbling the words Babd Catha, Mhor Rioghain,

Neman, which she shouted at them earlier. The day was moving on and it was about mid-afternoon when Seward returned. He had found them a way over by following a path to the bank. There was a raft hidden in the reeds. Two trips would get them over.

Ivar waited until Michael had finished with the wounds and called quietly for everyone to get ready for a move. He woke up the girl who was still dazed. They moved off quietly and slowly with Thorkil watching the rear. Not long afterwards they circled some fields and saw some men running.

"Scotti! Scotti! Cymbri!" said the girl. Michael didn't need to translate.

"They might be trying to get around the back of the fort. We ought to warn them, Ivar," he said.

"For a monk you're getting a bit warlike, I could get to like you. Let's get moving. How far, Seward?"

"Just in those bushes over there, down that bank."

The raft only just took four of them. Ivar, Seward, Thorkil and the girl went over first. Seward went back with the raft. They put Harald and Michael on it and the others swam with it. The ground was more open on the other side and they could see some cottages from the top of the bank and what could be Ryknield Street according to Michael. A little further and the fort came into view with ranks of men stretched out at the side at the top of the riverbank. Ivar saw the Edwinsson banner and ran to it as best he could.

"Mighty Odin! Am I glad to see you Ivar Grimsson! We need even you and seven men in this place," said Harald.

"I have only brought five, a monk and a girl, Lord Harald. One of the men is bleeding so badly now he can't fight. There are also some Scots and Cumbrians on the other side of the little river looking for a way over perhaps. Thorkil can show you where"

Harald shouted to some Frankish horsemen and one of them lifted Thorkil on to his horse as they rode off.

"Ivar, I couldn't think of dying without you and the lads by my side. I'm not sure I want the monk.......... and that woman you've found is a Picti."

"We rescued her from the Vikings. Anlaf's men seem to be turning on their own side. She says it is because we are winning. There are thousands dead down the river near that Roderham village, mainly Scots and Picts. We have met the king and that Bishop Odo. He wants us to spare the women we find fighting on the battlefield. They appear to be priestesses, a bit like Valkyries because the Picts believe they can't win unless they have them on the battlefield, encouraging the warriors and fighting. This one had already killed two Vikings near where we found her. She wounded another and I had to finish him."

"I am surprised Athelstan wants us to save the heretics and unbelievers as he calls them but you and her obviously make a good team," he said with a laugh. "To say this is a battlefield, we have had a good share of humour today. If any of us survive to tell the tale, the skalds will have lots to do.....If this young lady has been killing Vikings, we'd better not tell any of them. They'll say we stood by and she did it all."

"They'll make up the best bits as normal. This healer we have is a good one for a Saxon. He's stitched up a wound on young Harald the Ferryman's son. Both of them will certainly live past the ordeal."

Harald laughed and shouted over to another man. "Ivar Grimsson, meet Lord Karl of Tours, and here is what's left of his men."

Ivar looked around at the devastation and the bodies, dead and wounded and at a man only a year or two older than himself, perhaps.

"A poor day to meet, my lord!"

"It might be a good one to die with new friends, Ivar Grimsson," and shook his hand warmly.

Michael ran up followed by the girl complete with her sword and shield. Every few steps she poked him with her sword. "She wants Ivar, my lord," he whined.

By this time Ivar's cloak wasn't hiding much but Harald looked at the sword and then at Ivar.

"You gave Eric one like that in the battle at the top of that hill. The girl's sword is bronze and no good against our mail. He still has it by the way. He told us all about how you picked it up after the woman tried to strangle you. The one you gave him is steel."

In not very good Danish dialect, Karl said he had never heard so many funny stories on one battlefield, especially the one about the horse and the other about the Valkyrie strangling Ivar.

Ivar asked Michael to translate for her again, ignoring the laughter once again.

The girl said she had been thinking about what had happened during the battle and the time beforehand. She was convinced the Scots had forced them all to come just so they could get them killed. They could take more of the land in the north and that the Vikings were involved in the plan as well. So many of them had been killed and even if *Jarl* Anlaf won the battle and defeated the Saxons as he said he would, she didn't think any of them would be going home to defend their homes and families. Her father had been a chief and she thought it was her duty to consider things like this. Her twin brother had been chief but perhaps he was dead now. The survivors would look to her as the leader. She continued and this made Harald and Karl concentrate, Jarl Anlaf's brother had decided to try crossing the river by the fort with his men and the *Wealas* to go raiding. They tried it days ago but they couldn't get organised and made a weak attempt before they were ready because they thought the Saxons weren't prepared. They held the ford against them. Michael had struggled to interpret all this as she spoke quite fast.

In Latin and to the surprise of everyone, Karl asked "Princess, how do you know this?"

Similarly surprised she replied, "Our *Cailleach* has been sitting on Anlaf's council and she has told us. The Vikings wanted us to fight here in case we got the chance to move into the rest of the Saxon's land. They said we should fight the Saxons and we could have their land, but all they have done is kill our people because we had no armour."

Karl asked "do women fight in your country?"

"We did in our years of glory when we first conquered the north and were victorious. We drove the Romans out of the mountains back to their earthworks and then to their wall. The Christian Saint Adomnan made women give up war. After that we began to lose the battles and our land. The *Cailleach* formed us into another band in the name of the *Mhor Rioghain* and here we are, but I think we fight the wrong enemy……."

Harald Edwinsson thought to himself. There's one or two in this battle thinking they are on the wrong side. She may be only a bit more than a child but she's not stupid or without insight into the real world. The monks and nuns never changed her very much.

"……and I don't think I am ever going to see my home and family again."

Harald said, "Tell her, I think she is right in all she has said and she has spoken fairly with me and my men. If we win today, I would like her to come to my house and my wife will treat her as a sister and I as a daughter."

Karl said this to her and she said, she was grateful but really wanted to fight for them in the battle against her real enemies, the Vikings and Scots. She did not care about dying anymore.

When Karl translated there was more laughter from another man.

"The lads would love this, they already are calling her the *Valkyrie*" said a familiar voice to all.

"Eric, Eric, they haven't killed you so far. I am glad to see you," shouted Ivar.

"They are doing their best but it's not good enough"

"A bit like Michael's Latin" said Harald and everyone laughed again, except Michael and the girl. "She can fight if she wants and I don't think we could do much to stop her short of tying her up in the fort. She looks so resourceful, she would escape. Besides if Anlaf's men don't want her on the battlefield, her presence could unnerve them. Ivar, keep a watch on her, and look after yourself as well."

Michael grumbled again at this and went into a long tirade about heresy, civilisation, the holy saints, wrath of God only to be cut short by a shout.

"They're here again. They're coming and there's more this time."

CHAPTER 24

BEFORE THE ATTACK ON BRUNANBURGH

Charles de Tours, son of Count Henric, didn't need telling twice about the attack and nor did his men. He was relieved at the speed the Danes formed their battle line across the ford. His men and the Saxons he had previously commanded were narrowly beaten to their places, with a lot of good humour by all concerned. Karl, as the Saxons called him, laughed as well.

The battle, during the early part of the day, had been a hollow victory because of the casualties, much more wounded than dead and more to take care of. Athelstan had promised his father, Henric, he would re-enforce him as soon as he could spare men from the main battle, as no one seriously thought the northern allies would attempt a crossing at such a well defended place. Two attacks some days before had been repulsed by the Saxon garrison he was sent to re-enforce. The local commander had been killed and Charles was put in charge. The river was shallow at his point although at it's widest in the area. At either side of the fort were deep pools and steeper banks. There were marshes on both sides of the River Don and in places behind it as Rykneild Street passed south over the smaller river. Charles could see the fort had been larger in Roman days and how the Mercians had altered it. It was formidable but it hadn't put off the few Vikings and their Irish and Cumbrian allies who made up most of the attacking army.

Harald Edwinsson and his force were more than enough to make up the losses, and he knew more men were on the way. He liked how Edwinsson had kept his men away from the bank to avoid being spotted by the enemy. Uncle Athelstan, he thought, was always a bit despairing about the Danes but they were serving him well today. He was impressed by one of Harald's troop commanders who suggested they place obstacles just under the water in the ford to deter horsemen from crossing and slow up any men. The man, Eric, made an example out of wooden spikes, weighted down with a stone and it took him a few minutes. A couple of hundred appeared in no time plus some spikes to knock into the bank. Some were spread thinly within arrow range and others more densely to drive the enemy closer to the archers. Charles de Tours wished he'd thought of all this and began to understand Uncle Athelstan's suspicion of the Danes.

"Too well organised at times, but at least on our side," he'd said to Charles and his father on numerous occasions.

When he left home, his little sisters had said to him "find a princess to marry and bring her home for us to play with." All the Saxon ones seemed to have been married off already, although one or two earls' daughters looked good. The only exciting "princess" he had seen was from the enemy's side in the company of a Danish berserker and a miller's boy, when he wasn't out killing and murdering for his king. This would be a good story to take home. His sisters wouldn't have liked a princess carrying a sword and as for his step-mother, she would have taken a look at the princess's body decorations and gone into one of her faints.

Charles came out of his thoughts when someone said to him. "My lord, they've turned back."

"What? What are they up to? Harald, can you see anything?"

Another of Charles's men said, "They are leaving the water and going back on the bank and forming up again." Charles translated.

Harald ordered they send out patrols on horses upstream, just in case there is another crossing and sent some more to see what happening at the crossing over the smaller river. These went off and some time passed and so he stood down most of the men.

During this time Eric found Ivar again. His new battle companion was nearby and she was making him rest his leg with the rest of the wounded who could be counted on to fight if required.

"Eric, Brother Michael says this girl knows a great deal about medicine and she's helping him with the wounded. Now her hands have steadied she's sewing up wounds and she doesn't say prayers over everyone either. She treats more wounds that way."

"That'll please our lads, especially as she doesn't seem to bother about clothes."

"Well, I've got one of the boys from the fort to go for some clothes from his mother. She'll catch a cold if not something worse, but at least she's eating something. She's told Michael, they have been short of food for some time and she has hardly eaten for days."

"Ivar, if she insists on fighting, I have brought her the sword which was dropped by the woman who tried to strangle you. She could defend herself better with it but I think sometimes that such women intend to sacrifice themselves in battle in order to gain the victory."

"She is very unhappy because the Vikings started to kill the Picts despite being allies. I think they may have killed her brother and attacked the other women. She knows she can never go home, no matter who wins today. Harald has offered her a home but I think it is not what she wants."

"It's true Harald's family have a history of caring for the unfortunate amongst our own people and that is why many of us readily follow them. Perhaps we had better take her the sword and let her choose her own fate."

The girl looked at the sword and burst into tears and spoke for a long time in her own language, crying over Ivar. Charles who was checking his wounded came over and asked what was wrong.

He translated the Latin for her. "The sword belongs to the *Cailleach* who's our leader and priestess. Did you find it on the battlefield on her body, did you kill her?"

Eric answered by telling the story of how the King and Ivar had been attacked by some of the Picts and Scots and how a woman had nearly killed Ivar but had dropped the sword. She tried to strangle him instead. Eric had watched this but could not kill her. He pushed her off him and she ran away.

The girl cheered up a little bit and took the sword. Eric had found a sheath for it and she said she could now carry both into battle. "Swords are sacred "she said. "Whilst the *Cailleach's* is new, mine is many years old and was re-forged for me when I was dedicated to the *Mhor Rioghain*."

Ivar asked Charles to tell her he would be unhappy if she died and that Harald had asked him to protect her during the battle. She should not throw her life away because she was unhappy now. She could find happiness if she looked for it.

She looked very serious and said she had her duty to her sisters to take revenge. She believed they had not perished in battle as they wanted but had been murdered by their so-called friends. She gave Ivar a hug and a kiss which took him by surprise, and said. "Stay alive for me yourself but I must do my duty."

She ran off to Michael. Charles translated and then said to Ivar.

"Guard her well my friend and you could take a wife home to your mother. When this is all over find out her name and say 'amo' to her. It's Latin for I love you."

He went back to his men leaving Ivar with that amazing scrap of knowledge.

"Eric, we are going to have to find out her name"

"Ivar, what do you mean, we are?"

The opposite bank of the River Don was unusually quiet but what seemed a couple of thousand men and some horses were milling around on it. It was getting to the late afternoon. Charles and Harald began to expect some trick instead of a frontal attack. The scouts had returned with no bad news and the attack on the other ford had never materialised. The watch on the top of the hill looking down Ryknield Street reported some horsemen coming and soon about a hundred Franks wearing the de Tours badge were dismounting. A pale looking man without armour dismounted and walked slowly towards Charles.

"Son, the enemy have not claimed you."

"Not yet, father, but they have tried."

"I thought I might come for one last battle with Athelstan and yourself. Are we in good company?

"The King has put a lot of his old fighters in the fort. Twice they held off the northerners a few days ago. We're re-enforced with Danes and if they fight as good as they laugh, the victory is ours already. Come and meet their leader, Harald Edwinsson, but watch out for one his men, Ivar Grimsson, he's a man to get you killed if you stand next to him. His comrades say he is a man who death follows around today. He has a talent for finding the best part of the fighting. He's been trampled on by a horse and almost strangled by a woman. Nothing keeps him from the fight, however."

"Perhaps I may walk a bit with him. My pains do not ease and the doctors promise much with no results."

"We have a monk with us who seems to know his medicine, and we have a painted witch. Grimsson found her on his passage around the battle. She knows healing too."

"As long as she doesn't mutter and mumble over me, son, I don't care."

"You'll like her, Dad. She seems not to want to wear clothes anymore. She wants to fight on our side as well. The Vikings have been killing her people on their own side it seems, and this Ivar Grimsson rescued her from being raped and killed by them."

A short time passed and some more Franks turned up at speed with pack horses. In that time Henric had met Harald and confirmed the king's orders. Harald was to be in command of the complete battle at both the ford and the fort. The king now suspected this attack could be more than a diversion, and that an attempt to get a force to his rear or one to go south as raiders, could be part of his enemies' strategy. Athelstan could not understand why they had made a half hearted attempt to cross and take the fort. It gave the game away if that were the case. He concluded they hadn't a strategy at all and were just seeing what they could do with the numbers they had. He knew they outnumbered him but what a rabble and said this to Henric. They were dying in hundreds. Just to be on the safe side, he wanted the place on his flanks guarded by men who knew how to fight. He knew what the Franks could do and he'd fought with the Danes today, and against them before. Slyly he thought they would fight and die for him, and more who die, the fewer he would have to deal with after the battle. Henric had kept that part of the king's thoughts to himself. They had been friends many years.

Charles was happy at the sight of his father and more of their men. What they brought he welcomed almost as much. Ballistae! Small portable ones, just like the Romans had. Henric was also a Roman in re-incarnation, just like his old friend Athelstan. Henricus, he would call him on occasion. Both spoke good Latin.

"Assemble them quickly" he shouted. "Harald, you need them on the flanks so they fire across the attackers. They can be trained on those obstacles in the water or beyond normal arrow range where soldiers form up. There are five. You need the three to fire across on to your weakest side or where the banks are not so steep. They're no use really close up."

Harald had revised his battle lines. The Frankish cavalry were dismounted but with their horses hidden on the right. They might be need to ride into the water, and had two of the ballistae plus some archers from the fort. The bank here was not so steep. His men had the centre. The battered remains of the Frankish infantry with their re-enforcements were also on the right. He put the three ballistae and some more archers to deter anyone from climbing the bank. The Saxons in the fort could also cover the ford with arrows, and a number of them were in his second lines in the centre. Old soldiers prepared to die for their king. The ford had to pass down one side of the fort which was on a knoll out into the river. The sides had been made steeper a part of the original defences set out by Lady Ethelfreda. The other side of the fort was marshy but the wall and bank facing across the river, were steep and covered by the forts defenders. The original ford had been there but the river had moved since the fort was built, and a combination of marsh and deeper water had made that side impassable.

Henric thought, I am glad he's in charge as he looked at Harald. Charles is no coward but he hasn't the experience yet for a large command and he's going to be needed at home soon. I can't get him killed in this northern skirmish. We have an empire in the south to build and defend again. He thought what his first wife would have said, were she alive. Two of her sons were already dead from fighting in wars with their father, and he couldn't sacrifice the last one. All he had as an alternative were daughters to marry off and they were still children. He felt he hadn't long to go on and he needed Charles to look after them and the younger woman he married in the hope of more sons. There would, however, be no more now. He was dying and her body, and seemingly her mind, were ruined by continuous child bearing. It's going to be a good day to make an end of all this, he thought. I must meet this Ivar Grimsson.

Harald pointed him out amongst the wounded. He walked over towards him but stopped short and looked at two men talking together. Ivar was looking a little worse for wear and he knew that was him, torn clothes and battered mail shirt. He was, however, nonchalantly sharpening a sword, a strange looking lightweight thing. The other man was sharpening an axe and carried no sword. This man had various blood stains over him which on closer inspection, were clearly not from his own supply.

"Ivar Grimsson, my son Karl, says you are a man who cannot keep out of a fight."

"Not so, my Lord, he is confusing me with Eric Sigurdsson, even though he's hardly had a scratch in this battle so far."

"It's the way I swing my axe, no one comes near me," said Eric, giggling like some small child. "I keep out of the way of horses also."

Everyone else around them laughed at this, except Ivar who was tiring of this particular tale.

"Do you carry a toy sword to match your big axe, Eric? Does your little brother have to sharpen it for you?" asked Henric.

This caused more laughter but nothing could dampen Eric's humour and he replied.

"My Lord, this blade almost caused the death of my friend here and he's putting an edge back on it for the love of his life."

"I presume it wasn't she who tried to kill him"

"No, her best friend it seems."

"Ah, the mysterious painted witch. I suppose she's going to carry it in the coming fight."

Eric showed him the shield and the bronze sword which the girl had left with him.

"Eric, we have a collection of these in my castle at Tours. They go back to the days when the Gauls ruled the country. Some people in isolated parts have only recently stopped speaking the language. My grandfather collected them and I used to play with them as a child. Karl says she's a priestess of some sort. You call her a Valkyrie."

Ivar said, "She shouts something like Morrigan. She says she has to fight so her people win battles, but hasn't been allowed to, until things got very bad for them. Then it was too late."

"And she wants to kill Vikings now?"

"If they all went home," said Eric, "even we would forgive them and not kill any more."

More laughter and even Henric forced a smile.

Charles ran over. "They coming and they mean it this time. They have horsemen with them. Must have been what they were waiting for!"

Harald watched the mass of bodies advance. At least three or four times as many as we are, he thought. I wonder what's going on in the rest of the battle. Are we outnumbered three to one everywhere? Still, the Franks and Saxons were outnumbered this morning and managed to survive. The horsemen are at their rear. They want a breakthrough to get round the back of us. There seems only enough to deal with us or to go raiding, not enough to attack the main army. They may not have spotted our horses because of the trees. He told Charles his thoughts and he got his men ready to mount up in case of a break through. Everyone got into place as he was thinking and he turned back to watch three figures move slowly towards the lines. What's going on there, he wondered?

Ivar was limping forward supporting Henric. The girl followed behind them with her new sword in its case and her old one in her hand. Her shield was on a strap over her shoulder.

The girl was chattering in Latin to Henric. "You're too old and ill to fight. I know a remedy for the stomach pains and cramps. Don't listen to these monks they know nothing about how to get people better. They just want souls to go to heaven. This world is nothing to them. The next one is all they think about. They have all led my people astray. They got us killed for nothing fighting against the Scots and then fighting for the Scots. We can't even die with honour."

"I want to die myself but your chattering is killing me before I have a chance to find my sword." With a laugh he translated for Ivar who didn't see any joke.

"My lord, you've hardly the strength to lift it and none to wear any armour. Harald Edwinsson and Karl wouldn't want me to get you killed," said Ivar.

Karl knows what I have to do and Edwinsson has his hands full with this battle. Find me somewhere to die with honour. Don't you ever do what you are told?"

"Only when my mother tells me!"

"Don't be silly with me. Humour an old man, it's the only thing kept me alive the past few weeks this thought of a last battle."

A man of similar age to Henric came up with a sword. He was dressed like a warrior and looked menacingly at Ivar. He almost picked up Henric and they had a conversation in Frankish. At the end of it Henric said.

"This is Alain. He and I have been through much and he knows a soldier's duty to his commander. He only takes orders from me and even Karl knows that. Ivar Grimsson, find me a place to die."

Looking out over the River Don, Ivar said. "I think we only need to stand where we are, Lord Henric. You had better put on your sword."

The girl chattered on in Latin. "That noisy monk has all kinds of herbs in his pack. The first chance I get I'll make something good for your stomach to ease the pain and help you eat your food. He'll give me something for you..........."

"He most certainly will" muttered Alain under his breath. "I shall see to that."

"………..I can see what is wrong just by looking at you. You'll feel better soon."

"But I won't live," said Henric.

"A warrior does not fear death" said the girl. "I came here to die for a victory for the Scots, but that has been spoilt by our allies. All I have now is revenge on the people who have lost us the battle and our heritage."

"Dear God," said Alain. "I am with not only desperate and dangerous men to today, but women of the same like. Are the ways of peace lost in this island?"

"Alain, even the Romans needed more soldiers to hold on to Britain than any other part of their empire" said Henric. "And this was after they had killed about half of the population. The reason they lost the island was due to sending troops home from here to take part in civil wars, even the locals they recruited. The Britons will kill anyone for gold."

"A bit like us, my lord," said Alain with a smile. "We steal the land as well."

"I'm quite happy to die around here. I used to come this far north with my mother and her sister Helaine in King Alfred's time. There's a church and a shrine a bit further north just off this river dedicated to Sainte Helaine, the mother of Emperor Constantine. She passed through the place on her way to Rome with her son when he was to claim the throne and turn the Romans into Christians."

"There was a man who must have led a difficult and uncertain life," said Alain. "It must have been a little like ours, my lord."

"I can't remember what this place with the shrine is called either. I remember it's across some more marshes. It might have been more north of here."

"No point in you asking me to take your body there for burial then. You'll just have to live a little longer."

Ivar and the girl didn't understand any of this. They were anxious to get to the battle. Looking across at the enemy Ivar could see how slow moving they were. Speed is essential in battle was what his father Grim always said. Decisive movement is the key to winning, even if it's only a fight in your cornfield. Two old soldiers seemed to find time for a discussion about something and a thousand Scots were casually trying to ford a river. He would do it differently and be more decisive. He and the girl hurried to the front of the soldiers to get a better view of the river and face the enemy. The enemy didn't move through the water any faster.

She started to shiver and Ivar put his cloak around her again. Almost forgetting herself, she leant against him with a smile, hugged him, and then remembered what she was doing. She didn't break away but tried to concentrate her gaze on the men coming across the ford.

The men behind them had locked shields and those behind them were poised to raise theirs into the air to deflect missiles of any sort despite the advantage of higher ground. Eric's voice broke Ivar's concentration.

"Ivar, bring the poor girl back into safety until we see if they have any surprises for us."

Ivar ignored him and watched the enemy, still with his arm around the girl. He could feel her heart beating and her body straining to move off to attack.

CHAPTER 25

THE ATTACK ON BRUNANBURGH

Ivar Grimsson had been determined not to become the subject of heroic verse and said to himself. I think for the first time today, I'll let the enemy come to me and not seek them out. I just wish they would make better speed. He gave the girl another hug as she was shivering and stamping her feet in anticipation of the fight.

Harald Edwinsson was standing on a rock overlooking his men and staring into the ford across the River Don, thinking, come now, we're ready.

Eric Sigurdsson was stood quietly, thinking of Tildi and the children he had taken as his own with the new one on the way. He was still watching Ivar and the girl.

Henric of Tours was feeling as if he had more life left in him than he had had for weeks, and how proud he was of Charles who had done his duty to Athelstan, his benefactor.

The advance of the northern allies seemed slow through the water and Harald realised he had no idea how far it was to the other bank. He could see that the men weren't moving through too deep water. The river was low. It had been a dry, late summer. The coming autumn could be dry, even though there were rain clouds above. The column of men was widening out as it came forward, the same as the horsemen. They were trying to maintain the close ranks.

"Ideal target for the ballistas," said a nearby voice to bring him out of his thoughts.

A grizzled Frank nearby introduced himself as Alain de Briscourt, a supposedly retired soldier and nursemaid to Henri, le Sieur de Tours. Harald had seen him keeping a watching eye over Athelstan's friend, and even young Karl when they had arrived earlier. The urgency of the defence of the ford had prevented an introduction and the man seemed retiring, almost monk-like.

"This battle has brought many good warriors out of retirement," said Harald. "Has word gone around, its one too good to miss?"

"I crossed the sea to come here. My mother foretold if I crossed the sea, I'd die. I have crossed the sea many times. Perhaps she meant this time."

"You should have followed her advice and stayed in Briscot or are you like your lord, seeking a place to make an end to everything?"

"Oh no, I have several duties. You're only here to fight. I have to keep Lord Henri and his son alive.... and fight. La dame de Tours, the new one that is, wants father and son to return in one piece and here's me with the burden of prophesies on my mind."

"Well, Alain, next to me isn't going to be the safest place for an old soldier ....or even a young one."

"You could be wrong there. I've been in lots of battles and found the safest place is at the front. At the back arrows, javelins, stones and so on appear out of the sky when you least expect them. Usually when you're lost in thought!..... You look like a man determined to be in the thick of it."

"Fate and the command of a king have led me here. If you are determined you had better stand at the front with me."

They walked through the ranks and stood at the front. The sight of Alain raised a cheer amongst the Franks.

"I taught some of these rogues all they know about killing and murdering," said Alain proudly."

"I hope they learnt it well," said Harald. "Can you be ready to give the order to fire those big arrows? You seem to know about them."

"They are devastating when used against massed horsemen. That lot over there have no idea what to do with cavalry. They should be at the front or the flanks, not at the rear. I can't help thinking they are there just to keep the foot soldiers moving. Have your men ever faced horsemen by the way?"

"No....Never! The best action a few of us ever seen was raiding the Scots last year. They never put a large army together. The king didn't give them time or opportunity to put a lot of men together either on foot or on horses."

"Wise man, you were too far from home. Athelstan is like my lord and me. He learnt his war in a hard place."

"We only get a few pirates daring to sail up the Trent or land on the coast. They usually look for horses to move what they steal back to the boats. We keep a few for messengers and commanders. The king used them for transport on the raid but no one fought from them."

"We are starting to use them again, more as a force of armoured men as you can see from the ones here with us, just like the Romans. Those lads over there aren't even armoured properly. They'd be easy to knock over. Some even have short swords. If one comes close I'll demonstrate the best way to do it. There's bound to be one who thinks he's a hero."

"You should meet Eric Sigurdsson who is commanding my warband; he does things like that as if it came with mother's milk. You can't miss Eric, he has no sword. He's left it with his woman and stepson in case they need it, if he doesn't return. He'll be at the front swinging his axe."

"I have seen him, his friend Ivar Grimsson and the little girl he found. A dangerous looking young woman I have to say. She seems to know her medicine, however. Ivar's looking after Lord Henric at the moment. All of them look as if some sleep would do them good..... It would do us all good.......... I have asked him not to risk Lord Henric's life. He's done his share of fighting and should give someone else a chance. I wish he would go for a sleep in the camp."

Some of us may sleep for longer than we expect when that lot arrive, thought Harald.

Alain went on. "I can't understand why they keeping stopping. Are they trying to make us attack them?"

"We don't move off this bank and lose the advantage. They can stand in the water for the rest of the day and night," Harald bellowed to the men. Someone translated for the Franks.

"Alain, if I fall I want you to command this force. I think you are the only man to keep it together. I'll send a boy around to the others to tell them. I wish we could have met earlier and worked out some plan for this place."

"Dear Jesus, I thought I had given up all responsibilities for life and death. I was going to become a monk when this is over and I get Henric safely back home. She seems a silly little woman to some does La Dame de Tours but she's borne as many children for the family as she could to the point she's killing herself. She's told me to bring Charles home, if all else fails, or the family falls apart. She was so young and pretty until recently but the last two children nearly killed her. People say she's stupid but it's the veil behind which she hides her influence. She makes good decisions and understands everything. Henric can't last much longer but he should hold on for a while. He still needs to be alive over there while Charles takes over with Lady Isabelle to back him up. Pardon me, I could go on and on about this."

"Unless this lot in the water move soon, we shall be in need of entertainment, diversion and instruction," said Harald. "Anyhow you still have to take command this place. Your lord is too tired and his son too young, although a quick learner, I think."

"Shall we have a shot at them with the ballistae? It should irritate them enough for some hotheads to rush forward at the sight of a few dead comrades."

"Give that order, Alain!"

Alain walked over to the two ballistae stationed where the bank was the least steep and gave instructions to the men, then over to the other three and waited. Six shots from the left flank went out in succession to the middle of the northern force. Horses and men fell. Then order and counter order from the enemy seemed to ring out from over the water. The horsemen moved forward in the direction of the source of the bolts, leaving behind the infantry which they had trampled while changing position to the front, only to come up to the obstacles in the ford. At that point the others fired into the mass of horses and men. The archers joined in with a few aimed shots. The riders retreated and the unseated men still alive ran back though the water into the on-coming army. The horsemen were regrouping in the deeper water just next to the ford to give the others a chance to move, when the ballistae fired on them again with the same results.

By this time some control over the foot soldiers had been regained and they were marching forward with their shields up like the Roman's tortoise.

Alain had returned to Harald and said "the bolts will break through the shields when they reach the obstacles. We need to let them just come a little nearer. The men have their orders."

"They didn't kill that many horsemen but they made them run away," Eric Sigurdsson shouted in encouragement.

The men stopped just before the obstacle as if they suspected something in the water or the horsemen had told them, and moved carefully forward. Meanwhile Henric had moved to the front as he wanted a better look and had joined Ivar and the girl.

"Good tactics" he shouted to Harald, "but you need to get them to come forward."

The girl looked at the water and shouted to Henric in Latin. "This trap has no bait."

She took off Ivar's cloak and ran into the water up to her knees. She shouted several times. "Mhor Rioghain, Mhor Rioghain."

She ran up and down the front of the defences and in and out of the water, screaming and shouting.

"I am not sure what she's calling to them but they're moving" said Alain.

"Perhaps she's saying we're a weak and cowardly lot and they can come and take an easy victory," said Harald. "For one moment that's how I felt when I saw them form up."

"I think she's offering herself," said Henric who had returned to join him. "Here comes a taker."

A man left the front of the ranks but got stuck on an obstacle. She ran into the deeper water and stabbed him. The girl grabbed up his sword and threw it towards his comrades. Two men ran towards her and as she ran away, the rest followed. First the ballistas and then the archers fired as they reached the obstacles in the water. Bolts and arrows seemed to fly around her and she just stood there yelling. This was too much for Ivar who limped towards her.

"Stand fast the rest of you," shouted Eric. "You can't all be in love."

Ivar pulled her out of the water and they were followed by several of the enemy who were finding a way through the obstacles and moving them aside to let through the rest. Ivar's leg had given way again and he fell over.

The girl stood over him shouting "Mhor Rioghain, Mhor Rioghain."

He stood up and they began to fight with the northern soldiers. They were taken in by the speed of the girl, how light she was on her feet, a quick stab and if it didn't strike home she had moved. She fought with Ivar at her back. He moved as best he could to prevent them getting at her back. He stood and she moved. It began to work as the northern army just watched them whilst trying to move through the obstacles whilst under attack from the ballistas and the archers.

Ivar was knocked over by a big Cumbrian but held on to his shield. The girl jumped back to rescue him and diverted the soldier long enough for Ivar to bring his sword up to stab the man.

The enemy had almost circled them again and Ivar struggled to his feet, held his sword and stood back to back with her again. For a moment no one moved until their attention was diverted by a handful of horsemen charging down the water's edge. The northerners ran back into the water and the horsemen carried on to the other side. Ivar limped and the girl ran up the bank. The horsemen rode back as men ran out of the water again. By this time there were larger numbers coming through and forming up for attack. The ballistas fired on them again as they massed.

The girl ran out and shouted again. She picked up some abandoned weapons, swords and spears, and threw them at the men in the water.

All this was too much and men started to break ranks and attack the defenders of the ford in small groups. The enemy horsemen had reformed and moved over to where the bank was least steep. The ballistas fired on them again and again. Someone in the water was attempting some command, and their foot soldiers were concentrating their attack on the flanks where the ballistas were located.

Alain noticed this and shouted to Harald "this is what we want. I'll get the cavalry ready to go in the water once again."

The attackers at the steeper parts of the bank were beginning to realise they had a problem and were moving away to concentrate their efforts on the north east part where it was less steep. The obstacles in the water and the stakes in the bank were hampering their movement and they concentrated their effort again as the ballistas fired on them. The mass rush forward was met by arrows and as they tried to move down river, the Frankish cavalry met them in the shallows, driving them back to deeper water. Alain called the cavalry back and put more archers there. The northern allies withdrew to the middle of the river and then into the marshes on the far bank.

Harald observed all this in silence, thinking what a normally peaceful and lovely valley, so near to where I live and I've never visited it. He came out of his thoughts and then called for all the commanders. He asked Alain to translate for the Franks. "They tried us out there I think. They'll be back with a more measured attack now they know what we can do. We might have to arrange something a bit different next time to confuse them."

The Frankish soldier Gilbert LeVert, in charge of the ballistas, suggested they could engage them at a greater distance if required by Harald. The range might be improved enough to hit the opposite bank if they set them up on the fort. They wouldn't need troops around them on the walls. He did prefer them on the ground and thought they would be better served at medium range on cavalry. Both he and Alain thought they could expect more horsemen at a rush next time. Harald had already given orders for the obstacles to be extended along the bank and the Franks to patrol to the south again just in case there was somewhere else to cross. Unfortunately the conference was cut short as there was movement on the opposite bank. Everyone return to their previous places and Harald, Charles, Alain and Eric studied the opposing formation.

A broad column of infantry with rafts was entering the water.

"They are going to hide behind them when they get here," said Eric.

"They look like a different lot to me" said Charles.

"The eyes of youth prove an advantage once again," said Alain. "They certainly are by their speed and discipline. This lot look like the Dublin Vikings to me and some Welsh. The horsemen are keeping a distance and not concentrating. Someone has arrived who knows a bit about a fight."

"Ah well" said Harald. "Just when we though all we had to do was let the ballistae and the bowmen get on with it, we have to get stuck in ourselves."

More troops entered the water and formed up at the side of the newcomers.

"Where do they get the numbers," asked Henric? "They must have made some wondrous promises for all these to come without the money in their pockets. Where's the girl, I must ask her?"

She was at the back dealing with a few wounded. Brother Michael was looking a bit grim as the men preferred to go to her, even the Franks who professed to be Christian. Henric had recommended them to go to her. Michael didn't know. After a few words Henric returned.

"They have planned a full scale invasion of the middle of the country and then a return to York. I have to say King Athelstan expected this and even if we lose today's battle, they may not find a journey south as easy as they think. He would expect us to retreat into the fort if we cannot hold this river bank, and to delay their return."

"I do not plan any retreat or defeat" said Harald. "Those men are getting near enough for a shot from your big bows and arrows, Alain."

"Why not?" Alain went off to organise it.

Everyone else stood to and watched the numbers advance. The soldiers were recalled from the shallows where they had been collecting arrows, bolts, spears and anything else they thought useful for what was coming. Everyone stood waiting except for the girl.

After an hour's rest Seward and Thorkil decided now the time had come to do some more killing and despite the girl trying every language she knew, to stop them, they moved towards the front here they could see Harald and Eric. Michael had refused to intervene despite the seriousness of their wounds which had not been helped by the journey from the main battlefield. She ran after them and tried to get Henric to order them back. Instead Henric advised her to stay to the rear and reminded her of her narrow escape and how Ivar had risked his life to save her.

Harald intervened and asked Henric to translate. "Young lady, you seem to have a disturbing effect on the enemy and child or not, we have you on our side. If you want to fight you must be like every other warrior here and obey me. Get your gear and be ready to run into the water..... *when* I tell you."

With a big smile she ran to the rear. Harald shouted for Ivar.

"I know your mother is seeking a wife for you but only you would go looking for one on a battlefield. You are as stubborn as both your parents, especially your mother who we all love dearly. So no more unnecessary risks, she would be very sad if you get yourself killed foolishly fighting this bunch of pirates and cow stealers. I want the girl to act as bait again. This time she'll have some support and not take too many risks. You stay safe in the ranks. I have said before we have other battles after today's to fight."

Ivar looked at Harald, "Very well, Lord Harald.... but I am fighting here."

The hasty return of the northern allies gave Harald no time to rethink how his forces were deployed in any other way. His constant worry was encirclement now the enemy had discovered how difficult three frontal attacks had been. He ordered Charles to mount up his men when Alain suggested they could then be moved swiftly to any part of the banks and could also deal with a break though. They were set back a little in the trees. The northern horsemen could only come through the ford and they could be ready to challenge them. Harald stood again in front of his forces with Eric and Charles.

Eric peered out from under his helmet. "I cannot believe what I see. Three times or is it four, they have tried to storm this fort and its defences ...and they are coming back for another. They should try something else."

Alain walked up, snorted and said. "There is some vanity in the commanders on the other side of this river. There's perhaps a new one every time they try to cross and he thinks he can do better than the others who failed. It is because he has no respect for them as fighters. He doesn't put failure down to lack of numbers or a plan to deal with our defences. He sees it as an issue of will and leadership, lack of courage in the troops. This is playing into our hands and I think all we have to do is stand firm. They'll come to us and die."

"I wonder what to do if they fail and retreat again. We don't know what's happening over on the hilltops. Who is winning or losing," said Harald? "If they retreat again, should we follow?"

Alain agreed. "We must not follow the example of the enemy commanders and have no plan. I think we should follow them into the water with a small force and have the horsemen ready to cover a withdrawl back to here. The horsemen could also follow them further if it descends into a rout and they panic."

"We'll do that with the main force remaining in defence in case they see the error of their ways," said Harald with a laugh.

Brother Michael had been doing his best to patch up the wounded from the last attack There were only a few and most of them had preferred the girl or the women from the fort to tend them. Most of the seriously wounded had been moved into Brunanburgh out of the wind which was getting up and bring a chill to the end of the day. He was disappointed that they seemed to prefer remedies to prayer. He thought it was good that purgatory and hell were big places. They were undoubtedly full to the brim, he thought. Feeling rejected he decide to go and have a look at the river and the battle. He made his way into the Danish ranks to Ivar and Henric de Tours. He ignored the observations of many of the warriors about his piety and offers of a sword for the day.

Henric saw him and smiled and said in Latin. "Here at last, monk! You are going to need your bag of tricks when that lot get here. Look out over the water!"

Michael looked and winced. Henric translated for Ivar and the Danes who laughed some more. The attackers were very close, nearly up to the obstacles in the water.

"Dear God," said Michael. "I had no idea there were so many heathens come to plague our land."

"Don't be foolish, Michael, most of those men are Christian like yourself. God is on their side as well," said Ivar.

Michael was just about to enter his usual discourse on apostates, unbelievers and sinners when a figure slipped out of the front ranks She was naked and wearing a raven headdress, carrying two swords, shield and a couple of short spears. She ran into the water and threw the spears into the tortoise of shields. Surprisingly both found a victim as the men were taken by surprise, despite having watched her move with some fascination. The shields held in the air wavered and at that time and the ballistas fired. They fired more bolts and for a moment all seemed chaos. The force moved on into the obstacles where they put up the rafts as cover and began to try to move them. The girl ran deeper into the river and stabbed a soldier moving an obstacle. A couple of his comrades lunged out at her but she was gone. One followed, she turned and stabbed him. This was a bit too much for some of his friends and troops began to move through the works without clearing them, despite orders from their commander. The shields were coming down allowing arrows through the gaps.

After a short time the front of the force had cleared most of the hazards and was moving on to the bank under a rain of arrows and bolts. Ivar was hoping the girl would move away now. She had despatched another Cumbrian who wasn't quick enough but was being pursued by some others. None were fast enough and she disappeared down the front of the troops into the marshes. The attack moved up the bank. "Now for some serious slaughter" shouted Ivar. "Odin, grant us victory!"

"Sinner, unbeliever, devil worshipper," cried Michael! "How will God give us victory with you calling on the devil?"

"Very easily," said Ivar. "I'll kill more than anyone else." And with that he edged forward to the front, out of the ranks.

Michael went away in disgust at what he had heard, but thought he had better follow Henric's advice and get his medicines ready, especially treatments for sword wounds. He ordered some of the women and boys from the fort to collect wood for fires. They obeyed him reluctantly until he pointed out men need keeping warm if wounded.

Michael sat in thought for a moment wondering how he had found himself in such a place when all he wanted was to worship God. He was so tired all of a sudden but he thought for a moment, that at least all these people here needed him to heal their bodies, if not their souls. No one had really been too unkind to him but why did they persist in their heresies. He knew Ivar Grimsson was right about the other side. There were not many unbelievers on that side any more. His fellow monks had been successful for Rome and there weren't that many from Ireland. He knew the true church was making inroads there. Athelstan had more or less thrown out the Irish church from his lands and the Bishops were a bit angry when he wouldn't make it illegal. On matters of religion he was a believer in gentle persuasion, so strongly did he believe in the rightness of Rome, Michael reasoned. I will take all this as my quest and my test. He decided that painted witch and her Danish brigand are sent by the Devil to test my faith. She has the power of witchcraft and that is why all the sick go to her. They fear the power of prayer. They will only get better because the Devil allows it. The ones who die have resisted his power. The noise of the troops by the ford disturbed his thoughts and he decided to be grumpy again. He shouted at the people collecting wood and it reminded him of being at home with his parents in Gloucestershire. He had a vision of his now dead mother shouting at the servants and it made him sad, and much more bad tempered than ever.

Oswin, one of Ivar's companions on the journey to Brunanburgh who was not fit to fight was helping out with the other wounded, and heard all this. He came over and whacked Michael with a wet cloth.

"A sword next time! War is hard enough without monks grumbling. Let us all rest in peace. Get on with saving lives and souls, Monk. Then the rest of your life may not be in vain."

Michael became a bit apologetic and said. "I don't really want to be here, Oswin, but I think I have a duty to God."

"You could serve your God with better grace and if you think he has sent you to care for the people here, can't you at least show them a bit of love? Many are here out of duty to their king."

Michael felt a bit chastened and put his surgical instruments into boiling water to get ready. He couldn't hold back the tears, thinking why was he so ill at ease? He felt he was doing right by tending the wounded and most of them were good Christians. Even some of the Danes wore crucifixes. It was just that bunch, around Harald Edwinsson, and the younger ones were the worst of all, the ones from around the River Trent. A collection of the godless but he thought, I must try to befriend them and perhaps then they could be converted. They have shown compassion for each other. Many fight out of duty for a Christian Lord, Athelstan, their rightful king, ordained by God. They bear no real animosity for their enemy and they look forward to a return to the days of peace with their families. They must be good at heart but why then do I feel such rage. He began to look into his own heart and realised the problem lay with himself wanting too easy a life. His skills and his intelligence had ensured an easy rise in the Church. He must now seek more difficult tasks out in the world.

CHAPTER 26

BRIGID AT THE FORD

The Saxons were still in control of the ford when Brigid returned and the battle was moving a little away from the river bank. The Scots and the Welsh were having a final push against the Saxons on the higher ground but had not dislodged them from control of the river crossing. Men were crossing both ways up and downriver of the ford. Brigid had had enough and decided to swim over when a couple more of the priestesses appeared.

"What can you tell me, Annie," she asked quietly of one of them.

"We are losing. We attack and don't follow it up. The Saxons just stand and kill us. Then they move a little bit and someone decides to attack them again. All the clan leaders are dying. I think at least four of the king's sons are dead and that Welsh king, Eugenius, may also be dead. No one's in charge any more. We want to go home now, but how we shall, I do not know."

"I'll work out something once we are together. We must all come together and make the journey back overland. We cannot sail back with the Vikings or the Scots. They will blame us for their defeat. After they have enjoyed themselves, they will kill us or sell us to a slave trader. It might be a fight but I shall work out a way. Go and find everyone, as many as possible.

We meet on the opposite bank before dark and then move up the hill into the woods at the back of that fort."

Brigid looked about into the valley and how green it was except for where corn had been cut out of neat little fields. In her mind she took out all the sights and sounds of war and saw only peace. The Christians must think heaven can be like this, she thought. There's everything here you need to live: wood, water, good pasture, shelter from winds, some flat land. The thought of such bounty away from her native north began to irritate her and she walked off in a temper.

Dunstan was relieved that the casualties amongst his men were fewer in the afternoon than in the morning. They had come under attack themselves and he had been glad Thurstan was there with him. His men thought the Scots and Welsh had lost heart because many of their commanders had been killed. They had all stood and watched the chaos at the rear of the battle. King Athelstan had said before he had left them, he thought some of the Scots princes had been killed and may be even King Owen of Strathclyde. Many of the Vikings had been killed trying to lead their allies in counter-attacks which petered out almost as soon as they began. He and Earl Thurstan had been ordered to take the ford by the king. A good job Thurstan knew what he was doing, Dunstan reflected. Together they had watched the chaos of the battle and repelled two attempts to re-capture the ford.

Then the king had left them in charge of defending the ford and at Roderham which they had taken so easily during the day, but with instructions not to cross until they received orders from him personally. He and Edmund, his bodyguard as he now called him, looked at the bodies in the river. Suddenly in what was almost a temporary half light they saw a naked woman throw a sword and shield into it from the opposite bank. She was standing next to the track which led up the hill.

"She was saying something before she threw them," said Edmund. "The language was unlike anything I have heard spoken in Britain. It got darker just before she spoke and then became lighter when she had finished."

"I couldn't make it out," said Dunstan with a laugh. "The noise of this battle has destroyed my hearing."

"You have never been in a battle before, have you, Lord Dunstan?"

"No...Never!"

"But you are better with a sword than we thought, and you did decide to kill someone in the afternoon. If fact I counted five dead and four wounded.

Some of the men were worried you had become too monk-like, too bookish to be a warrior."

"I have had to defend myself before. Despite what the king says, the roads in his kingdom aren't all that safe, especially when folk suspect you of being on his business here in the north.... and I like to travel alone. He keeps telling me it's like in the days of the Romans when a virgin could travel the length and breadth, carrying a purse of gold but I don't believe him."

"Nor do I, but what do you think the woman was doing. The men are bound to ask what you think. They have all watched her. They'll expect you to know because you are educated and none of us can read or write."

"I think she was a priestess making an offering to her Gods or Goddesses. The locals hold this river to be sacred to the Goddess Brigit. Have you noticed how the land changes as you look across it? There is another world over there."

"Hmmm," said Edmund. "The lads will really wonder about that when I tell 'em. They will at least believe it as it comes from you. If we are crossing over tomorrow, they won't go without you, I know that. A lot of them were told by the women back home not to cross the river. No good would come if they did. It's a magical river dividing one world and another, they say. They say it wants blood every year."

Dunstan made no comment. He looked across and still watched the woman. She was still standing there with a couple more. He thought of the times he had been over there with his mother and aunts and his relatives over there. There definitely was another country over there. Different people, even the Danes on that side were different from those on this side. People ploughed their fields in a different way, had different words for the same thing. No wonder Anlaf thought he could carve it out from the rest of Athelstan's kingdom.

Brigid looked back at Dunstan but not knowing it was him. Her ribs they ached. She had been kicked by a Danish berserk whilst trying to strangle another. Why hadn't he just killed her and let her die with honour. She had dropped her sword and it had been picked up by the one of the Danes she tried to kill. Lost forever now, she thought. She had taken the bronze sword and shield off another girl who swam over to escape the Saxons. The girl told her the Vikings were killing all the Scots and Picts who tried to escape earlier in the day. Brigid had been at the front of the fight in the morning and the afternoon and had seen this for herself. She said she had seen them chase Brollachan after the men with her had fought back. All her brother's men were now dead. Brigid did not tell anyone she had followed Brollachan and seen her go off with some Saxons.

Thurstan took advantage of a break in the fighting to ask Dunstan if he had seen Aylmer since he had returned north.

"I haven't seen him for over a year. I saw him before he married Helena and went south with the king. The news of her death and the baby's reached us in Nottingham some months later. I did look for him but he was as always elusive, even under the best of circumstances."

"I wish they had not married, Dunstan. She would still be alive and she would have forgotten him by now. He did not realise she was not a warrior's wife. He is such a fighter and I am sure he still lives, although it is weeks since we have heard from him. Eventually she would have made him unhappy, you know. She could not have borne the separation. I should have told him before they married."

"Well, I am looking forward to getting married but I suppose I shall be content to live on the land. Father is not expected to live much longer, so everyone says..... Although I think he is good for a few more long years. He just can't fight any more."

"It's not what you're best at either," ventured Thurstan. "But you do know about looking after land and people. They say you are a good teacher and know a lot. You would have done well in the Church, but it is said you are not a fervent believer."

"Perhaps that's why I could have done well in the Church. I would have fitted in with the rest............It's not for me. A time will come when the religious will have to give up their control of knowledge. King Alfred was very learned you know. Athelstan is also.... despite his fame as a warrior. His Aunt Ethelfreda taught him much of what he knows."

Yes, thought Thurstan, and he is constantly telling us.

"Thurstan, are we winning today?" Dunstan asked out the blue.

"We are, and how I know is that, despite all their numbers, they have not routed us. We are standing still and they are wearing out. None of their commanders know what to do with such numbers. Athelstan knows what he can do with smaller forces. We have stood here and they have hardly attacked us but even we, a small number have prevented their use of this ford. Their troops are still moving both ways across The Don. No one is in charge. The much vaunted Anlaf seems to have disappeared. They have so many men. We could have been under constant attack and all been dead by now."

"I have heard from the king that his banner has not been seen this side of the river but having said that, not every leader needs to show off his presence everywhere he goes."

"Quite so, Dunstan. However, we need a banner for our men to follow."

Anlaf in the meantime was riding up and down near to them wondering if he could get some sort of order into the chaotic rabble their army had become. He stopped short of the ford and looked at Thurstan's little band standing firm by it. He shouted out some orders to the Picts around him but none seemed to understand him. Neither he nor any of his guard could speak any of the languages. He tried shouting louder and waving his sword at them but it made no difference. His men spotted one of Brigid's priestesses and dragged her over to him.

"Don't mess with me, girl! You priestesses all speak a variety of tongues. Tell all these men to form up to dislodge those Saxons," he shouted.

She looked blankly at him and he repeated his words several times in three languages.

"Good God, why ever did I come to this country? The hag speaks every language known to God but her minions hardly speak their own."

The two Vikings holding the girl relaxed their grip as they laughed at Anlaf's joke and she broke loose. She slipped off in the direction of the river, they followed her but she jumped in and swam across. As they stood by amazed at her speed, Thurstan ordered a couple of archers shoot them but not the girl. Anlaf watched all this near to tears. It's almost as if she purposefully led them within range of the enemies' archers, he thought. She knew what she was doing. Why do they hate us so much? Why won't they fight?

Anlaf and his men rode off to the rear of the main battle watched by the Saxons.

"That was Earl Anlaf gone for some help. He couldn't get the Scots to fight us" said Thurstan.

"They were Picts" said Dunstan with a smile. "How nice of that boy with the long hair to run by our front, when two of them chased him, it gave us an easy shot."

"Where have you been living recently, lad" said Thurstan with some humour. "That was a girl. I presume you can tell the difference close up or your new wife will be in for a big disappointment when you marry."

Dunstan's men laughed so much at this that the Picts milling around them stopped, and took notice, as if they were laughing at them. By some collective thought they all looked at the Saxons more intently and then they began to form up for attack.

"This is the last time I come to war with your men," said Thurstan. "They haven't learned to keep quiet on a battlefield. Sometimes if you don't rile the enemy, they ignore you."

Edmund, Dunstan's man laughed some more. "Let them come!.......If we cannot go home as heroes from a day such as this, we do not deserve the name of warriors. I have not yet had chance to blunt my sword."

The Picts preceded their attack with a hail of stones which bounced off shields and chain mail.

"Hold the line," shouted Thurstan."Let them come to us.........Archers get ready to fire!..........Archers, targets to your front, in your own time, pick your target and go on..... Shoot at will!"

The Saxons had anticipated this attack and grouped to repel it. The surprise was it came from the Picts and that there were so many. They just stood their ground and waited for the enemy to lose impetus. Eventually with a ring of dead and dying around them, they were relieved when the attack ceased. They had experienced fewer casualties than expected.

"Good armour and training, they have been the saviour of us today, Dunstan. If you ever have to do this again, remember that. You are a young man and the king or his brother may call on you again. Your experience today will stand you in good stead."

"Thurstan, I can do it but I don't think I like it. However, I do not see a time of peace ahead for us. This battle will not solve anything. The Scots will attack again and the Vikings will covet York and the rest of the country. King Constantine will somehow turn it all to his advantage as we cannot follow him home. The more we kill only means it takes longer for them to come back, when they have had time for more children."

"Well, that's true and to prove it, they are coming again."

Another attack was wasted by the Picts. Some Scots had come over the river and decided to show them how it was done. Their enthusiastic commander led a charge, only to meet with an arrow when he raised his shield too high, trying to encourage his men. The attack failed once again.

The late afternoon saw the Saxons more resolute and still in charge of the ford, watching their comrades move slowly down the hill to the flatter land by the river and their enemy retreating across it. Many were drowning on the way, despite the river being fairly shallow. It was wide with little islands dotted in the middle. The battle was still progressing to the north when all around the ford was almost quiet except for the cries of the wounded. Out of the chaos came one of the king's messengers with orders for them to hold the ford overnight with Dunstan in charge, and Earl Thurstan was to join the king without his men and attend his Council. They left at once stepping over bodies. The king's final order was to kill the enemy wounded except for any women or children they found unless they resisted. Dunstan looked ill at the prospect of watching over such a deed.

"Don't worry, my lord," said Edmund. "I can put the matter in hand. Your father said not to ask you to do it if we won."

"I think I could not have survived today without you, Edmund. I really must develop some military skills. Here I am saying what chaos will befall the land and not preparing for it."

"You were never inclined to fight much as a boy. You just followed your mother on her church visits, but you never seemed very godly to us. You once tried to teach me to read and write and I knew then, you would grow up different. I have never heard your father complain because you have never failed in anything you have done. He was worried you would never find favour with the king, but you have done that with more ease than most men. I have lived much longer than you and have known the king quite well. He chooses to have people in his life who are doing things he is not good at, or who do things he wants to do but doesn't have time, being king."

Dunstan thought on this in silence and wondered if war generally brought out such deep introspection and philosophy in men not used to considering these matters on a daily basis.

"Much to think about, Edmund. Let's walk around the men and see if anyone else has some thoughts they can spare on a day like this."

Brigid managed to get together as many of her priestesses as she could find in a reasonable time. Most of them thought they were the only ones left on this part of the battlefield. She counted twenty two, about a third of the number she brought.

"They won't all be dead.... or at least not yet," said Annie. "I had some difficulty getting the Saxons to fight me. Once they saw I was a woman, they just defended themselves. It irritated me they were so smug when doing it. It was like they saw us as no danger to them."

"We are going to set out early in the morning and make for the Humber. We can capture a ship and take it home. We'll probably have to fight for it. That will be easier than walking if we get there first. Travel light and fast.

We are used to being hungry, but get a good meal before we go, if you can. It might take us four or five days and we can travel just off the river valley. The first sea-going ship we see, we capture. All of you get hold of some warm clothes from these camps. Some better weapons if you can. We move before first light in case the Saxons invade tomorrow and the Northmen get organised. Let's get away from the river into the woods at the back of that fort."

"Brigid," said Annie. "Can we stay as a warband? Let's not pick up others, only our sisters, and just go together. It may be our best chance to survive without men hanging on."

"Good thinking, Annie. We all need to think differently now. Men will only blame us and enslave us. Our own side may treat us worse than the Saxons. We must try and find some more of our women. They may need to be rescued."

She thought back to the situation she saw at the spring by the Don. What was Brollachan doing? Why didn't the Saxons disarm her? Had she charmed them in some way even I could not understand? Brigid's mind had wandered off at this thought. She wondered if she would ever see Brollachan again. One of the best fighters and most spiritual of them all. Brigid felt she had been truly chosen by the Goddess.

"Oh! Let's get on and do this," said Annie, bringing Brigid out of her thoughts. "We'll be all dead if we don't. I can see men moving up the hillside away from the river. The Scots and the Seafarers are abandoning the battle. I think our people are all dead and so are the Welsh. We shall need revenge for this day on our friends as well as our enemies."

"Annie" said Brigid with a sigh. "Our friends have been the death of our dreams today. All our enemies have done is kill us."

CHAPTER 27

THE WELSH AND THE VIKINGS ATTACK BRUNANBURGH

The Northern Allies attacked as planned but the Saxons had as always second guessed them again as far as they could tell. The attack was repulsed not because the Saxons had a superior force but just because they defended it at all. Hakon and Idwal's men were so surprised at the determined defence, they lost heart when, had they persisted, the day might have been theirs. They achieved a foothold on the bank but were disheartened when Idwal was killed and Hakon was wounded by an arrow from inside the fort. To make matters even worse, as this was taking place, men from Wincobank raided their rear, destroying their camp. The surprise routed the few reserves, and then they escaped before anyone had time to react. The men Hakon had set to watch the fort had been picked off one by one to ensure the surprise was complete.

The survivors retreated and reformed. Hakon's second in command, Ragnold Tooligsson shouted to them all.

"Get in to some order..... and get your breath back. After a rest we are going to try again and this time we move carefully....shields up and over us. There are some re-enforcements coming.... and we are all going over. Anyone else who comes, will follow on."

More men were starting to arrive. The other crossings were blocked with numbers and men were just diverting to Brunanburgh. There were even some horsemen and Ragnold organised them immediately.

"Prepare for a breakthrough on our left flank and a move to their rear. Also get ready to keep our own men going, don't let them turn back. We need determination and we need momentum. Then we can do it. They have lost a lot of men and I haven't seen any more arrive except a few men with pack horses coming down the far hill."

He went to see Hakon.

"We failed again, Ragnold. What's wrong today?"

"We just need to keep up the attack. There seems to be some Franks amongst them. They are only fighting for gold and they'll run away if it gets too tough. The Saxons may be defending their own land but once the Franks run, they'll follow."

"Just like our men ran, once one lot started."

"Yes, Hakon, once it starts you have to stop it at once or a complete army will retreat."

"Ragnold, someone needs to take out this arrow and stop the blood or I'll die."

"We don't have anyone with the skill. I have only ever seen Sitric Oslacsson's mother do it and a man survive."

"Then remember how, and do it for me. She pushes the arrow through, someone told me."

"Hakon, the wound is only shallow, I'll have a go."

Ragnold looked at the wound and thought, the armour has taken the impact. If the idiot had worn his leather coat under his mail, he would be fine, it's not too deep. The arrow might not have entered the flesh at all through the leather. He now thinks himself too fine and has been wearing his embroidered linen jacket like a prince at a wedding. Pretending to look at the wound he felt Hakon relax and pulled. The pain and the surprise made him faint.

He only had Hakon's shirt to act as a pad to stop the blood. Fortunately it did stop, as Hakon came round.

"You didn't push it through then!"

"No, but I will do next time to teach you to wear leather under your mail. Your father will finish off where the Saxons have started when he finds out. However we'll get you back home, I do not know?..... I hope the rest are doing better against the main army than we are against that lot over there. Anyhow, we had better get on with another attack....and mean it this time."

Hakon sat amongst the trees just off the marsh, feeling just a little better. Some monks had appeared and had been directed to where he lay alongside the rest of the wounded who were rescued from the river. They went around tending them. Many of their wounded had drowned and the bodies were drifting downstream. The camp still showed the signs of devastation left by the Saxons from Wincobank. Hakon felt he had made the right decision sending more men to cover the fort up the hill. The men outside it had thinned out for some reason it seemed, giving the garrison a chance to help their comrades. No one's in control of this army, he thought, and even I am as bad as the others. I should not have disobeyed Uncle Anlaf. Did I spoil his chance to cross here? I think not. The Saxons have just outsmarted us again. They got wind of our intentions from the start from that Scots traitor. The defences here are the best in the east and what are we attacking....... a fort in a bog? All the men outside the fort have to do if they are defeated is move back along the track and hold the road through the bogs on the other side of that hill. They have set a trap for us here. I was stupid enough to fall for it. Uncle Anlaf was smart enough to concentrate his forces and bring the Saxons to a battle....... He could hear noises and thought we must be winning over that river.

He became faint and fell asleep. He was woken by a monk come to dress his wounds.

"How's the main battle going," he asked.

"Men were passing both ways across the river as we came" was the reply.

Strange, Hakon thought. Why is that happening but no good asking a monk and what appeared to be a Saxon, or at least a Danish one at that?

When the man had finished, he left Hakon and walked to the edge of the marsh. Slowly he walked back up to him and said.

"Your men are returning. God has not granted them a victory. They have left their dead in the water. The Britons say this river loves blood, but heretics and sinners have an excuse for everything."

"Just like the rest of us," replied Hakon, growing up very quickly. "Help me stand up and take me to the water's edge."

Hakon watched as the men returned through the marsh. He looked for Ragnold but only found Erik coming back.

"Ragi's dead. Some big Dane with an axe got him as he slipped in the mud. They had one of those Scots women with them as well."

"I knew we couldn't trust the Scots. We should have gone straight to York, stayed there and let them get on with their revenge."

"They had ballistas as well. It was a trap all the way." Erik began to cry at this point. "So many heroic men are dead."

Hakon knew how he felt and the monk helped him back into the woods.

"What are ballistas" Hakon asked the monk?

"They are a weapon used by the Romans against masses of soldiers or against forts. They have them on ships to shoot fire or large arrows at the enemy's rowers. The holy Bishop of Rome has decreed they should not be used against other Christians, only the unbelievers and heretics," he replied.

"That's how they see us, isn't it" said Hakon? "They'll kill the wounded and the prisoners. They won't even keep us alive and sell us for slaves."

The monk made no comment but thought, does he think my people uncivilised like Vikings?

Hakon settled down again and watched the monks deal with more wounded and dying. It was getting late in the afternoon and still he didn't know what was happening. Erik bought him a horse, one that was looking bit worse for wear. Erik had one but looked under horsed because of his size. Slightly comic, thought Hakon, he really ought to walk. He can take longer strides than the poor animal. Dear God, if I don't laugh, I'll cry on this battlefield.

Eric suggested they follow the river up to the next ford as it was the only way he had been directed to Anlaf's camp.

"We'll have to be careful and avoid the Saxon fort on this side of the river, Hakon. If it's defended like Brunanburgh, we are in trouble."

Hakon made no comment, feeling much too tired. He had to get off the horse and rest. They could see across the river the battle but couldn't make out anything, until some Vikings appeared. Eric recognised them as some of the Oslacssons' men.

"What's happening," he called over to them?

One of them came over and recognised Hakon.

"Your uncle has lost today, son" he said. "The Saxons have fought like demons and our allies have been no use to us. Our chief was even killed before the battle."

He then told them the story of how Sitric was murdered by a Saxon warrior pretending to be a trader and then how his son Guthric was killed by a Pictish witch.

"It was a fulfilment of Sitric's mother's prophesies. Nothing has gone right for us since we nearly all became Christians. It's not a religion for warriors. We need a go-between with death. All this love and forgiveness and turning the other cheek does us no good."

Hakon thought for a moment and said.

"Well, it's done the Saxons no harm…….perhaps we are the wrong sort of Christian?"

The man walked off at that. Erik put Hakon back on his horse as several more of his men walked up.

"Are we all who are left" he asked?

One of them replied. "There aren't many of us here, that is so. Many have gone back west to join the men on the Dee. It's a more direct journey home. We thought you might come back this way to your father and your uncle. We would prefer a boat trip and less fighting if you want to know the truth of how we feel."

"We appear to have lost and the Saxons could pursue us," said Hakon. "We do have some horses if we don't wear them out. All of them could do with a rest and a bit more than grass to eat. We'll have to do more walking than riding to the boats."

"We can only find your uncle or your father and see what the orders are before we go anywhere," said Erik.

They passed around a small Saxon fort with a number of dead around it, and made their way up a hill as it was getting dark. They met more Scots on the way who told them what had happened in the battle and how the Saxons had halted at the river when they had recaptured the crossings.

"It's clearly a plan they have" said Hakon as they rode on up into the woods. "It's all been worked out in advance and a trap we have fallen into."

"You've fallen into another now," called out a voice in Norse! "Drop all your weapons! Get off the horses at once?"

Through sheer tiredness and disbelief no one moved and a hail of arrows followed. After the arrows Brigid led her women in an attack on the remaining Vikings. Hakon was hit by another arrow in his side and fell off his horse. He looked around at the dead Vikings and recognised Brigid.

"Why, why, you traitor" he shouted? "We came to help your king."

Brigid stopped Annie from finishing off Hakon.

"You have been killing us all day in this battle, both our men and women, as you have done even in our own land. Your uncle is nothing but a thief and a murderer……and not even a good one. The Saxons have beaten him and killed thousands of us today and then his men have been attacking us. You can all suffer now. Kill the rest of them and leave this one to remind his uncle to treat his friends better in the future."

"No chance of me surviving" mumbled Hakon. "This is my second arrow today. How many more can a man take?"

"Brigid looked at his wound. Nowhere vital she thought, and pulled it out before he knew what she intended.

When he woke up from his faint, both his wounds were dressed properly and he was left by a track on the hilltop. He was left in a blanket but his sword and armour had gone.

No one will believe a word I say, Hakon said to himself aloud in the oncoming darkness. I wish they had killed me. Life can be as cruel as death.

Some Scots soldiers came along and noticed Hakon, one called over to an officer who recognised him.

"We can take him back to his uncle. He is with the king……Two of you, pick up this man! Support him as he walks."

They all walked up the hill past the earthworks into the head of a valley. Hakon recognised his uncle from a distance walking side by side with King Constantine. Anlaf looked at him as the two men took him over.

"Get him out of my sight," roared Anlaf, "or I'll finish what the Saxons couldn't do."

"Do as he says" ordered Constantine. "Take him to my camp up the hill…. Anlaf, don't be so hard on the lad."

"If he hasn't lost us the battle, he certainly has helped the Saxons."

"Anlaf, don't be foolish, he wasn't fighting on those hillsides over there. We could have done with some commanders capable of using their heads like him, even if they are a bit misguided. We'd have crossed into a bog if we had followed Rykneild Street. Athelstan knew that all along and nearly left that door open for us. He knew of our attack in advance and would have let us through to get us lost in the bogs, had he not been scared to let his only stone fort around here fall into our hands. The army needed to attack on a much broader front and not get narrowed in by marshes just as we did. Athelstan had that fort defended inside and outside by some of his best men. We could have put more men into attacking it. We had thousands standing idle on this side of the river, God knows this. Athelstan would have loved us to waste more of them on the fort."

"I don't suppose it helped by all the world knowing our plans…..Thanks to your traitors of one sort or another."

"Anlaf, we all agreed not to change the plan and Owen has paid for the decision with his life.... Anyway, I am going home with such men as I can put together and back the way we came. I may be able to persuade the Welsh to join with us now. Owen would have wanted that as it will keep them out of your hands and those of your kinfolk."

"Fine, but I'm for the sea. You can keep my nephew. A sea journey won't improve him. Send him to my brother if he recovers...... I can't understand why the Saxons aren't crossing the river."

"It's because they are making sure all our men on that side are dead before they come over here to start on us. We had best move on everyone while we can. We can only leave the dead and the dying. Those who can walk had better because the locals here are none to friendly. They may like us better in York or north of here beyond those Northumbrian forts."

"Then let us part, Constantine, and hope to better these Saxons on another day."

"Anlaf, that day can only come when Athelstan has gone to outsmart his God. Such a man as he, even then, will pull strings in heaven and do us ill. We haven't seen the last of the Saxons in our country, nor have you in yours wherever that might be."

CHAPTER 28

THE LAST BATTLE AT BRUNANBURGH

Earlier in the afternoon, Ivar had no sooner got out to the front of the battle line when two comrades pulled him back in.

"Eric's orders," one said. "He said he promised your mother to bring you back alive."

"I'm pleased to know she inspires the same fear in Eric as she does the rest of us," said the other.

"Thorolf Sigurdsson you are not my friend after this battle is over, and I'll tell her you said that and even though Eric is your little brother….."

"Your little friend is fine also. I can see her in the marsh. She's climbed one of the willows. If she's smart she'll stay there."

The two forces had come together again and Alain's words became truth. Despite the courage of the attackers, the defenders held the advantage in a frontal attack up the short slope. The attack was concentrated again on the northeast part and despite having brought the rafts as cover from arrows, they gave no real advantage. The hand to hand fighting and the constant bombardment from the ballistas on the troops at the rear, wore down the northern force. Their advantage of numbers was wasted when they attacked up the steeper bank adjoining the fort. As the fight wore on, the attackers could hardly cross the bodies of their comrades. The lines of Danes, Saxons and Franks held and never seem to waiver.

Any attempt to retreat was blocked by Vikings and the horsemen. Harald noticed them at the rear, a small number who had not engaged in the fight. The pressure on the front began to let up and he said to Alain. "Let's take the fight into the deeper water, direct the ballistas more on to the rear of the enemy."

The signal to move was the hoisting of his personal banner and the troops taking part formed up and moved. He moved to the front to his warband with Eric by his side. "Don't hit me with the axe, Eric. I can see how keen you are, find yourself a little more space" he said.

Eric moved a couple of paces right just in case and observed. "The Welsh are retreating now but the Vikings are in their way...... By Odin, this water's cold."

The concentration of ballista fire on the horsemen made their commander decide on a forward move, out first in to deeper water to get around the flank of the battle. Charles had been watching this and got his men ready to move. The northern attackers lost any semblance of order whilst moving and were in chaos by the time they were back in the shallows. The Franks charged. Their opponents were intending to use the horses to move to a place where they could fight on foot. The unexpected rush of an armoured enemy using the horse to fight from the saddle caught them by surprise and forced them back into deeper water under fire from archers. The ballistas were directed still on to the infantry but ceased as Harald and his men got closer.

The Vikings had been trying to prevent their allies from retreating and had killed some of them. When the Danes and Franks came to blows with them, the Welsh were unable to resist effectively and were being cut down. The Viking leader then shouted to let them through and then came face to face with his real enemies. Standing in cold water for a long time had not improved the fighting efficiency of his force. After a short but bloody interlude for both sides, their weight of their numbers failed and skill of Harald's men prevailed. The Vikings and what was remaining of their allies retreated in reasonable order. Harald ordered a return to Brunanburgh.

While all this had been happening Ivar had been watching the girl in the marsh. He had to remain behind. Northern soldiers had been slipping off into the marsh to avoid the fighting and Edmund Thorkilsson, the commander on the flank had been watching this. He watched as the girl kept slipping in and out of the tree to finish off one or two of the wounded ones.

"Ivar, your lovely new friend seems to like a killing from time to time. I don't think she should keep all this fun to herself," he bellowed to his men. "Rear rank with Oswin, go and clear the area. Ivar, fetch her back. Soon she'll have killed more than most men today. The skalds will say we were never here if this carries on. They'll say a northern Valkyrie did it all herself."

Henric decided to go along with Ivar. "Well, we never did get to shed blood together, my boy. I think it's looking over around here. Your Lord Harald looks as if he's winning out there in the ford. Your comrades are sorting out what's left in the marsh. Let's go and collect Morrigan as your friends call her."

"It's what she shouts, isn't it? I wonder if she would agree to be called that name. She won't tell us what her real one is or what she was called at the nunnery."

They found her trembling and crying in a tree. Ivar put his cloak around her again. He kissed her and soon she stopped shivering. She was covered in blood, fortunately very little was her own.

Lord Henric," said Ivar. "Tell her she is safe and she can come home with me as a wife. She can have a new family and a mother and father to love her, if she thinks she can be happy with a miller's son."

Henric told her and she replied, giving Ivar a kiss in return. "Tell Ivar, I will do all of that when I have seen this battle finish and found out what has happened to my sisters and to my *Clan*. If you and your friends want to call me Morrigan, it is a name I will be glad to have."

"Ivar," said Henric after he translated, "she's right, we should find out what going off on those ridges to the north....And if they faced the same numbers in Roderham as we have today, we may all be hiding in marshes before nightfall."

Harald's men were returning and they all walked back up to the bank outside the fort. Brother Michael was busy organising the lighting of a score or so fires and was mumbling.

"They'll all die of the cold tonight if they don't dry off." He shouted and was running up and down issuing orders. To his surprise they were being followed for care of the wounded. When he saw the girl, he became grumpier still.

"Returned at last, you painted witch, you will suffer in hell for your work today."

"Nonsense, I've added a few souls to the number to go wherever hell is for you. Your Devil will be grateful and we are all sinners to you anyway, you hypocrite."

"Her Latin is a wonder to hear. She must have had a good teacher," commented Henric. "She clearly doesn't like monks, however. I hope he's noticed she hasn't lost her sword. He could be on the sharp end of it............... Michael, we are calling her Morrigan, it means 'Great Queen' in the Welsh Languages."

"There is only one Great Queen and that is Mary, Mother of Our Lord, not this painted witch," wailed Michael.

Charles had returned by now and said, "Father, I will kill this monk myself if he doesn't talk less and help our soldiers more. I will kill him slowly too. He'll believe he is in Hell. Harald and the men are returning and since the good side of this monk's nature has got all these fires going to dry them, I shall resist roasting him over one for fun."

"Monk," said Henric. "I do not know what to make of you. I think you have had too much learning and think about more than is good for you. You think about too much at once. Concentrate on healing the sick and worry about their souls later....Charles, we ought to know what's happening in the rest of the battle. We are in an isolated corner here." Henric continued. "I am sure Harald will want a meeting when he is dry. I think you should be the one to ride over to see."

Harald came back and held the meeting while wet, saying they had some priorities. Charles and 10 men were to ride to find the king and give a report on the battle here and find out the situation in Roderham. He stood down half the men and reviewed the situation to Henric, Alain and his commanders Danish and Saxon.

"I don't believe they will try to attack us here again in large numbers. It doesn't mean they might not try and sneak over under cover of dark in smaller bands. We ought to do some reconnaissance on the other bank after nightfall but not unless we know there is victory in the main battle. We are low on arrows and bolts, until more are recovered from the river, although the enemy won't know that. Casualties are light for the last two meetings. It shows the virtues of armour. I noticed many of the *Wealas* and the Cumbrians didn't have much or none at all. They lost the advantages of movement in the water and coming up the slope. Had we been on flat land in open country or in woodland, there might have been a different tale to tell. Anlaf's commander spread his Vikings too thinly to make a difference. I think that had they been more and in the first or second waves, they would have taken this ford and let their friends across. The archers and the ballistas were the gift of the Gods. Their effectiveness was such a surprise to the enemy. I found it surprising they learnt nothing each time and agree with Alain about the commanders' thinking."

Eric said, "Lord Harald, this is the first time many of us have seen a real battle. I think had we known what was going to happen we would have stayed on our side of the Trent, king's money or none at all. We are all glad to be alive, those who have survived today so far."

"Harald, we should all get some food and a rest. Lord Henric here is nearly on his knees. His little nursemaid out there is cross he isn't resting and has threatened to chop me into little pieces, if I don't make him," said Alain. "If we have patrols on the banks from the men who are dry and horsemen with rested horses, we have done all we can."

"Sweet Freya," said Harald, suddenly noticing the girl! "The little one has survived. I thought she was going out to die."

"She's stitching up some of the wounded at the moment. She hid in the marsh when she wasn't sneaking out and killing the odd Viking or two. I did hear she let some of the Welsh live. They didn't survive your men, however. Oswin the Eeltrapper has talents eels have yet to learn. He seems so at home in a marsh, so do his men. I wonder where the young get their energy sometimes," said Alain and this time with a big yawn.

"I've nothing to add," said Henric. "Only my nurse, as Alain calls her, and Ivar Grimsson, have agreed they cannot live without each other."

"Fine," said Eric "but he had better hide her sword in domestic disputes. I'll swear she can use one better than him."

"Food and a fire call to me," said Harald. Let us meet and speak later."

It was getting completely dark when Charles returned, having found King Athelstan. Harald and Alain heard his report and then called all the commanders and as many other soldiers as he could gather.

"Comrades in arms, the message from the king says that we have won a victory. The main battle is over and the enemy are being pursued to the north. There is still some resistance at a more northerly ford crossing the river, as the enemy are trying to escape over it. The king has ordered that we do not cross the river in darkness. We do not know what enemy remains over there. There are, as some of you know the old defences up on the hills and these could still be formidable, if held by a determined force. All the forts have remained in our hands. The king believes we should hold our defensive positions until it is clear tomorrow what forces the enemy may still have. These may be capable of a fight against a smaller force. They still outnumber us and may come at us again. Tonight, he says, we need to be vigilant with sleep and food a priority for those men not on guard."

No one cheered or celebrated. Everyone walked away to find somewhere quiet. Small groups formed and a low hum of conversation could be heard around the camp. Morrigan had at last been found some ragged clothes which fitted her badly. There were no young women at the fort. She was still caring for wounded with Brother Michael but looking dead on her feet. She had obtained the herbs she needed to make up something for Henric and had stood over him whilst he drank it. He had gone to sleep at last. Morrigan told Charles she felt he had a chance for some comfort at last in the few months of life which remained to him.

Alain had surprised everyone by talking to her in Latin. "Well, I am taking holy orders when this is over" he said.

Charles was surprised most of all. "I was about to say something silly like I have known you all my life and never suspected you could speak Latin, but I have always known you to be a man of surprises. Always in adversity you come up with something."

Harald nodded in agreement at this.

"A man who has buried three wives finds himself in many dilemmas. I come from the same town as Charles' mother. My father was the steward to her father. I remember your father coming to ask for her in marriage. Although he was his overlord's son, your grandfather sent him away until he had proved himself a soldier. I think he and your other grandfather conspired in that decision. I thought he was going on some adventure and asked to go with him. It nearly proved fatal but it was much more exciting than supervising the servants in Briscourt."

Everyone laughed at that. Ivar observed it was still much safer grinding corn in Knaith, than taking a King's gold, provided that you didn't fall in the mill race. One poor child had recently and so his father Grim had insisted he teach all the children to swim. Fortunately his mother Emma had jumped in to rescue the child. No one realised she could swim. She said she couldn't but knew how to float. Seward said Emma had hidden talents with water. She once brought a drowning child back to life by moving the body to expel the water. She had jumped in the River Trent then. Ivar related the family myth about being related to water fairies on Emma's side.

He had often seen her swimming in the river with Grim his father on warm days. They all laughed so much; Henric woke up with a jolt. Then turned over and went to sleep again. Morrigan had fallen asleep by now and was far gone. One by one they all dropped off except Alain who lived with his memories and his demons. He watched over all of them, his lord and his adopted family at Brunanburgh.

The rain never arrived and next day came with some mist. Alain had slept at last when the demons from all his past wars had left him. He began to realise the despite one last battle, they would not leave him alone and not even a monastery wall would keep them out. He had only felt alive in that battle yesterday. What could he do until the next one?

He awoke with a start. Morrigan was there. "I have been for a wash in the river and found some hot water for my hair. I had forgotten I had all the blood over me from the crow I killed as a headdress. The wounded must have thought I had come for their spirits."

"No matter," he said, "many of them wouldn't be alive except for you and the monk. I think the women at this fort are not expert healers."

"Can you wake Ivar and ask him to come with me? This river is a sacred one to people of this island and the Goddess Brigit. She has had her blood sacrifice and now this sword should be given to her. This sword I brought south is old and cannot return to the north now. I know I shall never go back and must make a new home, for good or ill, away from the mountains I loved as a child. I intend to dedicate the bronze sword to the river goddess and ask her protection for myself and Ivar. Can you tell him what I intend to do? I am making the offering for all my people who died yesterday. The Goddess Brigit may be kind to them."

Alain woke up Ivar and explained. He and Morrigan disappeared into the mists.

On a little island in the marsh Morrigan removed her cloak and dress and stood naked in the water. She chanted in her language and all went quiet, no bird sang and even the river flowed a little quieter. The mist drew in closer and she threw the sword into it. Ivar heard no splash despite the quietness of the sunrise. She walked out of the water and held on to him. In her language she said she must make another sacrifice to the Goddess, but he couldn't understand the words, only the dedication as she removed his clothes. They made love and he was not surprised she was a virgin but began to understand why her clan had protected her; why she defended herself so well, and her confidence walking around naked. She was a walking sacrifice. Her Great Goddess had stood aside in this fight. Could a difference have been made to the result, had She, been invoked as Morrigan and her sisters had intended? He knew he had been chosen and now must carry the responsibility for Morrigan or Morgana as he preferred to call her. For now he just held her tight and kept her warm in the cold morning air. The mist was moving away except for a patch in the middle of the river which seemed to hang around.

They dressed and walked towards Brunanburgh hand in hand. No need of words.

CHAPTER 29

THE DAY AFTER THE BATTLE

Harald Edwinsson and Alain de Briscourt were looking out on to the river when they saw Ivar and Morrigan returning hand in hand out of the marshes. They said nothing until after the young people had gone into the camp. Alain explained what Morrigan had told him and Harald did not scoff.

"The old beliefs are not forgotten in Lincolnshire" he said. "I can still believe that if those women had done what they wanted there might have been more of us dead. I am not sure about the result of the battle. Many of us have called on the names of Odin as we fought. We are not like you Franks. The Christian teaching is only on the surface."

"The country people where I was born pay lip service when they pray," said Alain. "One part of me wants to take holy orders for the security and the peace. I tire of fighting but it's all I have known for most of my life. I cannot find any other hiding place."

"Don't seek to run, a man like you never has, why would you begin now? I think sometimes not only your lord came here to die and couldn't find a man to kill him. You both seek it because of pain of different kinds. Why not help Charles as much in the ways of peace as you have done in war?"

"Harald, you are wise beyond your years. If you give up war, you could take up healing of the souls of men with just your words. Priests and

Bishops would envy you. I think you would have to tell me more than once, however……But our war is not over. We need to secure this place for the King and see what is happening along the river bank in the direction of that village, Roderham."

"Young Charles can go there with some horsemen and a troop of infantry. Eric Sigurdsson can pick a force of men who are still in condition to fight well. They may be needed………… and I can no more give up fighting than you, but it is perhaps time for both of us to look carefully at what we do."

Harald went to issue his orders and they set off after a quick breakfast. Charles and twenty riders followed by forty Danes relatively unscathed in the battle. They marched just off the river, past where Ivar had met Morrigan. Eric noticed the dead Vikings, Ivar had described. They walked into the village of Roderham and stopped next to the ford and the little wooden footbridge, still undamaged, could be seen nearby. A three hundred or so Saxons were standing there. A man ran up to Eric.

"Mighty Woden's spared you, Sigurdsson. I thought your time had come when I heard you had gone to that fort. I thought they would have taken that easy crossing and not spent valuable hours fighting here……Could it have been because you were there?"

"Dunstan Edwinsson, I don't know why your mother called you after a saint. She must have thought you'd grow up a monk and not a berserk like the rest of us. You've hardly a mark on you that you didn't get brawling in Nottingham. You've been taking the blows on your shield like I taught you."

"Eric, you could take blows on your helmet from Thor's hammer and it wouldn't make your ears ring. Have you been trusted with the command of this bunch of murderers or is it the Frank on the pony? …Don't Franks ever walk anywhere?"

Eric shouted over to him.

"Charles de Tours, meet Dunstan Edwinsson, not a relative of Harald's. He's a Saxon with a big mouth even by their reputations for weighty words. He is a poet as well so don't encourage him to recite or we'll never find out what's happening. It will take him a full moon to compose it."

"Eric's right, I am composing the account of this battle, the heroic bits anyway and there were precious few of them. This is like no battle we have seen in these islands for many years. The slaughter has been unmatched since the Romans attacked the *wealas* and very little of it has been truly honourable fighting. Even though we have won, there is no glory in the deaths of so many. Come and see this river.

They walked over and even compared to the slaughter at Brunanburgh, the bodies in the river and on the bank sides seemed in the thousands. They were spread all around the ford and at the little footbridge nearby.

Dunstan continued. "We did not oppose this crossing when they came yesterday and the day before. As you know the King wanted them to be drawn into a battle. In their defeat they tried to re-cross and they were too crowded. Our archers fired on them and their allies tried to prevent them returning. Some of them did attack us. In their haste many fell off the footbridge into deeper water."

A priest nearby was praying and came over and spoke to Charles. "I am Brother Tobias and I know your father has influence with the King. You must ask him to establish a chapel here for prayers for the dead; even these heathens and unbelievers deserve this much."

"I will gladly speak with my father on this matter," said Charles. "These men I think were Christians and many of the Roman persuasion. I do not believe that they followed the Irish teachings, nor were they pagans."

Tobias went off to one side in a huff.

"There were some women here as well" said Dunstan. "They were smarter than the others and could swim. They escaped. I watched about a score swim over and one throw a sword in the river last night. I couldn't believe it, even a poet like me. I know the king ordered their capture but our lads were more concerned about staying alive. I can't believe they had so many men in the invading force. Where did they all come from? Even a poet like me, could not imagine so many men. If I talk about such numbers, people will say I lie. They tell me I do anyway. It's a good job we had better armour and a plan.........Even a poet like me............."

"The king's coming down the hill. Even a poet like you had better be on his best behaviour," said Charles, thinking he does go on. You can tell he hasn't seen much blood in his time.

Athelstan rode right up to them looked in the river and went pale.

"Speak no verse on this, Dunstan" he said grimly. "This day does no good for the office of a king."

"My Lord, this priest, Brother Tobias asks for a chapel to say prayers for their souls," said Charles.

"He shall see that come to pass," said Athelstan. "It will be as near to this spot as we can in that village and another near the fort on Ryknield Street for our own. None of us will get in heaven if some atonement for this slaughter is not made. I cannot believe the numbers who came to despoil our land, but God has delivered us and we must thank Him without being ungenerous to the souls of these dead. We have pursued the enemy to the north and east and there is similar destruction of life down river from here and on the hills behind us. King Constantine has much to answer leading so many to their deaths for the sake of pride. Earl Anlaf should not covet land already with a rightful king."

"I see precious few Vikings in this river, My Lord," said Dunstan. "I think Earl Anlaf may want to fight another day."

"We didn't kill that many Vikings at Brunanburgh either" said Eric. "They were directing the others and were everywhere, but not in row on row."

"Thank you for these observations, my good soldiers," said Athelstan. "This information fits with what I know. We may expect the good Anlaf to come calling again. You have all done well this day with your eyes as well as your swords and axes. We nearly captured King Constantine, I can tell you. He is an unhappy man for it is said six of his sons lie amongst the dead as well as the thousands of his people."

"I understand he is not short of sons or grandsons. On his death there would be many claim to take his seat, my lord," said Dunstan.

"I was sorely tempted to put an end to the vain old rogue and let them fight over his lands, but it does not bode well for kings to kill one another. If I had Earl Anlaf here that would be another matter. I have a bad feeling about that man. He leads a charmed life and so do the rascals who accompany him" said Athelstan.

"We did our best to discourage them," said Eric. "I had never thought I would kill so many men in my life, and not for you, King Athelstan."

"I saw you in this battle and your friend Grimsson. Give me comfort and tell me he survives."

"He does, my lord."

"Good, I owe much to his father who has led part of the defence of our eastern flanks while we fought this battle. His son's death would be a blow to him."

"He has even found love on this battlefield."

"Surely not the young lady who stood with sword and shield in a pool, cooling off after killing Vikings.... I was his age when I found a similar love sinking into the sea while out on some foolish venture with Charles' father. I wish him well with his love and hope he treasures her, but I need him to question her about what those women were doing. None have been found alive and one or two have been killed by their own side so I am told..... I am going to visit our wounded and then later in the day, or perhaps tomorrow, have a conference... Charles, ask your father to attend and bring Harald Edwinsson. He is to leave you in charge again at the brown fort....Bishop Odo's here again. I am sure he doesn't trust us to keep his priests and monks alive."

Odo came up and looked at the River Don.

"Sweet body of Christ!...............King Athelstan, what has happened here?"

"It's only war, good Bishop! Organise me a chapel for their souls and those of our people who have fallen today. Even the folk who live here need a good ministry after such a dreadful event by their homes. Find a truly good and dedicated man to serve them. But come with me now to other parts of our army.......Dunstan, again, no one is to cross this river, tell your men, no crossing either way until I command."

"No one shall, my lord," said Dunstan.

"Charles, get your men to patrol this bank down to the next ford northwards and up to the other river next to Brunanburgh. I know Harald Edwinsson will have patrols out beyond that. The Danes miss nothing. If any attempt to cross is made by the enemy, I must know at once. I am at the top of the slope at the head of the next valley. I am reserving some horsemen for re-enforcement at speed, just in case. Tell Harald his infantry will remain here to re-enforce Dunstan. The river is narrower here at this ford. This is where they could try again."

He then rode off with his guard at great speed minus the bishop despite his order to Odo to accompany him.

"The king has at this time withdrawn the main army from the river bank but left all the fords defended. This is so as not to tempt them to cross again to challenge our main force. From what we can see, there are many more over there who never took part in the battle. They have a choice of three places if they don't want to swim. Our force is hidden from view but can move at short notice. He's stood down the tired and the lightly wounded, all except for poets." Dunstan said this with a straight face.

Charles nearly fell off his horse with laughter and made his excuses to carry out the king's orders, leaving Eric and Dunstan looking at Brother Tobias and Bishop Odo.

"Eric, I cannot help but feel this slaughter has been so great because bishops have been inciting their flocks to excess, and this is so on both sides. Sensible men defeat an enemy and make a good peace. None can be made here. The Scots will seek revenge for this day's work when they have bred enough children who can grow old enough to carry a sword."

"They brought enough children with them. Almost as if they had come to settle. I presume they may have left their women up on those ridges over there."

"Eric, I think the king has ordered me to remain here for a purpose and that is at some time to cross over there to see what is happening. We have one of the smaller forts still in our hands over at Masborough. I think that is what the place is called. They have just passed it by. The defenders still signal to us by lights at night and I know the king wants to rescue them. I do know that part of the valley too well. I have in the past composed a poem about the ancient earthworks over there. People say the Romans built them and you may not know it, but the king likes anything Roman. There is a circle of banks people say was built by one of the Roman kings, Julius Caesar after he defeated one of the *wealas* queens. I do know that is not true. He never came this far north, but I have seen it. The king likes the poem, as you might expect."

"I like your poetry too, Dunstan, you make everything sound exciting. I would like my children to be educated like you."

"I'll educate them for you with mine, Eric, if we can both live long enough to have any. This war started just as I was about to make arrangements to marry. The girl is only sixteen and waiting for me to return. Both families are in agreement but as you know, father is too ill to lead the men and so I have come as leader. The king is happy with what I have done and I think this will not be the last time I will be fighting for him. Father will want me to carry on a warrior. I have a good man in Edmund to support and advise me."

"I am going back to forestry when this is over. Tildi is pregnant she told me before I left, and so I expect we shall handfast when I return. She has refused me before, having buried two husbands. I'll be related to the Edwinssons then."

"A noble name amongst any people"

"Don't be so boring, poet."

"I could do with a chance to be boring after yesterday........Anyway let's get your lads in place. Mine will feel a bit happier with a few extra swords and that axe of yours. We are all that are left of father's men. Not many killed but so many wounded who I have sent away for care. We are one hundred and eighty nine and two hundred and twelve of Earl Thurstan's. I came with four hundred and ten. It was mainly arrow wounds while waiting to engage the Scots. I think we have only about forty or fifty dead as long as we don't lose more to infected wounds. We took the precaution of bringing Aunty Elfreda and her three women to care for the wounded."

"Why didn't you just hold back the men and let her loose on the Scots and save us all this pain?"

"One day men will have rules about carrying out war and call themselves morally just, but it will not include letting loose the likes of my aunt and her three demons….. Let's get on with this defence before that bishop goes to tell the king that all we do is babble all day like his monks."

Bishop Odo and Brother Tobias stood and looked into the River Don.

"Bishop Odo, local people hold this river as sacred to Saint Bridget the Healer and say it has been sacred even before her. They are concerned that its bounty will no longer be there for them now it has been defiled by so much slaughter."

"We can only pray God does not allow this, Tobias. The people should be instructed not to associate saints with wells and water. I am sure when it is safe to do so the bodies can be recovered and buried. There is a man I know who could act as a priest here on a temporary basis, Michael of Gloucester. He is at the fort already and knows the area from before the battle. He also is a healer, so he should be a good choice to be near Saint Bridget, although we will not dedicate the chapel to her. I will organise this with him when it is safe for the extra forces to leave the brown fort."

"There is lots of that brown stone around here. I have never seen it before anywhere in Angleland."

"Tobias, don't let the king hear you say Angleland, he hates the word even though he's trying to create unity in these islands. He likes Britannia as the Romans called it."

"Lord Bishop, everybody is calling the country by that name and more will do so, especially after this battle, even though it's not yet over. They are only saying what they know. It's like the Scots and the Irish calling us all Saxons, even though some of us are Angles and Danes……. We're in charge anyway."

"Are we in charge? I haven't noticed, Tobias. Around here the Danes walk about like it's theirs. Let's go and talk to the locals about their chapel before those two berserks over there think all we do is babble all day."

Eric had taken the precaution of ordering his new command to bring all their equipment. Harald had given him the impression it was just a stroll to find out what was happening but he wasn't convinced. They had no food with them but had eaten a good breakfast. Dunstan's men shared what they had at midday and said they knew more was coming. They expected to be in position guarding the ford for a couple of days. A similar small force was down river at the other fords which were also difficult places to cross. The talk in the ranks was that any more crossings would be at the brown fort, a much easier place. This was until the Danes told the story of what had happened at Brunanburgh.

When Eric told Dunstan he was slightly amazed even for a poet, and he said. "Eric, after such a spirited defence, they won't try again there, they'll come back at us here, especially if they see how few men we have."

"They will think so few men are a trap after yesterday."

"Eric, the Scots can count. They may realise they have more men left than we have, and this, despite their great losses."

"Dunstan, they must have lost faith in their leaders. We still have faith in King Athelstan. Even we, the Danes, know he is greatest war leader, in the islands. Charles tells me one of the titles he assumes is *dux bellorum*, if I have the Roman language correct. We knew it before today as well. The Scots and the *wealas* knew too but were too full of pride to admit it. We are also still a fighting force and could hold this ford. It's narrow and deep. The one up river at the fort is nearly as wide as the river itself. We can burn the bridge if we must. I'll even stand on it with my axe and there is a room for a good swing on those planks. Do not be down-hearted by the sight of so much death. We may see more before our lives end, whether today or in forty years. You are a poet and think too much."

"You are right. I think I'll send a messenger to see when the food is coming."

Before he could, there came another messenger and with the food. One of the king's clerks appeared with a written order on the basis he knew Dunstan could read and not misunderstand any message given by word of mouth. Dunstan read it and looked a bit shocked.

He called all the men together.

"At the end of the day before sunset, the king will send more men to re-enforce us and then, when they are in position, eighty of us are to cross the river, relieve the Masborough fort… and take them some of these supplies. Every man, except for a few who I shall indicate, is to carry as much as he can and we shall move as fast as we can to the fort. We shall stay in the fort overnight, and tomorrow we shall try to find out what the enemy are doing and then return here. For the march to the fort, Eric Sigurdsson and twenty of his men will cross the bridge at speed and secure the other side of the ford. We'll do this when it's nearly dark but still light enough to see where we are going. Once the Danes are in position and the ford is secure, the rest of us will move more quietly over the bridge with bundles of food and head straight down the track to the fort. We move as a group and leave no one behind. Eric's remaining men will follow as a rear guard in case we are attacked in that direction. We can just see the fort from here when the lights are on. It's not far. Once we are over we need a fast pace and can run the last bit. Only if we get into a serious fight, do we drop the food. Remember, it's probably our breakfast we are carrying. I will take the first ten men and clear a path to the fort if necessary and get them to open the gate. Be careful when we get near, they might think it's a trap and let off some arrows…… Any questions?"

After a few questions everyone snuggled down in the bushes for a rest.

The evening came and a force of about five hundred men walked slowly down the hill and remained in cover behind the village. They had brought with them the reminder of the villagers who had not come with Brother Tobias, and all of them began to tidy up their homes and the area around them. A man who talked a language Eric thought was similar to what they all spoke but not quite, had a conversation with Dunstan.

"They're from Kent," he said.

"That would be the strange language."

"Ha, ha!…… It sounds just the same as everyone else's when you've heard it a while. Get your men ready, Eric and go over that bridge when I say."

At Dunstan's order they went over the foot bridge and took up position at the top of the bank and the rest followed, Dunstan and his men followed after but took up position at the front of the column when they had all secured their bundles. They set off down the track followed by Eric and his men. All was quiet.

The sun had not even looked like setting before they reached the fort. Dunstan was correct in assuming they would be suspicious and a few arrows, which were stopped by their shields, came from the wooden tower by the gate. Their march down the track had not gone unnoticed and a handful of Scots investigated. They were met by Eric's men and the fight could be seen from the fort. Someone ordered the gate open and the Saxons rushed in side, dropped the bundles as Dunstan led them out again to rescue Eric's men.

"Too late," said Eric. "What's not dead has run away. No glory today for you, poet."

"Where are the bodies then?"

"We don't need to kill any more, our reputation drives them away," said Eric as an arrow passed his ears.

"Their archers are brave again today, let's run!"

"Brave but not accurate, Dunstan."

Once inside the fort they had a look around from the tower with the warden, Wulfric Osbertsson. It was carefully built on a slight hill. It was actually higher at the palisade and bank than it first might seem. The invaders had wisely left it alone for the most part. Someone had given it a try and there were a few bodies with arrows which looked as if they had been there over a week.

"A bunch of crazy Vikings, we may look a bit past a pitched battle but there is nothing wrong with our arrowshot" said Wulfric. "We were more in danger of starving or dying of boredom before you came. Are we expecting another attack?"

"We have come to see what they are doing on these hills. We'll march out tomorrow to see and then go back to Roderham unless they chase us back in here. Do you know if they are massing behind the earthworks on the hill top," asked Dunstan.

"We know they have been camped up there behind them and have marched down the track outside of here. Our orders were not to fire on them unless attacked. They can see into this fort from the earthworks. There's no palisade on top of those banks. I think they were only for setting out a boundary but they are defensible by a determined force. Don't try to cross if there is a resistance. There are lots of places where the tree cover will allow you to slip over unseen if you are careful. Most of the locals are on our side. Some have moved across the river, others have gone deep into the woods and took their food with them. One or two have even joined us to defend this fort and the old *wealas* fort at Wincobank to the west. You can see the lights high up. You can't see the other one to the east from here it's around a bend in the river and there are hills in the way."

"There's not a lot of room in here now we have arrived," said Eric.

"Our well isn't deep enough to supply everyone in here now, only the normal garrison" said Wulfric. "I would think the enemy will go away now they have lost the battle. Clearly numbers weren't enough. Many of them had no armour to speak of. Plenty of weapons, however, and one reason we have no shortage of arrows is the numbers they fired at us which we picked up. They sent boys to keep shooting at us as if for practice. We had a number of fatalities at first and some wounded."

"We had many on the battlefield for the same reason and would have had more except for our armour" said Dunstan. "But when we attacked they ran away."

"We ran out of ale two nights ago," said Wulfric, changing the subject. "I can only offer you water to drink."

"Worst news a poet can hear," said Dunstan miserably.

The next morning as it was getting light the Saxons and the Danes moved out and into the woods. The few enemy about saw them but kept a safe distance. They reached the foot of the ridge, found a path up and at the top crossed the earthworks unopposed and stopped to look around. The men set up an all round defence while Dunstan and Eric climbed a tree. Sitting in the branches they hardly knew what of make of things they saw. In all the clearings they could see camps which looked unattended. A few people were about but looked as if they were preparing for a move out. The rest seemed to have gone and at some speed leaving things behind in their haste.

"Dunstan, we have to go and capture one or two of these people before they all disappear. Something is happening if they are still watching the forts and the fords."

"We are a large enough force to deter any of them from attacking us, if they are a small band and I don't see any large ones. We had better keep moving and not return the same way. Prisoners will slow us down now. In fact we might be best going to the west and returning through Brunanburgh. We'll have to cross the earthworks again but if all fails, we can try to get to Masborough. Let's go on to the end of this ridge and shadow the main track for a while. There is another valley to the south west which will lead us back to Brunanburgh. My mother and Aunty Elfreda used to take me to a church in the valley. It was one established by the *wealas* and considered a very holy place. If we can see it we know not to go too far north beyond it."

Dunstan ordered everyone up and to move out. They followed the path but saw no one until they saw a wide track going down the hill more directly north east. He sent ten men down it for a look and they came back and described a camp in some round earthworks but it had been abandoned.

Always wondered where Julius Caesar had been, thought Eric, just as in your poetry, Dunstan. They carried on until the ridge began to descend into another valley which was more open.

"This is turning us off our route. We can see where their camps are. It looks as if they are still occupied by their stragglers and wounded," said Dunstan. "If any of us spoke their tongues we could capture and question them. None of my men speak the languages and I only know Latin besides the dialects of our own tongue."

"You know, Dunstan, I haven't come across any Angles in this battle. I think they haven't joined against us in any great numbers, not even the Northumbrians."

"There were some in the main battle but not many and I thought they were from the very far north. We were too busy fighting to engage them in speech.......We are going to cross that main track over there into some of the open areas. I am not risking going back into the cover where we have been, as we could be followed."

He called to everyone to move and stay close together. They moved over the ridge down into the other valley which Dunstan had mentioned and he saw the church and its surrounding village. They turned south and followed a path down the hill till they came to a spring in the hillside which poured into a little stream. Eric thought to himself this is a bit like the one Ivar described where he met Morrigan. The one we passed yesterday. They could see the other fort at Wincobank and there were men camped around it packing up. These were organised, however, and had ponies with them.

"How many do you think, Eric," said Dunstan?

"Enough to avoid. At least three times what we are, perhaps four."

For a moment they watched them and saw some were setting out in their direction.

"We'll move up on to that hill to the south, it must be where the rest of the earthworks are located. We'll cross it and be in Brunanburgh in time for an evening meal," said Dunstan.

The men moved out carefully having filled up with water from the spring. They walked carefully to the earthworks at the top of the hill and found themselves looking at a camp of Vikings who had placed no guard to their rear. There were about thirty of them. Nice odds, thought Dunstan, as he signalled his men to encircle them.

"Eric, take ten of yours and take on the few watching the valley. I'll order an attack when you move in," he whispered.

Eric and his men moved around in the woods and sneaked along the bank. They leapt on the three who were sat talking on a log and silenced them without their fellows noticing.

"Let's just walk in and wait for the others," he said.

They walked down the path and the fight started. The Vikings had not put on their armour and it was a bit of a bloodbath, Dunstan recalled years later. Eric had gone berserk and had to be restrained, axe-crazy, said Dunstan. Eric recalled no such thing but said he calmly went about looking for who might be a leader to take back for questioning. A few were left alive and taken along.

Dunstan said the fun was spoilt by the arrival of more Vikings but they slew them as well. Eric said they saw us and ran, leaving behind some of their Scottish allies they had enslaved and had in chains. They were carrying some loot. They took the whole lot back down the hill to Brunanburgh. They avoided a camp near the ford in some trees where some monks were tending wounded. Eric waded first across the ford and shouted to his comrades. They all crossed safely.

In the camp the Vikings said nothing but the Scots who turned out to be Picts were quite content to describe what had happened. They spoke to Morrigan who translated for Dunstan. Dunstan rode off to the king with the information, missing his dinner.

Charles ordered the chains to be taken off the Picts and put on the Vikings to ensure they didn't escape until the king gave orders for their fate. Morrigan told the Picts to stay near the camp and not to run away. They would be safe and they would also get some food and a fire to sit by for the night. Brother Michael came up and castigated Charles for sparing the apostates and for the first time in his life but not the last, Charles de Tours took out his sword and hit a monk with the flat of the blade.

"You're lucky," said Morrigan to Michael. "I would have killed you."

CHAPTER 30

ATHELSTAN'S PLANS TO DEFEND HIS LAND

In the days after the battle, Athelstan brought together all his surviving senior commanders plus others who had proved themselves in the fight and men who knew the situation on the battlefield. His heart was heavy at the loss of so many of his good men, but most of all for Earl Thorolf. He saw him as his major link with his Danish subjects and he worried, even as he heard the news, what the consequences would be. Ordgar, his herald, had been around as much of the battlefield as he could to bring the men together. The only men absent were those defending key places or pursuing what remained of the battle. Athelstan had slept little overnight. His mind went over and over what he should say to his men. It was past midday by the time all were present. No one was talking very much as they waited for him.

"I have a plan to ensure we do not lose today what we won yesterday. I think we all know our army cannot fight another battle so soon and that the enemy still have large numbers of men.... I have not heard that Anlaf has engaged many of his Vikings in this battle but has been content to watch his friends' men and boys die in his cause. God will surely punish him for such a great sin with all the other punishments he will receive......I propose the majority of our army should camp along the Don valley to prevent any re-crossing of the river. The enemy may work out that despite such a huge loss; they still have more men than us. But if we set out our soldiers, as if we mean to put up a determined defence, they may go away. To encourage them we will send small forces to spy on them, attack where we have the advantage and give aid to our supporters north of the river. This we will do slowly and carefully. Yesterday I sent Dunstan Edwinsson his orders for the first patrol. The next will go north, once I hear how the pursuit of the enemy in the direction of the Humber has gone. I have issued orders no one is to be spared except women and boys who do not resist. I do not think it will be possible to consider sending the army home until after All Hallows and only then if the enemy are all gone, even out of York. I intend to personally go there and deal with that nest of traitors. If Anlaf tries to become king there again, he may find himself king of a wilderness, a king of nothing, just like he is now. He may find his supporters are fewer or conversing with Saint Peter from the ends of ropes."

There was a general murmur of approval by all present. Many felt too tired to argue even if they felt they had anything to say.

Count Henry of Tours got up to speak and supported Athelstan. "My dear friend, God has granted you a victory over your enemies. Do not waste it by reticence. Follow up by keeping the enemy on the move as you have suggested. We have many horses to follow them. They will move all the faster if they see us. Consider the success you had yesterday in pursuing them north. We are still following them, are we not?

"We are and great is the slaughter on the way. None are being spared" said Athelstan with a smile.

His aunt's voice was still in his head. "Kill all the traitors, all those not sharing your dream," she was shouting. "You'll never build Britannia without shedding blood."

Harald Edwinsson reminded the king of the west of the hills. "Have they attacked Chester or any of the western forts?

Athelstan thought even at a time like this, the Danes never miss a glance over their shoulders. Could this man replace the good Thorolf? I'll think about this man's place.

"They attacked Manchester, sat outside Chester and gave up for some reason and moved their men to the east to attack Brunanburgh. They failed to take it as you know best of all, Good Harald. They also did something else equally mysterious; although I think it comes of having more men than they know what to do with. They landed a force in the marshes near Chester, made up of Vikings and Irish. They did that when the others had left the area to come over to us in the east. The garrison at Chester and some local men are to attack it when they are sufficiently strong. I am sending some men to help. They may have been assuming the Welsh might come to their aid. The *wealas* would be too frightened while I live."

Athelstan went on. "It's a mystery to me why they have done this and all of all places. They land a force of men in the middle of a bog and then not move out of it for two weeks. I have been informed there are over five hundred well armed and supplied men. It's like they are sat there waiting to see what's happening here before they move out to attack us. They couldn't take Chester or Manchester with that number. What are they going to do, all puff at the walls to knock them over or blow trumpets like Joshua?"

This caused some laughter except amongst the bishops present.

Many of the Saxons had been too scared to ask Athelstan about the wider political situation and he knew that. Most thought he would have it under control anyway and so there was no point in irritating him. Several other suggestions came out but mainly to support Athelstan's existing plan and to add bits of information. All this went down well with him.

The meeting broke up and Athelstan called over Thurstan and Harald.

"It's a personal issue" he said. "Thurstan, I have not heard from Aylmer, your son in law. I hope he is not dead. Let me know if you have news and I will do likewise. Harald, I want you to tell Charles de Tours and his horsemen to go find him for us without putting his own life at risk. The men at the Wincobank fort may know something. Tell him to start there. His nurse and her husband live near but where, I don't know exactly. He may have gone there.... How about you, Thurstan, any ideas?"

"They might know at my daughter's property near Sheffield but Harald had better go there in force if he is to ask. There are mainly Danes around there and they have not been too friendly since she didn't marry one of them."

Harald laughed. "I'll do that visit myself then. Where is it?"

Thurstan grumbled and begged the king to excuse him before he gave any answer.

"Harald, I do think Thurstan resents not being able to collect his daughter's rents for himself but if he wants the return of the property his daughter held in her own right, he had best see his son in law as the heir to it. No formal complaint about the situation has been made to the Sheriff in Derby or I would have heard. The men at the forts at Sheffield or Brunanburgh will know where it is. I wouldn't bother asking Thurstan. A father's grief can do strange things to a man."

"If I can resolve it, I will, my lord, and I will do it peaceably" said Harald. "I have seen enough bloodshed these last days to see me through ten lives."

"Indeed, so have I" said Athelstan. "I wish you well in the future. There will be much to do now....Harald, walk with me and let us talk. You have been of great service to me and I want to know you better. I believe your father and my father may have been acquainted, although not under the best of circumstances."

When he returned to Brunanburgh, Harald carried out Athelstan's orders. Eric Sigurdsson went out with a force to cover the area where he had been with Dunstan. He took the four of the Picts they had freed as guides, as they knew the area also. One could speak some Welsh and so could one of his own men. Harald warned them of the king's order to kill all prisoners but assured them of his word, which to him was more important. Eric came back and reported the Scots and Welsh packing up to leave. He had let the men return to their own side with a warning not to come back. Harald decided that was a wise action and let the rest go with a similar warning.

Charles went over to Wincobank to ask about Aylmer Hansson, but he came back with no good news except an idea to ride to the north to a place called Bradfield. He was advised not to go there without a larger escort. Oswulf the local chief was formerly one of King Edward's personal warband and would be suspicious of anyone not Saxon. At the fort they believed if he was there, he was safe. Oswulf had reached the age when he did not look for a fight but would not run from one which came his way. He was taking care of the families of men who were in the forts at Wincobank and Sheffield. He had them scattered in the hills, but still sent messages to the forts when it was safe.

Harald decided to wait to see if the man turned up and not risk Charles. The son of the king's oldest friend was too precious in these uncertain times. The king ought to know better about the locations of his spies.

Over at Bradfield just a few days before, the defences had been quickly repaired and weapons shared out. Oswulf and Aylmer were training mainly women in their use. Kyra had decided eventually not to train women to fight. She wanted to spend more time with Hilda who had taken to heart the deaths of the women and boys.

Very early one morning they were talking. Kyra had put on the dress the girl had given her.

"Kyra, you look different in a nice dress. You look like another sort of person. You have a certain grace."

"I have had no choice. All my life from being a child to now, I have been trained to be mistress of a house and be the highest lady of my clan…. and have a position as a ruler. Even the nuns instructed me in this. I do yearn for the days when to be the queen was to lead warriors in battle. Those days have been long gone but it was nice to think for a while, we could have created them again. This was our last chance and it will never come again."

"Perhaps it is as well. The deaths of the women here will cause more problems than the death of any amount of men. We women are the real future. If we die, all the traditions have gone. Men have such short memories, especially Saxons."

"Hilda, you must not grieve for too long. Even in this place you are a queen, all count on you, don't let them down by being sorrowful in public for too long. Even I who am young enough to be your granddaughter, have learnt this well."

"I know child. I thought my last years would be filled with more peace. But I'm more content now I know my adopted son lives and that my own surviving children and theirs may do so."

Suddenly Wilfred appeared on his horse.

"The armies are crossing the Don………where's Grandpa? Where's Aylmer?" He called this out several times.

"Both still sleeping" said Kyra after Hilda translated for her into Welsh?

Aylmer came out into the sunshine moments later and yawned. "The day we have hoped for and dreaded."

Oswulf came from the grain store when he heard Wilfred shouting the news.

"Right, everyone listen to me, the tail of an army usually contains a lot of stragglers who will be preferring looting and rape to fighting with their braver comrades. A rabble such as we have seen around here will be no exception. We must try to do for Constantine what our king does with his renegades. Give God a chance to judge them!"

Aylmer translated this for Kyra whose response was to say, "I'll get my sword. When do we leave?"

Oswulf laughed when Aylmer translated. "She's a warrior's wife, my lad. Marry her after a decent time has passed. We could do with a good wedding when these days are over. She's right, it's time to arm and take our places. We must see what comes our way now."

Wilfred went off to do more watching with his comrades. Aylmer had asked him for information on the fort at Sheffield as he wanted to pass a message to the king. He thought Athelstan might send them some help. Not for one moment did he consider the king would lose the battle. He had always prepared for what he saw as the aftermath. Just as he knew he was not the only source of information for Athelstan, he also knew for some days, his friends would have to look out for themselves. He and Kyra were their help. The king would send more when he could. Athelstan did not desert his friends.

Kyra had sorted out some armour from the dead Vikings and padded it out as best she could. "I can't fight in this, it's too big, I can't move fast enough." She announced this to the other girls who had taken to following her. None could understand what she said and Ecbert wasn't there to translate. So she took it all off and danced around naked waving the sword and shield. The girls looked on in horror and ran away.

Aylmer arrived just in time to see it all. "Are the enemy at the door already," he enquired politely?

"Did you want a kiss, lad", she said sternly? "Or a poke with this sword?"

"Kisses at this time of day? The sun is hardly setting in the west."

She put her arms around him and he picked her up for a kiss.

"Aylmer, what's happening in that valley over there? The boys ride in and out of here all day to you and Oswulf. Tell me the truth, even if it's bad news."

"Until we know about the battle we do not know what to do. Oswulf is telling people to stay hidden. He has the boys watching rear of the battlefield and the old salt road to our north and east. This is the enemy's nearest safe escape route to the north and west. There is also one to the south of us. It takes in some of the old Roman roads across the hills. Whilst it's more direct it is not an easy road, especially in bad weather. No one uses it in winter unless they are really tough and hardened travellers. There is hardly anywhere to stay on the way. Oswulf has sent a message to the fort commander at Sheffield to suggest they try to block this route when we win."

"You really have faith in your king. He'll win against all those thousands."

"Kyra, he will. You do not know this king. Many of his people and his supporters do not either. They do not know of his determination. He is the greatest king of the Saxons in the whole of time. Even greater than his grandfather! When he has gone Britain will descend into chaos. He is the hope of all the peoples. While he lives we can keep out the Northmen. Your people, the Scots and the Welsh suffer from them as well as us. They are just waiting for his death to descend on us all like a pack of wolves. They have no ideas of justice or wisdom. Their kings all seek personal power and oppress their subjects. Athelstan must live forever."

Kyra began to understand that not only she had a dream, and that his might be also lost at Brunanburgh. He went on.

"After today life will not be the same for any of us. The Vikings and the Scots will come looking for revenge again when they lose. This may be sooner than later..... Kyra, I must return to the King as soon as I can, even if it is not safe to travel. You must come with me even though I know Hilda would make a safe home for you here. I cannot lose you now I have found you."

"I am glad you feel the same way as me. I thought that you might not when all these troubles are gone."

She hugged him some more and wouldn't let go of him.

"I have sadly learnt how happiness can be fleeting and sometimes not all you think it is. The king may be very angry when I return with a princess from the enemy and a pagan to boot. Athelstan is very quick to anger but also quick to forgive and understand."

"Aylmer, perhaps it may be best not to tell him too much of the details. If he is flushed with his victory, he may not want to know. I can pass myself of a believer of the Church from Rome, I spent long enough in a convent after all.....We shall be going tomorrow I suppose. I expect you and Oswulf have it all planned out. Just understand I shall miss Hilda. It's only been a few days since we met, but she has shown me more love and understanding than my own mother and a whole army of nuns. I can see how you acquired your contentment in life and your inner peace."

"I did have much of that till you came along, or at least I was regaining it after Helena's death. When we escaped the Scots, I found myself think more about you than our safety. When I first saw you watching me with that Viking, you nearly met the same fate as he did. I asked myself, why hasn't she run away and screamed? The whole camp would have rushed to her aid. So far in life I have tried to cause myself and others as little pain as possible. The monks have books from the Romans which tell of great thinkers from Greece who say that men should try to live peacefully and content within themselves.......... and not do harm to others unless severely provoked. I know the Church also teaches some of this but not in the same way. They say peace only comes through God and the Saviour. The monks keep these things too secret for their own good and then wonder why only ignorant men enter the Church? The king knows all about these ideas from the Romans and thinks more people should study them, but not to challenge the Church. They date long before Christ and go back to the Greek's Golden Age. Athelstan also seeks to create a Golden Age in Britain but none of the other kings are supporting him. He thinks they are ignorant barbarians just as the Romans did. The Welsh and Scottish kings chose Roman names but they have none of the aspirations of Old Rome for peace and prosperity."

"Aylmer, our children are going to grow up very wise with you to teach them. That was a long speech for you. I have never heard you talk for so long."

"My friend Dunstan will teach our children if he survives the battle. He is no fighter but he is a good leader, and is now with his father's soldiers. The problem is that you need to be both in Athelstan's Britain. I often say to him I will do the fighting if he can be the inspiration. The king approves of the arrangement and its one more reason I must return to help Dunstan. I also want to find out if my father has managed to get his other two sons killed, if only to save me the trouble of doing it. They were not anxious to fight and even my father will not allow such shirking of duty, despite their mother's pleadings. The king's aunt would have hanged them by now to show the rest an example."

"Aylmer, if we travel tomorrow, I go as a warrior, even if your king does not approve when he sees me... now, you mentioned a kiss!......... Perhaps something more too? Let's go for a walk in the woods, it may be our last quiet time together for a while. I want to hold you so much."

Aylmer picked up her cloak. "Here or you'll freeze. A wind's getting up."

"Don't worry, lad! I'll be warm enough, the way I feel about you," said Kyra. "We'd better practice producing those children."

The following day they left Bradfield as it was getting dark. The news of the Scots' defeat had reached them and the enemy was moving north in great numbers, although it appeared the king was not pursuing them across the river. Wilfred kept asking Oswulf why such a large amount of men should not reform and attack again. Oswulf was at a loss to answer except to say, Aylmer would return and tell him the full story when he had seen the king. A messenger had come from the Sheffield fort to say the area was relatively clear of the enemy. They seemed all clustered around Wincobank, Masborough and Brunanburgh. He offered to show them the safe route from Bradfield to get there and the journey passed without event, although slowly because of the dark. The lights of the camps and the forts to the east could be seen.

After a rest in Sheffield they set off at midday to Brunanburgh with another messenger and passed along the safer side of the Don. They could see the enemy still on the north bank but none attempted to cross. The fort and the land around were full of men still expecting an attack and all sides were guarded well.

The messenger was recognised by the Saxons and welcomed in with his companions.

"Aylmer Hansson," said a voice with authority. "The king's description fits you well which is more than you do that horse. We shall call you The Ganger for to walk would show pity for a dumb beast..........Welcome to Brunanburgh!"

"Harald Edwinsson, a man who thinks of everything, misses nothing and sees all, is what they say at Sheffield. From the extra height I have over most men, I can see you have been busy with the sword around here."

"We have had to earn the king's favour and he is not ungenerous. He had ordered me to find you but from your reputation, I had heard you were indestructible and would turn up....... if I had the patience to stand here and wait. So here you are..... And complete with your own northern princess, I see!"

"The Lady Kyra."

"One of my men, Ivar Grimsson, has done exactly the same in this battle. Have you fallen in love as well?"

Aylmer didn't have time to answer. A woman who could have passed for Kyra's sister to a Saxon's eye ran towards them, shouting. "Mairie, Mairie"," and chattering in a language alien to all the Saxons and Danes.

Kyra hugged her and said. "Broll, I have had a change of name and fortune. I was in a panic, running from the camp and I stumbled across this lovely man here, Aylmer, killing that Viking Sitric Oslacsson. You know the Viking whose men were continually harassing us. I thought Aylmer was going to kill me, but he didn't and the rest is that I've fallen in love. His wife and baby have just died, so we are seeing how things turn out. We've been in a fight with some Vikings."

"Well, I was attacked by some Vikings and rescued by one of the Danes here. He was even wounded at the time of the fight and I've looked after him. He's a bit indestructible. I have helped with the wounded here and I taken part in the big battle against the seafarers. The man who rescued me is called Ivar and I'm going home with him. I can't see any other choice even though we can't speak in a common language yet. He is a good brave man and kind to me. He fought for me in the battle and protected me despite his wounds……Oh! They call me Morrigan here because of our battle cry. He calls me Morgana, he says it sounds more like a name for a princess. So, don't tell anyone my real name. I also have had a change of name and fortune."

Ivar Grimsson limped up at this point in the conversation and was introduced to Aylmer by Harald whilst the two women went off to tell each other their stories.

"Aylmer and Ivar" said Harald, "the king has ordered that all the women brought by the Scots to fight should be taken to him. I think he is curious to know why they are here and that's all. He means them no harm and he is known to be a curious man, always eager for knowledge. He wants to see you Aylmer as soon as possible because of your work for him. Ivar you must go with Morrigan and you must be my representative with the king. There are messages I want you to take, and that monk Michael is writing them out for me. The king has great respect for your father and I know you have met him twice on the battlefield. I take it you can ride a horse as well as walk under one."

Ivar said nothing and looked stone-faced at Harald. Aylmer looked puzzled and asked if they were going tomorrow, not understanding the joke. Harald left them looking at the women and sizing up each other. Ivar was thinking, who's this Saxon lordling and Aylmer thinking, who's this Danish berserk?

Ivar broke the silence. "We usually eat before it gets dark and our food is better than inside the fort. The Franks are sharing with us as well. Their commander is Karl of Tours."

"I know his father but have never met him so far."

"He went to look for you at Wincobank. They said you were probably at Bradfield with Oswulf, and that he had better be careful if he went to find you there."

"We had our own smaller version of the battle there. Kyra fought very hard for us."

"Morrigan did the same here. Did Kyra wear any clothes?"

"No not a stitch and I think we had better hide that from the king, he will think it witchcraft."

"The king saw Morrigan when I found her and she wasn't wearing anything then. He didn't say a contrary word."

"That's strange" said Aylmer, "but let's go for some food. Do you have any cheese?"

On the way Ivar remarked. "You have a *langseax* and here I am thinking I was the only soldier still said to be encumbered by one in this battle."

"No encumbrance, my friend," laughed Aylmer. "It's saved my life a number of times. A family heirloom and I promised my Auntie who reared me, I would never pass into the wide world from out of her sight without wearing it. She has one to match and always says it's better than a sword at close quarters. Great Grandfather Ethelbert had the pair made and in the old fashioned way, welded not cast."

"Very good to follow up when you bang someone with your shield. A sword can be too long. Dad always swears by them for use at sea. He says when leaping from ship to ship carrying a shield and a sword, you could drop the sword. Better to keep the sword in the sheath, keep both hands on the shield to use as a batter, and then get out the *seax* quickly in the narrow spaces."

"He's right, Ivar. Surprise in battle even on a one to one basis, is essential. I can see you and I have something else in common besides being unable to resist those lovely women from the north of this island."

"Oh, I know what you mean! The first time I saw Morrigan standing in a pool of water, I just thought of all the stories my mother told me about water fairies. She is really quite as gentle as a fairy. I cannot believe I have seen her kill so many times, Aylmer. She has saved many lives after the battle amongst our men, having said all that. She has medical skills and can sew up wounds better than the monk we found.... and he's good. It's the small delicate hands in her case."

"Well, I thought Kyra quite child-like until we had to fight on those hills over there" said Aylmer pointing northwest.

Harald suddenly appeared. "You two seem to be getting on well. Perhaps Danes and Saxons being sworn enemies, isn't true anymore."

"We were talking about what we have in common," said Ivar.

"The love of beautiful women and fighting in battles," said Aylmer trying to keep a straight face and as if he were keeping a secret.

"Strange how some things never change down the years" said Harald.

The two women had never stopped talking about the last week of their lives.

"Broll, I know I love Aylmer. I almost felt it from the moment he first held me in that camp. For a man in fear of his life, he was so gentle, even holding a knife at my back. It was as if, once he realised it was me, the desire to kill left him. He told me he almost did kill me on the spot, as he thought I was shadowing the Viking as some sort of protection."

"Well, Ivar could have killed me any time if he had felt threatened. I was so weak with hunger and loss of blood. He wrapped me in his cloak every time I shivered...... You were lucky you found a man who cooked. All I got was one who was looking for a battle and with a monk who's done nothing but irritate me ever since."

Brollachan said this with a laugh and it made Kyra happy to hear her.

"I am glad your sense of humour has returned. Neither of us have too much reason to laugh. We are effectively prisoners in this land. I know I have found a good man and also a mother I could go to, if it doesn't work out, but it isn't our country. We can never go home. We wouldn't survive the journey with our lives."

"Mairie, we have been lucky to survive the last week. I dare not think about it.....How have you managed to find a mother?

"Broll, are you still a virgin," Kyra suddenly asked changing the subject?

She shook her head. "I threw my bronze sword in the river near here as a sign of breaking from my previous life and took Ivar with me to make another offering to the Goddess."

She told Kyra about the vision she had in the northern forest and how so much had come true.

"We'll I couldn't resist Aylmer and couldn't bear to see him unhappy. I just threw myself at him. I thought he was so lovely in all the ugly life I seem to have found for myself over the last years. Men really repelled me before, especially the ones which kept appearing at the convent......... It's really been the most contented week of my life. I was a child at the beginning................ His old nurse has become my mother. She lives up on that hill to the northwest."

"You are lucky. Perhaps she will take to me, although Ivar has said he knows his mother will love me. In many senses I think Ivar has made me grow up. He's a man used to taking decisions and risks despite his youth, I can tell that. I think I may grow to love him. He seems to want to take a chance with me and sees good qualities in me. But all we can do is talk through other people."

"Aylmer and I speak poor Welsh and better Latin, but he has had some education."

"I don't know yet about Ivar's learning but he knows a lot about life. Still, let's go back to our new men and have some food with them. We might have to have three- way chatter, and I have some things I would like to have said to my Ivar."

The four of them passed the evening quietly around a fire. Charles de Tours looked on from nearby in envy, but thinking eventually, no, a warrior princess and a future Comtesse de Tours are not one in the same....... Wouldn't it just be too exciting to find out?

Alain de Briscourt saw him looking longingly at the ladies. He reminded him he could cross the river to see if they had left any more behind, and if he did, could he bring one back for him.

"Charles, you could be a gallant knight rescuing these ladies in distress."

"Alain, the way my life goes, one of them would try to put a sword through me and I would need rescuing by another one. I think I'll go home to Tours and ask mother to find me a wife. She and father must have someone in mind......and if they have, they must have mentioned it to you."

"Well they have, but were waiting to see if we all came home from this war. Well, you and me anyway. Your mother will be glad your father is coming home to live a little longer. The lady they have in mind is from a good family in their eyes. She's a lot younger than you at fourteen, and if you wanted to teach her to use a sword and all the things these women know, well, you'll be Comte de Tours soon and in charge.... I'll be there to watch your back, you know that, and your step-mother is no fool, despite her act. She's just so very tired. Our country is getting so a woman can't stand up for herself without arousing suspicion of witchcraft...... enough of this for now. ....Let's go and see who's hiding the wine in that bunch of rascals pretending to be *les soldats de Tours!*"

The following day the party of travellers set off to meet the king and made their way slowly across the ford over the Rother and then up the hill to the kings camp in the next valley. The walk took most of the morning as they had left most of the horses behind with Charles as extra mounts for his soldiers. Some of the wounded who could walk easily enough were also moved away from the front of the battlefield. They rode and walked slowly and Aylmer insisted the party stay together.

Thurstan recognised his son in law from a distance and rode over to greet him. To Aylmer's surprise he greeted Kyra most graciously and winked at him.

"This has been a good meeting for you, lad…It is best not to grieve for too long in these bad times. Come for my support. I think I understand the situation and it is a good one for us all now."

Aylmer had not realised, the king had heard from Harald about Ivar finding Morrigan and what she had done at Brunanburgh. The king had also spoken to Thurstan about his attitude to Harald and Aylmer and to what the king saw as Aylmer's property now near Sheffield.

"Thurstan, its turning out that many of the enemy were not volunteers to fight in this battle and Anlaf's men were not good to their allies. I have brought Ivar Grimsson and his princess to meet the king. She can tell him much about this. My Kyra has been less involved in the main battle but will talk about what has happened before."

"Grimsson?...... He's the son of that pirate the king has allowed to work on our flanks," said Thurstan not realising Ivar was near?

"My father would be complimented by you, Lord Thurstan. Piracy is one of his more reputable activities. I think now he does only steal on the seas and rivers. He can leave a man on land in possession of his goods without a moment's thought."

"The younger generation are beginning to outnumber me," mumbled Thurstan as the king rode up.

With his usual approach to these matters the king went first among the wounded men. He greeted them and assured them they would have food and care in the camp and then directed one of his guards to take them to the monks. He turned to Aylmer with a beaming smile.

"We beat them, lad, didn't we? It wasn't easy but we did it" and he laughed. "A few times I wondered whether our plan would work. However did you guess they would lose confidence and control once they had crossed the river and get mixed up if we put pressure on them?"

"Dunstan has this theory men with wet feet are never happy. I think he read it in a book in a monastery."

"He reads too much does that lad, and I never read enough. Kings aren't allowed to do this by the laws of God and Nature, I think. Dunstan would no doubt have something to say on that, but he'll never make a strategist like you. I am glad you are back safe even though you look a bit battered and so does young Grimsson over there. But he looked exactly the same, the twice I saw him on the battlefield......... and by God, he's found another woman."

"No, the other lady is mine, but I have to say, she found me, my lord," Aylmer chipped in.

"They look like sisters, are they? I remember one speaks Latin, does the other?"

Kyra stepped forward and Aylmer introduced her. In Latin she spoke to Athelstan about how they met and what happened after at Bradfield.

Athelstan seemed quite pleased and pronounced.

"No one speaking the language of the Church and the Romans can be too far from our side. We must all dine together this evening before dark and I will hear from these ladies about how they came to be with Constantine's Army. This will be a meal with soldiers. No bishops and monks too distract us from talking about our battles and our lives... Now Ivar Grimsson, business! Do you have messages for me from your commander? Come with me! Your father has been killing my enemies for me since last you saw him. He's good at stealing ships, isn't he?"

"A pirate would be, my lord," said Ivar with a beaming smile and looking at Earl Thurstan.

They went off leaving Kyra and Morrigan staring at Aylmer and Thurstan.

"The king can be very concerned with detail at times", said Thurstan. "He treats Aylmer and many of the young men like sons or younger brothers."

Aylmer translated.

Kyra asked Thurstan if he was the father of Helena, and he replied he was but, she need not fear him or his family. He had realised, he was allowing his bitterness at the loss of his only daughter, spoil the happiness of the man who had loved her nearly as much as he did. Aylmer was surprised as he translated that, and afterwards they spoke separately.

Thurstan apologised for his apparent unkindness but his grief was still so great. Aylmer explained, he had thought much of what Thurstan had said about Helena but thought, whilst it could be true, she was now dead and he would never forget her. The war had brought Kyra and him together. She was very different from Helena and was perhaps the sort of woman Thurstan might think should marry a soldier.

Later in the day at the meal the story was told in detail. The king's younger brother and heir, Edmund, was present. Athelstan advised him to start building up a court around which he could administer the country for when he became king. Battles were taking their toll on his life and Edmund might find himself in charge any day. Athelstan heard the story from Kyra and Morrigan of how they escaped from the convent to go and fight as their ancestors did. Athelstan heard their words but saw only Juliana as they spoke. He thought everything was just put together by a group of feisty women seeking adventure. He was full of praise and convinced they could not possibly have influenced the course of the battle. Their adventures filled the evening hours, although Aylmer realised much had been missed out.

"A decent time must pass and you ladies must marry your men. Learn our language and bring new northern blood to us. Our land will be safe with you to protect our homes while we men deal with the Viking invaders. They are always waiting to bring their greed to our land with rape and murder. My brother will not be short of good men to assist him as king. What we have achieved today will not be lost. My Aunt was a lady such as you. Mercia was as safe as when the Romans ruled with Lady Ethelfreda in charge. My Uncle Ethelred of Mercia had truly benefited by such a woman as my aunt. She was as great a warrior"

And with those words from the king the evening came to an end.

Aylmer and Kyra went and sat together by some rocks overlooking the valley and looked down on Brunanburgh. It was dark by then but they could make out the lights of the fort and their friends camp outside it. They could see lights at Wincobank and Sheffield. There were still some lights on the hills over north bank of the Don. They could see to the south and west all the farmers and villagers in the area were lighting up now the news of the King's victory had made the people feel safe again. The land had previously been dark when they were fearful of invasion.

Aylmer was quiet for a while and then spoke.

"Kyra, the king looks tired, even though he is not an old man. He's just past forty years. I worry for us all when he's gone. His brother is not the same sort of man. He's a good man but not a true warrior. He does not attract good men to him. There are people waiting to pursue their own wealth at the country's expense when he becomes king. I am not able to prevent this as I am only a soldier. If I inherit from my father soon, then things may be different. Father is very healthy and good for many years, but he's not amongst the leading men of this land. He isn't an Earl and doesn't make attestations to the king's decrees. His death would divide our lands amongst me and my two brothers if they have survived these last days. I shall have what land my mother brought to the marriage as well as my share of my father's. I have Helena's land just over that hill. We could see it in daylight. In fact that is all I have in my own right at the moment. My family are Mercian and it's going to be the Saxons from Wessex and Kent, and Danes who hold real sway when Athelstan has gone and there are many of them who are jealous of my position in the army, especially the Saxons."

"There are lands up north" said Kyra. "A royal or noble husband of mine could justify a claim to them, especially if he could get rid of my unpopular brothers. You said you were descended from the Kings of Mercia."

"All on my mother's side," said Aylmer.

"That's the best side for my people," she said. "A good sword arm and descent from the royal woman is the all the support a man needs. Alternatively being the husband of the eldest daughter would help, or even the only daughter in your case. If things don't work out here for us we could move up north and if we could take a child to show the people, then that would help even more."

"Better a girl than a boy? Aylmer asked.

"Indeed, my love, and we shall have to keep working on that.... Let's go for a cuddle out of this wind. I've been so used to sleeping outdoors with you, I am sure I'll never settle in a house ever again. Have we ever made love in a bed? Not even at Bradfield as I recall. Whatever are we going to do when it snows? We'll think of something...... I hope we will, anyway."

CHAPTER 31

THE HOMECOMING

Emma stood at her door and looked out down the track to Torksey. Not a soul in sight, neither a husband coming back from returning the flour he had milled, nor a son coming home from the war. They had heard the Saxons won the battle but no sign yet of any men returning to the area. No one to come back to say her son was alive or dead. She looked around the farmyard and the mill for the hundredth time and all seemed in order. All the workers were going about their business. No building work needed for the winter remained undone. Everything tidy and in the weeks Ivar had been gone, it was all she had done. Tidy! Tidy! Tidy. Her life was on hold till he came home. She must seriously find him a wife. At past twenty it seemed wrong he should not have a wife. There was even a house for him, currently used as a store, but built for him, nonetheless. Even that rascal Eric, his friend was now settling down with his "widow." She hoped poor Mathilde was picking a durable one this time around, especially with another child on the way. Two dead husbands in a short life is bad luck. A third one would be a disaster. Two children are there already for Eric to care for. At least he does love them... a good and honest man.

Two figures appeared over the low hill. One with a staff was limping a little, clearly a man. The other was a girl or a child. Both carried packs. A couple of pedlars at the best, beggars at the worst she thought. A couple more mouths come to cadge for the evening meal. Another three men following, clearly having difficulty also in walking came over the hill a few moments later. My eyes are getting worse, she thought. She realised then she crying in the cold late Autumn breeze. Disappointed, it wasn't her son, just another band of beggars. Samhain was two weeks past and still no sign of him.

Ivar was walking and limping along with Morgana, both laughing and giggling. Just as they reached the brow of the hill, he saw the mill and the little hamlet next to the river. He pointed out the defences he had helped to construct, the rolling countryside and the big wide river flowing down to the Humber where she had first arrived. The landscape looked quite stark in the cold afternoon as it was getting dark. Ivar was glad to be home to his mother and father. As they walked along he stopped and pointed around again with the stick she insisted he used till his leg was properly better. In the many weeks since they met on the battlefield of Brunanburgh, her Danish language had improved sufficiently to give out advice on the medicine she had learnt at the convent and preparing for the invasion with Brigid. She had been taking care of the wounded on the march back and many of Ivar's companions remarked she would have come along to the next war. They had left Brother Michael behind at Brunanburgh to the great relief of all the Danes.

"I can see mother at the door" he said, thinking at the same time of all the things which had happened since he saw her at Lammas.

The weeks after the battle and their journey back home had been uneventful, just how Morgana wanted it. It had been pleasant and quiet. She wished it could have gone on forever with garrison duty at the Sprotborough fort and then brief overnight stays at Harald Edwinsson's, and then with Eric and Tildi. She had been given her chance to get to know Ivar and she felt not disappointed. He reminded her so much of Hamish in his good character and honesty. All who knew him told her he was a good man for her. But most of all she was glad to have the opportunity to look at what sort of life she could expect and know she had made the best decision to stay in the south. The Great Queen's prediction about the limping man was now properly revealed.

She was sad to part from Kyra who had left for the south west of the country. They both parted wondering when they would meet again. Ivar and Aylmer had given each other directions to where they lived and expected that they would try to visit when the war with the Scots was finally over.

She was feeling extremely tired and knew the reason. A dedication to the Goddess usually resulted in a child and she hoped it would survive to make Ivar happy. He already suspected something. They walked slowly and he pretended his leg hurt so she would rest as well.

Emma watched as Ulf the dog upped and ran down the track at the couple, on guard as always. They had stopped again and the man was pointing his stick at things around them. When Ulf got to them she could see he was jumping about and heard him barking a welcome. The man was hugging him. Then the five walked on slowly into the hamlet of Knaith with Ulf bouncing around for joy.

"Ivar, you are home," Emma shouted and called to all the others around. "My son's come home."

Then Ivar and what had appeared to be the child walked up to the door and Emma looked sternly at them.

"Son, you have come home to me from the wars, nearly in one piece. But who is this you bring dressed in rags, eyeing over the girl?..... You know we keep no slaves in this house if this is your war booty."

"Mother, I have brought you home a daughter. Ever since I was small, you always said you wanted one………… Her name is Morgana."

Emma still looked sternly at Ivar but turned to smile at the girl.

"A daughter is so very welcome."

She gave her a kiss and a hug and then clung to her.

"There's nothing to her, boy. Whatever has happened to her?"

She began to fire questions at her.

"Mother, she hardly knows our language, she's from the far north."

"Well, if she's a daughter, she must be a bride, bring her in the house in the proper way."

Emma looked sternly again at the other three men. "You three can come in later as well when you have had a wash….. And put your packs in the store over there!……. You can sleep in there tonight. Food will be ready soon…… You are all welcome. You've brought home my son."

They limped off with relief and without a word to each other, wondering what their poor friends had for a mother, a river dragon.

Ivar carried Morgana over the threshold and then brought in their packs as it was starting to rain. Although he was gone no more than a moment, Emma had sat her by the fire with a hot herb drink and was wrapping a blanket around her.

"Where's Dad?"

"Gone delivering flour! Tell me about her while she has her drink. You can have one as well."

So Ivar told her story and how she was given the name Morrigan by the Saxon and Danish soldiers and how he preferred Morgana. She wouldn't tell her original name or what the nuns had called her. She wanted a new start and she had been treating the wounded with the medicine she had learned in the north. Her skill had saved a number of lives especially preventing infections.

"I'll teach her more of our language and our healing ways," said Emma. "Go and see everyone and say the meal will be ready soon. Tell them of your adventures and don't make it sound too good, remember it was a war. My new daughter will be all better for a wash. Give me time to do it, son."

When Ivar had gone Emma hugged her some more and again called her "daughter." Then she asked her if she would like a wash and some new clothes, but suddenly realised she had none to fit her. She got a basin of hot water off the fire and started to wash Morgana who had never experienced such care and was a little frightened by it all.

Morgana then decided she liked it really and took off her rags. Emma winced at the remains of the cuts and bruises she saw and went to fetch some salve.

Emma returned and threw the rags on the fire. "A new start for you, daughter! We've no clothes for someone as small as you, however."

She wrapped her up again in the blanket after putting her salve on her wounds, even though most had completely healed. She fetched some more water to wash her hair and helped her comb it out. When that was done she said. "We'll have a dressmaking day tomorrow. You can wear one of mine till then although we can get two of you in it."

"Can I call you mother" said Morgana suddenly finding she knew the language of the Danes better than she thought?

"Of course, Child" said Emma.

"I have never had much of one I can properly remember."

"Did you know what happened to your real mother?"

"I think she returned to her family. She left me behind as I was to be a hostage with my two brothers. We were all members of royal clans and King Constantine needed to guarantee the loyalty of our families. I escaped when I grew old enough to find my way home. I didn't like the convent. The sisters beat me and all the other children when we wouldn't pray or get out of bed for matins. I tried to find my mother before I came south but she had disappeared. My aunt, her sister, did not know where she had gone. She did not think she was dead, however."

Emma tried to smile and said. "We only get out of bed for work here," being a woman of fewer words than her husband when the occasion called for it.

"That's fine" said Morgana and the hardly pausing for breath, "Ivar says the food here is worth is the work. He is so kind to me. Everyone has been. Brother Michael the monk has given me some of his special needles for sewing wounds. He still thinks me a witch, however. The Frank's *clan* chief, Henricus who is dying of the stomach sickness, has given me a gold chain. It was his first wife's who is also dead. I am going to wear it when Ivar and I give our vows. The poor man came to die in the battle but Ivar and his son Carolus wouldn't let him. He is using a remedy the sisters taught me to ease the pain and he may live a little longer. I think Ivar prefers to be a miller and Eric a forester, than warriors."

Emma thought there is a side to my son I have yet to discover and she has seen this already, trying not to be envious. She reassured Morgana. "You can be a witch around here if it involves doing good for people and loving them. We have no church here and you will not meet many priests. The old ways of all our peoples still survive but we do not shout about it."

Morgana chattered on, starting to feel comfortable with her new mother. "Carolus will be chief after Henricus but prefers his father to be alive. My eldest brother could not wait for my father to die, so he could become *Clan* leader. I think he may even have killed him………. Carolus really loves his father"

"You are very observant, child. I know Ivar loves Grim and me" said Emma and let her carry on.

She understood and carried on chattering. "I am so glad I met Ivar. I had nowhere to go and now I love him so much. He is such a brave man and he has said many kind things about you and his father. He said you would love me and not turn me away even though many would see me as an enemy."

"Child, Ivar knows I have never been able to have children of my own and would have adopted more if they had been around. I have looked forward to the day he finds a wife to bring me some grandchildren. I have never tried too hard to find him a wife knowing that one day he would do it for himself. You were not expected but you are welcome. I am concerned you are young for a wife and for proper child bearing."

"I am coming into my eighteenth winter."

"You don't look so old but you are so thin and tiny. Some more food and rest.... and you might still grow."

"The convent did not feed us well but we used to steal from the kitchen and the farm. When I was a novice with the Cailleach, we ate more but worked very hard. I do not intend to stop the training as a warrior. Ivar says the country around here may not always be peaceful. He says the Sasseneach want it back. A woman with a sword and shield could be useful to defend her home and children. I can also use a bow and a spear."

She took up the shield and the sword and was striding naked about the hut showing her new mother how to use them when Grim and Ivar walked in.

"Mmmm, hello, my new daughter," said Grim with a broad smile. "Ivar has told me all about you. I am pleased to say he did not speak in fantasies, although I was beginning to wonder... Everything he said was true about her, Emm, I can see that.... Have we no clothes for her? The workers will be here for food soon. The whole neighbourhood will think us so poor we cannot find a dress for a child......."

Emma and Morgana were hugging each other and laughing by then.

"......She can practice on the same day as the rest of us but she'll have to wear something or no one will be able to concentrate. They'll be stabbing one another."

He gave his son a hug and said. "She really is a Valkyrie, I can see that."

Emma laughed. "I fear she may be a little more and we may have much to be happy for, dear Grim. I think we have a grandchild on the way.... If your skills are such as you say, young lady, I think you already know."

"I do, Mother, but it is a little early to say whether the life may survive. I did not get much food over the summer and was weak when we came together after the battle. I do not want Ivar to be disappointed, although all this has been prophesied to me by the Great Goddess.... Oh, and I do have some clothes in my bag. Lord Harald's wife gave me some she had made for her youngest daughter. One is special for our vows, it's too good to work in, and there is another for everyday wear."

Emma smiled. "We must talk about this baby with the men out of the way. But let's now all be happy nonetheless and be hopeful some good to this family has come from the war. Our son has returned to us with you, a daughter, and perhaps a child for us to love."

Lightning Source UK Ltd.
Milton Keynes UK
23 December 2010

164824UK00001B/7/P